Marie Hansen Taylor

Letters to a Young Housekeeper

Marie Hansen Taylor

Letters to a Young Housekeeper

ISBN/EAN: 9783744649926

Printed in Europe, USA, Canada, Australia, Japan

Cover: Foto ©Andreas Hilbeck / pixelio.de

More available books at **www.hansebooks.com**

LETTERS

TO A YOUNG HOUSEKEEPER

BY

MARIE HANSEN–TAYLOR

(MRS. BAYARD TAYLOR)

" And true philosophers, methinks,
  Who love all sorts of natural beauties,
  Should love good victuals and good drinks."

THACKERAY

LONDON

SAMPSON LOW, MARSTON, & COMPANY

Limited

St. Dunstan's House

FETTER LANE, FLEET STREET, E.C.

1892

DEDICATED

TO

𝔐𝔶 𝔇𝔞𝔲𝔤𝔥𝔱𝔢𝔯

LILIAN BAYARD TAYLOR KILIANI

CONTENTS

LETTER VI

LETTER VII

LETTER VIII

LETTER IX

LETTER X

LETTER XI

LETTER XII

LETTER XIII

LETTER XIV

LETTER XV

LETTER XVI

LETTER XVII

LETTER XVIII

LETTER XIX

LETTER XX

LETTER XXI

LETTER XXII

LETTER XXIII

LETTER XXIV

LETTERS TO A YOUNG HOUSEKEEPER

LETTER I

'L'utile, pour moi, c'est le beau.
— CHARLES JOBEY.

SO you are going to begin housekeeping? And as I promised you a friend's advice whenever this event should
occur, I am ready to keep my promise. With the
exception that I have the advantage over you of
being older, and therefore, of course, so much the wiser, our
cases are almost parallel. We have not been raised in luxury;
we both have married worthy men, who have to use their
brains and energy to provide for bread and butter, and, since
our natures "cry for it," a great deal more in addition. Your
husband like mine furnishes the means for a modest but comfortable living, and you and I are bound in return to see that
the waste of force and brain-power he is obliged to undergo is
day by day restored, and his vitality kept unimpaired by those
chemicals of which our mortal frame is made up, and which
we call food.

Now do not think that what you have undertaken is mere
play. It is, on the contrary, a tolerably severe task — and a
great pleasure at the same time when you see that your efforts
are succeeding.

Do you believe that a morning's work can be done comfort-
ably on a gruel breakfast? Do you think a stomach would not
rebel against a continued diet of roast beef and chops? If you
wish your husband to be nervously debilitated by and by, dis-
heartened and the reverse of cheerful, give him breakfasts with-

Introductory.

1

out substance and dinners without variety.   Be they cooked as
well as you please, that will not tend to mend matters in the long
run.

Your task being not easy, I am going to be a severe teacher.
I require of you, my pupil, from the start that, being a housekeeper, you devote each day some of your best thinking to
the bill of fare and the meals to be served.   I do not think it
waste of time.   Try it, and you will feel satisfied with the
result.   With all that science and experience contribute nowa-
days, cooking is more of an art than ever, for an art it has
been considered ever since people became civilized.   Nor is
it a peculiarly feminine occupation.   There have been male
cooks always, — some of them famous, as we know, — and there
are not a few among men of genius and distinction who have
given more or less attention to culinary accomplishments.   In
Plato's opinion it brought no dishonor to a philosopher in case
of necessity to cook his own meal; and Baronius, a cardinal
and learned theologian of the Middle Ages, took pride in the
preparation of meals, writing over his mantelpiece with his
own hand: "Cæsar Baronius, permanent cook."   Richelieu,
also, and Mazarin, his successor, looked closely into the details
of their *cuisines*.   Rousseau was an expert in cooking eggs in
various styles, while Lamartine, the poet, was taught by his
tutor, the Abbé Dumont, to cook a plain dinner.   Our own
countryman, Rumford, who was made a count in Germany,
invented the soup which is called by his name, benefiting
thereby the poorer classes of the people.   And who has not
heard of the amiable and refined Brillat-Savarin?   You must
acknowledge, my friend, that we have a galaxy of renowed examples before us, whom to follow we need not be ashamed.
But, if an art, cooking is also a study, and my advice would be
to make it a study first and an art afterward.   This implies that
you are not to take what I say, or what the cook-books (a whole
host of them) tell you, according to the letter, but that you will
have to catch the spirit of it all, and do as it directs.   In this
way — the intelligent way — you will become the inventor, the
true artist, the benefactor.

This is my first injunction : To provide for your meals buy the best of materials; it is the cheapest, because it goes furthest in nourishing. This is especially true of the most important of all food, meat; inasmuch as the flesh of all the higher animals furnishing food contains nearly all the substances of which the human frame is made up. For this reason you must know how to distinguish between good and bad meat. In giving you the requisite indications I follow Dr. Wiel, whose "Diaetetisches Kochbuch" has been my teacher in many respects: 1, Meat when of a pale red color shows *How to choose meat.* that the animal had been ailing; 2, when of a deep purple that it died (was not slaughtered); 3, when healthy and well-fed the color is of a dark pink ingrained with white, which is fat; 4, the fat of a healthy animal is of a pure white, and hard; 5, the fat of a sickly one is of a yellowish white, and soft and watery to the touch. It follows that you have to do your own marketing yourself.

The two principal ingredients of the meat are the muscular fibre and the juice. In the latter is contained the albumen, which is of so much value in restoring us from day to day. The fibre, however, determines the relative nutritive properties of the meat. In this respect well-fed beef is highest in rank. And of the beef again it is the loin and sirloin which are the most nutritious parts as well as the easiest to digest. The poorest pieces are the flank, neck, and shank. Their nutritive value is about ten times less than that of the loin, sirloin, rib piece, and rump. The remaining parts are inferior to the latter and superior to the former; they are of more or less relative value; in the hands of an intelligent cook, however, the least nutritive piece even may be turned into good and palatable food. You must learn that even the best piece of meat is not fit for roasting or stewing unless it has been kept for some time after slaughtering. To give it the necessary *Meat must be kept till fit for use.* tenderness it has to pass through a certain process, which in reality is the first degree of decomposition. In this way an acid — the lactic acid — is developed, which tends to soften the fibre otherwise tough. This process, however, can take place only with meat kept at a temperature above freezing-point. If meat is frozen it has to be thawed gradually and then put to use at once, or it will soon be beyond the proper stage of ferment. The time necessary for the right sort of decomposition to set in is longer or shorter according to the different kinds of meat and the seasons. In summer beef is ready for use in one or two days, while in winter it takes about a week. Veal and lamb take two days in summer, and four to six in winter; mutton, one to two in summer, and three to six in winter; venison, four in summer, and ten to twelve in winter; poultry, one to two days in summer, and four days at least in winter; game, from one to twelve days. If at any time you should be obliged to use a piece of meat while it is still too fresh, you may remedy the case by pouring over it some boiling hot vinegar, then wiping it dry with a clean towel before putting it into your pan.

The time necessary for keeping meat.

This leads me to the kitchen fire, the importance of which is so little appreciated by our kitchen maids. The best of material is apt to be spoiled and made tasteless by either too hot or too slow a fire. A well-regulated fire is absolutely necessary in preparing good and nutritious food. It ought to be made a special study by each housekeeper, who, in turn, ought to instruct her servant. It is a known fact that water, after getting to the boiling point — *i. e.* showing an agitated surface — does not increase in temperature. As soon as this point is reached a slackening fire will do the same service as a lively one. The lesson to be derived from this is one of economy. The importance of the right sort of fire in preparing different kinds of food was known in ancient times. Some curious works have come down to us written by Greek cooks of old. One of them says: "You must see to the strong, the medium, and the slow fire according to the dishes you wish to prepare"; and then he adds: "Nor is he the genuine cook who handles the pan, swings the ladle or the meat-knife, or who serves up a delicacy; but he it is who knows to keep the right measure, and

Importance of the kitchen fire.

gives the necessary temperature to each dish of food he cooks."

Well, we have made a beginning of what we have to learn. We will proceed step by step, until we reach the top of the ladder, only to find that there is no end to the pursuit of knowledge — even in the matter of cooking.

LETTER II

Je crois qu'il est très bon de révéler aux hommes
Les secrets de se bien nourrir.
—CHARLES JOBEY.

YOU never had the benefit of a cooking-school? Neither had I. By-the-bye, I found out the other day that cooking-schools are by no means a modern institution; for during the reign of Louis XIV. of France Madame de Sablé distinguished herself among the court ladies — all dabbling in cookery — by establishing a cooking-school, where the Duke of Larochefoucauld was counted one of her best pupils.

I was going to say that although our cooking-schools are excellent, and are doing a great deal of good, a woman of common intelligence and good sense may never come near one, and yet become a good cook and housekeeper by the grace of her own ingenuity. Necessity and love of home combining, she will soon make herself acquainted with the first rudiments of cooking, and then her own experiences will teach her more and more. It is astonishing how many cook-books have been published of every size and kind. Still, many as there are, new and old, I think there is room for more of them; for cooking is gradually passing into a new phase by the help of modern chemistry. It was Liebig who first called public attention to the chemical process performed in every kitchen for the purpose of restoring the daily waste of the human body; who taught us in his "Chemische Briefe" how to roast meat, and why the piece of meat which has furnished us with a good broth is devoid of nutriment. Others have followed him, and intelligent housekeepers are beginning to see that they have to study in order to become adequate providers for their families. In my opinion the cook-books of the future will have

What Liebig did for the advance of cookery.

6

to take cognizance of the practical side of chemistry as demonstrated by modern scholars.

I touched on the subject of economy in my last in speaking of the kitchen fire, and now mean to impress upon *On the subject* your mind that in this word "economy," when *of economy.* coupled with intelligence, you have the key to the secret how to have a better table with restricted means than many a family paying large sums for no end of provisions. In the first place, it is absolutely wrong to be wasteful, and in the second place it is not ladylike to be so. This may comfort you when your servant, as ignorant persons are apt to do, will confound in her mind meanness with economy. Do not allow yourself to be troubled in the least by such a doubt on her part, for it is a matter of false pride to be influenced thus as long as you know better. Nor will you be able to carry out the principle of economy without making your servant your assistant. You will have to teach her imperatively that you will allow no waste of any kind — that no particle of food is to be thrown *Some ways of* away without your orders. Food, if left over, be it *economizing.* ever so small in quantity, is to be put on clean platters, and set away for your inspection next day. In this way, for instance, I have often made of little remnants of different kinds of cooked food the most palatable of soups. Bones left over, cooked or not, ought to be cracked, and added to the contents of the soup-kettle. The superfluous fat of a roast is better trimmed off when raw, and prepared for future use by cutting it in squares, and rendering or "trying it out." Have the clean drippings poured through a fine sieve into a bowl, and set away in a cool place. The fat left after the meat has been served may be appropriated to the same purpose, but it is inferior in quality. The drippings of different kinds of meat are better kept separate. Mutton drippings are only fit to use when fresh. If cooked up with a slice of onion, they are delicious to fry potatoes with. The fat taken from a chicken and rendered is nearly as good as butter for cooking purposes.

I want also to call your attention to the bread-box. Pieces will accumulate in it, and may be used up in different ways — the

nice pieces for various dishes, of which later; the odds and ends
to dry in the oven, and roll into crumbs for breading chops, etc.

Parsley, celery leaves and stalks, pieces of raw carrot left
over, may be dried, and kept — each separate — for future use.

These are merely hints on which to enlarge for yourself.

In marketing, look out for the best material. I said before
that it is the cheapest, because it contains the most nutriment;
About marketing. therefore, it goes the furthest to satisfy the appetite.
When you buy you should well calculate your needs
as to quantity. When brought home, all articles not for imme-
diate use should be taken care of at once and stored in proper
places. The next thing is to use your marketing in such a way
as to make the most of it. Even the best materials will be in-
sufficient to nourish if not put to their proper uses. To attain
this, each article of food has to be prepared in such a way as
to preserve intact the nutriments contained in it as much as
The way to pre- possible, and care has also to be taken to bring
pare food. out its particular flavor; this makes food palatable
and favors digestion. Too much heat will dry up the juiciest
of meat. The wrong kind of spice, or too much of it, will kill
the delicate flavor of animal or vegetable food, and rob it of its
wholesome nature.

Nor is it a matter of indifference what kind of food you provide, and in what way you combine the different kinds. There
Food is needed is a certain amount of waste going on in our
to counteract bodies day by day, which must be replaced by the
the daily waste
of the human same elements which have been spent, and which
body. are contained in the foods provided by nature.
These elements, and the manner in which they are distributed
in our foods, are a matter for you to study, in order to become
the judicious provider for your family.

There are two classes of nutrients which concern us mostly.
(1) The plastic materials, so called because they build up and
The chemistry repair the organs of the human body, and renew
of food. the life-giving blood. (2) The heat and breath
producing materials — the fuel by which the human machine is
kept going. Of the former the chief element is nitrogen,

which is furnished by the albumen in animal substances, by the gluten in cereals, and legumin in vegetables; by casein in milk, etc. They are classed by the name of albuminoids, or protein. The second class consist chiefly of carbon and hydrogen, and are summed up as carbohydrates. They are contained in sugar, starch, dextrin, alcohol, water, and in the fats of animals and vegetables. The fats, however, are often classed by themselves, and further on, in giving you the daily rations of food as set down by the latest investigations, you will find special mention made of them.

There is still another and equally important class of elements — anorganic substances — such as sulphur, lime, phosphorus, potassium, calcium, sodium chloride (common salt), ircn and other minerals, which enter into the composition of our blood and bones. Either one of these three (or four) classes of nutrients without the others will fail to nourish man or beast. But it is the first and second class which principally concern us, the fats being contained and distributed among the animal and vegetable food-materials in such a way as to need but small attention, while the anorganic and mineral substances are to be found so wisely mixed with the albuminoids and carbohydrates that we may let them take care of themselves.

Most scholars agree that for every part of albuminoids there must be four parts of carbohydrates in our daily food. Next we have to know how much of either of these food-elements is necessary to nourish human beings each day. The following is now generally accepted as being the daily rations on an average for persons of different sex and ages : —

The rations necessary daily.

	Albuminoids.	Fats.	Carbohydrates.
	Ounces.	Ounces.	Ounces.
For children up to 1½ years .	0.7 to 1.3	1 to 1.6	2.3 to 3.3
For children from 6–15 years	2.5 to 2.9	1.2 to 1.9	8.6 to 14.4
For a man	4.2	2	17.6
For a woman	3.3	1.5	14.4
For an aged man	3.5	2.4	12.5
For an aged woman . . .	2.9	1.9	9.3

This is meant for persons who work but moderately. A person of leisure would need less albuminoids ; a laboring man or woman would need more. Besides, there have to be considered the condition of health, the calling and temperament of the persons in question, as well as the climate and the seasons. It follows that a table may be loaded with luxurious dishes and delicacies, and yet fail to nourish properly those feasting on them. Unless they are so chosen as to yield in their combination the right proportion of the nutrients required to repair the daily wastes of the human body, they will do harm instead of good.

You might say, " How comes it, then, that mankind is still in existence, since the science of the kitchen was unknown heretofore? " It is, indeed, a fact to be wondered at when we consider the barbarities practised in the way of feeding and cooking even to the present day. There are two things, however, in favor of man : one is the toughness of his frame, which seems to be able to stand a good deal of abuse ; the other is that mysterious guide called instinct, which led people from the start to find out what is good for them and what not. But instinct, somehow, seems to beat its retreat when civilization advances triumphantly, and neither you nor I would fare well or be satisfied to rely always on that sort of leadership, when science is holding up her torch-light to show us the " how " and " why." Just think of all the persons we know, young and old, ailing of no one knows what — of mysterious troubles called anæmia, dyspepsia, liver complaint, etc. ! Who knows but that such persons are either half-starved or over-fed, for which ailments no physician can aid them ?

I would advise you to study this subject earnestly. There is many a spare hour in which to do it. And it pays. There are books to teach you — books which treat of the kitchen as a laboratory for preparing the chemical compounds necessary to preserve and foster life, but which so far, I am afraid, have not found many readers among our sex. Meanwhile the hints I give you may help a little to pave the way.

The following will furnish you with a rough estimate of the

nutritive values we have in our principal food-materials as to nitrogen (albuminoids) and carbon (carbohydrates).

These values may be divided into three different classes: First, food in which nitrogen and carbon are combined—the class to be rated as the highest; second, food which contains chiefly nitrogen, and therefore has to be complemented by articles of the third class; third, food which chiefly consists of carbon, and has to be complemented by food of the second class. Here follows a list to choose from according to the above values:—

Nutritive values in food-materials.

Food of the first class: Fat meat; beef-tea made without heat; milk; fat oysters; all unbolted flour, and gruel and bread made thereof; dried beans, peas and lentils; cabbages, especially cauliflower; kale, spinach, lettuce, string beans, and green peas; onions and leeks; mushrooms; tea, coffee, and chocolate.

Food of the second class: Lean meat; eggs; fresh fish; lean oysters and clams; cured fish, especially cod, herring, salmon, and sardines; cheese made of milk.

Food of the third class: Salt pork, very fat; wheat bread; wheat flour, corn meal; sugar; rice, sago, barley, farina, corn-starch; macaroni, vermicelli; potatoes, sweet potatoes, turnips, carrots, parsnips; fruit; fermented beverages.

Your task is to select from these three classes of food your materials and combine them in such a way as to give you, as nearly as possible, the correct proportions of albuminoids and carbohydrates demanded to supply the daily rations for the persons you have to provide for. In doing so, however, you have to bear in mind that what you buy is not food consisting of pure albuminoids and carbohydrates, but materials more or less mixed with refuse, like the bones and sinews of meat; and that in addition you have the mineral matters and the water, all of which tell in weight. C. Voit, the great physiologist of Munich, says that a full-grown person to get his full ration of albuminoids needs

C. Voit's estimate of a full ration.

at least 8.2 ounces of meat a day, of which there are bones about 0.6 ounce, fat 0.7 ounce, and pure muscle 6.9 ounces.

He adds that the latter may be replaced by poultry, or fish, and also either entirely or in part by cheese, and dishes prepared with milk or milk and egg.

I follow him also in stating that of the whole amount of food not more than one-third ought to consist of animal matters — the other two-thirds having to be made up from vegetable produce. A purely vegetable diet would require a considerably larger amount of albuminoids than is given in the table of daily rations, because the digestive properties of the nitrogen of vegetable food are from one-fourth to one-third less than those of the same substance in animal food.

It remains for me to give you an idea of the percentages of the different nutrients in the food-materials with which we have to work. But I prefer to do this as I go along, mentioning their proportionate values when I come to deal separately with the cooking materials and the preparing of them.

I may remark here that on the whole we eat too much meat. We would fare better if we relied for our animal food more **We eat too much meat.** on the products of the dairies. This cannot be preached enough to persons of moderate means, inasmuch as the dairies furnish us with a larger quantity of nutrients for the same money than meat does. Although your circumstances and mine are not so much restricted as to impose on us real privations, it is comfortable to know that, in reducing our butcher's bill and favoring the dairyman, we get a pleasant substitute for the same amount of nourishment, and at the same time are practising the virtue of economy. This method, moreover, helps us to a greater variety in our meals ; and variety of necessity promotes the appetite and aids digestion. You might succeed in putting on your table each day the exact amount of albuminoids combined with the right proportion of carbohydrates, and fail at the same time to satisfy the appetite of the consumer. Food, after being eaten, has to be assimilated — taken up by the system in such a way as to serve its purpose ; and to attain this effect in many cases the eye needs to be tempted as well as the stomach. Both easily tire if the same things are continually set before them. And there is the palate also, which is as severe a critic as you would wish to have. Therefore, you must have variety in your daily fare; it must look well; it must taste well; in short, your food must be cooked and served in the best possible way.

The cooking of it is what concerns us most at present. I am ready to step into the kitchen with you in my next.

LETTER III

L'appetit vient en mangeant.

FIRST of all you wish to know how to boil meat, and make the most of it for soup. Suppose you have bought a piece of meat for this purpose, and want to get from it as good a broth as possible. What we do first is to cleanse it. We do so by rubbing it off with a clean towel. If splinters of bone, sand, etc., have to be removed, we scrape it with a clean but dull knife. In extreme cases it may be rinsed quickly with water; but be sure never to immerse your meat. If you do, the surface of it will be robbed of its best juices. These we want as much as possible to preserve for our broth. To this end we take a soup-kettle with a tight-fitting lid, which we fill with cold water, and in this water we put the meat, adding a little salt. In allowing the water to get hot gradually the blood with the albumen and the mineral matters are extracted from the meat and imparted to the water. As soon as the latter reaches the boiling point the kettle has to be removed to a place where it will merely "smile" as the French term it; which means, of course, that it must simmer or boil gently. After a while we see a brown scum rising; this is the albumen, which coagulates in the boiling water and thus is lost as a nutrient. Consequently, meat or soup broth is not of great nutritive value. It is merely a stimulant on account of the so-called "extractives" in it, of which gelatine (or glue) is also a part, and, as such, important in the process of nutrition. The gelatine in the broth is the result of continued boiling, and proceeds from the tendons, bones, and gristle, or what is called the connective tissue of the meat. These extractives give the aroma to the broth.

How to boil meat and make soup.

14

The scum, or albumen, when coming to the surface, has to be removed by a skimmer in order to get a clear broth. To leave it in would make the soup unsightly, and besides albumen, when coagulated, is not easily digested. The meat which remains after all the good is drawn out is worthless, and if eaten will not be digested, even by a healthy stomach. Since this meat is refuse, I advise cutting it into small pieces before putting it in the soup-kettle, adding the bones separately. In this way there is no doubt of the meat yielding in the course of several hours all it contains. I must not forget to mention that for broth — but only for broth — meat freshly butchered is the best. And, now, before proceeding to tell you when to add the vegetables, which are to increase the flavor of the soup-liquor, and the proportions, I will stop and give you the recipe for making a broth which preserves all the nutrients of the meat and for cases of debility, sickness, or convalescence is invaluable. It is made without fuel of any kind.

To make soup, get meat freshly butchered.

Take three ounces of freshly butchered meat of the best sort, without fat or sinew (either beef or fowl) ; chop it fine, put it in a china bowl, and cover it with water which has been boiled and become cold (or better, distilled water from the druggist's), until one inch above the meat. Then add a pinch of salt, and five to six drops of muriatic acid ; stir well this mixture by means of a small glass spoon ; cover up the bowl and let it remain in a cool place for three to four hours. At the end of that time strain the liquid, which has a pale red color, through a hair sieve ; pour over the meat some more of the water, while pressing it down with a wooden ladle, until it gets entirely discolored and you have liquor sufficient to fill a large teacup quite full. This is enough for one portion. Two such cups are the most a person ought to take during one day. It is in liquid form the same as the meat itself.

How to make a broth preserving all the nutrients of meat.

I return now to the ordinary soup-liquor, and will sum up the whole for you thus : —

Take of lean meat freshly butchered one pound, of bones

one pound; cut the meat in large dice; crack the bones; put

Recipe for
the ordinary
soup-liquor.
all in a soup-kettle holding a little over three quarts; fill up with cold water nearly full; add one saltspoonful of salt.   Heat slowly, allowing it to simmer or boil gently; skim off the scum that rises.   After one hour add two more saltspoonfuls of salt, and continue boiling until the liquor is clear.   Then add your vegetables: a small carrot or a piece of a large one, a parsley root, the half of a celery root (the turnip-rooted), one or two of the large celery leaves, one small leek (it is more delicate than onion), half a turnip.   Allow it to boil one hour longer, or until the vegetables are done, when strain through a fine sieve; allow the fat to settle on top, and skim it off with care.

Some housekeepers are in favor of making their soup-liquor the day before it is to be used, in order to remove the fat more readily.   Except for economy's sake, or to save time, I prefer to cook it the same day I want to use it, because in reheating the broth some of its flavor is certainly lost.   With clean sheets of blotting paper the remaining traces of the soup-grease are easily and thoroughly removed.   The brown paper of the grocers will also do it.

See that your soup-kettle is always tightly covered, lest the aroma of your soup escape with the steam.   I will add, for the benefit of your economical propensities, that the soup-vegetables, by not being overdone, may be put to some further use. They have given, to be sure, their best properties to the broth, but in exchange they have taken to themselves the broth which has entered their cells.

For the benefit of the German middle classes, who make a meal of their soup, in which the meat and a vegetable are boiled, Dr. Wiel, in his " Diaetetisches Kochbuch," gives a recipe for "a better piece of meat, and yet a good soup." The sum of what he says is this: —

Divide your meat into two portions, one containing all the sinewy parts, and the bones with the meat next to them, while the other must be a piece of solid meat.   Chop the meat of the first portion, split the bones, and pour cold water over it.

For one pound of meat take three quarts of water, which will give you about one quart of good strong broth in the end. After putting in sufficient salt, some muriatic acid (from the druggist's) must be added. For one pound of meat about six drops, no more. Allow to stand in a cold place for a couple of hours; during this time the water will extract all the strength of the meat. Then heat it gradually, and when it comes to a boil, and not before, put in the second portion of solid meat, after tying it up tight with strong twine. By this process less of the surface of the meat is exposed, and the boiling water produces an impenetrable crust by coagulation, thus preventing the loss of the nutritive juices. Allow the whole to boil gently until the meat is tender. Put your vegetables in after the broth has been skimmed.

How to have a good soup, and save the meat for use.

It is well to know this recipe for economical purposes. A piece of meat boiled in this way makes a good dish for breakfast, either as a hash, a stew, or in the shape of croquettes. It may also serve to help out on the kitchen table. For economy's sake also, I would advise you (since we want a soup to begin dinner with) not to buy soup-meat oftener than twice a week. If a first-class broth is not needed do not exhaust the whole of your soup-meat and bones. Drain off the liquor wanted for the day, refill the kettle with water, adding such scraps of meat, cooked or raw, as have been left over or cannot be used in other ways; add bones also if you have them. Always crack the latter. Add some more salt and cook up. Let stand over until next day when fresh vegetables can be put in after it has come to a boil. I have often made a third edition by adding Liebig's meat extract. This you may always do if your broth is not of sufficiently good quality. Only be sure not to take too much of it. Meat extract — containing all the extractives, but not the albumen of the meat — is a stimulant rather than a nutritive, and as such is fulfilling an important part in the process of nutrition. As a stimulant, however, it is powerful enough to affect the heart if taken in too large a quantity. A heaped teaspoonful is sufficient for a quart of soup; or, take a lump the size of a dried bean for a plateful.

This may be the proper time to make you acquainted with the way Liebig himself had the meat extract used in his own household, instead of broth made of fresh meat : —

Take two quarts of cold water ; put in it either half a pound of cracked marrow-bones or one ounce of beef suet, and such vegetables as are handy ; boil until the latter are

Liebig's way of using his meat extract for making soup. done, which takes about one hour. Now strain the liquid, and add half an ounce good weight of meat extract, and the necessary salt. This is soup-liquor sufficient for seven persons.

The flavor of broth can be improved or varied by taking different kinds of meat at the same time ; as, for instance, adding a slice of ham to veal, or a piece of liver to beef. If amber-

Amber-colored broth. colored broth is wanted the vegetables may be sliced thin and fried brown with a very little butter before being added to the liquor in the soup-kettle. Fat meat is not the proper kind for the soup-pot. An old chicken makes an excellent soup of delicate flavor. Venison, game, and pigeons make as nourishing a soup as can be. In Catholic countries a good soup is made of various fish. But even water soups can be made exceedingly palatable. A good way to improve both the taste and nutritive value of soup, is to add one or more eggs. In doing so care has to be taken to prevent curdling. Beat up the egg thoroughly with a tablespoonful of either water, milk, or cream ; add slowly a ladleful of the hot soup after removing it from the fire, stirring all the while. Then add this to the soup, stirring also ; or, better, pour it into the soup-tureen, and add the soup to it while stirring. In using the whole egg we have the benefit of the white, which being largely albumen increases the nutritive value of the soup ; but in using the yolk merely, a velvety smoothness of the soup is attained, which is marred by the white of the egg. Therefore, you may choose between the two as you judge best. Whenever I take the yolk and not the white, I am in the habit of saving the latter, and using it with another egg, or with

two, for croquettes, pancakes, etc. When I have as many as
three or four whites, I use them for making a delicate white-
of-egg pudding — of which hereafter.

A small remnant of a vegetable dish added to a soup — it
must harmonize, to be sure, with the rest — is a good thing
often ; but the best vegetable to add is tomato, Occasional addi-
which never spoils a rice, macaroni, vermicelli, tions to soup.
or vegetable soup. Another very nice addition is " roses " of
cauliflower, or bits of asparagus boiled until just done in the soup
itself. In this way they impart their flavor and best properties
to the soup ; which is not so much the case if boiled by themselves in salt water, unless the water is added to the soup with
them. Certain soups are also improved by some minced parsley, which had better be put into the tureen just before the
soup is poured in, or it might lose its aromatic property. In
the south of Germany they add cives cut very fine ; but this is
a matter of individual taste. Bread is often added too. Cut
some of your stale pieces into either small dice or thin well-
shaped slices ; have ready a hot frying-pan ; put in a very small
bit of butter, or pork drippings (chicken fat is very good), and
after it is done hissing put in your bread, tossing or stirring it
frequently, until of a rich yellow or brown on all sides ; keep
hot and dry, and either add to the soup-tureen the last moment,
or have it served and handed around separately.

I might go on indefinitely to theorize in this fashion about
soups, and teach you the "composing " of them without giving
you a single recipe. I will, however, stop short, and give you
some detailed samples in my next.

LETTER IV

Je vis de bonne soupe et non de beau langage. — MOLIÈRE.

THE soup is, according to Brillat-Savarin, our philosopher of the kitchen, " la première consolation de l'estomac besoigneux "—the prime comfort of the eager stomach.   The French,

About soup in general.

Germans, and Italians have it on their table every day to begin dinner with.   As for their poor it is often all they have for their mid-day meal.   The middle classes are apt to make their soup the nucleus of their dinner by adding the rest of the meal to the soup-pot and serving it on separate dishes.   In the south of Germany soup is eaten at dinner and at supper by many a family of the upper classes — a custom which seems to be very old elsewhere, if we are to judge from a French proverb dating centuries back, which says : —

> Without his soup at eve and morn
> Is my good Christian all forlorn.[1]

I said before that soup-liquor is more of a stimulant than a nutrient.   It is owing to the substances you add that, as soup, it becomes more or less nourishing.   The following example will demonstrate to you how nourishing it can be made by study.   The recipe is called

Rumford Soup from its inventor, and is composed on the principle of getting what is necessary to nourish in the cheapest way.   It was for his merit in bettering the condition of the poorer classes that Benjamin Thompson, an American, was made Count Rumford by the Prince-Elector of Bavaria in the

---

[1] " Soupe le soir, soupe le matin,
   C'est l'ordinaire du bon chrétien."

beginning of the century. Being a scholar in national economy he found out by means of chemical researches how to obtain nourishment at lowest cost. It is by the Rumford Soup that he is now chiefly remembered. There are several versions of this soup. I have tried the following, and found it not only satisfying to the appetite but also palatable.

Soak three cups of dried peas over night ; put them to cook with plenty of cold water ; when they come to a boil add three-quarters of a pound of fresh pork, one cup of *Recipe for* barley, and the necessary salt. Now get ready *Rumford Soup.* four large potatoes, peel, wash, and slice them, and add them to the above about half an hour before meal-time. Allow at least three hours for peas and barley to get pulpy and for the pork to get done. Add boiling water if necessary to thin the soup, but it ought to be rather thick. When done remove the pork, cut it in dice and set it away in the covered tureen in a warm place. Pour the soup in a colander and strain, rubbing it through with a potato-masher. Heat up again the strained soup, add some minced parsley to the pork in the tureen and serve your soup over it.

Now let us see what nutrients we have in this recipe. The following table will show it : —

	ALBUMINOIDS.	FATS.	CARBOHYDRATES.
Peas......................	23 per cent.	2 per cent.	52 per cent.
Barley.....................	7.5 per cent.	1 per cent.	76 per cent.
Potatoes..................	2 per cent.	0 per cent.	20.7 per cent.
Fat pork (bones excepted)..	14.5 per cent.	37.5 per cent.	0 per cent.
Total.................	47 per cent.	40.5 per cent.	148.7 per cent.

In adding the fat to the carbohydrates you will find that the total is pretty nearly as one to four, which is the proportion necessary to give proper nourishment and keep the system in a healthy condition.

Since charity is a virtue to be practised in every household, you will remember this recipe when a poor man or woman, or whole family, is to be fed. Only see that they get enough of the ingredients to make up as near as possible the ration each person needs every day. I would advise to put this soup on your own table now and then when you happen to have but a slender steak to follow, or perhaps a dish made of some remnant of the day before — some croquettes, or a stew and no roast. For, mind you, we please ourselves (our husbands included) in this, that we do not ape the wealthy in a profusion of meats and courses, which would soon exhaust our funds and the capabilities of our husbands to furnish them. We are of one opinion in this, as you have assured me, that a simple meal, as long as it supplies the needful nourishment, is a comfort all around, if only prepared with care and served "with grace," as Brillat-Savarin ordains for the pheasant. It saves both time and labor. It promotes health and cheerfulness.

To be able to select the soup best suited for the day it is well to consider our subject under three different heads: Soups divided into three classes. soups made of preparations of cereals, those made of vegetables, and those made from animal substances. Fish soups, although properly included in the latter class, I will leave out for the present.

For the first kind of soups we have chiefly wheat flour, farina, barley, sago, rice, vermicelli. These are rich in starch, which belongs to the carbohydrates, as you know, and take rank in this way : —

	ALBUMINOIDS.	FATS.	CARBOHYDRATES.
Wheat flour	10 per cent.	1 per cent.	75.2 per cent.
Farina	10 per cent.	1 per cent.	75.2 per cent.
Vermicelli	9 per cent.	0.5 per cent.	76.5 per cent.
Rice	8 per cent.	1 per cent.	76.5 per cent.
Barley	7.5 per cent.	1 per cent.	76 per cent.

Of the vegetables as nutrients there is not much to say, their value as such ranking rather low, with the exception of dried peas, beans, and lentils. These three are valuable, as the following shows : —

	ALBUMINOIDS.	FATS.	CARBOHYDRATES.
Peas	23 per cent.	2 per cent.	52 per cent.
Beans	23 per cent.	2 per cent.	53.3 per cent.
Lentils	25.5 per cent.	2 per cent.	54 per cent.

But valuable as they are, they require good digestive capacity, and therefore may be kept in reserve, while preference is given to the more delicate although less nutritious vegetables for soups.

The third kind of soups — those consisting of animal substances — are the most nourishing if made of chopped meat, such as beef, venison, chicken, pigeon, game, sweetbread, calf's brain, etc.

Of each of these three kinds of soups you may borrow for the other two. You can add, for instance, vegetables to the cereal products; or animal matter to a vegetable soup; or you may mix ingredients belonging to all three classes of soups. Only take care that each substance is in harmony with the other, and that the whole is agreeable to the eye as well as to the taste.

To begin with the starchy matters, it is a safe rule to take a tablespoonful for each person of either farina, barley, rice, etc. They are added to the boiling liquor while stirring *Soups made* to prevent the forming of lumps. Boil gently. *of cereals.* As to time, farina takes about fifteen minutes to get done; sago, about five minutes, or until clear; barley, from one to two hours to get properly cooked. Rice takes about half an hour in soup. It has to be washed and scalded beforehand. Vermicelli, according to thickness, takes from five to forty minutes to get done.

I will remark here that I always mean my recipes for three persons, unless differently stated. I begin with some plain soup : —

Farina Soup. — Take the finest wheat farina, measure off your quantity (a tablespoonful for each person); stir gradually into your boiling liquor (about half a pint for a person); cover up, and let boil for fifteen minutes, stirring the soup every now and then with a spoon. Have the yolk of one egg beaten up with a tablespoonful of cream (or milk); add this at the last moment, proceeding as told before.[1] Salt to taste. This soup ought to be of a creamy smoothness.

Flour Soup No. 1. — Mix two tablespoonfuls of flour with a

[1] See p. 18.

little cold water, and stir until quite smooth; add to it gradually, and stirring all the while, one and a half pints of boiling
broth; flavor with a little lemon peel, which remove before
serving; put on to boil for ten minutes; then add butter the
size of a walnut and the yolk of an egg beaten up with some
cream or milk. Salt to taste; add a sprinkle of grated nutmeg.

Flour Soup No. 2. — Take butter, one and a half ounces
(or size of small egg); melt, and stir into it two tablespoonfuls
of flour. When bubbling up add little by little one and a half
pints of broth, stirring until quite smooth; add one teaspoonful
of minced parsley and one egg beaten up in two tablespoonfuls
of thick cream. Salt to taste.

To this soup as well as to those following you can make additions of cauliflower, green peas, asparagus, if they happen to
be handy, or whatever else you see fit. Remember also the
proportions mentioned before and apply them to the following
recipe. This is of French origin : —

Velvety Soup (*Potage Velouté*). — Take pearl sago (the
best), stir it into your boiling broth, and cook until clear; add
one yolk for each person (two will do for three persons), beat
it up with cream. Salt to taste.

Omelet Soup. — Make a pancake batter of one egg, milk,
flour, a little salt, and a sprinkle of either minced parsley or
cives, which bake thin and not too brown in a buttered frying-
pan; when done, put on a bread-board and cut into very narrow strips; put into the soup-tureen, and serve over them a
clear broth.

If you have mutton for the foundation of your soup, rice or
barley will be best to use. Take rather more than usual of the
soup vegetables for this broth, especially celery root and leaves;
also a clove, a bay leaf, and a few pepper seeds.

Barley Soup No. 1. — Take pearl barley; stir into boiling
water — nearly one pint to three tablespoonfuls — to which
add a small piece of butter, a little salt, and turnip-rooted
celery cut into small dice; cook gently (covered up) for about
two hours, seeing that the barley gradually takes up all the water,
but do not let it get dry. When done add your broth to it; let

come to a boil, and serve over one or two eggs beaten up with cream or milk.

Barley Soup No. 2. — Take the coarse-grained barley; do as before, leaving out the celery root. After the barley is about half done add the meat-liquor, and finish cooking it until quite soft. Rub through a wire sieve, add egg and cream, and serve over crisply fried bread, or little bread balls, of which later.

All these soups may be served without the egg, if the broth is a first-rate one.

Rice-flour Soup. — Take one ounce of rice flour (two table-spoonfuls); stir until smooth in one gill of cold soup-liquor; add to it one and a half pints of the boiling liquor, and cook for ten minutes, stirring all the while. Add now two or three tablespoonfuls of cream (hot), a sprinkle of white pepper or nutmeg, and salt to taste. After poured into the tureen put on top of the soup some custard, which is made in the following way : —

Custard for Soups. — Take two whole eggs and one yolk; beat well with one gill of cold soup-liquor (water will do), a pinch of salt, and a dash of grated nutmeg; pour into an earthen bowl or mug, place into a cooking-vessel with hot water, and allow it to be heated until the eggs have set, and no longer. Take out a spoonful at a time; or turn out the custard and cut it into small, equally long strips by means of a fluted knife.

This custard may be added to other soups, especially when clear and made of vegetables.

The above recipe for rice-flour soup is a German one. I have an English recipe which is the same, but leaves out the custard, flavors the soup with a saltspoonful of curry-powder, and a squeeze of lemon.

A very good and showy soup is the following : —

Soup with Moulded Rice. — Have a first-rate beef broth, amber-colored and clear. Take of rice, well washed and scalded, six ounces; of butter, three ounces; put into one quart of boiling broth, which may be of inferior quality (water

will do also) ; see that the liquid is salted exactly right ; boil
covered up for half an hour ; then set uncovered in a hot place
until all the liquid left is evaporated, when you empty the rice
into a deep mould.   Press it down to have it take the shape of
the mould.   Set it in a moderately warm place for a while, and
when ready to serve turn the rice out of the mould on a hot
plate.   Dust all over it some grated Parmesan cheese.   Or
have the cheese handed around separately, and pour over the
rice some melted crayfish butter, garnishing its base or not with
either shrimps, crayfish tails, buttonhole mushrooms, or forcemeat
balls, or with all of these.   Have the rice handed around with
each plate of broth from the tureen.   It is rice enough for six
persons.

The scarlet-colored butter made of crayfish or sweet water
crab, comes handy in tiny tin boxes.   Although an expensive
article, a small quantity will go very far both to color and to
flavor ; and put away in a cool place this butter will keep, after
the box has been opened, for weeks.   The crayfish tails are
also imported, ready for use, in small glass jars.

I will give you only one more recipe of this kind of soups, —
a vermicelli soup, to which we gave the name : —

Potage aux Voyageurs (Travellers' Soup).[1] — Take either
chicken or veal broth ; cook vermicelli in it, of the thick
kind, until soft, but not so that it falls to pieces.   When done
beat up one or more yolks of egg in half a cupful of cream ;
add to the soup with a squeeze of lemon juice, and serve
with grated Parmesan cheese.   If you take a tablespoonful of
sour instead of sweet cream, you will not need the lemon
juice.

Before I proceed I will make you acquainted with some
accessories to soups, which are apt to improve especially the

Accessories   vegetable soups, and often are the most nutri-
to soups.   tious parts of them.

Since you will need bread for nearly all of the following
recipes, I remind you that to be economical every piece and

---

[1] See Bayard Taylor's " Travels in Greece," p. 218.

chip of bread has to be saved, and kept for future use in a clean jar or box. The slices can be cut into any shape required, whilst the odds and ends after accumulation are to be put on the back of the stove or range to get perfectly dry, which makes them fit to be rolled into fine crumbs, by means of the rolling-pin. They ought to be kept in a covered glass or porcelain jar until needed. Just now we want some thick slices of stale bread to add — let us say — to a green pea soup.

Golden Dice. — Cut bread into large dice; beat up one egg in a few tablespoonfuls of milk, to which add a bit of salt; soak the bread in it for half an hour, then fry it until of a fine yellow in hot lard. Skim out of the lard on a piece of brown paper placed on a colander.

Cheese Crusts (*croutons*). — Cut some thin slices of bread into round or oval shaped pieces; dip the upper side into melted butter, and cover thickly with grated Parmesan or Swiss cheese; place these pieces on a sheet iron baking-pan or a pie-dish, and put into the oven until of a deep yellow. They are handed with the soup.

I was present at a dinner where the *croutons* were dry-toasted on the under side, while on top the bread was spread with fresh butter covered with grated cheese. They were handed with a Julienne soup.

Next we have forcemeat and bread balls. The latter are the easiest made, and the more economical additions to soups as well as to fricassees, etc.

Bread Balls. — Take two ounces of butter, and melt it; add four to five tablespoonfuls of fine bread-crumbs, a saltspoonful of salt, a little nutmeg or pepper; mix, then add one whole egg and one yolk; mix again, and stir until smooth and light. Form little balls the size of hickory nuts, and drop them either into boiling water salted or the boiling soup. Cover up, and allow to boil from ten to fifteen minutes.

It is always best to try one ball first by cooking it before the rest. If it cooks to pieces some more bread-crumbs, if too hard a tablespoonful of cream (sour is the best), has to be added. This rule holds good with all the recipes for balls and dumplings.

Sponge Balls. — Take the whites of two eggs and put them into a teacup; fill it up with milk, and pour the contents into a stew-pan; add one teacupful of flour and one ounce of butter (or size of an egg); stir well over the fire until the batter is thick and smooth; set it to cool, after which stir into it the two yolks, a few pinches of salt, a pinch of mace (if liked), and drop into the boiling soup a teaspoonful at a time. Cook from eight to ten minutes.

Marrow Balls. — Take two ounces of beef suet; soak in water for one hour to whiten it; chop fine; melt it over the fire, and strain into a large bowl. When nearly cooled off stir it with a spoon until creamy; drop into it the yolk of an egg and, after stirring a while, a whole egg, half a saltspoonful of salt, half a teaspoonful of minced onion, and one teaspoonful of minced parsley; at the last add three tablespoonfuls of fine bread-crumbs. Form into balls as big as a walnut by means of two spoons, which dip into boiling water every now and then. Place the balls one beside the other on a flat pie-dish which has been buttered previously. When ready to put them into the boiling water, or soup, heat the dish. The balls will drop easily into the cooking-vessel. Boil gently for about ten to fifteen minutes.

Forcemeat Balls. — Take half a pound of raw veal (or chicken); mince very fine; soak two ounces of bread (no crust) in milk; when soft put it in a clean towel and squeeze until dry; add two ounces of butter and the yolks of two eggs, pound the whole in a mortar, and force through a fine sieve; season with salt, white pepper, and nutmeg, and form into almond-shaped balls by taking a teaspoonful of it, heaped full, at a time, shaping it at the top into a point, and smoothing it down by means of a knife dipped in water. Cook about ten minutes in soup-liquor.

Ham Dumplings. — Proceed as above, taking raw ham instead of veal, and season with either minced onion or parsley, instead of nutmeg, leaving out the salt. Do not take the trouble to force it through a sieve, but stir until smooth and light. Form rather large balls — about the size of a small egg —

and cook for twenty minutes to half an hour. They must be as light as sponge when cut with the spoon, and are very good in a soup of clear broth. This is a recipe from Bavaria, southern Germany.

To-day's lesson having been long enough, I will stop here to continue in my next letter the chapter on soups.

LETTER V

They are very different thoughts born within man well nourished and
man miserable and hungry. — DR. J. N. VON NUSSBAUM.

YOU are right, my teachings are tinctured to some extent
by what I learned during the years I spent in Germany. I
there became acquainted with the thrifty spirit of the better
classes of the people, and with their ways of making a great deal
out of a very little. The French in this respect do the same.
Give them poor materials, and they will set before you a dainty
meal. We, who have the best of everything, ought to do
equally well, if not better.

Of a great number of recipes for vegetable soups which
I have at my command, I will select some typical ones,
leaving it to you to vary and improve on them.

Vegetable soups.
For you understand that it is not my inten-
tion to write for you a regular cook-book. After you become
familiar with the spirit of the art of cookery, you will continue
— after the beginning you have made — to teach yourself far
better than any one else could do it.

Julienne Soup. — Take one carrot, a quarter of a white
turnip, a quarter of a celery-root, half a parsnip, one small leek,
about four leaves of a head of lettuce, and a quarter of the
tender inside of a head of Savoy cabbage. Cut all this in narrow strips, about two inches long, stew for half an hour in one
ounce of butter; but see that it does not get brown or stick to
the vessel. Then add one quart of good, clear broth and boil
the vegetables in it gently for one hour. According to the
season, you may add to the foregoing vegetables some heads
of asparagus, tender green peas, and string beans, cooked separately. Observe that this soup, after adding the broth to the

vegetables done in butter, has to boil very gently to prevent the broth from getting cloudy. Serve with this soup some browned bread, or, if preferred, serve it over some boiled rice. A heaped tablespoonful of the latter will be sufficient for the above quantity of soup.

There is a general belief that herbs eaten in springtime are especially wholesome. The following recipe, taking this into account, is termed : —

Easter Soup. — Gather the young sprouts and leaves of wild herbs when their first shoots appear, such as dandelion, sheep-sorrel, yarrow, nettle, lady's-mantle (*Alchemilla vulgaris*), strawberry leaves, etc. Take a handful of each ; rinse repeatedly in cold water and drain in a colander. Do not squeeze them, lest you lose some of their juices. Chop fine ; put into some good broth, and boil gently for about half an hour. Mix butter the size of a walnut with a teaspoonful of flour and drop it into half a cup of boiling cream or milk. When cooking has dissolved it, add it to the soup. Serve with poached eggs on top, or the custard the recipe of which I gave you in my last.

Carrot Soup. — Take two large carrots, one small turnip, half a celery root, one leek ; boil in water which has been salted, adding butter the size of half an egg. When soft, drain and work through a sieve with a potato-masher. Add this pulp to the soup-liquor.

This soup is improved by an addition of rice. The latter in combination with Savoy cabbage is excellent if the whitish part of the inside head only is taken, and cut into fine shreds.

Asparagus Soup. — Take half a pound of fresh asparagus, cut off the heads, and boil separately in salted water until done, which will be in about fifteen minutes. Cut the rest into small pieces, throw them into boiling broth (which need not be of the best) and cook gently for one hour. Then pass through a fine colander ; put it back on the fire to boil up. Add the asparagus heads, and the yolks of one or two eggs beaten up in half a cup of cream.

Green Pea Soup. — Take half a pint of large green peas, and a handful of both spinach leaves and parsley (which serve as coloring-matter). Cook the whole in some weak broth until quite soft; rub through a fine colander; put back on the fire, and let it come to a boil; add a piece of butter the size of a walnut, and a handful of small green peas cooked separately. Some roses of cauliflower may be added; or some of the little balls I gave you the recipes for.

An Italian soup, called Risi-pisi, consists of green peas pulped through a sieve and mixed with boiled rice.

Corn Soup. — Take a couple of ears of corn; grate off the top skin of the grains all around them and by means of a tin spoon scoop out the milk and what is left of the grains. Stir the pulp thus obtained into boiling broth, and allow it to cook about an hour. Add a small lump of butter rolled in flour, and half a cup of cream or milk.

Some tomato, either fresh or left over from a previous meal, is a good addition to corn soup. To make it still better, take

Tomato, corn, and okra for soup. less of the corn, and add half a dozen okra pods sliced thin. Leave off the flour, and take of cream but one teaspoon, mixed with the yellow of an egg.

A tomato soup without any accessories but milk, butter, salt, pepper, and cracker-crumbs is a very simple affair, and very good, indeed, but I would class it rather with the water soups. Tomato soup with rice is excellent when milk is left out, and a good broth is used instead of water.

The following I consider a very good recipe : —

Tomato Soup. — Take about ten tomatoes; cut them in pieces; cook them with a quarter of a pound of ham, one onion in which stick a clove, a sprig of parsley, two pepper-corns, half a bay leaf (no salt on account of the ham) ; after half an hour drop into it butter size of a walnut mixed with a heaped teaspoonful of flour ; allow to dissolve while boiling, and rub through a wire sieve. Salt to taste. Add to a broth in which two or three teaspoonfuls of either very fine vermicelli or starlets of vermicelli have been cooked.

Tomato and okra seem to have been specially designed by nature to complement each other, the acid liquid of the one being in accordance with the glutinous and grassy insipidity of the other.   In the Southern States people found Tomato and this out long ago, and the result has been the okra combined. gumbo soup.   There are a great many varieties of recipes for this soup, most of them of an extravagant character.   Okra grows readily in our gardens North, and makes a first-rate soup in combination with a " Julienne," an addition of tomato, and a bunch of thyme, sweet marjoram, and parsley, the bunch being removed before serving the soup.   The following is a Georgia recipe for a plain

Gumbo Soup. — Take fresh tomatoes and okra in equal quantities, slice them ; cook gently in some beef liquor for several hours ; season to taste.   Boil rice separately, and serve with the soup.

Black Bean Soup. — Soak over night one teacupful of black Mexican beans.   Next day put them on to boil in three pints of cold water (if the water is hard add a pinch of baking soda, which will make it soft), and add any scraps of pork or ham you happen to have on hand.   Add the salted meat after the water is tepid.   Be careful in salting this soup.   After the beans come to a boil add one small onion, and one clove.   When quite done pulp the beans through a colander fine enough to retain the skins.   Add more water, or some soup-liquor, if too thick.   Serve over one or two hard-boiled eggs cut in quarters, and half a lemon sliced.   If liked, add a tablespoonful of sherry at the last moment.

The taste of this soup very much resembles that made of turtle.

We have got now as far as the bean, pea, and lentil soups —all three of them very nourishing.   You may use for them either broth or water, just as your judgment leads Soups made you to do.   If broth, scraps of meat left over, or of pulse. a ham bone, will be sufficient for it ; but water will serve as well.   It seems to me, therefore, that I might introduce the water soups here rather then later, since the best- Water soups. tasting of them are made of vegetables.   To begin with I have to give you two different recipes for an excellent foundation of a water soup.

Imitation Broth No. 1. — Take one pint of dried peas; pick out the bad ones and wash; put them to boil with three pints of water, and a saltspoonful of salt. When quite soft, pulp them through a colander. Use this liquid at discretion for the foundation of soups.

Foundation for water soups.

Imitation Broth No. 2. — Cook peas as above and strain them before they get soft, or rather as soon as the water turns yellow. Add to the latter such vegetables as carrot, turnip, onion, celery root, after they have been sliced and browned in a tablespoonful of butter, or fat. Add salt, and allow fully an hour to boil. If liked, a "bouquet," or bunch of thyme and parsley, some pepper seeds, and a small bay leaf may be added with the vegetables. The strained peas may be used up in some other way.

Another flavoring is obtained by adding the shavings and fibrous parts of asparagus. They ought, therefore, to be saved at the right season, dried, and put away carefully in the store closet.

Recipe No. 1 I found in a German cook-book, "The Perfect Lenten Fare," written by a "cook for many years" in a Catholic vicarage. She says this pea broth is the foundation for all lenten soups.

To make soup without meat, of either dried peas, beans, or lentils you wash them first, then soak them over night, and put them on the stove at an early hour, with plenty of cold water. (Remember that hard water, for cooking purposes, has to be made soft by adding a pinch of baking soda.) Do not let them get dry, but replenish the water if not sufficient. Pulse takes from two to three hours to get thoroughly done. To raise it to the proper standard of nourishment, the addition of fat is needed. Pork drippings are the best for this purpose. Both pea and lentil soups are improved by adding an hour before meal-time some soup-vegetables, sliced and browned in fat. If the soup, after being rubbed through a colander, lacks consistency, a little flour mixed with butter may be added to thicken it. The lentil soup is improved by some lemon juice

How to make a good soup of pulse.

or vinegar, which by softening the cellulose, or woody particles of this highly nourishing vegetable, helps the digestive powers to perform the heavy task imposed upon them by it.

Bean soup does not need the additional vegetables. If liked, a small onion and a slice of bacon cut in little dice may be fried crisp in a hot pan, and added to the soup after it has been rubbed through the colander.

All three soups are improved by serving them over bits of bread fried crisp in butter or fat. A sausage cooked, skinned, and cut into thick slices is also a pleasant addition.

In contrast to the above vegetables potatoes have but little alimentary value. Still, a soup made of them is often convenient, and palatable.

Potato Soup. — Take either cooked potatoes left over, and grate them, or peel, slice, and cook raw potatoes in salted water until quite soft. Add to the water a little bunch of sweet marjoram, an onion, and a small celery root. If grated potatoes are used which have been cooked before, stir them into the boiling liquid at the very last, and allow to boil up once or twice. For this sort of soup, imitation broth No. 2 is in order. The soup made of raw potatoes has to be rubbed through a colander. Add minced parsley to it, if sweet marjoram is not liked. One or two eggs beaten up in some milk or cream will greatly improve the nourishing quality of a potato soup.

By a simple process easily divined, a good many of the recipes for soups I have given you can be turned into water soups. Therefore, I will only add two more recipes.

A Green Soup. — Take one handful of garden sorrel and one of spinach — the stripped leaves only. Wash them well; chop them, but not too fine, with a sprig of parsley and a few lettuce leaves; toss them over the fire in hot butter the size of half an egg; then add one quart of boiling water, salt, a slice of stale bread, one onion, one clove, and (if convenient) a couple of pistachio nuts peeled and cut into shreds. Allow all this to boil gently for one hour, and no longer. Then rub the whole through a sieve, and add two eggs with some cream.

Serve either over some browned bread or some of the little bread balls mentioned before. Or leave away the latter as well as the egg, and serve the egg custard with this soup.

Pea-pod Soup. — Put to boil three pints of water; fill the kettle up to the water's edge with the well-washed pods of fresh peas after the latter have been removed; add one table-spoonful of drippings, some salt, and a few pepper seeds; also some thyme, parsley, and celery leaves. Cook until the pods are quite soft, when strain off the liquid into another pot, and pound the pods in a mortar to a pulp. Now put the latter back into the sieve and rub through into the liquid. Heat up again, and add either some of the peas cooked separately or some young carrots sliced and cooked beforehand; or serve over browned bread, etc., according to your own judgment.

The lesson of economy this soup teaches is evident.

We have come at last to the soups I have enumerated as those of the third kind. They are made chiefly of meat hashed very fine, and are generally called by the French term *purée*. There are a great many varieties.

Soups made of chopped meat.

If you mean to be economical, you will use for them remnants of meat. Trim it off the bones carefully, remove all fat and sinew, and chop it as fine as possible. The bones, of course, you will crack and add to the kettle in which the broth is simmering. Take the minced meat, toss it a few times over the fire in a little very hot butter. This is the thickening for your soup, which you may serve either white or brown, according to the meat you use. If white, you take half a cup of cream or milk; drop into it, when boiling, butter and flour rubbed into a ball; cook it until dissolved and smooth; then add the yolks of one or two eggs, beaten up. Put the hashed meat into the tureen first, then the whitening with the egg, and at last the broth, being careful to mix the whole gradually and thoroughly. Minced parsley may be added. If the soup is to be brown, take butter and flour of equal quantity, mix it in a very hot iron pan, and continue stirring over the fire until evenly brown. Add enough of the broth — a little at a time, and stirring well — to make a thick brown batter; add this to the broth for your soup, let it boil up a few times, seeing that it is smooth, then add your minced meat, and serve. With the white as well as the brown soup, an addition of either forcemeat, bread, or egg balls is in place.

The above gives you the generalization of this kind of very nourishing soups, to which I will add some special recipes. I begin with a soup which " Mademoiselle Françoise" (the pseudonym of a lady known in French society) invented for her frequent guest, Offenbach, the composer, after his years and labors began to tell on his health.

Raw Meat Soup. — Take a good beef broth ; boil in it some pearl sago ; when done, add the yolk of an egg mixed with a tablespoonful of tepid broth and a little grated Parmesan cheese. At the very last, when already in the tureen, add, while stirring carefully, some raw beef free of all fat and sinew, which previously has been chopped very fine.

The most delicate of this kind of soups is the chicken *purée*, which goes by the name of *soupe à la reine*. Of the different recipes I know of, I select the following as being, in my opinion, the best, and at the same time the most practical one.

Chicken Purée Soup (or *Soupe à la Reine*). — Boil an old hen in two quarts of water with a saltspoonful of salt, the usual vegetables, one bay leaf and about six white pepperseeds. When the meat is quite tender, take it off the bones, remove the skin and tendons ; chop it first very fine, then pound it to a pulp in a mortar with a little butter and six blanched almonds.[1] Meanwhile set on to boil three ounces of Carolina rice in the chicken liquor, freed of fat. When the rice is thoroughly soft, which will be in about an hour, mix with it the chicken pulp, and rub the whole through a wire sieve. This soup must have the consistency of thick cream. If too thick, add some handy soup liquor, or water, or milk. You may also add some yolk of egg, but it would change the color, which ought to be white. If you wish this soup to be particularly nice, take merely the white meat for the thickening, separating it from the dark

1 See p. 207.

meat, and using the latter for some forcemeat balls.   The above
is sufficient for from six to eight persons.

Game Purée Soup. — Take the bones and meat of any cooked
game ; also the heads, necks, and giblets of the same ; stew in
plenty of water, with a thin slice of fat bacon, an onion, half a
small carrot, one bay leaf, and a few black pepper seeds.   When
quite soft remove the meat to a chopping-bowl and allow the
rest to stew a while longer.   Chop the meat, then pound it to a
pulp in a mortar.   Brown a scant tablespoonful of flour in butter the size of a walnut ; add it to the liquor which you strain
off the bones, then add the pounded meat, and as much more
broth (or water) necessary to give to your soup the proper consistency.   Rub the whole through a wire sieve and serve over
browned slices of bread.

Sweetbread Soup. — Blanch and skin one sweetbread.[1]   Melt
a piece of butter the size of a walnut, and when hot put into
it the sweetbread with a pinch of salt, and one small onion,
whole.   Cover it up, and simmer over a slow fire until tender,
which will be in about fifteen minutes.   Then take out the
sweetbread, and cut it into small dice.   Remove the onion,
and stir into the hot butter one tablespoonful of flour.   When
well mixed add some light-colored broth, — either chicken or
veal ; let it boil for several minutes, stirring all the while to
prevent its getting lumpy.   Add the sweetbread, and last of all
the yolk of an egg beaten up in a few tablespoonfuls of cream.

If you leave out the onion, this is a first-rate soup for an
Soup for   invalid.   The next one, although very good, I
an invalid.   would not recommend for this purpose, owing
to the large percentage of fatty substance contained in the
brain.

Calf's Brain Soup. — Soak a calf's brain for fifteen minutes
in tepid water ; then pull off the skin ; heat butter the size of a
walnut in a frying-pan ; put in it the brain, and stir it with a
spoon until like mush ; dust over it some flour, and allow it to
simmer, stirring all the time, for about five minutes longer.

[1] See p. 72.

Thin it with broth, rub it through a fine sieve, and put it back
on the fire to boil up.   Add some egg and cream, and serve
over pieces of bread which have been fried crisp.

To conclude this matter of soups, I want to give you for your
edification — play after work — a sample of what our forefathers considered a fine bruce (broth) or soup.   An English
manuscript of the XV. century has the following : —

Take the intestines of a pig, and boil them gently ; cut them
into bits, and put them in a pot with some good broth ; then
take some white leek, peel it, and cut it into
small pieces.   Now with some chopped onions *Two old recipes.*
add it to the former, and set on to boil the whole.   Dip bread
in some broth, and make it tasty with blood and vinegar ; put
it into a pot, allow it to boil up with pepper and cloves, and
send the whole to the table.   With it was served an entire
pig's head.

Another recipe says : Take powdered rice and cook with
milk of almond until thick ; take also gizzards of capons or
hens, pound them in a mortar, mix with the former, put the
whole into a pot, adding powdered cinnamon and cloves ; and
dust some sandalwood over the whole.

Might this be the progenitor of our chicken *purée* soup?   I
leave it for you to solve.

LETTER VI

Too little can always take more,
But *too much* can never restore.

What say you to a piece of beef and mustard ?
— SHAKESPEARE.

YOU ask me for a rule in salting. This is slightly embarrassing, for there is really no rule to rely upon. Salt is a mineral (chloride of sodium) which exists in all animal substances as well as in all vegetable matters. But it does not enter into them in equal proportions. Therefore one kind of food needs more, another less salt added in cooking. Fat meat, for instance, has to be salted more than lean meat ; and of all kinds of meat, venison and other game has to be salted most sparingly on account of the larger percentage of salt contained in the flesh already. Of the vegetables, all grains and those rich in starch possess very little salt, while spinach, for instance, has 0.6 per cent, beans have 0.4, and figs 0.8 per cent of salt.

Difficulties in regard to the salting of food.

Another difficulty in giving rules about salting is the difference in the salt we buy. It is either good, *i.e.* pure salt, or bad, which means adulterated. The latter, of course, does not serve its full purpose. Good salt must be of a pure sparkling white ; its taste must not be bitter ; it must not be moist, nor pack into lumps ; it must dissolve in water without any visible sediment, for which trial you take one part of salt to three of water. Salt, if adulterated, is mostly mixed with gypsum (sulphate of lime), which, when added in quantities above five per cent changes the appearance of the salt to a dull white. If you dissolve this salt in water, the latter will remain cloudy. It is more easily tested when coarse, than when fine.

The qualities of pure salt.

40

It is safe in all cases to salt but slightly at first. More can be easily added if necessary, while an overdose of salt is difficult and often impossible to remedy. Any kind of food if salted too much is spoiled. Not only is it unpleasant to the taste, but it also has lost its wholesome properties. For scalding vegetables or boiling macaroni you may safely take a scant tablespoonful of salt to every quart of water; but in most other cases your taste has to judge how much or how little salt a dish of food needs.

Aside from making food palatable, salt helps to digest it on account of its dissolvent property. It assists especially to liquefy fatty and albuminous substances, which Salt assists then are more readily absorbed by the system. digestion. It is also well to know that salted water requires a higher temperature to reach the boiling-point. Thus it is a Salt will raise means, by increase of heat, to render any tough- the temperature of the ness of fibre softer and tenderer. boiling-point.

Salt, therefore, is the one seasoning cookery cannot spare. This accounts for the value attached to it in all ages, and by all nations. Aborigines have gone to war for it. High value Homer sings of it as the divine, the noblest of of salt in flavors; and in England, during the Middle Ages, past ages. the salt-cellar was a standard of rank. It stood in the centre of the table, and a gentleman sitting at the upper half thought himself too good to drink to one sitting at the same table "below the salt." A meal without salt — who would relish it? The best, however, of all dinners is the one where the "Attic salt" is not lacking either.

You have noticed that in all my recipes for broth and soups spice is used but sparingly. I mean by it, especially the exotic spices, the immoderate use of which is hurtful, The use and while a little of it, and of the right sort, im- value of spices. proves the flavor of a dish, and, like salt, helps digestion by promoting the secretion of the gastric juice. Therefore, a weak digestion is often benefited by the addition to food of pepper, allspice, cloves, ginger, nutmeg, cinnamon, etc. — each where it belongs, and in small quantities; while spice in excess will

always work harm in the long run by irritating the mucous mem-
brane, oftentimes causing malignant dyspepsia.

Too much spice is hurtful.

Besides, the art of cooking goes begging as soon as you overcharge your soups, gravies, etc., with spice. It makes all food taste alike in destroying the particular flavor of each kind. In following, for instance, most of the English recipes for soups, you will have generally a taste of something hot burning your palate and stomach alike ; but you are hardly able to distinguish any other ingredients except an overdose of spice.

I would warn you not to buy your spice, nor your herbs, in a powder. Buy them whole, and highest priced, to get them

Buy spices and herbs whole.

pure. They will be the cheapest in the end. If kept in tight-fitting boxes, and ground in a spice-mill when needed, spices will always have their fresh aromatic properties, and serve their purpose well.

Herbs, like thyme, sage, sweet marjoram, etc., I buy in market when fresh from the ground. After rinsing them well,

How to preserve herbs.

and removing what is imperfect, I dry them with a clean towel, and hang them up in a dry place, stems upward, and surrounded by a clean sheet of paper, which is left open below. The latter prevents the dust settling on them. When they are quite dry I tie the paper up all around, only to be opened when a sprig is needed.

With parsley and celery leaves I do differently. I dry them in a cool oven, and then rub them to a powder. In order to remove the stems remaining, I sift the latter through a fine wire sieve. It is quite economical to provide for parsley in this way as long as cheap. It is also very convenient to have it at hand in the shape of a powder, instead of having to mince it, although the dry article is not equal to the fresh in flavor.

Of lemons and oranges, when the juice is used for cooking, I cut off the peel with a sharp knife, quite thin, to be put in

How to keep lemon and orange peels.

corked bottles — each kind by itself — with some good brandy. More peel may be added at any time. This makes a pleasant flavoring for fruit sauces, puddings, and other desserts. In peeling be careful

not to cut off any of the white underlying the outer yellow.
It is of a bitter taste, and, in addition, prevents the aromatic
oil of the peel from yielding its aroma. The juice of a sour
orange is often preferable to lemon juice for cooking purposes.
It imparts a most delicate flavor even to sauces accompanying
dishes of meat or vegetables.

You are anxious, however, to have me tell you about meat
— the staple article of food whenever the question of good
nourishment is concerned. Of all meat, beef is Grades of
the highest in order. Next to it come venison nourishment
in meats.
and pigeon, especially squab, which is invaluable
for the sick and persons of weak digestive power. But, to
give you a clear estimate of the different grades of nutritives
in meats, it will be necessary to figure them out in percentages.
The following tables will show you that the fatter the meat is
the more its large percentage of water is reduced and replaced
by substance.

	WATER.	ALBUMINOIDS.	FATS.	MINERAL MATTERS.
Lean beef..................	76.5	21.0	1.5	1.0
Middling fat beef..........	72.5	21.0	5.5	1.0
Very fat beef..............	55.5	17.0	26.5	1.0
Lean veal.................	78.0	20.0	1.0	1.0
Fat veal..................	72.5	19.0	7.5	1.0
Middling fat mutton.......	76.0	17.0	6.0	1.0
Fat mutton...............	48.0	15.0	36.0	1.0
Lean pork................	72.0	20.0	7.0	1.0
Fat pork.................	47.0	14.5	37.5	1.0
Chicken middling fat......	75.0	20.0	4.0	1.0
Venison..................	75.5	22.5	1.0	1.0

I have demonstrated to you that meat when used for the
purpose of making broth or soup has to be treated so as to extract its juices, leaving the fibre as refuse. The The juices of
opposite treatment is necessary for all meats which meat must
be kept intact.
are to serve as roasts, steaks, cutlets, stews, etc.
With these the utmost care has to be taken that none of the
juices leak out of the meat. They must be kept intact. If
not, so much of the nourishment contained in the meat as will
escape is waste material and loss to the individual to be fed.

In order to show you how to proceed I will begin with a broiled beefsteak : —

Get a porterhouse steak an inch thick of about one to one and a half pounds.   If of a well-fed ox, it contains more nourishment in proportion than a lower-priced piece of the same weight.   See that your fire is bright and clear of smoke.   Have your gridiron hot.   Pour a little of the best olive oil into a cup, take a long-haired brush kept for such purposes only, dip it into the oil, and grease with it gridiron and steak.   Have the dish hot in which to serve the latter, and place on it a piece of fresh butter the size of a walnut.   Put your gridiron and meat on the fire, not so near as to burn it, and yet near enough for the meat to become seared over and browned in two or three minutes.   Then turn it and allow the other side to get brown as quickly.   In this way the albumen on the outside of the meat, by coming in contact with the heat, coagulates, and furnishes a crust through which the meat-juice cannot escape ; it stays inside, and thus is kept intact.   Place the steak on the dish ready to receive it ; put some salt on the upper side, and a sprinkle of pepper if preferred ; then turn this side downward to come in contact with the butter ; turn it back again and serve it at once.   With this recipe you have the principle to apply to all meats meant for food.

How to broil a beefsteak — a recipe demonstrating the principle of the art of cooking meat meant for food.

The roast is managed in the same way.   Take a rib piece. Have the butcher cut it as short as he is willing to do.   Or have him take the bones out (which you use for soup) and roll it up, fastening it tight with twine. Do not use skewers ; they make unsightly holes, and allow the juice to escape.   Have your oven thoroughly hot.   Put a teaspoonful of butter, or as much suet dripping, into your meat-pan, and when melted and very hot, put in your roast, and place in the oven.   Brown it on all sides as rapidly as possible to form that impenetrable thin crust, inside of which the particles of water contained in the meat will develop into steam. This in its turn permeates the meat-fibre, softens the muscle, and cooks the meat in its own juices.   As soon as this crust is

How to roast beef.

formed the heat of the oven has to be slackened. To prevent the outside from burning or drying up, a little melted butter has to be kept in readiness with which to baste the meat from time to time. It takes fifteen minutes for every pound of beef to have the roast done rare. A quarter of an hour before it is done sprinkle with salt. Do not do it earlier; for salt, being a dissolvent, softens the outside and extracts the juices. When the roast is done put it on a hot dish, clear the pan of fat, add a little boiling water or beef broth (one saltspoonful of Liebig's extract dissolved is an excellent addition) and a little salt; let it boil up while loosening with a spoon the brown deposit attached to the bottom and sides of the pan. Take care not to dilute it too much. Strain through a fine wire sieve, and serve this gravy with the meat. If you should prefer your roast without any other gravy than the juice running out in carving — which is the very best you could have — the made gravy can be kept over and used afterward in various ways, as, for instance, in hash or soup. I have purposely given you the recipe for roasting in the oven, and not on the spit before the fire. Although the latter is decidedly the best, the former can produce as good and nourishing a roast, if strictly done in the above way. It is the easiest way for young housekeepers who cannot afford to keep an experienced cook.

Be sure never to stick a fork into any kind of meat which is to appear on the table. By making holes for the juices to leak out, the nourishing properties of the meat will be reduced. I keep a pair of meat tongs in my kitchen for handling and turning steaks and cut- *Precaution in the handling of meat.* lets. For turning or lifting larger pieces of meat take two wooden ladles.

If for any reason you wish to use a lower-priced or indifferent piece of meat, you will do best to stew or braise it, observing the same principles as before. Use for it a stewing-pot with a tight-fitting lid. Brown the *How to stew or braise meat.* meat first on all sides in hot butter or fat. The highest temperature of fat is three times as hot as boiling water. The latter (or boiling broth) being added after the meat is browned will lower the heat in which the meat cooks considerably, which is necessary to steam the inside of the meat until tender. After adding the liquid allow it to boil up a few times; then secure the lid of the cooking-vessel as tightly as possible and remove the latter to a place where the temperature is kept somewhat below the point of boiling — where the contents will merely simmer. If allowed actually to boil, the juices inside the meat will dry up and the meat will be tough. From the time your meat begins to simmer, it will take from half an hour to one hour for each pound to get tender. A small piece will get done relatively sooner than a large piece. I will give you here a recipe of Mlle. Françoise's for braised beef.

Take four slices of fat bacon; brown them slightly in an iron pot; remove them, and brown in the fat remaining a

Recipe for braised beef. piece of beef (about four pounds of the round) on all sides. Then take the bacon, place two of the slices underneath and two above the beef. Have in readiness one tablespoonful of chopped mushrooms, one teaspoonful each of minced onion, parsley, chervil, and sweet basil; moisten all this with either a wineglassful of cooking sherry or a small cupful of broth. Add the whole to the meat, cover it up tightly, and let it simmer very slowly for from four to five hours. Be sparing with the salt on account of the salted pork. The liquid remaining in the pot, after the meat is taken out, will make a sauce to be served with it by adding some browned flour or *roux*, and some whole mushrooms, after the sauce has been passed through a wire sieve.

I have given you these three recipes to show the principal methods to be followed in cooking meats. Keep in your mind the law laid down in them and apply it to all other kinds of meat.

The time, however, which is required for cooking the different meats is not the same for all. Mutton has to be cooked

Time required for roasting other kinds of meat besides beef. more than beef; roast it fully twenty minutes for each pound, and five minutes more each pound for a large leg of mutton. Veal and pork must be well done to be wholesome; you may safely take half an hour for each pound, but twenty-five minutes only when

your roast is a loin.   Chicken and turkey require twenty minutes each pound, but spring chickens are done in fifteen minutes, and so are all small birds.   Pigeons and partridges require
half an hour, prairie chickens three-quarters of an hour.

I now return to the beef, than which for nourishment, if
properly treated, there is nothing better.   The rib piece, by
which I demonstrated to you the principle at the   Respective
base of roasting, is surpassed in succulence by the   value of differ-
                                                     ent cuts of beef.
sirloin and the filet, or tenderloin — respectively
the outer and inner parts of the loin.   The filet, bare of all
bone, by itself, is sold disproportionately high in price in the
large cities, and therefore is not recommendable for small
households like yours and mine.   But, after all, you might
some day have occasion for a filet-roast, and will then be glad
to have the following recipe for filet of beef *à la jardinière.*
For this piece of meat, eight minutes' cooking for   Recipe for
each pound is sufficient, if meant to be rare;   filet of beef
                                                  à la jardinière.
otherwise ten minutes each pound.   Remove both
fat and skin — the latter very carefully, with a sharp-pointed
knife, so as not to cut into the flesh.   Lard it on top as closely
as possible in several rows.   Have a dripping-pan hot, melt in
it some butter — a piece the size of an egg for every two
pounds.   When right hot put in your filet and brown it rapidly
on all sides.   Then continue to roast with moderate heat.
Baste frequently with the butter in the pan.   Sprinkle with
some salt when in the oven half an hour, and finish basting
with a cupful of cream.   If preferred, a few spoonfuls of beef
broth can be added to the butter in the pan, instead of basting
with cream.   Take the fat off the gravy, strain it, and serve it
poured over the filet.   Surround the latter with different kinds
of vegetables, as young carrots, green peas, Brussels sprouts,
" roses " of cauliflower, chestnuts, mushrooms, etc.   Arrange
them in little bunches, or bouquets, each kind by itself, and if
tomatoes are in season divide each bouquet by a large stuffed
tomato.

It is very likely that you will nave part of the filet left over,
of which remnant you wish to make the most.   This is the

special way in which I use up cold beefsteak or roast beef:

What to do
with remnants
of beefsteak
and roast beef. Scorch a scant tablespoonful of flour in a tablespoonful of drippings; add soup liquor sufficient to make a thick sauce, stirring all the while until smooth; add salt and pepper, a teaspoonful of lemon juice, and as much, or more, of mushroom catsup. When ready add the meat, either cut in dice or in thin slices, and stir until completely immersed in the sauce; cover up tightly, and set either on a vessel of boiling water, or on a place where the meat gets heated through, but does not boil. In fifteen minutes it will be ready to serve. Another way is this, which is given by Alexandre Dumas, who was never happier than when able to don the white apron and cook a meal for one or more friends : —

For "beef *en matelotte*" peel some small onions and put them in a saucepan with some butter; place them over a slow

Recipe for beef
en matelotte. fire until of a light brown; dust over them a tablespoonful of flour, and continue to cook slowly. After the flour is of the same color as the onions, add a glassful of claret (or a tablespoonful of orange juice), half as much broth, a few mushrooms, some salt, pepper, and a bouquet of one bay leaf and a sprig of thyme. Allow the whole to stew for a little while, then pour it over slices of cooked beef, and place for half an hour where the meat will be kept hot, and be saturated with the sauce without boiling.

In the foregoing you have means to prove the truth of what the famous Dr. von Nussbaum — of Munich, Germany — wrote : "All our thinking and doing is far greater in value when we are well nourished, than it is when we are poorly fed and not our real selves in consequence."

LETTER VII

Is not veal a calf?

Good pasture makes fat sheep.
— SHAKESPEARE.

YOU wish to know how much meat for roasts to provide for your usual meals as well as for company. Before giving you my opinion, I must remind you that there is waste material in what you 'buy, which tells in weight but does not count as food. Water is waste material, and so are bones. Then, also, meat when cooked weighs less than when you bought it; the loss in weight is different in boiling and roasting. When boiled, beef loses 15, mutton and turkey 16, chicken 13½, and ham 6 per cent; when roasted, beef loses 19½, mutton 24½, turkey 20½, lamb 22½, duck 27½, and chicken 14 per cent in weight. Considering all this, and that the larger your roast the juicier and better it is apt to be, I would advise, for a household of three, never to provide less than four pounds for roasting beef, mutton, and veal, and to take one-half pound more for each guest who dines with you. Of steaks, chops, and cutlets, as a general rule half a pound is sufficient for each person. In case of company for dinner, when you will have other courses besides, a large chicken or a capon is sufficient for six persons, a turkey for a company of ten to twelve, a duck but for three to four persons. The latter reminds me of a recipe quoted in C. Monselet's "Gastronomie."

It is equally good for a tame or a wild duck, and is called "duck *à la Portugaise*." Take the heart, gizzard, and liver, and mince them with three shallots (a small onion if you cannot get the shallots); mix with a teaspoonful of salt and half as much black pepper;

Waste material in food matters.

Loss of weight in boiling and roasting.

Recipe for duck à la Portugaise.

49

add a piece of table butter size of an egg and mix the whole with a silver fork. Then introduce the mixture into the inside of the duck, and sew it up at both ends. Take a large napkin, fold it in three thicknesses, roll your duck up in it and fasten it tightly all over with twine. Put it into boiling water well salted, and cover it up. Let it boil for thirty minutes if a tame duck, but thirty-five minutes if a wild one. Remove both twine and napkin and serve on a hot dish with pieces of lemon for a garnish.

I mention this only by the way; and since variety is the spice of life, you will not object. Later on I intend saying more of poultry, but first I mean to talk to you about the kinds of meat on which we depend chiefly for ordinary use.

Veal is much less nourishing than well-fed beef. It has less muscle, about one-third less iron, and is poorer in alkalies. If, *General remarks about veal.* however, the animal is not too young, and has been well cared for, it furnishes the table with a variety of food which in the hands of a clever cook may be turned into a great many pleasant surprises. La Reynière, who wrote the famous " Almanac des Gourmands," calls the calf "the chameleon of the kitchen," on account of the number of different dishes into which it can be turned. The tenderest parts of the calf are the loin, with the kidneys attached, and the breast. The latter is cheaper than either the loin or leg, and therefore an economical piece of meat. It may be stuffed and roasted; or stewed, and served with a white sauce; or made into a delicious " roulade " for slicing when cold. In case you have a loin of veal, and you wish to make the most of it, you can use the kidneys for a savory breakfast dish in the following way: When the roast is *Breakfast dish of veal kidneys.* about half-done, remove the kidneys embedded in their fat. Mince them with one shallot (or a bit of onion) and a sprig of parsley; melt a teaspoonful of butter in a skillet, add the mince when the butter is hot; cover it and allow it to stew for about fifteen minutes over a very moderate fire, shaking the skillet with its contents from time to time to prevent the latter from burning. Add a pinch or two of salt to the mince, and after you take it off the fire a little white pepper and a few drops of lemon juice. Set aside until next morning, when add one egg, and mix it in well. Now cut some slices of bread, brown them slightly in a little butter, then spread over one side of them the prepared kidneys, about half an inch thick; dust over them some grated Parmesan cheese, and over it some fine bread-crumbs. Sprinkle over the whole some melted butter, place the slices on a tin dish, and put them in a quick oven to get a light brown on top. Serve hot.

A roast is not always desirable for a small family. Veal cutlets have the same nourishing properties, if prepared in the right way. The cutlets from the loin are the best, but those cut from the leg may be made just as savory, *Veal cutlets.* and are the cheapest. Have the butcher cut you one pound off the leg in slices one-third of an inch (half a finger's width) thick. Divide this meat into pieces as large as the palm of your hand. Remove skin and bone, *Veal cutlets à la parmentière.* pound the cutlets with the flat side of a kitchen knife, and turn them in some flour. Then heat a teaspoonful of butter in a saucepan and throw in a teaspoonful of minced onion. When the latter begins to turn yellow put in your cutlets, one beside the other, and add a few small slices of thinly cut ham. Let all get brown first on one side and then on the other. Sprinkle a very little salt over the veal, add some pepper, and a few squeezes of lemon juice. When the ham is tender take it out and cut the lean in as many small diamond-shaped pieces as you have cutlets, and keep hot. Add a little water to the cutlets, cover them up and allow to simmer on a slow fire until quite tender, adding more liquid if necessary. Serve them on a bed of mashed potatoes, place a piece of ham on every cutlet and pour the gravy around the potatoes.

When in Carlsbad, Austria, I learned from the bill of fare that this dish was called veal cutlet *à la parmentière*. After giving you this particular recipe in which you have the base for cooking veal cutlet, I leave it to you to vary according to

your own good judgment. You might have peas instead of
potatoes ; or you might leave out the ham and
garnish the cutlets with capers and slices of lemon,
serving the vegetable separately. The latter way is called
Vienna *Schnitzel.*

Vienna Schnitzel.

If parts of cooked or roasted veal are left over, you may use
it to advantage for a baked hash, called *miroton :* Chop fine
the veal and, if on hand, some fat ham or bacon.
Mince a slice of onion and a few sprigs of parsley. Take bread-crumbs, about a third of the amount of
chopped meat ; soak them in milk, and squeeze dry by means
of a clean towel. Add some salt and white pepper, and one egg
beaten light beforehand. Mix well all these ingredients, then
warm — but do not cook — them in a saucepan. Now taste
the hash, and see that it is right in salt and spice. Put it into
a deep dish, well buttered, and bake it in a quick oven. It
ought to turn out whole. A tomato or a caper sauce served
with it will greatly improve this dish.

Miroton of veal.

A great delicacy are the sweetbreads. They are both nourishing and easily digested, therefore invaluable for the sick.
But, unfortunately, they are so high-priced in our
large cities (even in the country butchers no
longer throw them away, as they used to do) that
they belong to the luxuries. A calf's head also is not cheap ;
it, however, furnishes us with enough material to permit even
an economical housewife to purchase it now and then. Beside
the meat and skin there are the brains and the tongue for use.
Since all gelatinous matter — and the calf's head has a great
deal of it — is not easily digested, the addition of a slight acid
is necessary either in the preparation of such matter or in
what is served with it. To increase the nutritive properties of
calf's head, eggs are a first-rate complement.

*Sweetbreads
and calf's head.*

I have two recipes which I would recommend
both for their simplicity and wholesomeness.

*Recipes for
calf's head.*

After the head has been properly scraped and cleaned
(which the butcher generally does), have it split in halves,
giving particular orders not to split the tongue as well. Soak

the whole in cold water for about two hours, then remove the brain and set it aside. Put the halves, with the tongue, on the fire, with cold water to cover it; add salt in moderate quantity; add one or two pounds of beef bones, if you wish to make your dish particularly nourishing. After the scum is removed add two carrots, one turnip-rooted celery, one onion, a bunch of parsley, eight white pepper seeds, and half a cup of vinegar. Allow to boil slowly until soft, which will be in about two hours. Now take the fleshy parts off the bone, also the ears, and peel the tongue (unless you wish to save it for a special dish later on, when it will keep fresher in its skin). Cut all this into nicely shaped pieces and set to keep warm as much of it as you wish to use for your dish presently. The rest you cover up with some of the strained liquor and set away. In cold weather it will keep for weeks. It can be used in various fashions, for soups, ragouts, etc.; or it may be baked.

Although the brains may be used for a soup or fried in a batter, etc., I propose that you should use them for a dish of "baked calf's head." Take as much as about half of the above cooked head. Cut the pieces rather small. After the brains have been well soaked in salted water, scald them in boiling water, and remove all skins and veins; then mash them through a sieve, mix them with a cupful of cream, half a teaspoonful of flour, two eggs well beaten, a saltspoonful of salt and a sprinkle of nutmeg. Butter a dish in which to serve it, put in it the pieces of calf's head and pour over them the above mixture. Bake in the oven until brown, and serve the following anchovy sauce with it: Take a teaspoonful of butter; when hot mix it with a scant teaspoonful of flour; add gradually and stirring all the while about half a pint of the liquid in which the calf's head has been boiled, or any other broth (water even will do). When well mixed add four sardines out of brine, which have to be well washed and bones removed beforehand. Or, if more convenient, add instead half a teaspoonful of anchovy paste. Add also one small onion, the peel of a quarter-lemon, and allow the whole to boil from half an hour to one hour. Put through a wire sieve, then add some lemon juice and a tablespoonful of capers ; set it again on the fire, and as soon as it comes to the boiling-point stir in the yolks of two eggs beaten up either in a little cooking wine or cream. Serve in a boat.

The other recipe is called calf's head *en tortue*. Use for it, we will say, the other half of the calf's head you have in readiness. If you wish to use the tongue as well, peel it and slice it evenly. Set it to get warm in some of its own liquid. After that prepare a sauce in this way : Melt a piece of butter the size of an egg, mix with it one teaspoonful of flour ; then stir into it half a pint or more of the liquid in which the head has been boiled, and which, of course, has been strained. Let it bubble up and stir over a moderate fire until quite smooth. Then add half a teaspoonful of Liebig dissolved in a little boiling water, and the prepared pieces of the calf's head. Have the whites of three hard-boiled eggs chopped fine ; add them and a tablespoonful of capers. Put the whole on a moderate fire and, stirring repeatedly, allow it to simmer for five minutes longer. At the very last add the juice of half a lemon and a saltspoonful of white pepper. Stir to get it well mixed in and remove from the fire. Serve in a hot dish, placing the nicest pieces in the middle, with skin uppermost, the tongue, if used, in a circle next to them ; pour over it some of the sauce ; and serve the rest in a boat. Garnish with slices of lemon and parsley, or water-cress.

To be economical you will save the tongue for a breakfast dish. It will suffice for two, if the calf was a large one. It is
Breakfast dish of calf's tongue. very nice prepared thus : After the tongue is boiled, and the skin peeled off, cut it in two lengthwise, turn the halves in sweet oil or melted butter, then in some fine bread-crumbs which have been mixed with a little salt and some minced parsley. Broil them over a bright fire until they are light brown.

To make a *roulade* of veal, take the breast. Have your butcher take out the bones. Then separate the upper from
A *roulade* of veal. the lower part in such a way that both hang together and form one thin square piece when opened out. Lay it, inside uppermost, on a meat-board, and

dust it over with salt and pepper. Now make a forcemeat in the following way: Take half a pound of veal freed from fat and skin and mince very fine. Take also some suet, and mince it as fine as possible. Mix the two, and add half a teaspoonful of minced shallot (or onion) which previously has been steeped in hot butter until yellow; also two eggs well beaten, a sprinkle of grated nutmeg, and a saltspoonful of salt. Mix the whole thoroughly and spread part of it over your veal to the thickness of half a finger's width. Cover this layer of forcemeat with oblong strips (about half an inch thick) of fat bacon, boiled ham or tongue, and red beets, some parsley leaves, small gherkins, and slices of hard-boiled eggs. Arrange all this tastefully as to colors and distances. Then spread over the whole another layer of forcemeat, which press down to secure the pieces underneath. Have a flat surface. Now roll up the meat so as to have the filling all inside. Roll it tight, sew it together with needle and thread, and string it around with twine. Take broth enough from the soup-pot to cover the rolled meat. Place a tight-fitting lid on the stew-pan in which you cook the meat, and boil it over a gentle fire for about three hours. When tender take it out of the liquor, put it between two boards, and place a heavy weight (a flat-iron, for instance) on top. Let it remain over night, and the next day it will be fit for slicing. As long as you cannot afford boned turkey, this is a good substitute when you have company for tea or luncheon. If the slices are *Roulade of veal to take the place of boned turkey.* arranged in a ring, and the centre filled either with a mayonnaise salad or a slightly acid meat-jelly[1] broken up in small pieces, it makes a very palatable and at the same time ornamental dish.

Mutton is easier to digest than veal, if the meat is of a young and well-fed animal. In boiling or roasting mut- *General remarks about mutton.* ton or lamb, a bouquet of thyme and sweet marjoram should be added, which improves the flavor of the meat. A leg of mutton can bear even a button of garlic.

[1] See p. 79.

To boil a leg of mutton, crush to a coarse powder a twig of thyme, a bay leaf, and six black pepper seeds ; chop coarsely an onion and a clove of garlic ; mix the whole and add a teaspoonful of salt. Rub this mixture into the outside of the mutton, lap the latter tightly around with a napkin, and sew it up with thread and needle. Place it in a pot with a tight-fitting lid, and no more than còver it with boiling water. Add to the latter a teaspoonful of salt and the same vegetables as for soup-liquor, with the addition of some thyme and sweet marjoram. Do not let it boil violently. A leg of about seven pounds ought to be done in one hour and three-quarters to two hours. Take the napkin off just before serving. A *purée* of white turnips or a white caper sauce is a fit accompaniment.

Recipe for boiling a leg of mutton.

The loin makes a savory roast. Add an onion cut in two and a bouquet of sweet marjoram and thyme after the roast has taken color. But the best roast of mutton is the saddle. This is the two loins without being separated. Have the butcher trim off the flaps, the tail, and the shoulder-blades. It requires a brisk oven and ten to fifteen minutes roasting for each pound. Add the bouquet required for mutton and an onion. Peel off the skin which covers the top of the saddle when nearly done (about twenty minutes before) ; sprinkle the fat which remains with salt, then with melted butter, and cover it all over with finely sifted bread-crumbs. Now continue the roasting, top part uppermost, until done, when the meat ought to be covered with a crisp brown crust. Garnish this delicious roast with small potatoes browned in butter, and small glazed onions,[1] all of one size. Have it accompanied by green peas.

Loin of mutton.

To roast a saddle of mutton.

Apply the same process to a quarter of spring lamb, than which there is nothing more delicious.

Spring lamb.

The cheapest pieces of mutton are the shoulder and the breast. As to the former, let the butcher take out the bones, which, of course, you use for soup. Put bits of bacon here

---

[1] See p. 125.

and there over the inside of the meat, and sprinkle over it some salt, black pepper, minced parsley, and a little crushed thyme. Roll the meat up tightly and fasten it with twine. Put it into a stew-pan, in which has been heated a tablespoonful of butter. Brown it rapidly on all sides. Then add boiling water enough to cover it about half. Salt but slightly, and put around the meat a few onions, some carrots and turnips, a bay leaf, one or two cloves, a bunch of parsley, and thyme. As soon as the whole comes to a boil, remove from the top of the stove to the oven, and allow it to stew there slowly until done. Place the meat on a hot dish and arrange the vegetables around it. Add a scant table-spoonful of flour to the liquor remaining in the pan. Let it boil for five minutes, while stirring; taste if it needs salt, and pour this gravy over the meat.

Recipe for a shoulder of mutton.

A breast of mutton you may treat in the same way, or you may boil it with soup vegetables and salt until tender; then drain it, turn it first in melted butter, and after-wards in a mixture of bread-crumbs, minced shallots and parsley, salt and pepper, over which you sprinkle some more melted butter. Place the whole be-tween a double gridiron and broil it until light brown over a quick fire.

Recipe for a breast of mutton.

Mutton chops are always best when broiled. Apply the same principle to them as I demonstrated in regard to beefsteak. If you wish them extra fine, do as follows: Mince a small onion, and as much as a tea-spoonful of parsley for about four chops. Mix both with a scant tablespoonful of olive oil, and rub your chops with this mixture. Place one upon another, and leave standing for five minutes. Broil them over a bright fire, sprinkling with salt and pepper when done. Or in this way: Turn your chops first in melted butter, and then in part bread-crumbs and part grated Parmesan cheese, the two mixed together. Then broil.

Broiled mutton chops.

The kidneys also furnish you with a good breakfast or lunch-eon dish. Divide them into halves, but so as to let them hang together. Dust over them salt and pepper, and turn them well in bread-crumbs. Then broil them over a quick fire until light brown. Be careful not to expose them to the heat too long : they must be soft and juicy. Have ready a mixture of fresh butter and minced parsley (to which you may add tarragon and cives, all minced very fine) ; form the mixture into little balls as large as a pill ; put one inside of each kidney ; squeeze a few drops of lemon juice on each, and double up the halves. Serve while hot.

Breakfast dish of mutton kidneys.

I give you in all these recipes only an outline of what can be done with meat. You understand that it is for you to enlarge on them, and apply the rudimentary rules to all other dishes on which you wish to try your skill. It is the "spirit of cookery," which I principally want to instil into you.

LETTER VIII

I HAVE come now to the most despised of animals — the pig, which in spite of all the ignominy heaped on it, lavishes on us an abundance of acceptable gifts in the shape of pork, ham, sausages, etc. Grimod de la Rey- nière, in fact, calls the pig " *l'animal encyclopé- dique par excellence*," and in an old German cook-book of the XVI. century we read, " If a sow were feath- ered and would fly over a fence, she would be superior to all poultry and birds of the air." But pork of all meats is hardest to digest. This is chiefly owing to its toughness of fibre, which resists mastication, and thus causes larger particles of food to be conveyed to the stomach than is otherwise the case. There is, however, a great difference in pork according to what the animal has been fed on. The sweeter its food was the better the meat will be, and the healthier at the same time. Pigs fed on chestnuts are considered the best. The ancient Greeks ate pigs' livers only if the animals had been fed on figs, and wine made of honey. And the " Edda " tells us that the heroes in Walhalla are treated by Odin with meat of wild boar, who is the progenitor of the pig. All this goes to show how much pork, and all derived from it, has been esteemed in all times and ages.

General remarks about pork and the pig.

Nevertheless you would hardly treat your dinner guests with a dish of pork, but rather keep it for the family meal. A rib roast, if tender is, indeed, succulent and deli- cious of flavor. Always roast it with an onion cut into halves, and a clove stuck in each half. Sprinkle plenty of salt over the upper crust of fat, and let it get well done, with-

Roasted pork.

59

out drying up the juices. Some people like a layer of brown
bread-crumbs put over the top of the roast after it is done.
Sprinkle over it a little fine sugar, a pinch of ground cloves,
and lastly some melted butter. Put it once more in the oven
to take color. A Cumberland sauce goes well with this roast.

Recipe for Cum-
berland sauce.

To make it, pour the fat from the pan in which
the pork has been roasted, and add to the brown
sediment in the bottom of it half a cup of broth, a wineglassful of claret, a tablespoonful of French mustard, and as much
of currant jelly. Let the whole boil up, and strain through a
fine sieve. If any fat remains skim it off the top.

A filet or tenderloin of pork is an inexpensive piece of meat
inasmuch as there is no waste. Take either the pair of them

How to roast
tenderloin
of pork.

— since they are excellent for slicing and eating
cold — or only one if it is large, which will be
sufficient for your dinner of three. It must be
well skinned and not entirely bare of fat. Boil a cupful of
vinegar with one small onion sliced, one slice of lemon, one
bay leaf, one sage leaf, one sprig of thyme, six black pepper
seeds, one clove, for five minutes. Pour it boiling hot all
over your pork, turning it in this liquid a few times. Have a
piece of butter the size of a walnut heated beforehand in a
small dripping-pan, and when hot put in the filet, browning it
quickly on all sides. Then continue to roast slowly for about
one hour, adding a spoonful of the strained vinegar from time
to time, to keep the bottom of the pan moist. Sprinkle with
salt and baste frequently. A quarter of an hour before it is
done, pour over your meat a gill of thick cream. Baste it a
few times. This helps to make the sauce ; remove all but a
little of the fat on it, and serve either poured over the filet or
in a boat.

A very economical roast is the spring or the foreloin of pork.
Let the butcher remove the bones, and prepare the following

Recipe for
stuffed fore-
loin of pork.

stuffing : Cut two French rolls into thin slices,
pour over them a cupful of boiling milk ; let soak
a while and get cool. Then add three eggs, half
a teaspoonful of salt, a teaspoonful of minced onion, as much

of minced parsley, a slight sprinkle of grated nutmeg, and beat the whole until light and smooth. Fill this stuffing in the inside of the meat, where the bones have been taken out, and secure it by sewing the edges of the meat together. Roast it in the usual way.

If you wish to cook pork chops, I would recommend to have them well pounded on both sides, then turned in bread-crumbs, in an egg beaten up and salted, and once more in bread-crumbs. *Sauté*[1] them in a **Pork chops.** little hot butter, shaking them frequently to prevent their scorching. They take from twenty minutes to half an hour to get done, and must be of a light brown on both sides.

A favorite with all of us is the ham, and for good reasons. Although in the process of curing some of its nutritive juices are lost, it is made fitter for digestion by means of the **About ham.** salt entering and softening the tough fibres and tissues. If not too large, a ham, even for a small family, is no piece of extravagance. In cool weather it will keep for a week after being cooked, and will help out in many ways. You know how nice it is when cold and sliced. Served with a green salad it makes a nice dish for lunch or supper. It may also be served with a cold sauce made in this way: Take about an ounce of lump sugar, rub into it the outside of half an **A sauce for cold ham.** orange and squeeze over it two tablespoonfuls of its juice. When the sugar is melted, add to it a heaped teaspoonful of French mustard, two tablespoonfuls of salad oil, and as much good vinegar. Mix thoroughly. Or serve with your cold ham the following horseradish sauce: Take two tablespoonfuls of sweet cream; one tablespoonful of best vinegar, half a teaspoonful of sugar, and as much of **Recipe for horseradish sauce.** salt. Beat it up, and add as much grated horseradish as it will take to make a thick sauce. You may also combine these two sauces, by leaving out the cream and mustard. They both go equally well with cold corned beef, with boiled fish, and poultry.

[1] See p. 76.

In case you wish to serve your boiled ham heated over, I propose the following way: Cut it into even slices, soak

Boiled ham heated over. them in cold milk for about half an hour, then wipe them dry. Make a brown *roux*,[1] add to it some broth (or water if you have none), a little lemon peel, a blade of mace, and six black pepper seeds. Let all this boil slowly for half an hour, when strain and add a wineglassful of port wine or sherry. Put the sliced ham into this sauce, place it over boiling water, cover it up, and let it get hot. Serve it in a rice-ring[2] dusted over with grated Parmesan cheese, if you choose to do so.

You may also mince some of the lean part of your boiled ham, and serve it dusted over a dish of boiled macaroni; or,

Other ways of using up boiled ham. in layers between boiled rice, and baked *au gratin* — *i.e.* browned on top and served in the dish baked in. There are, in fact, so many different kinds of nice dishes to be made of ham that in mentioning some of them I forgot that I have not told you as yet how to boil a ham — which is quite important to know. Buy only the best of ham, and then do not soak it in water over

How to boil a ham. night, as a good many cook-books tell you, but have it washed and scrubbed with a brush in lukewarm water. Put it on the fire in cold water, which must cover it entirely. Have a tight-fitting lid for the pot in which you cook it. Let it come to a boil very slowly, then change the water for fresh which is boiling when poured over. Place the pot now where the water will not boil, but merely simmer. The ham is done when the skin, being lifted at the end, will pull off easily. It will take from four to five hours to cook a small ham.

To roast a ham, cook it as above, and after the skin has been

How to roast a ham. peeled off, put it in a dripping-pan with a bottleful of prime cider, and place it in a moderately hot oven for another hour. Baste it occasionally with the liquor in the bottom of the pan.

---

[1] See p. 70.   [2] See p. 73.

Speaking of ham, I am reminded that of cured food a boiled beef's tongue is a very good thing to have now and then, although it is less economical and not nearly *How to* as wholesome as ham. Beef tongue is extremely *boil a tongue.* fat, and there is the root of it, which counts in weight and is nearly all refuse. In boiling a tongue do as in boiling ham, with the one exception that a tongue is better for being soaked over night. If any cold tongue is left over, it will serve for a breakfast dish, done in the following way, given by Dumas : —

Cut your boiled tongue into very thin slices ; take the dish in which it is to be served, put in a few tablespoonfuls of broth (or a saltspoonful of Liebig) and a few drops of *A break-* vinegar or lemon juice. Have a mince made of *fast dish of* pickled cucumbers, parsley, shallot (or onion), *cold tongue* chervil, some black pepper, salt, and bread-crumbs. Spread a thin layer of this mixture first, then a layer of sliced tongue, and so on, finishing with the mince. Dust over the whole some bread-crumbs, and put in a quick oven for about ten to fifteen minutes, to heat through and get brown on top. Just before serving, moisten it with a little more broth (or water).

I have come now to poultry, and particularly chickens, than which there is nothing more delicate and wholesome in the way of meat. I am not going here into details *About poultry* about drawing, singeing, and trussing poultry. You *in general, and* will find that described in every practical cook- *how to buy.* book. But I will give you a few hints, which may be valuable, as to making the most of the poultry you buy and of the great variety of dishes furnished by the barn-yard. When marketing, see that your chickens have flexible bones, that a duck's bill is not too hard to the touch, and that the feet are of a light yellow. You are sure, then, that both chickens and ducks are young. A young turkey has a more delicate skin than an old one ; nor are the flaps about its head of so dark a red. The barn-yard pigeons, if young, have very small heads, thick bills, a light skin, and a delicate yellowish down about head and breast and underneath their wings. An old fowl or old pigeons furnish an excellent broth for soup. Remember this in case of sickness.

If you have a chicken which is not very fat, you may tie some thin slices of fat bacon or salted pork over its breast, and lay another couple of slices underneath while roasting. In respect to pigeons, squabs, and game in general, this process is invariably the best, since all birds lack in fat. They are best enveloped all around in slices of bacon, which König, in his famous "Geist der Kochkunst," calls their *habit.*

If you have a very young chicken, it is best to split it down the back and broil it. It is also good dredged with flour and

About cooking young chickens.

browned in an iron pan in some hot butter, first on the outer side, then on the inner, sprinkling with salt after the former is turned uppermost. When done and removed to a hot platter, pour a little cream into the frying-pan to boil up and mix with the brown deposit in it; salt it slightly, add a few drops of lemon juice, and pour over the chicken. Serve it trimmed with bunches of parsley, either fresh or fried crisp in some boiling lard. I have had the breasts of a large chicken served in this way for two persons, while I kept the rest of the chicken for stewing on another day.

The flavor of a young roasted chicken is greatly improved if you place inside it a piece of fresh butter the size of a walnut, and with it a bouquet of parsley and a small onion. If you like, you may also add the giblets to it, sprinkled with salt. I must not omit to tell you that the inside of poultry, after being drawn, ought always to be rubbed with some salt.

Not merely a good, but also a good-looking dish is the following: Take a well-prepared chicken, put it in a stew-

A dish of stewed chicken and rice.

pot with four ounces of washed rice, half a dozen mushrooms — if you will go to this extravagance — a sprinkle of salt, a blade of mace, four ounces of butter, and enough boiling water to cover the whole. Cover with a tight-fitting lid, and allow to boil over a moderate fire until chicken and rice are tender. Add more water if needed; or substitute beef broth for water, if you have it on hand, which will make the dish more nourishing. The liquid must nearly all have been taken up by the rice. Remove the mace, and serve the chicken with the rice around it.   Garnish the dish with an outside rim of roses of cauliflower boiled in salt water.

A fricassee of chicken is stewed chicken of a higher order. The following is a good recipe for it : Divide a chicken into four parts, put it in a pint and a half of boiling water, to which add a piece of butter the size of a walnut, an onion cut in two, a few sprigs of parsley, half a bay leaf, and a teaspoonful of salt.   Allow it to stew gently until the chicken is done, when remove and strain the liquor all but a little, in which you keep the chicken hot. Bring the strained liquor again to a boil, when drop into it two ounces of butter kneaded into a ball with one tablespoonful of flour.   Let it boil five minutes when the ball will be dissolved ; then beat into it the yolks of one or two eggs which have been mixed with a little milk.   If too thick, add some of the broth left on the chicken.   At the very last add the juice of half a lemon, a very little white pepper, and another piece of butter the size of a walnut.   Stir the same vigorously over the fire until quite hot again, but do not let it boil.   If you wish to make it very nice you may add some button mushrooms, or a dozen oysters, or some crayfish tails.   But should you think this too extravagant, you merely add some wheels of oyster-plant (salsify) which have been cooked by themselves in salt and water.   This vegetable harmonizes very well with the sauce and chicken.   Have rice or macaroni served with it.

Recipe for fricassee of chicken.

In the south of Germany, and especially at Vienna, a favorite way of cooking young chickens is to fry them in lard.   They are called *Backhaendl* (baked cocks), in true Viennese dialect, and are delicious.   The *haendl* or cocks must not be older than two months, and well fed.   Cut them into four parts ; first, lengthwise, then removing the spine, divide each half so as to have the breast and wing and second joint and drumstick each by itself. Take two eggs for two chickens, add to them two tablespoonfuls of water and a saltspoonful of salt, and mix.   Dredge the chickens first with flour, then turn them in the egg, and after that in fine bread-crumbs.   The latter must be of bread one

Backhaendl.

day old, when it will not take up fat as much as crumbs
from staler bread. Lay all the pieces thus prepared on a
platter, side by side, and put a deep pan on the fire with one
pound of lard (or half lard and half butter). Heat it until a
thin piece of bread, when thrown in, will turn light brown in
a few seconds. Then put into it one half of the chicken,
and shake the pan gently until the chicken turns to a rich yellowish brown, which ought to be in two or three minutes.
Remove the chicken with a skimmer to some blotting-paper.
Repeat the same procedure with the other half of the chicken,
Fried parsley.   after which throw into the hot lard a handful of
                       parsley. In one or two minutes it will be as crisp
as the chicken ; skim it out of the fat on to the paper. Dust
over it some fine salt, and serve on top of the chicken. Green
peas are the vegetable best suited to accompany this dish.

    Remnants of poultry may be done up to advantage in various
Various uses of   styles, either cut into small pieces and heated
remnants of   in a white sauce, or as croquettes, or a *ragoût*,
poultry.   or a salad with mayonnaise dressing, etc.

    A turkey you will provide but for special occasions. I think
it worth while to give you for a trial the following, which is the
very recipe for cooking a turkey as fancied by and served to
Stewed turkey.   the late German Emperor Wilhelm I. : Take a
                       deep oval pan with tight-fitting lid, large enough
for the turkey to fit in. Heat half a pound of butter in it, and
when hot put in the turkey. Add half a pound of ham cut in
pieces, a plateful of sliced onion, and one pint of boiling water.
Allow to stew slowly from two to three hours. Put the gravy
through a sieve, and pour it over the turkey. Serve macaroni
with it.

    The turkey drumsticks, if left over, you may serve up the
second time " devilled." Make a cut down the side, take out
Devilled   the bones and cartilage carefully, dip in melted
drumsticks.   butter ; dust the inside over with salt and pepper,
sprinkle it with lemon juice, and spread some mustard over
the whole. Broil over a quick fire for a few minutes, and serve
hot.

I have given you already a recipe for a duck. If you prefer
to roast it, it is best to stuff it with a chestnut filling. Pigeons
you may stuff and roast ; or you may fricassee them,
adding some forcemeat balls to the sauce. When *About a duck.*
you serve them with boiled rice, proceed in the following way :
Cut your pigeons into quarters, and *sauté* them to a light
brown in some butter. Then add a slice of onion
minced, the juice of one or two tomatoes strained *About pigeons.*
through a sieve, salt, a little white pepper, a bouquet of parsley,
and a little broth (or water). Stew them, cov- *Pigeons*
ered up, until tender. Serve them on top of some *with rice.*
boiled rice, and pour the gravy over the whole.

I add a few recipes for the stuffing of poultry. The following you may use both for chicken and turkey : Take two
French rolls, soak, and squeeze dry ; beat until *About various*
light with two whole eggs and the yolk of one egg. *stuffing*
Mince the liver ; add a tablespoonful of minced *for poultry.*
onion and as much parsley, a teaspoonful of salt, a little
ground mace, and two ounces of butter, which melt. Mix
the whole thoroughly, and heat, but do not let it come to the
point of boiling. To this stuffing you may add also as much
as one pound of sausage-meat, which makes it rich, and imparts a flavor in harmony with poultry.

A chestnut stuffing for either turkey or duck is made thus :
Take a dozen large chestnuts, boil, peel and mash them.
Cook the liver of your turkey or duck ; mince it very fine ;
add a tablespoonful of minced ham, a teaspoonful of minced
shallots (or onion), as much both of minced lemon peel and
salt, a very little white pepper, two ounces of melted butter,
two tablespoonfuls of grated bread, and the yolks of two eggs.
Mix the whole thoroughly.

A stuffing of oysters, to which you add bread-crumbs, melted
butter, and a little ground mace and minced parsley, is perhaps
the most delicious of all stuffings for either chicken or turkey,
with the exception of truffles — an ingredient by far too expensive for any sensible mortal to think of in a country like
ours, devoid of this precious fungus.

I will close with a stuffing for pigeons, and then release you for to-day. For three pigeons take one ounce and a half of bread, soak it in milk, and press it dry ; pour over it two ounces of melted butter ; add to it the minced livers of the pigeons, a slice of onion, and a few sprigs of parsley minced, a scant tea-spoonful of salt, a sprinkle of grated nutmeg, and three eggs. Mix well and fill it into the breasts of the pigeons from the neck, by means of a teaspoon.

LETTER IX

Thy spirit be thy guide.
— FRIEDRICH VON SALLET.

THERE is one branch of cookery which I might call the flower of the culinary art. This is the making of *ragoûts* and their attendant sauces. An ordinary cook has not the faintest idea how to produce them; it requires both taste and study to achieve success in this line. I want you to devote your best mind to the production of *ragoûts* and sauces, since they may be adapted at the same time to the requirements of a luxurious dinner and of a modest one, as I am going to show you. Suppose you have a remnant of chicken left, too insignificant to put on the table either cold or warmed up. Take it, every scrap of it, except the skin, and cut it in tiny pieces—squares if possible. If the liver has been saved, so much the better; cut it in tiny squares likewise, and set both aside. Now make a thick white sauce (of which later), which you flavor with some anchovy paste as large as a pea, and a sprinkle of lemon juice. With this sauce you mix your meat. Then pour a teaspoonful of olive oil in a saucer, brush it over the inside of some scallop-shells (one for each person), fill the latter with your *ragoût*, which must be quite hot, sprinkle some dry bread-crumbs over it, and then some grated cheese. Put a few flakes of table butter on top of each; place the shells in a sheet-iron pan, and brown them in a quick oven, which will take about five minutes. They must be watched, lest the *ragoût* dry up. Serve the shells immediately over a folded napkin on a china dish.

They make a nice appetizer when eaten between the soup and meat course; and they furnish the best and nicest way of using up meat as well as fish.

A ragoût, while artistic, serves also economical purposes.

Now you can take the same recipe and, for a special occasion, turn it into a

Salpicon Royal. — Cut into small dice the breast of a chicken, some sweetbreads and mushrooms, all cooked beforehand; add a *bechamel* sauce, in which some crayfish butter has been melted; pour this mixture either into shells of pastry or small paper cases, and serve hot. Or, more luxurious still, prepare a

Salpicon à la Condé. — Take equal parts of prepared sweetbreads, the reddest of beef tongue, the blackest of truffles; cut them into small dice, and moisten well with a thick white sauce flavored with lemon juice and mushroom.

The term "salpicon" is generally applied to a *ragoût fin*, the ingredients of which are cut into fine squares. A *ragoût*

What a salpicon is, and the requisites of a ragoût. always requires a savory or piquant sauce, and mostly is composed of mixed materials, which, however, have to be so assorted that they blend harmoniously. The greatest care must be bestowed on the sauce which completes the whole. It is either a brown or a white sauce, according to the solids used. If remnants of cooked beef, mutton, or venison are to be turned into a *ragoût*, a brown sauce is required; for veal, poultry, fish, etc., a white sauce is needed. The foundation of a sauce is flour and butter mixed, which is called a *roux*. The proportions are one spoonful of butter to one spoonful of flour. Melt the butter, mix it with the flour, and stir over the fire a few minutes only, if the sauce is to be white. Do not allow it to

How sauces are made. take color. For brown sauce, set this mixture on the back of the stove until it turns to a rich brown. Stir it frequently, and do not allow it to become attached to the bottom of the pan (one of sheet-iron is best) or to get black in any part. Now, to get the consistency of sauce, add to the *roux* the liquid required. Add it lukewarm and little by little, stirring all the while in one direction; thus you avoid getting lumps. When properly thinned, stir over the fire until it begins to boil; then set it on the side of the stove and allow it to continue boiling gently until the flour is cooked, which will be in about fifteen minutes. To keep the mixture for use later in the day, put it in a saucepan with tight-fitting lid, which you place in an open pan filled to reach three-quarters up the saucepan with boiling water. This you put on a place where the latter will keep boiling hot, but not boil. The liquid to be added to the *roux* varies as to the sauce to be made. A white sauce requires either a clear, mildly flavored veal or chicken broth, or it is made with milk and cream, sometimes with the addition of an egg. A brown sauce ought always to be more or less piquant; the broth used may either be of beef or from scraps and bones of dark meat, flavored with spice, onions, pickles, or other accessories of the kind.

Professional cooks keep "stock" on hand for the making of sauces, but this is far too expensive a way for you and me. The contents of the soup-pot are all we need, and, by adding afterward to the above white or brown sauces the condiments needed to suit the kind of food they are to accompany or form a whole with, we can make with ingenuity as good a sauce without stock, as the best of professional cooks can with stock. A brown sauce, however, can always be improved in looks as well as in regard to its nourishing qualities by adding to it at the last moment some of Liebig's extract.

With the plain white and brown sauce you can manage to produce pretty nearly any kind of sauce that you will need. If you wish to serve some slices left from cooked beef, mutton, or tongue, the following is a good recipe for a

Brown Ragoût Sauce. — Prepare your sauce in the way demonstrated, then add one onion, one bay leaf, one clove, four allspice, six black pepper seeds, a bouquet of parsley, summer savory or sweet basil, and continue to let it boil gently for half an hour longer, stirring from time to time. Strain through a wire sieve, and half an hour before serving add some lemon juice or a little vinegar, and either capers, slices of pickled cucumbers, or mushrooms — or, if preferred, all three of them. At the last you add the meat, which must be fully covered with sauce. Cover it up tight and place it over boiling water, where the meat will get heated, and blend with the

sauce without coming to a boil. Cooked meat heated over
must never boil, or it will get tough.

Of white sauces the *bechamel* is the most useful. The
original one, invented by Louis XIV.'s famous chef, M.
Bechamel, is a very elaborate one, of which there are many
descendants of high and low degree. The latter, however, are
by no means to be despised. I have, in fact, a special fond-
ness for the following one, which I recommend to you for its
simplicity, tastiness, and wholesome as well as nourishing properties.

Plain Bechamel Sauce.—Make a *roux* as for white sauce,
substitute milk for broth, add one onion, a flake of mace,
and a bunch of parsley. Let boil for fifteen minutes, then
strain.

This is a very good sauce for poultry, sweetbread, and ham,
and also for certain vegetables. For a *ragoût* or a *salpicon*,
take half milk and half veal (or chicken) broth, and flavor
with a few mushrooms instead of mace and parsley.

I can recommend also the following

Sauce Allemande. — Make a white sauce with either chicken
or veal broth, add to it one onion, half a slice of raw ham cut in
squares, a few white pepper seeds, the peel of one quarter
lemon ; allow it to boil for half an hour, when strain and flavor
with lemon juice.

To this sauce, as to any other, you may add any accessory
which serves your purpose, if you merely take care that nothing incongruous enters into your dish. I use it for a

Mixed Ragoût in a Pastry Shell (*vol au vent*). — Take two
calves' tongues ; boil them in your soup-pot. When done,
peel the skin and trim off the roots. Prepare one or two
sweetbreads in the following way : Wash them well, put them
in a saucepan, cover with cold water, let them simmer—not
boil — for one hour until they are well blanched. Meanwhile
put water on to boil in another saucepan, and throw into the
boiling water the blanched sweetbreads ; let them boil for a
few minutes, removing the scum which rises ; then put them
into cold water, and after they get cool take them out and

trim off the skin and cartilage. Both tongues and sweetbreads are now ready for use. Cut them into slices and put them into the above sauce, which must be rather thick; keep hot over boiling water. Add some mushrooms, either canned or fresh.[1] If you wish to make this *ragoût* first-rate, you add at the very last some forcemeat balls boiled in broth. Serve the whole in a shell of pastry, with a cover of the same, which you can order of a baker or confectioner, heating it in an oven for five minutes before use.

You can also dress the *ragoût* inside a rim of *croutons*. Take slices of stale bread, cut off the crust, shape it either in square, triangular, or circular pieces, throw them into boiling lard until they are of a deep yellow, when remove them to a piece of blotting paper to drain off the grease. *How to make a ring of croutons.* Have ready a mixture of white of egg and flour, by means of which you fasten the lower edges of the *croutons* to the rim of your dish (which must be slightly warm) so as to form an inclosure for the *ragoût* to be poured and served in.

You may also serve a *ragoût* in either a rice or a potato rim; this is, however, a somewhat tedious process. I therefore prefer for a change to make a rim of boiled rice in a plain way, by boiling the rice until quite thick and soft, then filling it hot into a well-buttered *How to make a plain rice-ring.* ring-shaped mould made of tin. Now, by pressing the rice down, it can be turned out on a warm dish, and is ready at once to be filled with anything you please.

I have been writing at length on the subject of these mixed dishes, because I consider them a very valuable chapter in cookery. Far from being unwholesome if composed of wholesome food, they, on the contrary, are apt to tempt even a delicate and dainty stomach, and by their nutritious contents to benefit a reduced system. Then, what a field for invention these dishes are, and with what comparatively small expense they furnish the showiest and most palatable *entrées* for a company dinner!

[1] See p. 96.

Since I am writing on sauces, I will add here a few more cold sauces for serving with both cold and warm meat. They also have the advantage of keeping for days after they are made. The simplest is the

Maître d'Hotel Sauce or Butter. — Take four ounces (four tablespoonfuls) of the freshest butter and either one teaspoonful each of minced parsley and tarragon or, if the latter cannot be had, two teaspoonfuls of parsley. Beat the butter with a wooden spoon, mixing well with it the minced herbs, and adding gradually the juice of one lemon. Add a little salt if the butter is not much salted already — or add a flavor of anchovy paste, which gives an agreeable piquancy to the butter. A spoonful of this butter heaped on a broiled steak or fish is very good. It can also be used as a beautiful garnish for a dish of either meat or fish by putting as many small egg-shaped lumps of this butter as there are persons, inside of curled lettuce leaves; place them here and there on the edge of the dish.

An excellent appetizer, when desirable, is the

Sauce Tartare. — Chop very fine two shallots, mince also some tarragon and chervil, and mix with one heaped teaspoonful of French mustard and the yolks of two eggs, to which add one teaspoonful of vinegar, one tablespoonful of oil, a little white pepper and salt, stirring all the time in one direction. If you notice that the sauce begins to curdle, add a little more vinegar. Taste to see whether it is sufficiently salted; if too much salted, remedy it by adding a little more mustard and oil.

This is Alexandre Dumas' recipe.

A more pretentious sister to our excellent mint sauce is this :

Herb Sauce (*Sauce à la Ravigote*). — Chop fine equal parts of chervil, pimpernel, water-cress, cives, parsley, and tarragon. Mix with them the hard-boiled yolks of two eggs, add one scant tablespoonful each of French mustard and oil, a teaspoonful of vinegar, some white pepper and salt, and stir for half an hour.

I do not mention the sauce mayonnaise; I will do so

when I come to speak about salads.   For the present you have quite enough matter to try your hand on.   But let me advise you, before I close this letter, to use for your sauces always the best of butter; otherwise all your trouble will be in vain.   I have for that statement, outside of my own experience, such an authority as Gouffé.

LETTER X

Dost thou know the art
Of butter and of lard ?
In finger-tips canst feel
How much pepper and salt to deal ?

WHEN I told you about the cooking of meat by means of boiling, roasting, stewing, and broiling, I made no mention of frying, or *sauté*ing. I kept it in store for a separate demonstration. For to fry as it should be done, is not only a difficult process, but in regard to a rational diet, it is undesirable to indulge in fried food more than occasionally. In case the distinction between frying and *sauté*ing should not be quite clear to your mind, I will explain here that the latter means browning in a small quantity of fat, while the former requires immersion into hot fat. Fat, which is capable of a temperature three times as hot as boiling water, answers well to perform the urgent office of cementing at the very start the outside of the meat (or some other food-matter), in order to preserve the nourishing and juicy substances within. But the nature of the fat itself, which of necessity becomes a part of the food fried or *sauté*ed, causes the latter to become somewhat more hard to digest. I would, therefore, class a *friture* as a relish, in order to distinguish it from necessary food. Of the two, frying and *sauté*ing, the former is preferable, inasmuch as the process, if carried out correctly, causes much less fat to attach to the object than will adhere in the slower process of *sauté*ing. The latter, in fact, is only admissible if the pan is thoroughly heated beforehand, and the fat, after being put in it, is made so hot as to surround the food instantly with a sort of crust. If this were not done, the fat

Difference between frying and sautéing.

76

would penetrate through the pores into the inside, destroy
the juices, and make the food unpalatable, as well as decidedly
unwholesome. ..

It is with the manner of frying, or immersing, that I wish to
make you particularly acquainted. For some of the greatest
triumphs of culinary art are to be gained by it. In
the first place you want a deep casserole of good   How to fry.
metal, and then the right sort of fat. Leaf lard, and suet rendered, or half and half of each, are equally good. Take a large
enough quantity of it to fully immerse what you wish to fry.
Let it melt and get hot. To know when the right temperature
is reached, watch and see when the air above it begins
to waver. Then take a small piece of bread sliced thin,
and throw it into the fat. If it sizzles and takes color in
about five seconds, immerse at once the substance to be fried.
Brillat-Savarin calls this the " surprise," and your whole success
depends on its taking place at the right moment. If your fat
begins to smoke, that moment is past already : you will then
have to remove your casserole with the fat from the fire, add
some fresh lard or suet, and watch again for the exact moment.
After the surprise is effected, you slacken your fire to prevent
the food from carbonizing. When the *friture* turns to a
golden brown, and rises to the surface, it is time to remove it
with a strainer-ladle to a piece of blotting paper, which you
place on a warm plate. All superfluous fat will enter into the
paper and leave the *friture* dry and crisp. For frying you
may use almost any kind of cooked meat or vegetable, and
fish when raw. Cereals, if fried, have to be cooked beforehand, but not so farinaceous food made of dough. Some of
the finest *fritures* are croquettes, for which remnants of poultry, veal, beef, fish, etc., may be appropriated. The foundation of croquettes is a thick sauce, for which take How to make
a gill of sweet cream, butter the size of half an egg,   croquettes.
one tablespoonful of flour, a little white pepper, salt, and a
piece of lemon peel. I do not repeat how a sauce of this sort
is made ; you know it already. When done, add to it, cut into
tiny squares, whatever material you wish to use. Set it on ice

to get cold.   Then take as much as a tablespoonful of it at a
time, mould it into pear-shaped or cylindrical forms, by rolling
it lightly on a baking-board with your hand.   After your
croquettes are all formed, roll them in fine bread-crumbs, then
in a beaten egg slightly salted, and once more in bread-crumbs,
when they will be ready for immersion.   Remember what I
said about bread-crumbs *apropos* of fried chickens in my last.

Croquettes of sweetbread are among the most delicate.
Calf's brains are best fried in batter, when they are very
good indeed.   Treat them like sweetbreads,[1] and boil them
with an onion, a few pepper seeds, one bay leaf, and a little
vinegar in salt and water.   Divide them into pieces as large as
an egg, and make the following batter: Beat over the fire
until hot one cupful of milk, one whole egg, the
Recipe of a batter.   yolk of another egg, half a saltspoonful of salt,
and one tablespoonful of olive oil.   Let it get cool, when add
sufficient flour to make the batter thick, but not stiff.   Stir
until smooth.   The same batter also serves for fried vegetables ;
as, for instance, roses of cauliflower, pieces of squash, etc.
Even flowers may be fried in it.   The vegetables, as I said,
have to be boiled beforehand.   As to flowers, I found it
stated in some German cook-book, that "white roses, elder-
berry-blossoms, and nettles," fried in batter, are very good ;
but I will not vouch for it.   I myself have eaten in Italy, while
staying in a primitive place among the Apennines, a *friture* of
pumpkin-blossoms, and acknowledge that I quite relished it.

There remains now for me to tell you something about that
particular substance in the flesh of animals which is called
glue or gelatine.   It is derived principally from
About gelatine.   the tissue, the cartilage or gristle, the tendons and
bones.   But the bones, skins, and fins of fish also furnish
gelatine.   It is extracted from meat or fish by prolonged boiling in water at the highest possible temperature.   The latter is
reached by preventing the steam from escaping from the pot in
which the gelatinous matter is being boiled, and by the addition
of salt.[2]

[1] See p. 72.   [2] See p. 41.

Now, as to the use of glue or gelatine for nutritive purposes, the scholars are somewhat at variance. Some authorities hold that, although gelatine is rich in nitrogen (two parts of gelatine are equivalent to one of albumen), it is hard to digest, and, therefore, as good as useless for the organic building up of the system. Others, *The nutritive quality of gelatinous substances.* on the contrary, claim that gelatine, if it does not build up, has, at least, the valuable property of economizing the albuminoids demanded by the animal system, so that a minimum of them in connection with gelatine is well calculated for a time to provide proper nutrition. These same authorities claim also that gelatine, because easily dissolved, is easily assimilated. In order not to be lost between these opposing teachings, I think it best to be on the safe side, and follow the precept of adding to a dish rich in gelatine (like calf's head, etc.) a slight *Acid acts as a dissolvent to gelatine.* acid, acting as a dissolvent. If gelatinous substances are used for a jelly, make it just stiff enough to stand, which will render it more palatable, and easier to digest, than when surcharged with them.

To make meat-jelly or *aspic*, you have at your service the skin, nose, and ears of a calf's or a pig's head, the feet of both calf and pig, the skin of pork or a boiled ham, the wing-ends, legs, and feet of poultry, etc. Such *Substances yielding material for jelly.* a jelly will enable you to produce plain dishes, as well as *plats de goût,*— highly fanciful and ornamental dishes. It is used, also, for garnishing, and, when broken up into irregular pieces, is very effective. Meat by itself will like- *The uses of meat-jelly.* wise yield up the gelatine contained in its cellular tissue, if boiled long enough for the process to take place. The meat in this case will be quite worthless, but the jelly will be of the best and most nutritious, albeit the most expensive. I will give you first a recipe for *aspic*, and later two for jelly.

For *aspic*, to make it economical, take a couple of calf's feet, and any odd pieces of raw veal and beef, as *Recipe for aspic.* well as remnants of bones or gristle which you may have on hand. Bring it to the fire with three pints of cold water and a teaspoonful of salt. Skim well, and let it boil for three hours. Then add to it one small celery root, one small onion, half a carrot, a bouquet of parsley, one bay leaf, and six black pepper seeds. Allow to boil for about an hour longer, or until the meat of the calf's feet is ready to drop off the bones. Now strain it through a hair sieve, and let it stand over night. The next morning remove all the fat which may have collected on top, and test it as to its consistency. If it should not have jellied sufficiently, you will have to boil it a while longer; if it is too stiff, add more water, and test it once more. To clear the jelly, dissolve it, and when nearly boiling, add to it the whites of two eggs, beaten to a slight foam, and the crushed egg-shells. Stir until it begins to boil, then remove it to the side of the stove, cover it up, and let it remain there without boiling for about half an hour. It is now ready to receive whatever acid and additional spice (powdered, of course) you might wish to add. The juice of a lemon or a sour orange will make it pleasantly acid. Tarragon vinegar also gives it a pleasant flavor. By adding spice and acid the last moment, their characteristic flavor will be preserved, while, if allowed to participate in the process of boiling, their fine aroma would evaporate into the air. To give your jelly a good color, add also at the last moment two saltspoonfuls of Liebig, and see that it dissolves and mixes evenly with the liquid. Now cover a colander with a clean napkin, place it on a bowl large enough to hold your jelly, filter the latter through the napkin, and repeat this process if the jelly is not quite clear the first time.

How to clear broth or jelly.

This jelly will keep for at least a week in winter, if kept in a cool place. But, in case it should begin to show specks of mould on its surface, it may be purified and saved for use by melting and bringing it to a boil. The scum then rising to the surface will have to be carefully skimmed off, and the liquid poured into a clean vessel for preservation. Broken up (as I said before) into small lozenge-shaped pieces, *aspic* or meat-jelly is a delicious accompaniment of cold sliced chicken or veal and, in fact, any kind of meat.

A very nice dish, either for luncheon or supper, is chicken in jelly. To make it economical, and yet preserve all the nutritives pertaining to it, do as follows : Boil the chicken whole with just enough (boiling) water to cover it. Add salt, and the vegetables and spice as for *aspic*. When the chicken is tender, remove it from the pot to a meat-board, cut the meat off the bones, and divide it into small pieces. Then take the bones, break them up with a cleaver, add the head and feet of the chicken, and put them back into the chicken broth. Let them boil for an hour longer, when you had better test it by taking out a spoonful, which you put on ice in a saucer. If it jellies when cold, you stop the boiling ; if not, you allow it to boil a while longer, until you obtain the desired result. Taste it now, to see whether salt or spice ought to be added. A slight addition of lemon juice is desirable, but not necessary. If your liquor is not muddy-looking, you need not clear it. Strain it over the pieces of chicken, which you place in a mould. They must be covered and no more. After turning it out on a flat dish to be served, you may trim it with sprigs of parsley, lettuce leaves, and slices of lemon. The choicest accompaniment for chicken in jelly is a mayonnaise celery or lettuce salad.

Recipe for chicken in jelly.

Once your *aspic* is made, you may appropriate part of it for embedding meat of any kind, as, for instance, slices of cold roast beef, veal, pork filet, or any remnants which you wish to serve the second time in disguise. To make these dishes more fanciful, you put your mould on ice and fill it half an inch deep with liquid *aspic*. After this is tolerably, but not quite firm, you arrange upon it a pattern of either slices of lemon, sprigs of parsley, capers or wheels of pickled cucumbers, pieces of cured and boiled tongue, slices of hard-boiled eggs, etc., according to choice and taste. This pattern shows when the jelly is turned out of the mould. Now pour some more of the liquid jelly into the mould, and when nearly firm, place a layer of meat well arranged on top of it, and so on until the mould is almost, but not quite full. Let it stand on ice for two hours before turning it out.

How to make a plat de goût.

The latter way, to be sure, is troublesome, and you will not often resort to it, but it goes to show what can be done, after all, with comparatively small means, if we want to make some extra exertion to please the guests we entertain.

It is often convenient to have on hand something special for slicing down cold. For this purpose I recommend to you the

Recipe for head-cheese.

following recipe for head-cheese : Take a calf's head, and boil it in salt and water until quite tender; then take it out, and after it is somewhat cool cut the meat into dice. Boil in another pot four calf's feet and one pound of pork, in just enough water to cover the whole. Add one onion, one bay leaf, the peel of one lemon, a dozen black pepper seeds, three cloves, a sprig of tarragon, half a pint of vinegar, and a teaspoonful of salt. When done cut the meat into dice and mix with those of the head. Now filter the liquor in which the calf's feet and pork have been cooked over the meat. Stir the whole until well mixed, put it in several small forms, and when cold set it away for future use.

The remaining space of this letter I will devote to the promised recipes for meat-jelly. They are both given by Dr. Wiel. The following he recommends for enriching gravies and soups, and to eat with cold meat. He finishes by designating it as " an invaluable refreshment for fever-patients ! "

Take three ounces of butter ; put in a large cooking-vessel, and let it melt, when add to it first one pound of lean ham

Two recipes for meat-jelly.

sliced, then four pounds of lean, gristly beef, the same amount of gristly veal, and, if you should have it on hand, any bones or extremities of poultry. Add also three carrots, one yellow turnip, one celery root, three large onions each stuck with two cloves, a large sprig of tarragon, one teaspoonful of white pepper seeds, and a blade of mace. Add but little salt (about a teaspoonful) at first, since the ham is salted. If not sufficient, salt can be added, but remember that it cannot be taken away. Allow all this to cook for about half an hour, while moving the contents of the vessel to and fro from time to time. As soon as a light brown sediment is noticeable in the bottom of the vessel, add cold water enough to cover up completely the meat and vegetables. Let the whole boil now uninterruptedly over a moderate fire for five hours. Skim well, and filter through a napkin. An addition, at the last, of a scant tablespoonful of Liebig increases the piquancy and nutritiousness of the jelly. In cold weather it will keep for a long while.

I have tried this recipe over and over again, and found it delicious. But I have never made any more at a time than half the quantity, which is all that is required for ordinary purposes.

The second recipe is Dr. Wiel's jelly for persons suffering with stomach complaint.

Take four calf's feet, two pounds of beef, and an old fowl. Boil them for a whole afternoon in five quarts of water, to which add half an ounce of salt. Skim well. An hour before it is done add a small pike. Drain, and let get cool over night. Next morning take off the fat, melt the jelly, and clear it with the whipped whites of six eggs and the crushed egg-shells. When as clear as wine, filter it, and add a good half ounce of Liebig. Put the jelly in small moulds (or bowls) and set it away in a cold place.

This makes a large quantity. For one person about a fourth of all ingredients is more than sufficient.

In my next I hope to get done with meat, of which you may be tired already.

LETTER XI

Enough is as good as a feast.

YOU are right, my friend, man cannot live by meat alone, but needs to complement it by juicy vegetables. Still, I want you to be patient for another little space, and let me tell you first of some more mixed dishes, wherein you have combined foods which complement each other, and which, therefore, as good as represent a whole dinner in themselves, containing all the food-matters necessary to sustain a healthy organism. They are invaluable where time and money have to be saved. I mean the combination of rice, or macaroni, with meat and other substances rich in albuminoids.

You remember that rice contains 8 per cent only of albuminoids, 76.5 of carbohydrates, and 1 of fat, to which I add here the volume of water, 13 per cent. Rice, in consequence, is deficient in albuminoids, which have to be replaced by food rich in them, but poor in carbohydrates. The ancients knew this. Ask your husband, and he will tell you that in the old Indian epos "Ramayana" there is mention made of a cousin to our rice pudding, dear to our grandmothers and little children. It is called there "krisharah," and was made of rice, milk, sugar, and cardamon seeds, boiled thick. We would hardly want to make a dinner of it, but what I can highly recommend to you for this purpose is the pilaff (or pillaw) of old Persian origin. It is to-day one of the best dishes you get in the Orient.

Before I proceed to explain to you the pilaff, I have to say something more about rice itself and the way to cook it. We are favored by producing in the United States the best of all the different kinds of rice — the Carolina rice. Its seeds are

General remarks about rice, and how to cook it.

84

of a pure white, long and narrow, and almost transparent. The East India rice is only third in quality, the Italian rice being superior to it. The most inferior of all is the Brazilian rice. I advise you by all means to buy only our excellent domestic Carolina rice. It is not only better in taste, but also richer in nourishment. Now, rice before being cooked has to be washed in cold water at least twice, then drained, put in a china vessel and scalded by pouring over it some boiling water, in which it is to remain for about fifteen minutes; then drain again. To cook it, throw it into boiling water, one quart for one quarter-pound of rice, and two teaspoonfuls of salt for this quantity. Allow it to boil rapidly for twenty minutes, then drain the water off and remove the rice, uncovered, to the back of the stove, where it must remain about fifteen minutes to get dry. In this way the seeds remain entire, and do not impart to the water their mealy substance and sweetness of taste. To see whether the rice is sufficiently done, take a seed and press it between your fingers; if it flattens easily, the rice is fit to drain. Do not stir it, it would spoil the looks of it; each seed ought to remain separate and intact. Thus prepared, it is ready for use in various ways. If you wish to serve the rice cooked merely as a vegetable, add to the water in which you boil it a piece of butter the size of half an egg for the above quantity.

For the genuine pilaff you need rice, and either mutton or chicken, and you boil the rice in water only five minutes, in order to finish it in the juice of the meat. There is a great variety of recipes to choose from; I give you first, because very simple, the following " Oriental pilaff" : *The genuine pilaff; and a recipe for it.*

Take two pounds of mutton (either breast or loin), cut it into squares the size of walnuts; put it in a stew-pan over a slow fire; cover it up tightly and allow it to stew in its own fat until brown, adding from time to time a few drops of water to prevent scorching. Add pepper and salt, a little thyme, and one onion. Meanwhile parboil half a pound of rice, and, after draining it, set away to dry. Remove the mutton when quite tender, by means of a skimmer, into another vessel.

Keep hot and well covered.   Then substitute the rice for the meat, and let it stew slowly until done and saturated with the juice and fat of the mutton.   Serve on a hot dish, the rice first and the meat on top of it.

This same recipe may be followed, by taking chicken instead of mutton, with this difference, that the chicken is browned first in butter, then stewed by covering it with water, and that the thyme is omitted.

Of all the many variations on the same theme, I give you the following one as well worth trying.   It is by M. Casimir, chef of the Maison d'Or of Paris, and is called "Turkish pilaff" :

Take a chicken, divide it into pieces, stew it with butter, some chopped onions, thyme, and bay leaves.   When it is of a deep yellow, add a quarter-pound of well-washed Carolina rice.   Put it over a slow fire, and allow the rice to swell and absorb the chicken broth.   Add some salt, pepper, a pinch of cayenne, and nutmeg.   Cut a few parboiled tomatoes into dice, and add them also.   Moisten the pilaff with good veal *consommé* and allow the whole to stew for twenty minutes longer.   Add a piece of good butter and a tablespoonful of veal suet, then take out the pieces of chicken from under the rice, heap the pilaff on a dish, and put the chicken on top.

Various other recipes for pilaff.

You will notice that here the rice is called "pilaff" aside from the meat.   This agrees with my recollection of the pilaff we used to have served at Athens, which, being in close proximity to Turkey, is half Oriental in its customs and habits. Our pilaff consisted of rice heaped up, dry and yet moist, and having the aroma of the meat broth in which it had been steeped.   It was besides highly colored a deep orange hue, which seemed to be the combined effect of tomato and saffron. And this puts me in mind of a recipe for "*le pilau*" in verse, by Mery (I found it in Monselet's "Gastronomie"), which he ends by saying : —

> "Add last of all, to perfume and color the rice,
> The finest saffron — then of a truth you will have
> A pilaff for Mahomet in Paradise ! "

Based on the same principle and similar to the pilaff is the Italian rice dish called *risotto*.

After the rice has been properly scalded and dried, put it on the fire with a piece of butter until it begins to turn slightly yellow. Then add to it, little by little, some Recipe for chicken broth flavored with onion. Wait between *risotto.* each addition of broth until the rice has taken up every drop of what has been put on already. Continue this' until the rice is sufficiently done and fully saturated with the meat-liquor. Then mix it with bits of poultry, particularly liver, or whatever else of suitable accessories you wish to use. Serve it heaped up in a dish and dust over it some grated Parmesan cheese ; or you may also mix some of the cheese with the rice at the last moment. It always looks well to cut the meat in dice for this dish. It is excellent also made with pigeon or sweetbread, or both sweetbread and chicken. You may also add to the chicken, boiled ham and mushrooms cut either in little squares or narrow strips, and then call your rice *à la Milanaise*. The most luxurious way would be to add bits of truffles.

I return, however, to daily common sense, and give you a plain recipe, in case you have some ham left over, and wish to use it in a new shape. It is called baked rice.

Take some boiled rice, let it get cool ; mix it with a table-spoonful of melted butter, one or two eggs well-beaten before-hand, some boiled ham chopped fine, and some Recipes for grated cheese. Put the whole in a buttered form, baked rice. dust over it some more cheese, and bake it in a good oven. After about fifteen to twenty minutes, try with the clean straw of a broom, which you stick into the middle of your dish, and see whether it comes out without anything adhering to it. If so, the egg is done ; and when the egg is done, your dish is done.

You may prepare the above in a still simpler fashion thus : Take one quarter-pound of rice, which you boil with a piece of butter, and a small onion stuck with one clove. When done and dry, remove the onion, and mix the rice by means of two silver forks with six ounces of boiled ham, either chopped or

cut in little squares (or narrow strips). Mix just before serving, set it in the oven for five minutes in order to heat it over,
and heap it on a hot dish.

The giblets of poultry, especially the liver, harmonize well
with boiled rice steeped in butter. They will have to be
minced, and then mixed with the rice. To vary, you may
either moisten your rice with tomato sauce, or have the sauce
served with the rice and giblets separately.

There are more recipes I might give you, but I will rather
leave it to your ingenuity to improve on the foregoing, and
invent your own variations, in order to devote the remaining
portion of my letter to macaroni, which is as useful in nourishing, if not quite as digestible, as rice. The best macaroni
comes from Italy, where it originated and is the
national dish. The best macaroni, again, in
Italy is the Neapolitan. I have heard it said
there is something in the quality of the flour raised in Italy which
makes the Italian macaroni so superior to that made in other
countries. Whether this is true or not I do not know, but it is
a fact that the French and German macaroni does not compare
with the Italian, and that there is none superior to the Neapolitan. It is not even higher-priced than its imitations, when
bought of one of our Italian grocers. Its percentage of carbohydrates is 76.5, the same as rice, while it is slightly richer
in albuminoids, containing 9 per cent. In fat it is poorer,
having only 0.5 per cent. Its percentage of water is the same.
(13.0) as rice. On account of the lack of fat it is even more
in need of butter and cheese than rice is. The cheese, especially, heightens the nutritive quality of macaroni, by adding
the casein to its floury substance. La Reynière, in his famous
"Almanac of the Kitchen," says that macaroni is one of the
most nutritious *entremets*, if neither butter nor cheese is spared.
Then he adds, that if one must needs be economical he may
take of Swiss cheese and Parmegiano (Parmesan cheese) half and
half, since only the keenest gourmets will notice this stratagem.

When I have macaroni to accompany a roast of beef I use
cheese but moderately, since the meat supplies abundantly the

(margin note) General remarks about
macaroni.

lacking albuminoids.   I prepare it in this case in the plain
way I learned in Italy when I was young.   But first of all I
have to tell you how to boil the macaroni, be- How to
cause a great deal depends on this.   The cook- boil macaroni.
books generally tell you to boil it for fifteen or twenty minutes, but I have found that this leaves it tough and raw in
taste; nor is it the length of time it is boiled in Italy.
Have plenty of water in a deep pot (two quarts for half a
pound), add salt enough to have the water taste, let it come to
a sharp boil; then put in your macaroni, — which you break
in pieces as long as you like, — and see that the boiling takes
place again quickly, and continues without interruption until
it is done, which will be in not less than three-quarters of an
hour, if the macaroni is of the large-piped kind; if of the
thin kind called *spaghetti* it will be done in slightly less time.
I have for this as good an authority as Dumas on my side.
To test it you have to try a piece of the macaroni between
your fingers; if it mashes easily, it is done; you can also tell
by the taste.   Do not let it boil too long, else it will give its
best nutritives to the water, getting reduced to an almost worthless paste.   For the same reason never wash it before boiling.
As soon as done, drain on a sieve, and use at once.   There
are ever so many ways in which to serve it, each one more
appetizing than the other.   Macaroni presents, in fact, an
open field to an inventive genius.   Proof of this is that such
creative spirits as Dumas, Rossini, and others, bestowed their
tender cares on macaroni, and were as proud of their successes
in that line as of their masterpieces in literature and music.
You are waiting, however, for my "Italian recipe for plain
macaroni": —

After it is boiled and drained put a layer of macaroni
in a deep dish, heated beforehand; sprinkle with browned
butter, and then with grated cheese; add another Italian
layer, sprinkle with butter and cheese, and con- recipe for
tinue until all the macaroni is used up.   Do not macaroni.
cover the dish, and serve at once.   The proportions are generally two ounces of cheese and a quarter-pound of butter for

half a pound of macaroni; but you may take less of butter and cheese if you choose. Simple as this recipe is, I have rarely found a cook who could prepare the dish as it should be. There is judgment required to get the right proportions of macaroni, butter, and cheese. If you have not got them in your hands and eyes, no recipe can teach you. If to accompany veal or poultry, which is less nutritious than beef, it is best to have a " macaroni with gravy " (*al sugo*).

After the macaroni is ready for use, return it to the pot and add a meat gravy, which is quickest made by reducing to about a cupful (by sharp boiling) some broth made of a slice each of beef and veal, a few scraps of ham, and a bouquet of herbs, one onion, one clove, and a few pepper seeds. Shake the macaroni until it is thoroughly moistened with this gravy; then serve in a hot dish, accompanied by grated cheese.

If a sufficient quantity of a dish of macaroni is left over, you will do well to serve it for luncheon the following day in this way: Take one-half can of tomatoes and put them on to boil with one saltspoonful of salt, a few black pepper seeds, a bouquet of parsley, and one small onion stuck with one clove. Let boil for fifteen minutes, then add a heaped teaspoonful of butter which you have mixed with a teaspoonful of flour and formed into a ball; allow to boil until this is dissolved, which is sufficient time to cook the flour. Now pass the whole through a wire sieve, and take of it what you need to moisten well your macaroni. Heat the sauce over again, then add the macaroni. If the latter is in a lump it will fall apart when getting warm in the sauce. Do not let it boil, but set it covered up on a hot place until thoroughly heated through. The tomato sauce which is left will keep for several days, and is very useful also as an addition to either mutton, chicken, rice, or a soup.

A luncheon dish of macaroni with tomato sauce.

I intended to devote this single letter to rice and macaroni, but I see how unjust to my theme I was; I have only begun on the latter, and my time is up for to-day. Still, I consider it so important a subject, and I have such delicious recipes in store for you, that I will venture to crowd them into my next.

LETTER XII

THERE are accords and discords in the composition of human food. As to macaroni, there is a striking harmony in its union with the sweetest of butter and the spiciest of Parma cheese. Now add to these the white meat and liver of chicken, and fresh mushrooms; moisten the whole with a tomato sauce, and you will have almost an ambrosial symphony. In this strain, at least, the praises are sounded of the dishes of macaroni the great Rossini used to have served to his enthusiastic guests. He, however, when asked about the secret of his culinary composition, was said to be mute "like Jupiter Olympus." Why macaroni should have such great attractions for musical genius I cannot tell, but we learn also that Lablache, the great singer, was an expert in macaroni, and that he took his secret with him to the grave. Then there was Isouard, the composer, who invented the stuffed macaroni pipes, and who used to prepare with his own hands the stuffing, which consisted of beef suet, venison, goose liver, truffles, and oysters. Rossini, however, it appears, was not always as close-mouthed as stated, for, if we are to believe "Mlle. Françoise," she is in possession of a recipe in Rossini's own handwriting for a dish of macaroni of which she partook at his villa at Passy, in company with Auber and Meyerbeer. I give you this recipe here as published in her "One Hundred Recipes." It is called *stufato à l'italienne*, with macaroni.

Cover the bottom of a stew-pot with half a pound of chopped bacon; when melted, brown in it four to five large onions chopped fine. This done, remove the onions with a

skimmer, put them in a teacup, and fill it up with hot water;
then set aside.   Take from four to five pounds of

Recipe for
stufato à l'Itali-
enne, with
macaroni.

the round of beef, pound it well on all sides with
a wooden mallet, and lard it with square strips
of bacon half an inch wide, which have been turned over and
over in a mixture of salt, pepper, three cloves powdered, and a
minced clove of garlic.   When thus prepared, put the beef into
the hot fat left in the stew-pot, and roast it uncovered on the
top of the stove, slowly for two hours.   It must be of a nice
brown all over.   Then add to the meat the onion water, a
pound of the knuckle of veal, and one cupful of thick tomato
sauce; cover the pot with a sheet of paper, and then with the
pot-lid, and allow it to continue to stew very slowly for four
hours longer.   Meanwhile boil your macaroni (we will say
half a pound) in salted water; drain and serve in layers, each
of which you cover with part of the gravy left in the stew-pot
after the meat has been taken out and the fat removed, and
with plenty of grated Parmesan cheese.   Meat and macaroni
are, of course, served together.

I give you now the recipe of Alexandre Dumas for "macaroni à la ménagère" (of the good housewife) : Boil your

Recipe for
macaroni à la
ménagère.

macaroni for three-quarters of an hour in salted
water with a piece of butter and an onion stuck
with a clove.   Drain well, put it in a casserole
with a little butter, plenty of grated cheese, half Gruyère and
half Parmesan, a sprinkle of nutmeg and coarsely ground pepper,
a few teaspoonfuls of cream, and allow the whole to sauté for a
couple of minutes; then serve.

For "macaroni au gratin," fill a buttered dish with the
above macaroni, dust over it some sifted bread-crumbs and

Macaroni
au gratin.

some grated cheese, and put it in the oven for fifteen minutes to get light brown on top.   Serve in
the same dish.   This is also Dumas' recipe.   You can improve
it by adding some boiled ham chopped fine.

If you have some meat-liquor to spare, you can enrich both
the flavor and nutritiousness of your macaroni by using the
broth instead of water.   In that case you put it first in salted

water and allow it to boil for ten minutes. Then you drain and put it into the boiling broth, which ought to be no more than sufficient to be absorbed by the macaroni at the time it is done. Shake it occasionally to prevent its getting attached to the bottom of the pot. .

Cook it in this way for preparing the following dish : Have ready soaked for a couple of hours half a cupful of dried mushrooms (which are to be found at the Italian groceries), and boil for fifteen minutes in the same water it has been soaking in. Use some chicken broth for boiling half a pound of macaroni called *spaghetti*, until properly done in the above way. Take the giblets of a chicken, which you have cooked previously with an onion, six pepper seeds, and one clove ; chop them fine, as well as some small remnants of chicken meat, if you should have it. Make a tomato sauce of about half a canful, and have it hot. Add a piece of good butter, size of an egg, to the cooked *spaghetti;* mix it thoroughly ; then add the mushrooms and a few table-spoonfuls of the water in which they have cooked ; next add the chopped meat and one ounce of grated Parmesan cheese ; and lastly the tomato sauce, of which you stir into the whole just enough to moisten and bind it sufficiently. Place it in the oven with the door open for about ten minutes, then serve in a deep dish previously heated. This is quite a meal in itself, and very good. If you have it the day after you dined on a chicken, you will find this dish a very economical one. Appropriate the bones and giblets to furnish you with the broth for the macaroni, and then stomach, heart, and liver, with some remnants of the meat, are ready at hand for your needs. I will add, lest you should not know, that while it takes an hour or more to cook the stomach and heart of a chicken, the liver will be done in five to ten minutes. More cooking would make it tough.

I call the above macaroni *à la milanaise ;* it is, however, a recipe of my own, concocted from hearing enthusiastically described a similar dish served at an Italian restaurant. I have made it a number of times, and have been always successful in pleasing whoever happened to dine at my table.

[margin note] Another Italian dish of macaroni.

I now will give you a recipe for a macaroni pie for five persons: Boil half a pound of macaroni in salted water;

Macaroni pie. drain; mix with five ounces of raw pork chopped fine, five ounces of raw ham cut into tiny squares, one ounce and a half of grated Parmesan cheese, and two ounces of melted butter in which a teaspoonful of minced shallot (or onion) has been *sauté*ed until yellow. Take a deep pie-dish, butter it and dust it over with fine cracker-crumbs. Line this dish with puff-paste, and fill it with the above after mixing it well. Cover the whole with puff-paste, and bake in a moderately hot oven from one hour to one hour and a half. A gill of cream added to the macaroni just before putting it inside the crust, is a good addition. After the pie is baked turn it out on a hot dish, and serve either with a tomato or a white sauce.

An equally good and rather simpler recipe for baked macaroni is the following: Boil half a pound of macaroni in salted

Baked macaroni. water; drain, and let it get cool. Meanwhile, take four ounces of butter, beat it to a cream, add very gradually, stirring continuously in one direction, two whole eggs, a gill of thick cream slightly sour, half a cupful of cooked ham chopped fine, a saltspoonful of salt, half a teaspoonful of minced onion, two tablespoonfuls of grated cheese. Last of all add the cooked macaroni. Pour this into a buttered baking-dish and bake half an hour. Turn out and serve.

A dish for Any portion of it left over may be cut into thick
luncheon. slices on the following day, and *sauté*ed a light brown. It makes a nice dish for luncheon, especially when served with tomatoes or green salad.

To believe an Italian enthusiast on macaroni, it is the most difficult thing in the whole art of cookery to produce a dish of perfect macaroni. He exclaims, "If you only knew what juices of meat, *purées* of tomato, delicate creamy paste, and what point of cooking, what constant watching and minute care this complicated dish exacts, you would never resort to those piteous counterfeits which bring discredit on the French *cuisine* — the first one of the whole world!"

I quote this, not to discourage, but rather to spur you on, and show what culinary genius may accomplish in any country in the world, whether in France, Italy, or America.

In conclusion to my lessons on rice and macaroni, I have to say something special in regard to mushrooms, the flavor of which is essential for the production of a dish of About either when of the highest order. Mushrooms, if mushrooms. not found sprouting wild, are the product of painstaking culture and are correspondingly expensive to buy. They are light, however, in weight, and a quarter of a pound will be sufficient for your purposes. The cultivated mushrooms are inferior to the wild ones in flavor and aroma, but they have this great advantage, that you can be sure they are genuine, while in gathering them in copse or field, you are always in danger of confounding them with poisonous fungi, unless your botanical knowledge and experience are a sufficient safeguard. There are a large number of eatable fungi growing wild, and their flavor is in most cases particularly spicy and agreeable. But in our country we only know the mushroom, which is one of the most delicate of eatable fungi. When I was in the mountains of Thuringia, Germany, in summer time, some little peasant girls came to offer me for sale several kinds of strange-looking fungi, which they said were very good to eat. On my asking them how they came to know that they were not poisonous, they replied: "We learn that from our schoolmaster; he teaches us. He shows us which are the good and which the bad ones." My trust in the schoolmaster's teachings, and the intelligence of the pupils, did not mislead me; every one of these fungi was good and wholesome.

The wild mushroom (*Agaricus campestris*) is apt to sprout up suddenly after a warm shower on meadows where cattle, and especially horses, have been pasturing. They also appear sometimes on the grassy bottom of a woodland, where it edges out toward the open field. The mushroom comes up like a little white ball, or button, and is at its best before it grows up to have much of a stalk, which will be in a very short time, since in the course of a day it passes through all the stages from childhood to old age. It is all over white at first. Later on, a white skin, ringed around the upper part of the stalk, frees itself from the edge of the vaulted top, or button, and the latter shows a lining of pinkish scales, which become darker and at last black. As the mushroom grows older, the outside of the top gradually spreads and flattens out. Its surface is silky to the touch, and sometimes is covered with tiny, hardly perceptible scales. The flesh of the stalk and top is of a solid texture and exhales a peculiarly agreeable odor.[1] There is a toadstool, *Agaricus muscarius,* and a globular agaric very similar to the mushroom, which are both poisonous. It is said that both an onion and a silver spoon will turn black if cooked with poisonous fungi; but I am afraid this is more of a legend than of truth.

The danger of confounding the poisonous and the eatable fungi is so much the more to be regretted, since the latter are not merely highly palatable, but also very nourishing. They have, in fact, pretty much the same nutritive properties as meat. On an average, they have as much as 3 to 8 per cent of pure nitrogen, besides being rich in alkalies and phosphoric acid.

The canned mushrooms, which come either in tin or glass, are not to be compared with the fresh ones. The most delicious way to cook the latter is to put them in a saucepan with a little butter, a taste of vinegar, an onion halved, a few pepper seeds, a little salt, and to let them stew for just five minutes. They must be served at once, with all their juice. If they are to be added to a sauce, they may be done in the same way; and be sure to add their strained liquor likewise.

How to cook mushrooms.

I have, however, not told you as yet how to prepare the mushrooms for cooking: Peel off carefully the thin, silky skin covering them on the outside, and scrape away with a small knife or teaspoon the scales visible underneath the top. Now, since mushrooms are

How to prepare mushrooms for cooking.

---

[1] The stalk, which must never be hollow, is eaten as well as the cap when young, but had better be omitted after old age has set in. If the mushroom has become wormy it is not fit for use.

a luxury, we must make the most of them on those rare occasions when we indulge in purchasing them. Therefore, take the skins and scrapings, wash them in cold water, drain them, and dry them either in the sun or in the oven after the fire gets low, and put them away either in a clean paper bag or a glass jar. They will serve as a mushroom flavoring for soups, sauces, *ragoûts*, etc. Soak them in water over night before you use them, and then simmer them in the same water for about an hour. Strain, and use the water only, which will be of a rich brown color.

What to do with the skins and scrapings.

Of the truffle, which is the costliest of all fungi, I have not much to say, because it is in reality out of the reach of people like you and me. Nor need we care; for the truffles, which have to be brought to our country from over the ocean, are generally of a very poor and adulterated kind. Truffles grow as much as one foot deep underground in France, Italy, and Germany, where sometimes dogs and sometimes pigs are used to "hunt" them up. Those of Périgord in France are considered the best. The recipes say, cook them in wine, or in champagne. Brillat-Savarin calls the truffle *le diamant de la cuisine*, and, to hear him and others, you might think that a pheasant and even a turkey are not fit to be eaten, unless stuffed with this precious growth.

About truffles.

Have I been digressing too much? Or will you charitably consider this little deviation as my introduction to the vegetables, of which you will think it high time to speak?

'Twas thought one hundred years ago
  Good food for pigs (and that was all),
But now the gentry love them so,
  The big, and eke the small.
                    —GERMAN FOLK SONG.

OUR forefathers, the Anglo-Saxons, knew in the dark ages that vegetables by themselves are poor food. They liked them best accompanied by milk, butter and cheese — how correct the guide of instinct! In our enlightened times we have sure knowledge that vegetables are not able to nourish man, unless complemented by other foods which contain what they lack. On the other hand, also, vegetables are necessary in connection with animal substances, since they furnish the acids, the alkalies, and mineral matters of which the latter contain but a scant measure. Vegetables are, in fact, indispensable to a healthy diet. Their mild acids act as a dissolvent on the albumen, often so hard to digest in its solid form, *i.e.* after being cooked; and green vegetables in their cooling and refreshing effect are invaluable as a part of our daily fare. Last, but not least, they are pleasing to the eye, as well as to the palate, since with their gayer colors they are apt to relieve the sober hues of the meats. Therefore, we may gladly be content with their poverty in albuminoids and carbohydrates — which is accentuated by their enormous percentage of water — as long as we do not neglect to complement them by those nutrients they lack.

The value of vegetables in nutrition.

Of all vegetables, those styled pulse (shelled beans, dried peas, lentils) are the most nutritious[1] — so much so that they furnish with very slight additions all that is needed to nourish a

---

[1] See p. 22.

person. In their unripe state we know them as string-beans and green peas. Lentils, on account of their indigestibility, we will not take into account here.

Next to them in rank, but indeed far inferior, come potatoes. They are, in reality, as " feeders " not the cheap food they are commonly thought to be. This is chiefly owing to their large percentage of water, *i.e.* refuse. About potatoes. They contain 75.5 per cent of it. You see, it leaves but little for the food-matter, which consists of 2 per cent albuminoids, 20.7 per cent carbohydrates, and no fat at all. This poor showing accounts for the immoderate use of tea or coffee among the poorer classes who feed on potatoes. Their craving for the lacking nourishment leads them instinctively to make up for it in the best way they can. You will know from this, that potatoes are not worth their money, unless they are accompanied by that kind of food which supplies the nitrogen they are devoid of. Yet despite all this, potatoes are a general favorite on our tables, and their prosaic nature does not prevent their being transformed into a variety of very nice dishes. The chapter on potatoes in the literature of cookery is quite a voluminous one, but I intend chiefly to tell you how to treat potatoes in boiling, roasting, and steaming, and then to give you a few nice recipes not commonly known. You would smile, very likely, at my wanting to teach you how to boil potatoes — "such a simple affair" — if you had not complained that your potatoes were not always what they should be, sometimes watery instead of dry, and then again soapy rather than mealy. Even poor potatoes can be made to be the proper thing if properly cooked. Only you must know how.

To boil potatoes, wash them very clean through several waters ; any dirt remaining will enter into the potato through the medium of the water. Wash them only just before boiling them. Cut away an inch wide of How to boil potatoes. the skin around the middle of each potato ; this facilitates the escape of their poisonous substance called solanine, which is next to the inside of the skin, and is most hurtful in potatoes not entirely ripe, or in those sprouting toward spring. It is this poison which causes the obnoxious smell of the water in which potatoes have been boiled. Although they get done sooner by being put on to boil in cold water, it is advisable to put them into hot, or boiling water, because it saves as much as possible of their small amount of nitrogenous substance. Boil them in plenty of water and keep the steam in by covering the pot tightly. Add some salt after they are half done. They need a half-hour's boiling. Try them by sticking in a fork; if soft all through, remove them at once; if you allow them to boil longer than needful, they will take up more water than they need to soften them and will get watery. Pour off all the water and put them, with the pot-lid slightly to one side, on a hot place for a short while to get entirely dry. Serve them at once in a folded napkin. Another way to boil potatoes is to peel the potatoes, have them very clean, put them in boiling water, salted, and cover them tightly. They will be done in about twenty-five minutes. Pour the water off at once; do as before to have them dry.

To steam potatoes, peel them, and when very clean put them How to in a colander over boiling water; cover tightly steam potatoes. with a lid and leave them until done.

To bake potatoes, wash them very clean, dry them with a towel and lay them in a good oven. They will need about one How to bake hour to get done. By baking them the water potatoes. evaporates, and you get all the nutriment they contain. They are also the most wholesome, since in baking a part of their starch is already turned into sugar, and thus some of the work to be done by digestion is performed beforehand.

For mashed potatoes, take potatoes boiled as in second recipe; add a good-sized piece of butter, some salt, if needed, A few vari- and while mashing them, a little hot cream or eties of mashed milk from time to time. Work them over and potatoes. over with the masher until quite smooth. If you take cream instead of milk, you will need less butter. A very wholesome variety is made with the addition of green herbs: Take one half of spinach leaves, the other half equal parts of

sorrel, chervil, parsley, and tarragon (the latter is optional) ; parboil them with a little good broth, but so that they keep their
green color.   Then chop them, taking care to save their juices,
and mix them into your mashed potatoes, in which you omit
cream or milk.   Another variety is the following : Press your
mashed potatoes through a colander into the dish they will be
served in.   They are called *à la neige*.   Mashed potatoes
ought always to be served at once, but most particularly the
latter kind.

If you have boiled potatoes left over, a very nice way to use
them a second time is this : Grate them into the dish they are
to be served in, put bits of butter here and there,   Mashed pota-
and dust a little fine salt over them ; then put   toes *au gratin.*
them in a hot oven for five minutes.

New potatoes, boiled either in their skins and then peeled, or
peeled first and then boiled, are excellent served with a plain
bechamel sauce[1] poured over them.   Or chop   A few other
some parsley, heat it in some melted butter, and   varieties of po-
when it bubbles up take it off the fire and pour it   tato dishes.
over the potatoes ready for serving.

For roasted potatoes, take either small potatoes, raw, of an
even size, and peel them ; or scoop little balls out of large
potatoes, with the help of a potato-cutter.   Pour   How to roast
boiling water over them, cover them up, and leave   potatoes on
them standing for ten minutes.   Then drain them,   top of stove.
put them in a large colander, and put them on a hot place till
they are dry.   Put butter in a pan, — about two ounces for one
quart of potatoes, — and when very hot put in the potatoes, one
beside the other.   Sprinkle some salt over them.   Cover them
up at first, giving them a toss from time to time.   When getting too hot, leave off the cover, shake them frequently, and
turn them when brown on the under side.   Finish them on a
slow fire.   It will take from one to one and a half hours before they are done.   If you wish them glazed, dust some fine
sugar over them after they are tender.   These potatoes are
very nice for garnishing.

[1] See p. 72.

From the untold number of recipes I know of, I select the following ones:

Potato Pudding with Cheese. — Take one quarter-pound of potatoes boiled in their skins, peel them, and, when they are entirely cold, grate them ; add one ounce of grated cheese, one-half ounce of butter, and one-half pint of milk. Put all this in a stew-pan, and stir over the fire until it turns into a stiff mixture. Then pour it into a deep dish, let it get cold ; add the yolk of one egg one scant tablespoonful of cream, and beat the whole for a while in one direction. At last add the stiff snow of the white of an egg. Butter a mould, dust it over with fine cracker-crumbs, fill into it the above, and bake in a slow oven. Serve as soon as done.

Potato Croquettes. — Take butter the size of an egg, beat it to a cream ; add gradually two eggs, one teaspoonful of flour, one saltspoonful of salt, and six heaped tablespoonfuls of grated potatoes which have been boiled and then peeled. Form this mass into sausage-shaped croquettes the size of a large thumb ; turn them in beaten egg, then in fine bread or cracker-crumbs, and fry them in plenty of hot lard until of a golden yellow.

Potato Noodles. — Take six large potatoes, boil them, peel them, and place them while hot on a baking-board ; mash them with a rolling-pin. To one heaped soupplateful of them add a good sprinkle of salt, two tablespoonfuls of flour, and one egg. Make a stiff dough of it, which you manipulate with your hands, until a long sausage-like roll about one and a half inches in diameter is formed. This you cut into sections of a finger's width, and these again you lightly roll with the tips of your fingers until the ends are rounded off, by which process the noodles get slightly longer and thinner. Now take a large iron frying-pan, put into it nearly three tablespoonfuls of lard, and when very hot put in your noodles side by side ; let them get brown first on one side, and then on the other, turning them with a fork. Take them out with a skimmer, and place them on a piece of blotting-paper before serving. This is a favorite dish in the south of Germany, and, when successful, as nice as any Saratoga potatoes. They can also be warmed over the following day by putting them in a hot oven for a few minutes before serving.

Another delightful dish of the same origin is the following, called " potato balloons." Make a thin batter of two cupfuls of flour, half a pint of milk, the yolks of two eggs, and a saltspoonful of salt. Beat it well ; then add *Potato balloons.* six potatoes which have been boiled the day before and grated while warm. Add also at the last moment the stiff snow of the two whites of egg. Take a spoonful at a time to drop into plenty of boiling hot lard. It will form into balls, which are to turn to a deep yellow before you remove them with a skimmer to be served immediately.

I never throw away a single potato which is left over ; there is always some use for it. If even one or two only are left, I grate them and use them to thicken a soup. If *How to use po-* more, they can be *sauté*ed the next morning for *tatoes left over.* breakfast, or cut into dice and heated up with hot milk, to which some salt and a piece of butter has been added. By putting them in a hot oven and allowing the milk to be partly absorbed by the potatoes, this makes a very good plain dish.

Another way is to transform them into *"potatoes à la maître d'hôtel"* : Cut your boiled potatoes into slices, fry them in hot lard, then put them into a stew-pan with some *Potatoes à la* fresh butter, chopped parsley, salt, pepper, and a *maître d'hôtel.* few squeezes of lemon juice. Let the whole get hot, and leave it on the fire until well commingled ; then add a very little hot cream, and serve. This latter is Alexander Dumas' recipe, which warrants its excellence. You can also do the way I learned in Switzerland and have " potatoes with cheese." Slice some potatoes rather thin. Put them in layers into *Potatoes with* a buttered dish, alternating with layers of thinly *cheese.* sliced cheese, finishing with the latter. Put small pieces of butter on top. Bake in a slow oven until of a light brown. The cheese underneath ought to be no more than just dissolved.

If you wish for one reason or another to render a dish of potatoes more nourishing than ordinary, select either one of the two following recipes : —

Potatoes stewed in Milk. — Peel raw potatoes and cut them into slices; put them in a saucepan, cover them up with milk, add salt (a teaspoonful to a quart of milk), and boil them slowly until done. Be careful not to let the slices drop to pieces. Meanwhile take some butter — two ounces (or size of an egg), for two pounds of potatoes — add to it half an onion (whole), and half a tablespoonful of flour; mix over the fire, and when quite smooth add the milk strained from the potatoes. Cook, while stirring, for about five minutes, when you will have a thickish sauce which you strain through a sieve over your potato slices. Should your sauce be too thick, add a little more milk, and some salt if necessary. Place the whole over the fire once more, and let it get hot, without boiling, shaking the contents of the saucepan every few seconds.

Potatoes in Broth. — Take a neck piece of beef weighing about a pound and a half. Put it on to cook with boiling water, and treat it the way I have taught you.[1] When done, put it in another pot with a little of its liquor, and keep it warm. Have ready some potatoes boiled in their skins, but not quite done. Peel and slice them, and put them into the beef broth with the addition of a few onions thinly sliced (the latter are not essential and can be omitted). Cook them until entirely done, when add some minced parsley. Do not stir, but toss the stew-pot so as to mix the contents. Serve with some of the broth poured over the potatoes. Surround the latter with the boiled beef sliced down. Have the dish accompanied by French mustard and cucumber pickles.

Both these recipes are well to remember on days when not much attention can be paid to cooking. But the best of the kind is the following, which in regard to nutrients gives you in itself all that is required for a whole meal. Dr. Hermann Klencke, from whose book on domestic chemistry I take the

---

[1] See p. 17.

recipe, says this dish represents "nourishment of the highest order." To prepare it, you will have to take a stew-pot with a well-fitting lid, which you make air- and steam-tight by tying a folded and dampened towel right over and around the crack between pot and lid, closing it up thereby completely. Before you do this, put into your pot alternate layers of sliced raw potatoes and slices of uncooked mutton. Sprinkle each layer with a little salt, pepper, and minced shallots (or onions, but shallots are preferable). Begin with a layer of potatoes and finish in the same way when about three inches from the top, to leave room for the swelling of the food. Finally add a scanty gill of cold water, and close your pot as described. Put the latter into another and larger pot in which a sufficient amount of water is boiling to reach up to three-quarters of the height of the inside pot. Now cover up the larger pot with a lid. Let it remain boiling from two and a half to three hours, then take out the inside pot, and allow it to get cooled off somewhat before removing towel and lid. If you should open the pot at once, before the steam had time to condense and form itself into a liquid, a large part of the food-aroma would escape with the steam, and the food-matter would become dry. The contents of the pot, when served, will contain all the nutrients of meat and potatoes, without loss of anything. Each will complement the other, and satisfy both palate and appetite. The juice surrounding the dish is the pure juice of the meat, and better than any broth can be.

With this plain but excellent dish I will close my lesson on potatoes; for I know how anxious you are to have a variety of vegetables from which to choose for your table.

Sameness in one's food brews mischief.

— DR. WIEL.

I WILL now tell you of vegetables more delicate, which are chiefly valuable on account of the various mineral matters Vegetables and and alkalies contained in them. To give you a their food-values. comparative idea of their food-values, I will formulate for reference a table of those vegetables which have been analyzed.

	Albuminoids.	Fats.	Carbohydrates.	Water.	Cellulose.	Mineral Matters.
Green Peas	6. 4	0. 5	12. 1	78. 0	2. 0	1. 0
String Beans (very young)	5. 5	0. 5	7. 0	84. 0	2. 0	1. 0
String Beans (older) . .	3. 0	0. 0	6. 5	89. 0	1. 0	1. 0
Kohlrabi	3. 0	0. 0	8. 0	86. 0	2. 0	1. 0
Cauliflower	2. 5	0. 0	4. 5	91. 0	1. 0	1. 0
Spinach	2. 5	0. 5	6. 0	88. 0	1. 0	2. 0
Asparagus	2. 0	0. 0	2. 5	94. 0	1. 0	0. 5
Cabbage	2. 0	0. 0	5. 0	90. 0	2. 0	1. 0
Carrots (young ones) . .	1. 0	0. 0	9. 0	88. 0	1. 0	1. 0
Turnips	1. 0	0. 0	7. 5	89. 5	1. 0	1. 0

If you deduct the percentage of water all these vegetables contain, you will know how small the amount is of their dry substance in every hundred parts, and how necessary it is to make good their shortcomings by combining them with complementing nutrients. The elements of which they are composed have to be economized so much the more because of their small proportions. Their relatively large percentage of mineral matters is most essential for supplying vital power to the blood, and helping thus to restore day by day the waste

of our system. Therefore, like meat, they cannot afford to lose
any of their nutritive substances. Consequently we must not
keep them soaking in water, nor put them on to boil in cold
water. In regard to onions, cabbage, and string-beans, it is
advisable to throw away the first water, after they have boiled
up once or twice; it renders them more wholesome, inasmuch
as these vegetables contain some sulphuric gases inimical to
digestion, which thus are got rid of. In all available cases,
however, I am in favor of serving the vegetables with the liquid
they are cooked in, for only in this way can we get the whole
benefit of their delicate and volatile mineral constituents, and
preserve their original and characteristic flavor.

The worst vegetables in the world are those prepared by
English rules, when they are boiled in water until done, and
the latter is thrown away, after having extracted all the good
the vegetable food contained, leaving it insipid and flat-tasting.
It was this style of vegetables which made a German author,
Ludwig Boerne, who was condemned to a life of exile, say
that they reminded him of Etruscan vases, the designs of which
showed only the first and rudest principles of art — an expres-
sion almost too good for that sort of misused food.

We will see now how to make the best of it. You notice
that among the vegetables enumerated in our table, green
peas make the best show as to nutrients. They are also the
most digestible of them all, if not too old. In
our country they are generally too mature when *About peas,
and how to*
picked for use. To get the best they contain *cook them.*
and have them tender, cook them as follows: After they are
rinsed in cold water put them in a saucepan in which a little
butter has been melted; let them stew for several minutes,
shaking them a few times to prevent their sticking to the bottom;
sprinkle with a little salt; add some boiling water from time
to time — not more than just enough to keep them moist.
This water must be for the most part absorbed, and the rest
served with the peas. If thrown away, the best of the latter
would be thrown away with it. Shake them occasionally, to
have all the peas come in contact with the liquid. They

ought to be done in fifteen to twenty minutes, if young. If your water is hard, add a saltspoonful of baking-soda to it in the beginning. Serve the peas with a piece of fresh butter on top.

I will mention here that, in order to preserve the beautiful green of peas, string beans, spinach, etc., it is necessary to cook them uncovered, and to add salt to them as soon as put on to boil.

Green peas need no accessories of parsley or mint, as French and German cookery prescribe. They are of such fine and delicate flavor that any kind of spice, be it exotic or herby, would merely deteriorate them.

It is a curious circumstance, which might interest you, that, although the ancients knew them as pulse, peas were unknown for culinary purposes in their green state until the time of Louis XIV., when they at once enraptured the court circles. Madame de Maintenon writes at the time (1696) : "The subject of peas continues : — the impatience to eat them ; the pleasure to have eaten them ; and the delight to eat them again, are the three points our princes talk about for the last few days. It is a fashion, a craze ! "

They have continued favorites ever since, and deserve it. Now let us see what they agree with and what are their complements. They assort with asparagus, cauliflower, young squash, and young carrots, in which they find increase of their mineral and other values, besides harmonizing with them in taste ; while lamb, mutton, and poultry not only are in harmony with, but complement peas in regard to fats and albuminoids. To obtain a dish of almost perfect composition you might do as follows : —

Take a round platter, place in the middle of it a fine head of cauliflower boiled in salted water with the addition of a piece of butter the size of half an egg. Encircle it with a wreath of green peas, which in turn you surround by a rim of boiled rice. Put outside of it a circle of boiled carrots cut into wheels, and surround the whole either with lamb chops, or stewed sweetbreads.

A dish composed of vegetables and meat.

Next to green peas come string beans when quite young, which, however, if maturer, are surpassed in their nutritive qualities by kohlrabi, — a vegetable introduced from
Germany.   Cook string beans thus : String them
from each end twice, *i.e.* four times altogether.

String beans, and how to cook them.

For nothing is more disagreeable than to eat beans not
entirely freed of their strings.   Wash them very well through
several waters, rubbing them through your hands to get rid
of parasites which are apt to cling to them, and are invisible
to the naked eye.   This done, you cut them slantwise into
pieces an inch wide, and parboil them as stated before ; then
drain and put them into boiling mutton or beef broth enough
to cover them.   They need more or less boiling according to
their kind or age ; not less than one hour.   Some need two
hours, some even more ; but I would say the latter are not
fit to eat because too hard to digest.   By slow boiling and
evaporation the most of the liquid ought to disappear ; the rest
must be served with the beans.   They need more fat than
peas, not having any themselves.   Serve them with beef, mutton, or pork.

In the tables at my disposal some of our most favored vegetables are missing.   I cannot, therefore, give you the nutritive
values of Lima beans and some others, but I judge from the
mealiness of the Lima bean that it must have a large percentage
of carbohydrates.   Cook them in boiling water, slightly salted.
Do not take any more water than will cook them,
and when tender add a little hot milk, in which a

How to cook Lima beans.

good-sized piece of butter has been melted.   Add some salt.
Leave them standing in a hot place for a short while to get
saturated with the milk.

Kohlrabi are only fit to eat when quite young ; later they contain much fibrous matter which is indigestible.   Peel them,
halve them, cut them into thin slices, parboil in
salted water, and drain them.   Stew them slowly

How to cook kohlrabi.

in some light-colored broth.   When they begin to get tender
add the heart of the green leaves growing at the top of the
kohlrabi, after cutting them into shreds.   They are of fine

flavor, and will color the dish slightly green. When done, drain the vegetable and use the liquid in which they have cooked for a *béchamel* sauce, which you pour over your kohl-rabi. Let them get right hot in it, and serve.

Taking into consideration the downward ratio of nitrogenous substance — which is the guiding standard — I have next to

About spinach.

mention spinach, then cauliflower, cabbage, aspar-agus, carrots, and turnips. The two latter show more carbohydrates — owing to the sugar contained in them — than any of the foregoing, except green peas. Spinach is a highly valuable vegetable because of its mineral matters, espe-cially iron and lime. Therefore, you must be most careful not to waste its precious juices by throwing away the water it is cooked in, or pressing its leaves before chopping it fine. Some, indeed, prefer not to chop it at all, and they are no doubt right ; but table fashion will have it chopped.

For a *purée* of spinach, pick the leaves over carefully, omit-ting the coarse and thick-ribbed ones ; wash them several times,

A puree
of spinach.

throw them in plenty of boiling water, well salted ; leave them in a few moments, then drain, and cool them off in cold water, from which drain them again. Now chop them very fine in a wooden bowl. Take a saucepan, put in a piece of butter, and when hot add to it your spinach. Stew very gently in its own juice, merely adding a little boiling water, if necessary, to prevent scorching. When done, which will be in about one-half hour, the spinach ought to have suffi-cient consistency to serve it heaped up in a dish, or to use it as a garnish around any kind of meat.

If spinach is served as a course by itself, a garnish of *croutons*, or quarters of hard boiled eggs, or both is in place. A *purée*

Spinach as an
entremets.

of spinach is suitable for an *entremets* — a course between the roast and dessert — and as such is nice accompanied by either poached eggs, or pancakes[1] rolled up.

A cupful of spinach *purée* left over will furnish you with material for a spinach pudding on the following day.

[1] See p. 169.

Take butter the size of half an egg, and when melted and hot, add to it a slice of onion and some parsley, both minced ; one stale French roll, of which the crust is _{A spinach} grated off, and which has been soaked in milk _{pudding.} and pressed dry. Mix well over a moderate fire, and let it stew for about five minutes. Have some remnants of cooked meat chopped fine — half a cupful is sufficient — and beat the yokes of four eggs until light. Add both meat and yokes to the foregoing. Taste it, and see that it is salted just right. Finally, add the whites of the four eggs beaten to a stiff snow.[1] Put the whole into a well-buttered pudding form, and either steam it, covered up in a vessel with boiling water for one hour, or bake it in a moderate oven until by inserting a broom-straw nothing will adhere to the latter when pulled out.

This excellent dish requires a sauce for serving with it. A white sauce with a flavor of lemon juice answers the purpose. An addition to it of mushrooms is, of course, better. Still better is a thickening of coarsely chopped chicken, cooked beforehand.

Spinach will bear warming up the next day; although I do not quite agree with the French canon, who ate spinach only after it had been cooked up for six consecutive days, with the addition, each time, of a fresh lump of butter. This canon's name was Chevrier, who also invented the hermetically closed stew-pot.

A very pleasant combination is that of spinach and sorrel ; especially, in spring, when the young leaves of the latter are not as acid as the later growth. Sorrel by itself is a delightfully refreshing vegetable for those who like the _{Sorrel.} acidity of it. You treat it exactly like spinach, but to bind it, add the yoke of an egg beaten up in a little cream, at the last moment.

To boil cauliflower, put it upside down into cold water strongly salted ; this destroys the insects apt to vegetate between the

---

[1] See p. 183.

roses or flowerets. Leave the head in but a short time, then rinse it off, and put it into boiling water slightly salted, top

Cauliflower.

downward. See that it is fully covered with water, and boiling continuously. It will be done in twenty to thirty minutes. It gets tasteless if you cook it after it is tender, which you can test with a larding-needle thrust through the middle. Lift it out carefully, and place it on a platter, then pour over it a *béchamel* sauce for which you use some of the water it was boiled in. Or you may use the fol-

A sauce for cauliflower.

lowing sauce : For a small head of cauliflower take half a pint of the water in which it was boiled (or the same amount of veal broth) ; add to it two ounces of butter, a teaspoonful of flour, a taste of nutmeg, and the yokes of two eggs beaten beforehand. Stir the whole over the fire until it just comes to a boil, and no longer. Continue to stir for several minutes after you have taken it off the fire, to avert all danger of curdling.

To cook cauliflower with cheese, take a dish and moisten it with a thick *béchamel* sauce ; dust over it some grated

Cauliflower au gratin, with cheese.

Parmesan cheese ; then arrange on it a layer of large flowerets of cauliflower boiled beforehand, and spread over them more of the sauce, and cheese thickly sprinkled ; put in a hot oven until of a golden yellow, and serve in the same dish.

A head of cauliflower divided into its different roses before

Cauliflower, with lobster.

being boiled, and then served on the same dish with boiled lobster, produces a good effect, and tastes well. Serve it with an herb sauce,[1] to which add the minced coral of the lobster.

Cauliflower served with either pigeons, chickens, veal cutlets, or roast beef, is a good combination.

To prepare asparagus for boiling, shave off with a sharp

Asparagus.

knife the fine outside fibres, beginning below the head downward, and cut away the woody end below. Do it just before needed. Rinse in cold water, then tie

---

[1] See p. 74.

the stalks together by the dozen, and put them in plenty of boiling water slightly salted. They ought to be done in twenty minutes. If left boiling too long, they will harden, and, moreover, lose their flavor together with their delicate mineral matters, which render asparagus so valuable. Remove the strings after they are placed on the dish they are to be served in. Have with them some melted butter, or a *béchamel* sauce made slightly acid, and thickened with the yoke of one or more eggs. A *sauce Hollandaise*[1] agrees well with them. But whatever sauce you make, always use for it some of the water in which the asparagus was boiled, because it absorbs part of its flavor and wholesome properties.

There is a great deal of difference in asparagus, for it is very particular as to the soil in which it grows. It likes sandy soil much better than clayey soil, and fashions itself accordingly. In southern Germany the asparagus of Ulm on the Danube is especially famous; but at the town itself the highest priced is that grown on the left bank of the river, because superior to the asparagus grown on the opposite bank.

When asparagus begins to appear, and is high in price, the thin kind, which is cheapest, may be appropriated with advantage for a dish of asparagus *en petits pois* (in shape of peas). Cut the asparagus into sections as large as full-grown peas. Cook them in salted water, drain them when tender, and take the water to make a sauce in this way: Melt a tablespoonful of butter, mix with half a tablespoonful of flour, to which add, when bubbling, asparagus water sufficient to make a slightly thick sauce. Add the yolks of one or two eggs at the last moment. Pour this sauce over your asparagus, and allow it to stand in a warm place covered up for about ten minutes before serving.

Asparagus assorts best with the more delicate kinds of meat, but it is also acceptable with boiled ham.

Among the cabbages, Brussels sprouts are the aristocratic branch of the family. They are a very sweet and delicate

[1] See p. 131.

vegetable. Take the little roses, rinse them in cold water, and throw them into boiling water salted. Let them boil up once, and no more. Drain and pour cold water over them ; then melt a small piece of butter, in which you stew them gently until tender. If they should get too dry, add a very little beef broth. They go with any kind of dark meat, as well as with boiled ham or tongue. They are delicious, accompanied by boiled chestnuts, either as a *purée* or whole as a garnish.[1]

Brussels sprouts.

To boil cabbage, cut the heads into quarters, taking out the stalks inside. Treat it like cauliflower in cleansing it. Boil it in broth ; that obtained from pork is the best, for cabbage needs plenty of fat to make it digestible. The most economical way is to stew it with ribs of pork, covering both meat and cabbage with boiling water, and cooking them gently for two hours, allowing the water gradually to be absorbed and serving the pork on top of the cabbage. By adding a few small sausages, which also garnish well, this dish, followed by a pudding or some sweet pancakes, is quite a dinner for days when time is precious.

Cabbage.

An economical dish.

For cabbage, *au gratin*, I use what is left over, and put it in a buttered china dish ; then I pour over it a white sauce mixed with the yolk of an egg. On top of it I put a thin layer of fine bread or cracker-crumbs, over which I dust some grated cheese. A few flakes of butter distributed over the whole, finish the dish, which has to be put in a hot oven to get brown. It is served in the same dish it is baked in.

Cabbage au gratin.

A more delicate kind, and much more to be recommended, is Savoy cabbage. It is especially good prepared in the following way : —

Take young and firm heads, and after removing the coarser outside leaves, cleanse them well, and parboil them. Then cut them in halves, take out the woody insides, and fill them with rice cooked in boiling water for five minutes. Put a good-sized piece of butter in a stew-pan,

Savoy cabbage with rice.

[1] See pp. 125, 126.

and when hot put in your halves, rice uppermost, side
by side. Put some bits of butter on top of the rice,
and dust over the whole a little salt. Let it stew, with
the addition of some beef broth, until quite tender, then
serve carefully, either by itself, or around your dish of
meat.

To prepare a stuffed head of cabbage is more troublesome,
but pays well. For it you may take either kind, but Savoy cabbage is preferable. Take a large head. Boil it
whole in salted water until the outside leaves get   Stuffed cabbage.
tender. Then pour off the water, taking care not to injure the
head. Place it on a meat-board, and carefully unfold the leaves
— turning them backward leaf by leaf, until you get to the
heart. Remove it as well as the hard inside part. Chop the
tender leaves of the heart, and add to the stuffing, which you
make of two ounces of fat pork and two ounces of beef, both
chopped fine (any remnants of meat partly fat will do) ; one
ounce of butter beaten to a cream ;[1] the yolks of two eggs; a
teaspoonful of minced onion ; a scant teaspoonful of salt; the
same of minced parsley ; one French roll soaked in milk and
pressed dry. Mix the egg and bread, and add them to the
butter; add the other ingredients last, and heap up the whole
in the centre of the cabbage head. Turn back now each leaf
in its proper place, thus enveloping the stuffing and reshaping
the entire head. Now take a baking-pan, heat in it a piece of
butter the size of an egg, place the cabbage in it, and bake in
a moderately hot oven. Baste from time to time, and add a
little water when there is danger of scorching. It will take
from two to three hours to get done. Serve on a round
platter, and pour over it the gravy which will be in
the bottom of the pan. Besides, you may serve with this
dish a white sauce, made slightly *piquant* by the addition
of a small amount of anchovy paste and lemon juice.
The head is to be carved in sections cut, like a cake, from
the centre towards the outer circumference.

[1] See p. 183.

The famous *"Bombe à la Sardanapale,"* which was served one day to Frederick the Great, of Prussia, by his *chef* Sieur Noëls, was nothing more nor less than a stuffed cabbage head, with slices of cooked ham and bacon underneath and on top of it, and a small sausage folded up in each leaf. The king was as great a *gourmet* as he was a great leader, and felt so delighted with this surprise prepared by his *chef*, that he wrote and dedicated to him a poem of 137 lines.

Red cabbage is finer and more delicate than the white kind. In Germany it is cooked in the way which follows, when it is served with partridges in their proper season. It **Red cabbage.** is very good, also, with roasted pork, or boiled ham. Cut a large head, or two small ones, into quarters, and after removing the hard parts, shred fine with a sharp knife. Put it in a stew-pan, in which a tablespoonful of lard, or the same amount of pork-drippings, has been heated. Cover it up, and let it stew over a moderate fire, shaking it and tossing it from time to time, for half an hour. Then add half a cupful of beef broth, and an hour later a wineglassful of cider-vinegar and twice as much claret. Add also a teaspoonful of salt and the same amount of granulated sugar, and continue stewing until quite tender. The longer you boil this dish of cabbage, the better it will be ; only be sure and do not add the vinegar and wine too long before serving, since they lose by cooking. If you prefer not to use wine, you will have to double the quantity of vinegar, and increase that of sugar also. The claret, however, gives this dish a special flavor, which is very pleasant. I can also recommend adding a Baldwin or Spitzenberg apple — peeled, cored, and quartered — half an hour before the cabbage is done.

In many families the great objection to boiled cabbage is the odor which it is apt to send to the upper regions of the house. I have already mentioned that cabbage gets rid of some of the obnoxious gases if parboiled before cooking it. But, to fully prevent any odor penetrating further than the pot in which the cabbage is being cooked, place over it a towel folded treble or quadruple. I can vouch for its effectiveness.

Here I am at the end of my letter — and a whole string of vegetables waiting for me to discourse on. You have, however, plenty on hand now, to secure a variety for your table until I continue the theme in my next.

LETTER XV

Dis-moi ce que tu mange, et je te dirai ce que tu es.
— BRILLAT-SAVARIN.

I BEGIN at once with the root vegetables, which contain the least nourishment. Still, they come in for their share of usefulness also. Carrots make the best show among
Carrots. them. Next I would place salsify or oyster plant, which is certainly the most agreeable of all the roots. Carrots are generally discarded as a vegetable by themselves, but if treated in the proper way they are both palatable and wholesome as long as they are not too old. Scrape them clean with a sharp knife, and rinse them in water. If quite young cut the carrots into little wheels, but if grown large cut them first into thin wheels and then into narrow strips. Put them into boiling water, barely enough to cover them, and add a piece of butter as soon as they begin to boil. Allow the liquid to soak in gradually. They will be done in an hour's time, if young. Add some minced parsley and serve. You may cook turnips in the same way as carrots, merely cutting them thicker ; or stew them in mutton broth, leaving out the butter, and omit in any case the parsley. To press the water out of boiled turnips is to rob them of all the good which is in them. They are about the poorest vegetable as it is, and though for the sake of variety I allow them on my table, it is only when cooked in the following manner, which I learned in Italy.
Turnips. Cut them into slices, stew them in water, adding a little butter and salt. When tender drain off what liquid is left and use it for a sauce, which you make of a heaped teaspoonful of flour and the same of butter. Now grease a dish, put in a layer of the sliced turnips, dust with pepper and spread some of the sauce over it, then another

layer of turnips, and so on until they are used up. Dust some grated Parmesan cheese over the top, and put flakes of butter here and there. Bake in the oven until light brown and serve in the same dish.

I have also eaten cucumbers cooked in this way, and found them very good. They were quartered and had the seeds taken out.

Salsify is invaluable in winter, when fresh vegetables are scarce. It is both delicate and easily digested. One might call it the winter asparagus. To have it of a pure white, throw it into cold water made slightly acid *Salsify.* by the addition of some vinegar. Add also a teaspoonful of flour to it. Before you do this, however, you have to scrape off the black outside. Cut the roots into pieces one inch long. Leave them in the above water for a little while before you throw them into the boiling water. To make *Salsify à la* " salsify *à la poulette*," boil your salsify in water *poulette.* with a little salt and butter. It needs one hour to get tender. Then drain and put in a sauce made of chicken broth and white *roux* in the usual way. At the very last add the yellow of two eggs, beaten up with some cream. A slight addition of lemon juice is an improvement. Have the same quantity of small pieces of boiled chicken as you have of salsify, and add it also to the sauce. You can, of course, leave out the chicken if you want to use it for something else. Or you can make your sauce with cream instead of broth, and leave out the egg.

You know that salsify fritters are similar to fried oysters in taste, hence the name of oyster plant. They are, of course, not nearly as wholesome as the vegetable when merely boiled or stewed, yet, if *sautéed* with care, *Salsify fritters.* they are not any more risky for a sound digestion than other food cooked in fat. For fritters, boil the salsify until soft ; drain, and mash it with the addition of a lump of butter, salt and pepper. (To a dozen roots take a tablespoonful of butter.) Form into small cakes, turn them in flour, and fry them in butter or lard.

The root vegetables all need to be complemented by fat meat.

A highly medicinal root is celery, *i.e.* the soup or turnip-rooted celery. According to Liebig, it contains the astonishing amount of sixteen to twenty per cent of mineral matters and alkalies in one hundred parts of its dry substance. Its taste is a peculiarly spicy one, very agreeable to some persons and distasteful to others. It is certainly very wholesome when young, and devoid of coarse woody fibres. To eat celery root as a vegetable, have it well scraped and cleaned and thrown into the boiling liquor for soup, to which it will impart its flavor at the same time. When nearly tender remove from the soup-pot, cut into slices, and put them to stew in either some broth or cream (a gill to two good-sized roots). If cream is used a teaspoonful of butter, mixed with a little flour, will have to be added. Serve with the liquid around them.

Celery root.

Parsnips, like carrots, contain a good deal of sugar. In the case of carrots, parsley mollifies their sweetish taste ; parsley, however, is out of harmony with parsnips : they need cream, and are better in taste for being boiled in slightly salted water — which throw away — until tender. Then, prepare a cream or plain *béchamel* sauce, and allow the parsnips, which you have cut either into wheels or thick strips, to be steeped in this sauce for a while before serving. Parsnips are best, perhaps, as a *friture*.[1] Or, take one parsnip, one small celery root, and half a dozen salsify roots ; cut them into even dice and stew with a piece of veal and a few slices of salt pork or bacon, in a little water. Serve the veal in the middle of a dish, and the vegetables around it. The juice remaining in the stew-pot will serve to be poured over the whole. A squeeze from a sour orange added to it will improve this dish.

Parsnips.

A dish of mixed roots.

The root containing the most sugar is the beet. There are several varieties, of which I prefer for a vegetable the dark red

[1] See p. 77.

kind. When quite young they are very tender and delicious. Later in the year and in the winter the large red beets will make a nice salad. To preserve their color, you must prevent their "bleeding" by carefully keeping _{Red beets.} intact their skin, and not interfering with their tops and tails before they are cooked. Wash them very clean, put them into plenty of salted and boiling water, and let them boil for one to three hours, according to size. Test one of your roots with a skewer to see if tender to the core. Drain, peel, place in a hot dish, and pour over them some melted butter. Slice them if they are not very young and small. In Italy they put the beets in the oven after the bread has been baked, and leave them in until tender. They are best in this way.

I will say a few words here about sweet potatoes. I have not seen them analyzed, but judge from their components of starch and sugar that their nutritive properties might be slightly superior to the common or _{Sweet potatoes.} white potato. It is to be regretted, therefore, that they are heavy to digest, and, in the same measure, decrease in value as food ; for only in so far as we digest food are we nourished by it. Boil or bake sweet potatoes as directed about white potatoes. They need, however, a longer time to get done. They are nice cut into slices lengthwise — after being boiled — and *sauté*ed until light brown.

Green corn and egg-plant ought both to have good nourishing properties, if we consider how they satisfy one's appetite. The former, after being freed of its husks and tassels, is done in fifteen to twenty minutes after _{Green corn.} being put into boiling water salted, and allowed to boil uninterruptedly.

For corn fritters — which also taste a good deal like fried oysters — grate the green corn off the cob, and for half a pint of it take the yolk of one egg, a heaped tablespoonful of flour, a tablespoonful of cream, and a _{Corn fritters.} saltspoonful of salt. Mix well, and *sauté* in lard, dropping into it a tablespoonful at a time.

For canned corn take half a cupful of cream (or milk) for

half a can. When it boils, add butter the size of half an egg,
mixed with a teaspoonful of flour. When dissolved pour it
over the corn, which you heat in a separate sauce-pan. Let
the whole simmer together for a few minutes.

In summer, when you do not care for much meat, egg-plant
furnishes you with a nice breakfast dish. Cut it into slices
about a quarter of an inch thick; sprinkle each
slice with salt; heap up the slices, one above the
other; put a board on top, and press it down by the weight of
a heavy flatiron. Let them remain thus for about an hour,
when most of their bitter flavor will have oozed out. Now
turn each slice in some flour, and *sauté* in a little hot butter or
drippings to a dark brown, first on one side, then on the other.
Serve very hot.

Egg-plant, sautéed.

For baking egg-plant take either one large or two small
ones. Pare them, cut them into thick slices, and boil in salted
water until quite soft. Then drain and mash
them. Add half a cupful of bread-crumbs soaked
in milk, a scant tablespoonful of butter, a teaspoonful of minced
parsley, half as much of minced onion, a little pepper, and salt
to taste. Beat together, and put into a buttered *gratin*-dish.
Cover the top with bread-crumbs, and bake until nice and
brown.

Egg-plant, au gratin.

Before speaking of our great favorite — the tomato — I will
hurriedly mention the summer squash, sometimes called patty-
pan squash, on account of its shape. Although
not much more than water, squash, for a change,
is quite refreshing. When it is very young and tender, you
need not pare it, nor take out the seeds. Wash your squashes,
and quarter them; cover them with boiling water, slightly
salted, and boil them until they mash easily, which will be in
about half an hour. Then put them into a sieve, and, with a
large and flat spoon, press the water out of them. Return
them to the stew-pan with a good-sized piece of butter, a little
salt, and some cream, if you choose. They need a good deal
of butter to make them palatable.

Squash.

Now for tomatoes, this always welcome and refreshing vege-

table.   Like the potato, it belongs to the family of night-
shades; but how different from that common-place relative
it is, both in nature and in looks, drawing nurture
and color from the rays of the sun, while the
meaner cousin is sticking to the clod and
vegetating in darkness. The sunny offspring, to be sure,
does not give us nearly the amount of actual food we get
from the darkling; but what other vegetable is there so cooling on hot summer days, so refreshing always, whether summer
or winter, so much so, as to tempt us to call it a fruit rather
than a vegetable?

Tomatoes and the various ways of cooking them.

If you pour boiling water over the tomatoes and allow them
to stand awhile, you can easily remove their skins.   Then take
each between your hands, and press out some of the watery
inside and as many of the hard seeds as possible. Don't rob
them of too much of their juice; it contains highly valuable
mineral matters and the very acid which produces their refreshing and cooling effect.   Put your tomatoes prepared in the
above way into a skillet, and allow them to cook twenty minutes, no longer.   Add plenty of salt, and shortly before they
are done a good-sized piece of butter and a sprinkle of pepper.
If you like them thickened, add some water-cracker dust or
fine bread-crumbs.

To bake tomatoes, cut them into halves and place them, with
end downward, side by side on a layer of bread-crumbs in a
buttered *gratin*-dish.   Sprinkle with plenty of salt and a little
white pepper.   Cover up with a layer of bread-crumbs, and
put over it as many little pieces of butter as you have halves of
tomatoes.   Bake them in a moderate oven for from half to
three-quarters of an hour.

Fried tomatoes are most delicious for breakfast or supper.
I have eaten them in perfection in southern Pennsylvania and
Delaware, where there is a wealth of rich cream.   Cut the
tomatoes into rather thick slices.   Have some hot butter, or
the best beef drippings, in a large frying-pan; put your slices
into it, one beside the other, and *sauté* until brown on both
sides.   Then pour over them plenty of rich cream to make a

gravy. When bubbling up, remove the tomato slices carefully with a skimmer into a hot platter. Do not heap them up, but place them side by side. Now take the yolks of two or three eggs, beaten up in a little cream, which you have gotten ready beforehand, and stir into the cream gravy after it has been removed from the stove. After stirring it well, replace it on the stove for a few minutes to get hot, without boiling, stirring all the time. At last pour it over the tomatoes, and serve.

It was Grimod de la Reynière who invented stuffed tomatoes. I give you his own famous recipe : Make an opening at the stem end of the tomatoes, press the latter, so as to relieve them as much as possible of their seeds without injury to their shape. Fill into the cavity thus obtained a stuffing of either sausage meat or chopped meat of any kind, or of different meats. Mix with this stuffing a *soupçon* of garlic (or rather rub the dish in which you mix the stuffing with the inside of a clove of garlic), some minced parsley, shallot, and tarragon. Put the tomatoes side by side into a buttered *gratin*-dish, which they must fill out. Dust bread-crumbs over the top to cover the whole ; place bits of butter on it, one for each tomato. Bake in a hot oven for about half an hour. The top ought to be of a light brown.

Stewed tomatoes left over can be served again in many ways. They may be added to rice, or macaroni, or eaten with eggs, or added to a soup or a hash. They are always in place, with whatever meat or cereals you serve them ; and they are pre-eminently suited to go with eggs in any shape.

To make my list of vegetables complete I must not omit onions. If you like them, you will do well to have them now and then with roast poultry. Boil them in two waters, salted. Throw away the first water after they have boiled about five minutes, and renew it. They will be milder in taste this way. Boil them for an hour or more, until they are perfectly tender. Drain them. Boil some cream, to which add a piece of butter, salt, and pepper, and pour over the onions for a dressing. Steep them in it for a little while. Then serve. Or, make a *purée* of them, by chopping them fine

Onions.

after they are boiled and tender, which moisten with the same dressing, adding to it a little thickening of flour.

For a garnish of roast duck or beefsteak, do as follows: Take a dozen small onions, all of one size. Be careful in peeling not to cut them too close at the root end, or they may fall to pieces in cooking. Boil them in the above manner for half an hour, then drain, and put them in a sauce-pan with butter the size of a walnut, a scant teaspoonful of sugar, two or three tablespoonfuls of good broth, and a little salt. Keep them over a lively fire for about ten minutes, shaking the sauce-pan frequently to prevent scorching. Then remove them to a moderate fire, and let them stew until they become brown and glazed over. They must be perfectly tender.

I would be at the end of enumerating the different vegetables for table use were it not for my classifying chestnuts with them rather than with fruit. In our country we have Chestnuts and not yet made such use of them in connection with how to use them. meat or other vegetables as is done in Europe. One reason for it, no doubt, is the high price paid for the large imported chestnuts, and the tediousness of peeling for cooking purposes the puny little ones growing wild on this continent. The chestnut, on account of its mealiness (starch) and sweetness (sugar), is very much like the sweet potato in its compounds. Its flavor, however, is far superior, and its fibre much more delicate. In the south of Europe, where chestnuts grow large and abundantly, they are part of the daily food of the common people. On the Isle of Corsica the latter make them serve as bread, and speak of the bread tree when they mean the chestnut tree.

Chestnuts assort especially well with cabbage, Brussels sprouts, and other greens. They need fat to make them easier of digestion. For a garnish do as follows: Peel the chestnuts, throw them into boiling water, cover them up and allow to stand for five minutes. Then remove the inner skin by rubbing it off with a clean towel, and throw the peeled chestnuts into cold water. Drain and rub dry with another towel; then put them into a sauce-pan side by side with a little salt, a good sprinkle of granulated sugar, a small piece of butter, and broth half an inch deep. Cover them up well, shake them from time to time, and cook over a moderate fire until they are light brown and tender.

They make a very nice *purée* by preparing them as above, and cooking them until quite tender in broth sufficient to cover them (veal or chicken broth is best). Then mash them well, adding some boiling hot cream, a good-sized piece of butter, and a little salt. This *purée* is particularly good with duck, mutton, and meat croquettes.

Before closing I will repeat what I indicated in the beginning when speaking of vegetables: that two or more of different kinds will make with ingenuity and judgment, a most appetizing-looking mixed vegetable dish,[1] or what is called a *macédoine*. It will give you some extra trouble, to be sure, and also cause a certain expense. But once in a while, for some desired guests, you would take this upon yourself willingly, and the effect produced will repay you. At the time of spring and early summer, when vegetables are freshest and in plenty, a *macédoine* is in its proper place: Take only

A *macédoine* of vegetables.

the best and freshest you can get: carrots, turnips, green peas, asparagus, string-beans or any other vegetables which will match. Cut the roots into fancy shapes, the beans into lozenges, the asparagus into one-and-a-half-inch pieces. Cook each by itself in salted water until just done. Drain them; put a good-sized piece of butter into a stewing-pan; when melted, put in your vegetables and stir them gently over a not too lively fire. There must not be any more butter than sufficient to encase with it the vegetables. When they are thoroughly heated, moisten them with some thick *béchamel* sauce and serve them heaped up, pyramid-shaped, on a hot dish.

This is Dumas' recipe, on which you may improve by stewing each vegetable, after parboiling it, in butter and a little water, except asparagus and cauliflower, which you boil in

---

[1] See also filet of beef, p. 47.

some broth.   Then you might either mix your vegetables in
the above way, or — what would look nicer — arrange them
wreath-like, each vegetable by itself, as demonstrated before ;
or in different sections around some kind of meat, or a head
of cauliflower.   By adding stewed mushrooms, shrimps, or lobster claws, you will raise it to a first-class dish.

If from the abundance of vegetables at your command you
make wise selections, and have a variety for your daily fare
accompanied by well-assorted meat, you will not run the
danger of being reproached one day by a squib like that of the
boy averse to turnips : —

> Turnips, turnips day by day,
> Drove me surely off and away.
> If for dinner mother had
> Meat, good meat, at home I'd staid.

So many fishes of so many features.

—DU BARTAS.

YOU have reminded me in good time that I have not said anything as yet about fish. It is not equivalent to beef, and hardly as nourishing as the lower grades of meat; still, it contains nutritives enough to warrant using it in place of meat.

Food value of fish. It also produces a pleasant change in one's diet, and is enticing to the appetite, often much more so than meat is. Then, it offers a variety incomparable to the latter. The Neapolitans, who eat everything living or breathing within the briny deep, call it *frutti di mare* (fruit of the sea), a fit figure of speech, it seems to me, for shell-fish of any sort. In thinking about the abounding food offered by sea and river — salt and sweet water — and the succulent meals to be derived therefrom, one might rather wish for the strict Lenten fare of former times. We owe many a first-rate recipe to those days.

To make it clear to you what nutrients you have in different kinds of fish, I again give you a table : —

	ALBUMINOIDS.	FATS.	WATER.	MINERAL MATTERS.
Pike...................	18.5	0.5	80.0	1.0
Salmon	16.0	6.5	76.5	1.0
Codfish	17.0	0.4	81.0	1.6
Eel.......	13.0	28.5	57.3	1.0
Green herring..........	17.8	10.3	70.0	1.9
Pickled herring.........	19.0	18.0	46.4	16.5
Smoked salmon.........	24.2	12.3	51.5	12.0
Sardines, salted.........	23.0	3.0	54.0	20.0
Salted codfish..........	30.0	0.4	49.6	20.0
Dried codfish, not salted..	80.0	1.0	17.5	1.5
Smoked herring........	21.0	8.5	69.3	1.5

You will notice that fresh fish contains a larger percentage of water than does meat, while cured fish makes a strikingly good show of albuminoids and mineral matters. The latter, however, are largely owing to the salt used in preserving them. The highest percentage of nutrients is found in dried codfish, and both it and herring furnish the greatest amount of nourishment for the least amount of money. They have, however, to be accompanied by an adequate percentage of carbohydrates to satisfy the demands of the human system. Thus the poorer classes of Europe instinctively eat their salted herring with potatoes; while in this country we have the codfish-balls, consisting of part potatoes.

You will also notice the large percentage of fats which is found in some fish, especially eel. Fish of that sort is harder to digest, and on that account not rated as high for nourishing a tender stomach as fish less fat (for instance, pike), even if their nitrogenous substance should be of a lower grade.

Fish is either boiled, broiled, baked, or fried. In all cases it is to be treated on the same principle as meat. When put to boil in cold water, fish, like meat, will part with its best substances, which will go to enrich the *How to cook fish.* water it is cooked in. To make a soup of it or a fish-jelly (which is very delicate), this would be the right way; but to boil fish which is to be eaten, it is necessary to put it into boiling water. To know the right moment when a fish is done, is not such an easy affair as you might think. It depends not merely on the size of the fish, but also on its kind, on the nature of the water it has lived in, on the time passed since it was killed, and on the water in which it is boiled. An underdone fish is disgusting, while an over-done one is tasteless and mostly tough. After fifteen minutes from the time a fish has been put on the fire, one has to be on the watch. If the fish is small or thin, it most likely will not stand a second's longer cooking. If large, it may need half an hour to be well done, or even more. Experience and a certain fine instinct have to guide you. One sign — and a pretty safe one — is to try a fin. If it gives way easily to a slight pull, the fish is done. Fish, like meat which is to be dished up, has to be kept simmering rather than boiling after its first immersion in lively boiling water. After it is cleaned, it must not be kept soaking in cold water. Some salt-water fishes are better for sprinkling them with salt inside and outside for about one hour before cooking them. The salt, of course, has to be washed off again. Be sure that your fish is always as fresh as possible. It decomposes quickly, and then is very harmful. Never buy a fish whose eyes are dull-looking, or the gills of which are not of a fine red color. It is best, of course, when put on the fire as soon as caught and killed ; but this luxury is within the reach of but a minority of people.

To boil fish, well-salted water with the addition of a cupful of vinegar is generally the right medium. In some cases, however, the addition of a bouquet of herbs, an onion, and a little spice is preferable. A good recipe for this "cradle " of boiled fish, as Grimod de la Reynière calls it, is the following : —

Court-Bouillon to boil Fish in. — For three pints of water take one-half pint of cider vinegar, one large carrot, two onions, two cloves, one teaspoonful of pepper seeds, two bay leaves, and enough salt to make it strongly taste of it (about three table-spoonfuls). When it boils put in your fish.

Keep this in mind, and all I have said before, and you will be able to boil pretty nearly all kinds of fish without trouble. Fish is nice enough boiled whole, well garnished, and served with potatoes and a good sauce ; but it is pleasant to vary the method, for the sake of which I proceed to give you some special recipes which will enable you to diversify the process by applying the given methods to other kinds of fish, or to alter them according to your needs and likings. A few of them will be convenient for breakfast. I take for granted, of course, that you get your fish of the fish dealer, well prepared and cleaned.

Striped Bass, stuffed and baked. — Make a stuffing of one stale breakfast roll, one tablespoonful of butter, the roes of the fish (or if it has none, of a carp or some other sweet-water fish), two eggs, a teaspoonful of minced parsley, and a salt-spoonful of salt. Soak the roll in milk, and press it until dry in a napkin ; melt the butter, and pour it over the bread. Mix well; then add the eggs, stir until light, after which you add the roes chopped beforehand, the parsley, and salt. Try a little of this stuffing by putting it into boiling water for five minutes. If too soft, add some bread-crumbs, if too stiff, a little cream. Fill it into the fish, and sew it up. Now put a tablespoonful of butter into a dripping-pan, slice one onion, one carrot, one celery root, and add to it some bunches of parsley; arrange so as to make a bed of them for the fish to lie on, and cover the latter up with a sheet of paper buttered on both sides. Bake for one hour in a slow oven, adding a little water from time to time, and baste the fish frequently. When done, lift it on a hot platter, carefully remove the stitches, and garnish with parsley, pieces of lemon, and anything else your taste dictates. Serve it with a sauce; we *Sauce Hollandaise for fish.* will say a Hollandaise. To make it, put the yolks of two eggs into a skillet, which you place in a vessel with boiling water. Add a cupful of the liquid left in the fish-pan, after it has been strained and the fat taken off. Stir all the while with a wire whisk. Cut a tablespoonful of butter into little pieces, and add them one by one; salt to taste; put in a sprinkle of nutmeg, and the juice of half a lemon, if liked. Stir until thick; do not let it curdle, and serve as soon as done.

In the same way you can bake red-snapper, carp, shad, and lake-pike.

The best lake-pike I have ever eaten was in Switzerland, near the lake of Geneva. I asked for the recipe, and here it is: —

Stewed Pike. — Take a good-sized fish; put it whole into a fish-kettle with about a quart of good rich broth, two onions, each stuck with one clove, a bunch of parsley, and four or five thick slices of bread as large as the palm of your hand. Cover it up well. When half done — that is, in about a quarter of an hour from the time it began to boil — add a pint and a half of some good white wine (cold). When entirely done, place the fish carefully on a hot platter, remove onions and parsley from the liquor in which the fish was boiling, and add to it the yolks of about three eggs beaten light in a little cream (or milk). Do not let it curdle, and do not break up the bread any more than you can help. Put the latter around the fish by means of a cake-lifter, and pour as much of the sauce over it as the dish will hold. The rest you serve in a boat. I have cooked shad this way, and also found it delicious.

By boiling pike simply in salted water, you can have a very pretty dish, if you put the tail of the fish into its mouth, thus **Ringed pike.** shaping it into a ring. You have to do this when raw, before putting the fish into boiling water. In this case you need, of course, a round pot in which to boil your fish. When done, serve it on a round platter, and fill the space inside the ringed fish with small round potatoes cooked in salted water. Pour over them some melted butter, in which a table-spoonful of minced parsley has been cooked for one or two seconds.

Boil codfish or haddock in salted water, with the addition only of a little vinegar. Of cod the tail-piece is the favorite **Cod and haddock; how to boil and stew.** part. It is nicest served whole, with oyster sauce. For stewed codfish, cut a small cod into three or four equal-sized pieces, wash them in salt water, and put them into a kettle with no more water than will cling to them. Add a blade of mace, a wineglassful of white cook-ing-wine, and two tablespoonfuls of butter divided in halves, one of them having a scant tablespoonful of flour rubbed into it. Add salt to taste, and at the very last a little white pepper (powdered). Let it cook slowly and well-covered for fifteen to twenty minutes, and serve the fish and sauce in the same dish.

For a sauce to accompany either pike, cod, or haddock, I would recommend a mustard sauce. It is made simply by **Mustard sauce.** mixing and stirring over the fire two tablespoon-fuls of butter and one tablespoonful of French mustard, until just before the point of boiling.

For boiled salmon take a middle piece, because there is little waste. Two pounds will be sufficient for eight persons. Take a heaped tablespoonful of butter, work one heaped teaspoonful of flour into it, and place it in the hollow side of the fish. Tie a napkin around it with twine, and boil it covered up with court-bouillon, to which add some wine, if you wish to indulge in such luxury (for, accord- ing to Grimod, salmon — which he called the prince of the sea — is somewhat addicted to the use of spirits, and only cares for the best). Your salmon needs about twenty-five minutes' gentle boiling. Take it out of the napkin, place it in the middle of a platter, and garnish with the finest sprigs of curled parsley you can get, to which you may add some pieces of lemon, little potato balls, lobster claws, or anything harmonizing in taste and color. Serve it with a

Boiled salmon with parsley sauce.

Parsley Sauce. — Take the yolks of two eggs, half a table-spoonful of flour, two tablespoonfuls of minced parsley, and one heaped tablespoonful of butter. Melt the butter, put in the rest and stir, with a little water, until quite smooth ; then add gradually, stirring all the while, three-quarters of a pint of the boiling-hot liquor in which the fish has been cooked. Allow to boil up just once, and serve in a boat.

Another most delicious sauce for salmon is the following, the recipe of which I owe to the wife of the landlord at Bad Gries-bach, in the Black Forest,. Germany. She called it *sauce Génoise.* Chop the lower tail-end of a salmon into several pieces, and *sauté* it in a little butter, with the addition of one small onion, half a carrot (both sliced), a little bunch of parsley, half a bay leaf, two pepper seeds, one clove, and a mite of garlic. Take it off the fire before it gets brown ; pour off the butter, add one pint of good red wine, one salted sardine, and let it boil continuously for a quarter of an hour. Then pass the whole through a wire sieve, stir into it a piece of butter the size of half an egg, and serve. If a salted sardine cannot be had, a little anchovy paste added at the last will do instead.

Sauce Génoise for salmon.

If any cooked salmon is left over, use it next day in this way : Divide it into nicely trimmed pieces, *sauté* them quickly on both sides in a little hot butter, then serve them with a cold

A luncheon dish of salmon.

Sauce Remoulade. — Take the yolks of two hard-boiled eggs ; when cold, press them flat with a spoon, and stir them with a teaspoonful of vinegar until smooth. Add little by little one tablespoonful of olive oil and two tablespoonfuls of French mustard, then one teaspoonful of minced onion, two teaspoon-fuls of minced parsley, a pinch of white pepper, salt to taste, and, if not sufficiently sour, the juice of a lemon. This sauce will keep for days.

Filet of Flounder à la Joinville is an extremely nice dish. Take two flounders, skin them, and cut the flesh off the bones with a sharp-pointed knife. Divide it into eight filets, which you roll up into eight little turbans. Fasten each with a wooden toothpick, to be removed before serving. Stew them slowly in one tablespoonful of butter, to which add a wineglassful of cider champagne, one small onion, a little lemon juice, three pepper seeds, and a pinch of salt. When done (in about fif-teen minutes) take out your filets carefully with a skimmer and arrange them on a hot dish. Place a button mushroom, heated in its own liquor, on top of each turban. Now throw a ball of butter and flour the size of half an egg into the boiling liquid, and when dissolved strain this sauce. Pour some of it around the filets and serve the rest in a boat. A very nice addition is to have some oysters cooked in their own juice with which to trim the filets. You may also color your sauce with a table-spoonful of melted crayfish or lobster butter.[1]

Fried fish is very good turned in salted flour, or salted egg and bread-crumbs, and then put into boiling hot fat to get

To broil fish.   brown. But most fish are really too fat to be treated in this way ; they are much better broiled, as, for instance, shad, if not too large, mackerel, and eel. In broiling you follow the same rule I gave you for broiling

Broiled mackerel.   meat, merely seeing that the fire is rather slow and keeping the fish roasting on it until thoroughly done. Mackerel is best in the spring. The Spanish mackerel, coming up from the Southern States, is the most delicious,

---

[1] See p. 146.

but also the most expensive.   Even the common kind is very acceptable when broiled.   Wipe it dry with a towel after washing it.   Rub the inside with some salt and pepper ; brush the fish on both sides with some olive oil (or melted butter) ; wrap it in a piece of white paper which is well oiled or buttered, and put it on the gridiron.   It will take from twenty to twenty-five minutes to get done.   Then remove the paper, put the fish on a hot dish, and serve it with *maître d'hôtel* butter[1] spread over the top.

To broil bloaters, soak them in half milk, half water, for an hour; then pull off the skin.   Wrap them in buttered paper and broil on a slow fire for five minutes on each side ; or divide them down the middle, remove **Broiled bloaters.** the bones, put them on a flat dish, and pour on them some olive oil. At the time for serving put them on the gridiron and keep them on the fire for one or two minutes on each side.

A halibut steak turned in salted Indian meal, **Fish steak** and *sauté*ed in hot lard, is a nice dish, espe- **sautéed.** cially when served with oyster sauce.

As it is a matter of importance to an economical house-keeper to know what to do with remnants of fish, **How to use** I mention the following ways in which to use **remnants of fish.** fish left over : —

No. 1. — Butter a dish ; put into it in alternate layers thinly sliced boiled potatoes and fish picked into small pieces. Spread over each layer some plain *béchamel* sauce.   Dust bread-crumbs over the top, and put in the oven to get brown for ten or fifteen minutes.   Serve in the same dish.

No. 2. — Remove carefully skin and bone of boiled fish ; cut it into nice little pieces and pile it up pyramid-shape on a flat dish.   Now pour over it a *béchamel* sauce, made with cream or milk, to which a saltspoonful of anchovy paste has been added.   Dust over the whole some grated Parmesan cheese, and sprinkle with melted butter.   Put in a quick oven for a few minutes, or until of a nice brown color.

[1] See p. 74.

No. 3. — Put mashed potatoes rim-like in a dish ; place some nice large pieces of boiled fish in the middle ; drop flakes of butter between the pieces here and there ; pour over it some thick cream, and dust it over with two-thirds bread-crumbs and one-third grated cheese.   Put it into the oven to get heated and take color.

No. 4. — To a cupful of shredded fish take a cupful of mashed potatoes.   Put both into a wooden bowl, and work them to a paste with a potato masher, adding to it successively one egg, a tablespoonful of butter, and a cupful of milk.   Add salt to taste, and continue working the whole until quite light. Fill it into a buttered *gratin*-dish and bake in a quick oven until light brown.   Serve it either with a green salad, French dressing, or with a sauce of your choosing.

No. 5. — After your cooked fish is freed of all bones and skin, cut it into small dice, and put these into shells.   Make a white *roux*, thin it with broth and a little white wine (which may be replaced by lemon or orange juice) ; add salt, a sprinkle of white pepper, a little minced parsley, and a few mushrooms also minced.   Cover up the fish with this sauce, put on top of each shell a flake of butter, and put in the oven for five minutes.

There are some excellent French ways of stewing fish which we might appropriate to our use.   Famous among them is the

Bouille-abaisse.

Bouille-abaisse of Southern France, which inspired Thackeray to write his ballad of that name.   But this dish, after all, seems to have been more a convivial memory than a real enthusiasm, or he would have done better in describing it : —

> "A sort of soup, or broth, or brew,
> Or hotchpotch of all sorts of fishes,
> That Greenwich never could outdo."

It sounds much more appetizing when we read of it in Méry's long poem, given by Monselet, which begins : —

> "Pour le vendredi maigre, un jour, certaine abbesse
> D'un couvent marseillais créa la bouille-abaisse,
> Et jamais ce bienfait n'a trouvé des ingrats
> Chez les peuples marins, qui n'aiment point le gras.
> Ce plat est un poème." —

[For a Friday's fast one day the abbess good
Of a convent in Marseilles created *bouille-abaisse*,
And the boon she conferred is remembered with praise
By the men of the sea, who are partial to fish.
The dish is a poem. —]

Then he goes on and describes in the most enticing manner how, at first, a wonderful *coulis* is made of numerous little fish and spice, and how, in this carefully prepared liquor, about half a dozen different kinds of fish are cooked and then served. The vulgarized recipes for *bouille-abaisse* are nothing compared to it, and, on the whole, since we do not live on the borders of the Mediterranean, we had better leave this dish alone, and turn to the simpler and less expensive matelote, for which I will give you two different recipes to choose from.

Bluefish en Matelote. — Cut the fish into pieces, put it into a stew-pan, add a bay leaf, six pepper seeds, a sprinkle of salt, one clove, and pour over it sufficient cheap claret to cover the fish. Let it come to a boil as quickly as possible. Meanwhile take a dozen small onions and *sauté* them in butter until turned light brown. Take also a dozen small button mushrooms, a saltspoonful of salt, a sprinkle of pepper, a teaspoonful of lemon juice and the juice of the mushrooms; add all this to the onions, and allow the whole to stew until about three-quarters done. Now, when the fish has come to a boil, skim it, and add to the liquor about a tablespoonful of butter, and as much of flour, both kneaded into a ball. This makes the sauce, which must neither be too thin, nor too thick, but have the right consistency. After the butter and flour have dissolved, you add the onions, the mushrooms, and their liquor to the sauce, and allow the whole to simmer until the pieces of fish are quite done. You may add some shrimps at the last. Serve the pieces of fish wreath-wise on a round dish, and pour the sauce over it and into the centre. You may cook other kinds of fish in the same way. Or make a matelote of several kinds of fish. Take one fat, and the other lean, as for instance pike and whitefish, or salmon-trout and shad.

Matelote of Perch. — Melt some butter in a stew-pan, and add some minced parsley and onion, and then your fish. Pour over it a pint of cider champagne, and when nearly done add a dozen or more oysters, a dozen clams, and some shrimps if you choose ; then let the whole simmer until done. This is a French recipe (called *matelote normande*), as is also the foregoing one.

I end this letter with a recipe for fish in jelly, which is well worth the trouble of trying. I have found it useful many a time, when I wanted a pretty dish other than meat on my tea or luncheon table. You can make this dish also of remnants of boiled fish, if they are left in good shape. Cut your fish into thick slices and boil them with several onions, pepper seeds, a bay leaf, salt, and some vinegar. When done and cool, arrange the pieces in a mould, placing in the bottom of the latter first of all some thin slices of lemon. Allow the liquor in which the fish was boiled to continue cooking, with head and tail of the fish added. After an hour's lively boiling strain it, add a cupful of good broth in which you have dissolved a heaped saltspoonful of Liebig, and the juice of half a lemon. Taste it if salt is needed. Place a tablespoonful of it on ice to see if it will jelly. If not, add some gelatine to stiffen it. Clear it,[1] and pour over the fish in your mould. If you should be able to procure some branches of fresh tarragon, you will produce a very pretty effect by arranging them inside your mould, but outside of the fish, in the form of a light wreath. This you do before you fill up the mould with your jelly. The tarragon in addition will add its flavor to the dish.

Fish in jelly.

Of all the wealth of the fish-market, and the abundance of good recipes, I have shown you but a glimpse. You will learn by experience, and, to guide you on the road to it, I believe I have told you what is needful.

---

[1] See p. 80.

LETTER XVII

A dish that I do love to feed upon.
—SHAKESPEARE.

I WOULD rather commence at once to tell you of shell-fish — a delightful subject — if my conscience would let me. For I have not given you any instruction as yet about the prosaic, but very useful, cured cod. To prepare it for use, *Cured cod, and how to cook it.* put it in cold water (skin upward, to allow the salt to leave the fish), which change a few times, and soak for from twelve to twenty-four hours, according to the thickness of the fish. To cook it, put it in plenty of cold water (no salt), and place it on the stove, where it will get hot very slowly. It must not boil, or it will be tough. When quite hot, move the pot with the fish to a place still further removed from the fire, and let it steep there for half an hour longer. If the piece is from a fine large cod, it is to be served whole with a *sauce Hollandaise*.[1] At a New England coast town I have eaten it thus cooked, when it was exceedingly nice. It was served with two sauces, one of drawn butter, and the other consisting of the pure fat rendered from salt pork, cut in small dice, and the cracklings left in. Besides, there were the mealiest of potatoes (cooked in salted water), sliced beets in vinegar, and hard-boiled eggs. It was a perfect meal.

In a Capuchin monastery in southern Germany, dried codfish, after being freshened and cooked, is served with onions cut fine and fried in butter until yellow, and with a *purée* of dried peas.

You may also shred salt codfish, after being cooked, into small pieces, and treat it like recipe No. 4 for using up remnants of fish.[2]

[1] See p. 131.   [2] See p. 136.

139

For Codfish Balls, chop even quantities of cooked fish and potatoes. Cut fat salt pork into dice, and render until partly melted; then chop fine what is left of them and mix with the fish and potatoes. Form into balls and fry in the fat rendered from the pork scraps. This recipe will also make a nice hash. I owe it likewise to a good New England housewife.

What has been said in praise of codfish as a nutrient cannot be said in favor of oysters; and yet who would be willing to do without this "fruit of the sea"? Their large percentage of water (from 80 to 85 per cent) is the reason why oysters rank low in this respect. Still they make a show of about equal percentages of albuminoids and carbohydrates — a little more perhaps of the former than the latter — and a very fair show as to fat and mineral matter in proportion to them. If eaten in quantities they do very well for nutriment. They are easily digested if eaten raw, but less so when cooked. Oysters, therefore, ought never to be more than just made hot; the longer they stay on the fire the more the albumen they contain will harden, and be apt to interfere with a comfortable digestion.

Oysters may be cooked in so many different styles, and are so easily gotten ready, that they are most convenient, and at the same time always welcome, for helping out Oysters, and the different ways of cooking them. when an unexpected guest comes to share a meal with us, or when provisions happen to run short for our daily fare. They are so delicious in taste and flavor that I would prefer to have them cooked mostly in their own liquor; and if spice is to be used, to take a blade of mace only, since it seems to harmonize better with the aroma of the oyster than other kinds of spice. The addition of a little lemon juice, however, is to be recommended, since a slight acid helps to digest the albumen.

The one way in which the flavor of the oyster when exposed to heat is preserved almost intact, is to roast them. To do this, get them on the half-shell with whatever juice they have, and place them side by side on a gridiron over a bright fire. Leave them on it just long enough to get hot and plump; then serve on their shells. The next best way is to pan them.

Take the oysters with the juice that will adhere to them and put them in a shallow pan, in which a piece of butter has been melted. Put them in a moderately hot oven, and leave them in it until the beards begin to curl; then serve. Always taste the oysters to see whether salt is needed. For broiled or panned oysters, a slight dusting over with white pepper might be liked.

For tea or supper a dish of scalloped oysters is very nice. Drain your oysters, and see that no fragments of shell are left clinging to them. Take a *gratin*-dish; butter it; put in a thin layer of rather coarse bread-crumbs, then a layer of the oysters with some bits of butter, some more bread-crumbs, and so on, until the oysters are all used up. Put a thick layer of crumbs on the top and sprinkle with melted butter. If the oysters appear rather dry, add some of their juice before putting on the top layer of crumbs. Some substitute a small wineglassful of sherry for the oyster liquor; but this is a matter of taste. Bake the oysters in a moderately hot oven for about one hour.

To make a plain oyster stew, boil and skim the oyster liquor first. Add a thickening of flour and butter rubbed together, or one of cracker-dust, adding the butter afterwards. Some like milk added to the juice of the oysters, and some do not. By adding milk you increase, of course, the nourishing properties of the oyster stew. After the liquid is ready, put in your oysters, and let them get hot. If you intend to have a more perfect oyster stew, proceed in this way: Cut the beards off two dozen oysters. Sprinkle some lemon juice over the latter. Put the juice of the oysters and the beards on to boil, and skim well; then add a blade of mace, a few pepper seeds and the peel of half a lemon shaved off; let it boil slowly for half an hour from the time it was put on the fire; then strain the liquid and when boiling again put in a scant tablespoonful of butter, into which as much flour has been rubbed. Add also half a pint of cream (or milk) made hot beforehand. When the butter and flour is dissolved and the sauce quite smooth, put in your oysters. Allow them to get hot, but do not let them boil, and serve at once.

If you wish to fry oysters, take large ones, drain them, turn them first in some flour, then in an egg beaten up, and lastly in some bread or cracker crumbs. Throw them into some boiling hot lard and leave in only long enough to turn light brown.

For broiling oysters also take large ones ; turn them in breadcrumbs, and put them on a well-greased, double wire gridiron. Have a bright coal fire, and broil them for one or two minutes, first on one side, then on the other. Have a hot dish, with a piece of butter melting on it, to receive them, and serve at once.

For an oyster fricassee proceed as for the oyster stew second in number, with this difference, that you add the yolks of two or three eggs, beaten up beforehand, to the liquid, and stir it over the fire until it thickens. Add also a little lemon juice. Do not let it boil, or it will curdle. This recipe you may use likewise for oysters on scallop-shells. Strew bread-crumbs over the oysters and sauce with which you have filled your shells, and place them in the oven to brown on top. Or fill with them some puff-paste patties, which are exceedingly nice. You may serve an oyster stew on pieces of toast, which makes a nice breakfast dish. If you have some oyster liquor left, thicken it with flour and butter rubbed together, add milk or cream, and pour it over some hot toast for breakfast or luncheon. If you wish to keep the oyster liquor until the following day, be sure and scald it, or it will not keep. You may also add it to a soup made of broth. If cooked oysters are left over, they give a pleasant flavor to a hash made of meat, if chopped fine with it.

For oyster sauce, make a *béchamel* with the juice of the
Oyster sauce.   oysters and add some cream. Season with a little
mace and white pepper, and when done put in
some oysters, taking care that they do not harden.

Clams have the advantage of being fit to eat when oysters are not. They afford a good broth, especially for invalids ;
Clams.   but clams themselves are hard to digest, unless
they are boiled just two or three minutes, and
then even the soft part only is fit to eat. A clam chowder is delicious when made as I once ate it in New England.

Clam Chowder. — Take a quarter of a pound of fat salt pork, cut it into small dice, and put it on the fire until brown and crisp. Chop a small onion, and throw into the pork fat to turn yellow. Have ready a soup-plateful of raw potatoes very thinly sliced. Put them into a deep stew-pan, strain over them the fat from the pork, and add the liquor from a quart of clams. Boil slowly until the potatoes are quite done. Meanwhile take your clams and boil them for three minutes and no longer in one pint of water, adding one teaspoonful of salt. Drain them; but keep the water. Cut off the hard part of the clams and chop, then put them back into the strained water, and let boil for at least a quarter of an hour longer; then drain them again, adding the water to the potatoes and clam liquor, and throwing away the hard part of the clams. Take their soft parts, and chop them also, but coarsely. Add a gill of boiling milk (or cream) to the potatoes, half a dozen water crackers, and lastly the chopped clams (soft parts). Season with pepper if you like, and a little powdered thyme.

A lobster furnishes you with a very ornamental and palatable dish. To boil a lobster, have a large kettle three-quarters full of boiling water; add four onions halved, a large bouquet of parsley, twenty pepper seeds, two bay leaves, salt at the rate of one heaped tablespoonful to every quart of water. Put in your lobster. Do it quickly, head foremost, which will kill it and end its torture at once. Let it boil for fifteen to twenty-five minutes, according to its size. When done, take it out, twist off the claws and tail, cleave into halves (lengthwise) body and tail, and remove from the latter the dark, stringy vein called "lady-fingers," which is poisonous. Crack the claws on their lower sides and be careful not to disfigure them. Thus prepared, you may serve the lobster hot or cold, scalloped, as salad, croquettes, or in various other ways. If you wish to serve the lobster whole, you reconstruct it from its separate pieces, masking the flaws with sprigs of parsley. Serve it on a folded napkin in the middle of an oval platter; garnish with parsley laid wreath-like around, and have either a tartar sauce or a mayonnaise accompany it.[1]

I will now give you some specified recipes for dishes made of lobster.

Lobster Cutlets. — Take the meat of a boiled lobster and pound it in a mortar with one ounce and a half of butter (size of an egg), a saltspoonful of salt, half as much white pepper, and the coral of the lobster (if there is any). When it has turned to a smooth paste, it is ready to be formed into small cutlets, with a small lobster claw stuck in each. Dip into a beaten-up egg, and then turn them in some fine bread-crumbs. Repeat this after a minute or two, then *sauté* the cutlets in hot butter, and serve them as a course by themselves.

Lobster Stew. — Cut the meat of a boiled lobster into slices, put it into a stew-pan with a saltspoonful of salt, a teaspoonful of French mustard, a tablespoonful of good cider vinegar, and two ounces of butter. Cover it up, and allow to stew over a moderate fire for about six minutes. Then add a wineglassful of white wine, and let stew another four to five minutes. At the last, sprinkle over with white pepper, then serve, and garnish with parsley and slices of lemon.

Lobster Fricassee. — Cut a boiled lobster into pieces about an inch square, and break up the shells into little pieces by means of pestle and mortar. Melt and make hot three ounces of butter; add to it the shells, and when the whole bubbles up stir into it a heaped tablespoonful of flour. After it thickens, add broth sufficient to give it the consistency of a sauce, and let all boil slowly for half an hour, then strain through a hair sieve. Return it to the fire, add the meat of the lobster and the yolks of two eggs beaten up in a little cream. Stir over the fire until hot, but do not let it come to a boil. You may add to the sauce some asparagus points cooked beforehand in salted water, or some balls made of bread-crumbs[2] or fish; or both, balls and asparagus. The fish balls you make in this way: Take three tablespoonfuls of bread-crumbs; moisten

---

[1] See pp. 74 and 153.　　　　　[2] See p. 27.

them with broth, and stir over the fire until bubbling up. Then remove from the fire, and mix into them about six ounces of cooked fish freed from skin and bones, one whole egg and the yolk of another one, some salt and Fish balls. pepper, a little grated nutmeg, and a teaspoonful of minced parsley. Make a thick and smooth paste of all this by working it over and over with a wooden pestle. Then form into little balls, which boil in some broth for about five minutes, or until done.

Baked Lobster. — Chop the meat of a boiled lobster. Chop also two or three shallots (or a slice of onion) and put into three ounces of melted and boiling hot butter. Then remove to the side of the stove, and let the shallots simmer until soft, when you add the chopped lobster, a saltspoonful of salt, a sprinkle of pepper, a teaspoonful of minced parsley, a little minced tarragon, if you have any ; and, lastly, four eggs beaten light beforehand. Stir and mix over the fire, without allowing it to boil. Put this mixture into a buttered *gratin*-dish, cover it with bread-crumbs, sprinkle with melted butter, and bake in a moderately hot oven. You may serve with it a *sauce Hollandaise* [1] colored with some of the lobster coral. Should you have the right number of lobster-shells — one for each person — fill them with the mixture, and bake it in them.

Creamed Lobster. — Chop the meat of the boiled lobster, put it into a sauce-pan, add a saltspoonful of salt, half as much white pepper, a tablespoonful of white wine, and as much vinegar. Let it get hot, then add one ounce of butter (size of half an egg) mixed with a heaped teaspoonful of flour and a gill of cream. Stir the whole over the fire, allowing it to cook gently for ten minutes. You may serve this also in lobster-shells, but do not bake.

Lobster is delicious with a mayonnaise sauce, and as a salad. But I defer giving you the recipe for it until I talk to you about salads in general and in particular. I will add, however, the recipe for a

Lobster Sauce. — Chop very fine the coral of a boiled lobster, together with two anchovies. Moisten it with some broth,

[1] See p. 131.

and add a piece of butter the size of a walnut. Rub it through
a hair sieve.   Take as much of the coral as will give a fine red
color to a *béchamel* sauce.   Flavor with a little lemon juice, and
add to it a heaped tablespoonful of the lobster meat cut into
small dice. If you cannot procure any anchovies, take anchovy
Lobster butter. paste the size of a large pea. What is left of the
lobster coral you may mix with some more melted
butter and set away for further use.   It will do instead of crayfish butter which I recommended to you for some recipes.

Now, before closing my lesson on fish, I want to say something about a generally discarded amphibiam, — the frog, of
Frogs' legs. which the hind legs alone come in question. They
are said to be nourishing and very easily digested.
Dr. Wiel, who was a famous specialist for diseases of the
stomach, recommends them highly for invalid diet, either
stewed or in soup.   I give you the following recipe for stewed
frogs' legs, which I take from a German cook-book devoted to
Lenten fare : —

Remove the toes of the frogs' legs and wash them clean.
Make a sauce of butter and flour, thinned with water and flavored with lemon peel and juice.   Put the frogs' legs into this
sauce and let them stew until tender.   When done, add the
yolks of two eggs.

They are also good this way : Cook the frogs' legs until
tender in some water, to which you add salt, a bunch of thyme,
an onion, and a little vinegar.   Do not use any more water
than just enough to cover them.   Strain the liquid and pour
over the frogs' legs before you serve them.   *Sauté* some
bread-crumbs in a little butter, and, when brown, spread them
on the top.

You may also treat them as a *friture*, either dipping them
in batter,[1] or merely turning them in egg and fine bread-crumbs,
before frying them.   But, of course, cooked in this way they
are less digestible.

"*Basta !*" says the Italian — "enough for to-day."

[1] See p. 78.

LETTER XVIII

Let olives, endives, mallows light
Be all my fare.
—HORACE.

Eat cress, and have more wit.
—GREEK PROVERB.

I AM glad to hear that now you think yourself prepared with all my teachings to give a dinner party. There is, however, one thing more which you have first to learn, and that is to plan and dress a salad. I have a long lesson in store for you, — a pleasant task, — for I count it a very important part of culinary art, and a delightful accomplishment, to make a salad in perfection.

There are raw, cooked, and mixed salads. But lettuce is the salad *par excellence*, and cannot be recommended sufficiently for its refreshing, its wholesome, and cool- ing qualities. Cooked vegetables, fish, and meats, when made into salads, either by themselves or mixed, can be made very tempting; but for a healthy diet I would recommend only the green salads and the cooked vegetables simply dressed. They yield material for a large variety of salads and give you an opportunity for testing your talent.

General remarks about salads.

In our country, with its succulent vegetables, green salad is not yet introduced as generally as it deserves. During our hot summers especially it ought to be part of the principal meal, at least. Brillat-Savarin says: " Salad refreshes without debilitating, and comforts without irritating. I am in the habit of saying that it is rejuvenating." We find, however, a much earlier appreciation of salad — the *lactuca* of the Romans — in Greek authors, where it is praised as soothing, fortifying the stomach, and favoring sleep.

147

This latter, by the by, reminds me of a little incident occurring years ago. It was June time. We lived in the country and had a guest at our table,—a distinguished pioneer and general. At dinner I had served with the roast a lettuce salad, which was fresh from the garden, and prepared and dressed with my own hands, — as I thought, in the most tempting way. But, when offered, our guest declined to take it, remarking that the opium contained in the lettuce leaves was apt to make him inopportunely drowsy. This was news to me; nor do I find it stated anywhere that opium really exists in lettuce. The milky juice of the stem, because resembling that of poppies, seems to have led to this belief. This juice, most likely, is the vehicle for the nutritives contained in salad, and the fresher the latter, the juicier and consequently the more nutritious it is. According to Liebig, lettuce has of alkalies 23 to 24 per cent of its dry substances. But when we consider that it has 94 parts of water in every 100, we cannot place it very high as a nutritive. Its usefulness, like that of other green and vegetable salads, lies in another direction, as indicated above; while the defect of it, and of all of them, is easily remedied, if we add the nutrients they are deficient in. The best accompaniment, therefore, for green salad is eggs in any form you please; and is there a prettier sight, on the table, than a dish full of green curly leaves of lettuce set off with quarters of hard-boiled eggs?

Aside from lettuce, we have herbs for salad. An old parchment volume of 1691, in my possession, enumerates sixty-two kinds of them for a famous herb salad. I would not want you to go to that extent; nor would you be able to procure most of them in our days. I merely wish to call your attention to certain tender herbs which our markets now afford. They are principally water-cress, peppergrass, field salad, borage, chicory, dandelion, and they make a nice salad each by itself, as well as intermixed *ad libitum*. With the exception of dandelion they also garnish beautifully every kind of salad. The latter in its wild state makes a wholesome salad in the spring, when the first fresh shoots appear on meadows and fields, and you dig for the plant deep enough to get part of the root.   The tender, clover-like leaf of the oxalis (*oxalis acetosella*), which is to be found in the woods during the summer, will also furnish you with a slightly acid and refreshing salad.   The following herbs are what the French call *"fournitures de salade"* (trimmings for salad): water-cress, peppergrass, chervil, chives, tarragon, pimpernel (garden burnet), balm-mint and borage. Add to all these the orange-tinted flowers of nasturtium and the blue blossoms of borage, which you may either make into a salad by themselves, dressing them with oil, vinegar, and salt, or use for a garnish, and you must acknowledge that you never need be in trouble about having an enticing and even artistic dish of salad on your table.   The Italians, who are extremely fond of salad, use for it almost anything green they can find.   When in Northern Italy once in early spring, I met during my walk a little black-eyed peasant girl filling her apron full of the sprouting shoots of clematis growing on a hedge.   I curiously inquired the purpose of it, to which she replied, *"Per far insalata"* (to make salad of).   But the French were the first to excel in salad-making.   Many a distinguished Frenchman prided himself on his proficiency in this art; and let me tell you here of my belief that it takes the fine sensibilities of a gentleman or a lady to make a really good salad.   Ordinary cooks and servants are incapable of comprehending even the first principles of it.   When the French Revolution drove the aristocrats from their country, some of them made their living, and even their fortunes — like D'Albignac — by the making of salads.

> "Tu sais que pour la salade
> J'ai les soins d'un émigré"
> (You know I have for the salad
> The emigrant's cares),

writes Monselet in "*Le diner que je veux faire*" (the dinner I want to devise).

To dress a salad is not as easy a task as you might think. The so-called " French dressing," of oil, vinegar, and salt, seems to be such a simple affair; but unless you take each of these elements in exactly the right proportion to each other and the salad to be dressed, the result will not be the desired one. To be an expert, you have to divine by instinct how much to take of each. I never allow a servant even to touch the leaves of the salad I have served at table, for to have the salad to perfection the touch must be light, the fingers to trim and arrange must be nimble. First take leaf by leaf, throwing away the outside and coarse ones, and removing all imperfections of those fit for use; then put them in a deep dish full of cold water to rinse them, one by one, transferring them at the same time into a large colander. This done, take the latter with both hands and toss the leaves lightly up and down in it, which will free them from the water clinging to them. Now put the colander on a plate and remove the whole to the refrigerator; but do not let it come in contact with the ice, which would chill the salad to such a degree as to rob it of its characteristic flavor. There you leave it standing for an hour, or until near dinner-time, when it will have turned deliciously crisp. Then take up once more leaf after leaf, dividing the larger ones carefully into halves and arranging them in a salad-bowl, wreath within wreath, like a full-blown rose. It will depend on your skill and inspiration to vary your salad by intermingling or garnishing it with one or more herbs of a darker green, the white and yellow of eggs, the tender pink of radishes, the pale green of thinly sliced cucumbers, the flowers of nasturtium, etc. Suppose you have done this to your satisfaction, you put your salad-bowl once more in the refrigerator, with distinct orders to leave it there until the time comes for placing it on the table, to be dressed dexterously with your own hands, to the delight of your husband and your guests, if guests there be. As to the dressing itself, I have told you already that instinct will have to teach you more than any recipe can do, but, in a general sense, I can recommend the following proportions for a plain French dressing: Take, for a heaped soup-plateful of salad, a heaped saltspoonful of salt,

How to prepare lettuce for salad, and how to make a plain dressing.

three tablespoonfuls of oil, and one tablespoonful of vinegar. Put the salt in your spoon first, then the oil (which must be of the best) ; mix-the two with your salad-fork, and pour over the salad ; then mix with the latter, and after adding the vinegar, mix again thoroughly. If the vinegar is not very sharp, add the juice of half a lemon. A sprinkle of white pepper mixed in with the oil is also recommendable, as well as a slight addition of mushroom catsup mixed in with the vinegar. Whenever I want to add some other ingredients to the plain dressing, I mix them beforehand with the vinegar needed, and pour the mixture, ready for use, in the empty vinegar-cruet of the caster.

If you wish to dress your lettuce salad with mayonnaise, it is best to put the latter in the bottom of the salad-bowl and to arrange the salad on top of it, allowing the sauce to show in the centre. In that case you have but to mix the salad after it comes to the table. I will give you some recipes for mayonnaise and other salad sauces by and by.

A salad of herbs — endives (of which the escarol is the best kind), water-cresses, dandelion, and field (or corn) salad — is always at its best when merely dressed with salt, vinegar, and oil. Endives are improved by putting them into warm (not hot) water for a short time, then rinsing them in cold water. It somewhat lessens their bitter flavor. Dandelion ought always to be a salad by itself. Its bitter and pungent flavor does not harmonize with any other herb or vegetable. Tarragon vinegar, substituted for plain vinegar, is the only deviation in the above dressing which is permitted. Field (or corn) salad does not allow as much oil as other salads do. It is improved by the addition of a cooked potato, grated and mixed into the plain dressing. Water-cresses are spoiled by too much vinegar ; they bear but a sprinkle of it. A famous firm of gardeners in Germany, who make the culture of water-cresses one of their specialties, give the following directions for dressing them : Pick and rinse them two or three hours before meal-time. Shake them dry, and squeeze the juice of half a lemon over a quart of them. Add one tablespoonful

About the dressing of herb salads.

of oil, and a small onion minced fine.   No vinegar.   Mix well
and let stand in a cool place until served.

Apart from the exceptions stated, you may, of course, vary
your dressing as much as the composition of your salads.   I
More substantial will give you now a small number of varied salad
dressings.   dressings or sauces to use at your own discretion.
I begin with the oft repeated, because never to be forgotten,
recipe of Sydney Smith : —

> " Two boiled potatoes pressed through kitchen sieve
> Smoothness and softness to the salad give.
> Of mordant mustard add a single spoon,
> Distrust the condiment that bites too soon;
> But deem it not, thou man of herbs, a fault
> To add a double quantity of salt.
> Three times the spoon with oil of Lucca crown,
> And once with vinegar procured from town;
> The flavor needs it, and your poet begs
> The pounded yellow of two well-boiled eggs.
> Let onion atoms lurk within the bowl,
> And — scarce suspected — animate the whole.
> And lastly, o'er the flavored compound toss
> A magic spoonful of anchovy sauce;
> Then, though green turtle fail, though venison's tough,
> And ham and turkey are not boned enough,
> Serenely full, the epicure may say, ·
> ' Fate cannot hurt me — I have dined to-day.' "

This recipe, in its quaint form, gives you the base for other
varieties of salad dressing when you lack time to make a
mayonnaise, and yet wish to have something more than a plain
dressing.   A very excellent variety is the following : —

Take two or three hard-boiled eggs, rub them to a paste,
and add gradually about five tablespoonfuls of oil, one teaspoonful of French mustard, a sprinkle of white pepper, three
to four tablespoonfuls of vinegar, and either a tablespoonful of
minced cives, or capers.   You may also leave out the mustard,
take less oil and vinegar, and add half a cupful of cream.

A very excellent dressing, also, is the following : —

Take the yolks of one hard-boiled and one raw egg, one teaspoonful of French mustard, one saltspoonful of salt, three to

four tablespoonfuls of oil, one tablespoonful each of cider and of tarragon vinegar, half a teaspoonful each of anchovy essence and mushroom catsup, and one heaped tablespoonful of minced parsley, chervil, pimpernel (garden burnet) and tarragon mixed. Stir until perfectly smooth. The herbs you may omit, if you choose.

The mayonnaise dressing or sauce has to be prepared with greater care to make it a success. For a fish or meat salad I prefer the following mayonnaise : Boil four eggs for fifteen minutes ; put them in cold water, and when cool take the yolks and mash them to a paste. Now take two ounces of freshest butter ; let it get soft enough to beat it to a cream (always beating in the same direction). Add to it, little by little, the above egg; and afterward, also very gradually, the raw yolks of three eggs, stirring vigorously all the time. See that the raw eggs are not cold, lest your butter should curdle. If it does, add the raw yolk of another egg. Add salt and vinegar (or lemon juice) to taste. If the mixture has not enough consistency, add some olive oil, drop by drop.

Three different mayonnaise dressings.

Another very excellent recipe is this : Take four raw yolks and put them into a porcelain dish. Place this dish on ice. Stir into the yolks half a pint of olive oil by taking a teaspoonful at a time and allowing it to mix drop by drop with the egg. Just as soon as the latter begins to thicken, add a few drops of lemon juice ; then proceed to mix in another teaspoonful of oil and more of the lemon juice, until all the oil is absorbed. The occasional adding of the lemon juice prevents the curdling of the sauce. Add salt to taste, and, if you like, a little tarragon vinegar. Keep in a cold place until used.

For a quickly made mayonnaise I can recommend the following recipe : —

Take the yolks of two eggs and the juice of half a lemon. Stir until thickening, when add salt, oil, and vinegar in proportions given above. If made in this way you need not be particular about adding the oil drop by drop : be careful only not to add it in larger quantities than a teaspoonful at a time.   This is the best mayonnaise dressing for green-salads.

All these recipes you had better follow closely at first, until by and by you may vary them at your needs, or as your inspiration leads you.

A slight addition of wine is often a great improvement. Some experts also will put a small piece of brown or rye bread in the bottom of the dish to give a peculiar flavor to the salad, and for those who like a taste of onion, or garlic, you may either rub the bread or the sides of the salad-dish with a slice of onion or a bit of garlic.   These little fine touches, and how and when to apply, you have to learn by yourself.   This is the case also in regard to mixed salads, for which I will give you a few recipes merely as suggestions upon which to produce your own variations and "compositions."

I begin with some plain ones and keep the more elaborate recipes for the last : Take some endives, well blanched ; separate the branches from the stem, cleanse and rinse well, then put in warm water for a short time.   Drain well, and arrange in the centre of a salad-bowl.   Then surround it with watercress dressed beforehand in the shape of a wreath.   Finish the dish with an outside rim of beet salad.

The latter ought to be always at hand in your store-closet. In winter, when green salad is scarce, beets can be resorted to. Combinations in salads, and how to pickle beets. They make a salad, either by themselves, or in combination with potatoes, celery root, meat, or fish.   Take for this purpose the large, dark red beets, and boil them as indicated in my instructions on vegetables.[1]   When cool, peel them and cut them into slices a quarter of an inch thick.   Have a stone jar ready, and place into it your beets layer-wise, putting between each layer a few scraps of horse-radish, and two or three black pepper seeds. Pour boiling vinegar enough over the whole to cover it.   It will keep for months, if put in a cool place.   When needed for use, take out with a silver fork the desired number of slices, and dress with salt, vinegar, and oil.

[1] See p. 121.

A combined beet and celery root salad is very palatable. Boil the latter, after cleansing it well, in slightly salted water. Do not let it get too tender. Drain and remove all specks and fibrous matter on the outside. Cut into slices like beets, and pour over them while still warm a dressing of a good deal of oil and vinegar, and a sprinkle of pepper and salt. If kept in a cool place, this salad will keep for two or three days.

Celery root, on the other hand, combines well with red cabbage, which you shred as fine as possible after removing the thick ribs. Mix into it a plain dressing. Do *About cabbage* it a few hours before use, which will improve the *salads.* salad. Heap up the cabbage in the middle of a dish, and let the wheels of celery root form the outer rim. This, also, is a nice winter salad, when green things fail or are too high-priced.

A cheap salad is made of white cabbage. Take a firm head only. For a family of three, one-quarter of it will be sufficient to make a good dishful. Shred it fine, and, if very young, dress it a couple of hours before meal-time with a plain dressing. Some boiled potatoes sliced and minced with it are a good addition. You may also combine white and red cabbage in different rims, and have the potato salad in the centre. In winter, when cabbage is old, it is better to scald the white cabbage by pouring over it some boiling water, in which to leave it for about fifteen minutes. Then drain the water off, and pour over your shredded cabbage, while still warm, the mayonnaise dressing quickly made, for which I gave you the recipe. This is a slight variation on the " cold slaw " (the proper name in Dutch is *koolsla*), known among our country population, especially in Pennsylvania.

Other vegetables, also, may be appropriated for salads after they are boiled. Some roses of cauliflower left over, some asparagus, string-beans, even carrots, green peas, *Boiled vegetables* and dried beans, you may use, either by them- *for salad, and* selves or in combination, for an attractive-looking *rules to follow.* salad. Be sure, however, to have all these vegetables dressed a while beforehand, in order to have them impregnated by their dressing. If you omit this, they will taste flat. And never have them icy cold. It kills their flavor. A certain medium between cold and warm favors them best. Keep the latter rules in mind, also, for potato salad, for which I will give you some recipes in my next letter. For the present I close with one more recipe — and a very good one — for a combination salad, which will at the same time teach you a few more things.

Take cucumbers, string-beans, and lettuce of equal proportions. Peel and slice cucumbers from the stem downward.
An excellent combination salad, and how to treat cucumbers. When you get near the end, taste it to see that it is not bitter ; it is generally the end only which is apt to be so, while the rest is perfectly good. Slice them very thin. Do not follow the old-fashioned way of salting the slices and extracting the juice. The latter is the only really useful and digestible part of the cucumber and the very substance of it which is so refreshing and cooling when eaten. The rest is merely fibrous matter. On account of its highly cooling quality, the cucumber sometimes causes catarrh of the stomach ; therefore do not increase this danger by chilling it through contact with ice, but rather alleviate it by a free use of pepper. Use cucumbers only which you know are fresh, and prepare them just before dinner. The string-beans must be fresh also and very young. String them well on both sides, and, after washing them, throw them into boiling water, slightly salted, and boil until just tender. Then drain, and cut into lozenge-shaped pieces one or two inches long. Dress them while warm with oil, salt, and vinegar. Do it a couple of hours before meal-time, and when arranging your salad for the table remove the beans to the salad-bowl without their dressing. Stir into the latter one or two grated potatoes boiled the day before, and use it with some additional oil, salt, and vinegar for the dressing of your well-arranged dishful of the above ingredients.

LETTER XIX

Let none assume the art of entertaining at table,
If he has not penetrated into the secret of tastes.
— HORACE.

WHEN I began to tell you about salads, I meant to have
done with them in one letter. But very soon I found
that to do it justice, and instruct you thoroughly, another letter
would have to be written. If I read your mind rightly, you
will submit to this infliction with grace — I hope, maybe, with
gladness.

Now, to lose no time, I at once proceed to teach you how
to make the homely potato salad, which during the last thirty
years has found so many friends in our country. Various ways of
It serves as a base for a number of excellent making a potato
combinations. There are two ways of making salad.
a potato salad : one is to have it in distinct slices, when
you have to make it of cold boiled potatoes; the other is to
slice and dress the potatoes while hot, which is rather apt to
break up the slices into smaller fragments. The latter method
renders the salad mellower, and certainly wholesomer than the
former. Yet this is rather a matter of taste. It is my way of
doing. In either case you have to take potatoes of a certain
firmness — I mean not too mealy — and boil them in their
jackets. When drained, peel and slice them into a rather flat
dish, and pour over them enough of hot meat broth to moisten
them. It gives them a better flavor, and makes them more
nourishing. Cover them up and let them steep for about five
minutes. Have a little onion minced fine, add it to the
potatoes, and dress the latter now with plenty of vinegar, oil,
pepper, and salt. Add the vinegar before the oil. To mix the
salad without breaking it up too much, place a platter over

the dish which holds the salad, and give it a good tossing.
Then remove the salad into the dish you mean to serve it
in, and trim it according to your fancy. To vary the dressing, add a teaspoonful of French mustard, or some capers, or
both. Or replace half of the vinegar by as much claret. In
that case, beets cut in small dice are a good addition. So are,
at another time, white celery stalks cut into shreds. A sprinkle
of minced parsley will accentuate the color and flavor. Part
of a salt herring, skinned and boned, and cut into small dice,
will give to potato salad a pleasant piquancy, as will also pickled
cucumbers cut into shreds. There are, in fact, very few things
which you cannot add to a potato salad. This makes it an
economical one, since remnants of food will serve for its
composition.

Potatoes are necessary also for an Italian and a Portuguese
A Portuguese salad. For the latter take stewed mushrooms,
salad.   boiled potatoes, and raw tomatoes. Cut into thin
slices; dress with oil, salt, and pepper, and add last of all a
small glassful of sherry, but no vinegar.

The following is one of a number of recipes for "Italian
salad": Take boiled potatoes, sour apples, pickled cucumbers,
An Italian salad. and cooked veal (one cup of each); cut into
small dice. Add half a cupful of beets, three
hard-boiled eggs, and ten anchovies, also cut into dice. Mix
all this with one and a half cupfuls of oil, one small glassful of
sherry, one to two tablespoonfuls of tarragon vinegar, salt, and
pepper. Cover up the whole and allow it to stand in a cool
place for about three hours; then mix it once more thoroughly,
put it in your salad-dish and garnish with anchovies, pickles,
capers, and corned beef or ham cut into even shreds.

The following is an excellent appetizer: Take the breast
An appetizer. of a roast chicken, one salt herring, one anchovy,
some boiled ham or tongue, and two hard-boiled
eggs; chop fine and dress with oil and vinegar.

I must not fail to give you the recipe for a real sardine salad.
The sardines needed for it are the salted ones, which come in
little kegs and are sold by weight. For a large dishful of salad

take half a pound of them. Soak them in water for about an hour, changing the water several times. Then divide them into halves by pulling them apart from head downward, removing the spine. Take about half of the filets thus obtained, and cut them into narrow strips an inch and a half long. The rest you roll up turban-shaped, and set aside for garnishing. Take also small gherkins, pickled mushrooms, crayfish-tails (which come in little glass jars), smoked salmon, some mixed pickles, and cut them likewise into strips. Add capers, and mix the whole with oil and vinegar. Heap it up on a salad-dish, and garnish with small triangles of smoked salmon, the sardines rolled up, capers, pickled cherries, stoned olives, and pickled oysters,[1] finishing at the base with a rim of boiled tongue cut in imitation of cocks' combs, alternating with thin slices of lemon similarly frayed.

As a sample fish salad I will give you a Venetian one : Take two herrings out of brine, and after they have been well soaked, skin and bone them ; take also one pound of Venetian fish pickled eel, half a pound of salted sardines, which salad. soak and then halve, and cut all this into small dice. Mix with part of a mayonnaise sauce. Now take the middle piece of a cauliflower, a handful of tiny green peas, about as much of small string-beans, and boil in salted water until done. Take half a carrot, and a small celery root, slice them, and with a tube cut them into cylindrical pieces as large as your peas. Boil them also until tender. Then drain, and cool them off in cold water, drain again, and dress all these vegetables with oil, salt, and vinegar. Now heap up your mayonnaise salad in the centre of a dish, cover it up with more mayonnaise sauce, and trim it all over with your vegetables, arranging them symmetrically and well assorted as to color. Place the cauliflower on the very top, and garnish the edge of the salad with quarters of hard-boiled eggs, allowing their whites only to show.

Now, suppose you take boiled salmon (canned will do pretty nearly as well) instead of salt and pickled fish, as above, and you

[1] See p. 201.

will have an extremely nice variation. Salmon harmonizes particularly well with mayonnaise, and if you relieve it by a rim
A salmon salad. of crisp, green lettuce leaves, and inside of it
put a border of broken-up amber-colored aspic,
you will have a most refined as well as a beautiful-looking
dish of salad. By adding to a mayonnaise for salmon a little
anchovy paste or essence, you will give it a slight piquancy,
well in accord with that fish. Instead of salmon, any other
kind of cooked fish will do for a salad ; and a sauce *tartare*,
ravigote [1] or *remoulade* [2] will serve instead of a mayonnaise.

If you wish to try a lobster salad, ask your fish dealer for a
female lobster. Take the eggs, — which will give a fine flavor
A lobster salad. and color to your dressing, — pound them in a
mortar with as much oil as they will take up,
and add them either to a mayonnaise or the following dressing : Rub to a paste the yolks of two hard-boiled eggs, add
three tablespoonfuls of oil, one tablespoonful of tarragon vinegar, a teaspoonful of English mustard, two or three minced
shallots, a teaspoonful of minced tarragon leaves, salt to taste,
and a sprinkle of white pepper. If not acid enough add some
lemon juice, and stir the whole until thoroughly mixed and
smooth. Cut your lobster into small pieces, saving some of
the claws for garnishing, dust them over with a very little salt
and white pepper, and pour over them some tarragon vinegar.
Let them stand for about an hour ; then heap up on a flat dish,
pour the dressing (which meanwhile has been kept on ice)
over and around the lobster. Then trim, using crisp lettuce,
or endive, stoned olives, slices of hard-boiled eggs, tiny pickled
cucumbers, capers, etc., etc. I might suggest here also for an
outer rim to use nasturtium flowers arranged wreath-like, and
leave it for you to go on improving on this suggestion.

You know already how good a salad can be made of cooked
vegetables. You may dress it plain or with a mayonnaise. In
the latter case I advise to have the dressing served separately,
while the vegetables are kept in a marinade of lemon juice and

[1] See p. 74.   [2] See p. 134.

salt for about an hour's time, and then drained, previous to
serving.   In Switzerland the carrots boiled with the meat are
frequently served as a plain salad with the *bouilli,*   Cooked vegetable
the boiled beef, and eaten while still warm. They   salads.
are quite good.   But a plain vegetable salad served to us at
a cosey little restaurant at Paris, at a time when the Anglo-
Saxons had not invaded its secluded precincts, was by far a
superior one.   It consisted of green peas, carrots, and celery
root, the two latter cut into very small dice, which were
arranged in three sections of a circle, running to a point in
the centre. A mayonnaise would have completely hidden this
pretty effect of geometry and color; but it might have been
a tasty accessory, if it had been served with it. We, however,
did not miss it, for it was palatable enough without.   I would
suggest to improve this salad, by placing some roses of cauliflower — put together like the centre of a head — in the middle,
and then having the other vegetables start from this centre
piece, widening towards the rim of the dish. You might try
this some day when you have some cauliflower left over. Then,
in winter, when an open can of vegetables will keep for several
days, you might take some green peas from one can, some
string-beans from another, some asparagus tops from a third,
a carrot from the soup-kettle, and a boiled potato from the
day before, cut and trim it all in the right shape, and you
would have a salad in a very short time, and at little expense.

Still another variation is the salad *à la Nostiz,* — called after
a German nobleman : Take equal quantities of asparagus tops
and roses of cauliflower, about half the quantity of young
string-beans cut into lozenge-shaped pieces, and as much of
carrots and celery root, cut into small dice. Boil all these in
salted water until tender, drain and cover them with vinegar
and oil dressing, then set them aside for an hour. Take
meanwhile about half a dozen heads of lettuce and remove all
the leaves, making use only of their firm and white hearts.
Dress them separately with plain French dressing. Put them in
the centre of a salad-dish, and arrange around them the
cooked vegetables. Garnish the whole with hard-boiled eggs

cut into quarters, and with claws of lobster. Cover with a mayonnaise sauce.

The Dumas, father and son, have been inventors of salads. To the Japanese salad of the younger Dumas is attached both literary and culinary celebrity. It belongs to the extravagant ones, which are not within the scope of my advice. But as a A Dumas salad. fair sample of a Dumas salad I give you this recipe : Take one egg for each person, and boil hard the number needed. Rub the yolks to a paste ; chop the whites, and mix both with a spoonful of minced chervil. Add some French mustard dissolved in a little vinegar, oil, pepper, and salt. Cut into fine shreds a pickled cucumber, an anchovy or two, a small red beet, to which add some capers. Finally have some crisp lettuce washed and well drained, mix all together and serve.

Of all meat salads, that made of chicken or turkey is the best. To be economical, however, you can take part veal or, Chicken salad. better still, rabbit, and mix with the former. It will hardly be detected. Take equal parts of meat cooked tender and cut into dice. Cut celery stalks into thin pieces. Keep some of the tender white celery leaves for garnishing. Mix the meat and celery, add a good sprinkle of salt, a little white pepper, and the juice of a lemon. Let stand for about two or three hours in a cool place. Make a thick mayonnaise, adding some cream at the last to make it as white as possible. Take a few tablespoonfuls of it to mix with the salad, which heap on a dish, and cover with the rest of the mayonnaise. Garnish with celery and lettuce leaves, beets, stoned olives, capers, little pickled cucumbers, or anything else that will be pleasing.

Any other cold meat will make a nice salad. You can mix with it almost any pickled fish, cucumbers, beets, as well as Other varieties of potatoes, herbs, mushrooms, etc. A bit of dark meat salad. meat left over is speedily transformed into a nice salad by cutting it into small dice or thin shreds, and making a dressing for it of a saltspoonful of mustard, a tablespoonful of sour cream, two tablespoonfuls of vinegar, some pepper, salt, a bit of minced onion, minced tarragon, and any other herb you may have at hand.   Trim with peppergrass or watercress if convenient.

I was about to close, when it occurred to me that in all these pages I have mentioned tomatoes but once (in the Portuguese salad).   It does not require, to be sure, any especial art to slice tomatoes, and pour over them a plain dressing or a mayonnaise.   Still, it would seem to me that I ought to give you a few hints about making a perfect tomato salad.   Select firm ripe tomatoes of equal size.   Pour boiling   Tomato salad. water over them, and after a few minutes change to cold water.   Peel them, and cut out the hard parts of the stem with a sharp, pointed knife.   Then place the tomatoes on ice to get thoroughly cold, and, just before serving, slice them with a very sharp knife, and not too thin.   Place the slices in a glass dish, sprinkle them thick with salt and some pepper, and pour over them oil and vinegar in great moderation.   In the South of Europe the bottom and sides of the dish in which tomato salad is served are rubbed with the inside of a halved clove of garlic.   A mixed salad of tomatoes and lettuce has found great favor of late years, and is so delightful to look at that we often do not realize the actual incongruity between the two as to flavor and taste.   Their union is improved, however, by the binding quality of a thick mayonnaise.   A very pretty way to serve the three combined is to take a flat dish, place the skinned and cold tomatoes on it whole, each on some crisp leaves of lettuce curling around it, while the top of the tomato is hooded with a teaspoonful of thick mayonnaise.

If, after all the foregoing, you are in need of a deep breath of relief, I am ready to grant it by closing this long chapter on salads.

LETTER XX

Man cannot accomplish much on an empty stomach.
—GERMAN PROVERB.

YOU have been waiting patiently all this while for a lesson on eggs,— this very important article of food. For its com-

Food value of eggs. ponents are not very different from those of fairly well-fed beef. In the white we get mostly albuminous substance, in the yolk chiefly the fat contained in the egg. The minerals are principally sulphur and phosphate of lime. But I had better give you a little table to make it more comprehensible and exact : —

	ALBUM.	CARBOH.	FATS.	WATER.	MINERALS.
Eggs (whole) ..	12.5	0.0	12.0	74.5	1.0
Whites	11.0	0.0	0.0	87.5	0.5
Yolks	16.0	0.0	30.0	51.5	1.0

Dr. Wiel says that a man can hold his own on a daily diet of eight eggs and four-fifths of a pound of bread. This ought to be taken into consideration by the provider of a family. Eggs

Various ways in which to cook eggs, and how to do it. are also easily digested, if not cooked too much. They are best when boiled soft. A good digestion, however, can manage even hard-boiled eggs. The former need three minutes' boiling if put into boiling water ; the latter five minutes. If you wish them neither too soft nor too hard, allow them four minutes. Eggs to be used for mayonnaise or to be stuffed, have to be boiled ten to fifteen minutes. All this, however, is no sure guide in cold weather, unless the eggs have been allowed to remain in a warm place for a while beforehand, to take off the chill.

Try your eggs as to freshness before you boil them ; put them into cold water, and if they sink to the bottom they are

164

fresh. An egg more than a week old will not sink, but swim on top. Wash and clean them before boiling. This is very important, because the dirt clinging to them will enter the inside through the many small pores of the shell. When in doubt as to their freshness, it is best to open your eggs and use them for poaching, frying, scrambling, etc. They will thus furnish you with the daintiest of breakfast dishes.

To poach eggs take a wide, flat stew-pan and put into it one quart of water, one cupful of vinegar, one tablespoonful of salt; when it comes to a boil, open your eggs one by one into a cup; drop them into the boiling water; but not more than two or three at a time. Take a spoon, and try to keep each egg in shape, by pushing the whites toward the yolk. As soon as the whites are firm, take out the eggs carefully with a skimmer. Place each on a slice of buttered toast. Now, if you have a tomato sauce at hand, and pour it around the eggs and toast, you will have a most delicious dish to serve. But you may also pour hot milk over the toast, in which some butter has been melted, and, of course, omit the tomato sauce.

Fried eggs are best and nicest done in little egg-moulds, which are made for the purpose. They come in pairs or threes, and so on up to six and more. I have a mould of six, and if I have fewer eggs to fry, I fill the other forms with water. Put a tiny little piece of butter in each mould, drop in the eggs, and, while cooking, loosen the whites at the edges every few seconds to prevent the under side from getting too much done. Sprinkle the eggs with salt — and pepper, if you like. As soon as the whites are firm, take out the eggs with a spoon. They are nice with spinach, sorrel, and green salads, the acids of the two latter, especially, helping to digest the albuminous matter of the egg, each one complementing the other in a very desirable and palatable way.

For "panned eggs," take a porcelain pie-plate, butter it, pour in thick cream enough to fill it half full, drop in some eggs (four or five) side by side; place on each Panned eggs. yolk a few capers; dust over them some minced parsley (or cives) and some fine bread-crumbs, and put flakes of butter here and there.   Place in the oven and let the eggs get firm and slightly brown on top.

For "eggs on shells," butter some scallop-shells, fill them partly full with smoked salmon or bloaters cut in small dice, Eggs on shells.   and drop an egg on top of each without breaking the yolk.   Put in the oven until the whites have set, and serve at once.

And now you want to try your hand at an omelet.   This is no easy undertaking, but I do not see why you should be less How to make an successful than others who have tried and come omelet.   out victorious.   First of all, have a good, brisk fire, and a frying-pan well heated.   Break your eggs into a basin, add a small pinch of salt, and a teaspoonful of cream (or milk) for each one.   Whisk them until whites and yolks are mixed; it makes the omelet light.   Put a piece of butter (very fresh) the size of half an egg for every three or four eggs into your pan, and when sizzling hot pour in your eggs.   Be quick now, and shake your pan with one hand, while with the other, holding a silver fork, you turn up the egg which is coagulating.   When every part is equally cooked and creamy, you allow the eggs at the bottom to get firm, but not brown.   To prevent the latter you have to keep shaking the pan, and with it the omelet, which must stay creamy on top. Then with a spatula you turn one-half of the omelet over the other half and, placing a hot plate over your pan, you toss your omelet upside down into the middle of the plate.   Thus you will have the omelet "*charnue et dorée*" (fleshy and golden yellow), of which a French poet sings.

This plain omelet you can diversify in very many ways, of which I mention a few to indicate how to do it.   Make thus A variety of an omelet *aux fines herbes :* Mince some parsley, omelets.   tarragon, and shallots — or parsley and cives — and mix with your eggs.   Or chop fine equal quantities of spinach, sorrel, parsley, chervil, and cives; *sauté* them for a few minutes in a little butter, let them get cool, and then add your eggs before making the omelet.   For an omelet with bloaters, skin and take the bones out of a fine Yarmouth bloater; cut the flesh in tiny dice. Mix it with some parsley and one shallot minced, which slightly *sauté* beforehand in a little butter. Then moisten the whole with one tablespoonful of brown gravy, heat it up and place it in the middle of your omelet before turning it over.

Here is an omelet with bacon: For four eggs take two ounces of breakfast bacon, cut it into small dice, *sauté* it until light brown, and mix with your eggs before baking. And here is an omelet with tomatoes *à la Provençale*: Take two middle-sized, very firm tomatoes, and cut them into dice. Put one teaspoonful of minced onion into a frying-pan in which you have heated one teaspoonful of butter and one of olive oil. As soon as the onion turns yellow, add the tomatoes. Cook them on a quick fire until their watery substance is somewhat reduced; then season them with salt and pepper, and lastly add a teaspoonful of chopped parsley, with a taste of garlic (the latter to be obtained by rubbing the board, on which the parsley is chopped, with the inside of a clove of garlic). Make an omelet of five eggs for the above. The recipe says to take olive oil for it, but in our country I prefer to take butter. Put the tomato in the middle of the omelet, and take care when you fold it that the rims are closed tightly. Serve it on an oval dish, with parsley or water-cress around.

After you have mastered these different omelets, you will be able, with a little thought, to make any other kind you wish, only taking care that the ingredients blend. Such are: ham, kidneys, mushrooms (all cut into small dice), green peas, asparagus points, and others. All these, suitable for omelets, will do also for stirred (or scrambled) eggs. I prefer the latter to the former for every-day fare, because they are quicker done — can, in fact, be cooked in a chafing-dish at table, where they are best, because served as soon as done.

Stirred eggs also are more wholesome than omelet, which requires more butter to get it perfected, and does not permit the same creamy consistency of the egg all through it. This is the recipe for stirred eggs: Break the Stirred eggs. eggs into a bowl, add a little pinch of salt and a scant tablespoonful of milk for each egg. Give it two vigorous beats for each egg, with a spoon ; melt a little butter — about the size of a small hazel-nut — for each egg in a hot pan; pour in your eggs, and with a spoon loosen them from the bottom as soon as they begin to thicken; do it only in one direction, toward the handle of the pan (which you hold with your left hand), and each time in another place. In this way your eggs turn out in large flakes, as they should. Remove them from the fire just before the eggs are all coagulated and while some liquid is left. Unless you catch this very moment, your eggs will be either too soft or too hard for perfection. Whatever ingredients you wish to add you mix with your eggs while raw; or put them into the melted butter first, and then pour in the egg.

A nice way to serve stirred eggs is to heap them in the middle of a platter, and garnish them all around with thin slices of smoked salmon, which have been dipped into melted butter and then allowed to *sauté* slightly on a slow fire.

After you have mastered the omelet, it will be easy for you to produce a nice, tender Roman *fritata* and wafer-like pancakes. Here are the recipes : For *fritata*, whisk five or six eggs until light ; add two tablespoonfuls of raw ham cut in small dice or chopped coarsely, some minced parsley, or parsley and cives. Pour the mixture into a hot pan, in which a good-sized piece of butter has been heated. Shake to prevent its sticking, and when slightly brown on one side, turn it with the help of a warm plate, and brown also on the other side. The *fritata* ought to be thick, not thin like a pancake ; the pan, therefore, must be of small circumference for the quantity given above.

A Roman fritata.

As for the pancakes, a small iron frying-pan is the best to bake them in. To make four or five pancakes, take half a pint of milk, three eggs, about four tablespoonfuls of flour, and a little salt. If the batter is too thin, add a little more flour. Whisk until light. Put a piece of butter the size of a walnut into your pan, and when quite hot, pour into it about a cupful of the batter. Shake it ; and from time to time lift it at the edges with the round point of a knife to prevent its sticking. When light brown on the lower side, give the cake a toss with the pan to fling it upside down, — this is the correct way; but as long as you have not practised it, you

Pancakes.

had better turn your cake with the help of a plate. Slip another little piece of butter — about half the quantity as before — under the turned cake and let it get light brown. Put it on a hot plate, and place it where it will keep hot. Put the other cakes on top of it as they are finished, and serve. If you wish your pancakes sweet, add a tablespoonful of sugar to the above quantity. This recipe is a first-rate one. You can make very good pancakes, however, by taking but one or two eggs for the same amount. I have even made them in winter with a few heaped tablespoonfuls of clean snow and no egg at all. They were pale, to be sure, but light and good.

A very nice dish for breakfast or luncheon is the following : —

Pancakes Filled with Meat. — Mix, for pancakes, three-quarters of a pint of flour, three eggs, two tablespoonfuls of olive oil (the very best), a little salt, one tablespoonful of brandy, and half milk, half water, to get a batter not too thin. After beating it well allow it to stand for two or three hours. When baked let the pancakes

Pancakes filled with meat.

get cold. Meanwhile take some remnants of any kind of meat (or of several kinds), chop them fine ; mince one small onion (or a shallot), some parsley, and a little cives. Take a little piece of butter, heat it in a pan ; put in the onion first, and when it gets light brown, add the meat, parsley, and cives. Stir until hot. Allow this hash, too, to get cold. Then spread one or two tablespoonfuls of it on each pancake and roll it up so as to make it look like a sausage. Now heat some butter in a pan, put the rolled pancakes in, side by side, and brown them slowly all around. Do it only just before serving, allowing about fifteen to twenty minutes to *sauté* them. They must be very hot when served. They are excellent with a tomato sauce, or even with plain stewed tomatoes.

For a mere relish I can recommend the following : —

Farcied Eggs à la Fauvel. — Boil eggs hard; put them in cold water; they will shell better. Take them out before quite cold, and when shelled, cut off the tips in

Farcied eggs.

order to stand them up; then cut them into halves, take out the still warm yolks; mash them; mix them with some oil, a very little vinegar, season with salt and pepper, add a taste of onion, and a little minced parsley. The mixture must be stiff and smooth. Fill it back into the whites and serve nicely garnished. I call them " Fauvel" after an American boy in England, who taught me this recipe.

There is one combination — that of eggs and cheese — in favor of which I can merely say that it is a very

About cheese.

palatable one. For, although rich in nutriments, as the following table will show you, it seems somehow to be in league with nightmares.

	ALBUM.	CARBOH.	FATS.	WATER.	MINERALS.
Cheese, rich	25.0	2.2	29.0	39.2	4.6
" middling rich .	27.2	1.5	23.7	43.2	4.4
" least rich	30.0	5.1	13.4	46.5	5.0

Although cheese is prized as a digester, it is equally certain that "cheese digests everything but itself." If, however, a kind

A fondue.

is used which is neither too rich nor too poor (such as Parmesan, Gruyère, Chester, or our American imitation of the latter), and great care is taken to cook it no more than just to melt it, the dishes made partly of cheese may be partaken of with impunity by persons of tolerably good digestion. I give you a few recipes because your husband, like other men of intellect, may be fond of such *piquant* delicacies : For a *fondue* take three eggs, beat them well; add two ounces of grated Gruyère, one ounce of melted butter, and one tablespoonful of cream. Pour the butter into the cream to cool it, before adding to the cheese and eggs. After it is well mixed, pour the whole into a china *gratin*-dish — or into little paper boxes — and put into a slow oven until of the firmness of custard. Serve immediately.

This is not the famous *fondu* of Brillat-Savarin, which you find in most cook-books of modern date, but equally good if done with due care.

To Toast Cheese. — Take three eggs, a cupful of milk, and a teaspoonful of flour; beat and mix well. Melt a small piece of butter in a skillet; put in about two ounces of Toasted cheese. cheese cut into thin slices; pour the above mixture over it (it ought just to cover the cheese) and stir over a slow fire until the cheese is melted and the mixture has thickened. You can do this in a chafing-dish at the table, which will insure its success. In Chester County, Penn., I have eaten this dish mixed with "cottage cheese" (curds), instead of flour, which is a great improvement. In this case more of the cottage cheese and less of the real cheese is to be taken.

For *ramequins*, put a tablespoonful of butter into a *gratin*-dish, then a layer of bread cut into thin slices; on top of it put a layer of sliced cheese, and over the whole Ramequins. pour a mixture of three eggs and a cupful of milk. Bake in the oven until light brown on top. It needs very little heat underneath and ought to brown in fifteen minutes. It is delicious if the oven is in the right condition.

You would not wish me to continue, and give you all the 543 different dishes made of eggs which Grimod invented, or tell you how J. J. Rousseau excelled in cooking eggs in various ways, nor of the dish of eggs the Duke of Soubise placed before Louis XV., which cost him 75 *louis d'or*. I hear you say, "Oh, no, please do not."

I might now leave you to your own devices altogether; for I believe you are equipped sufficiently with material to furnish your table so as to please a capricious as well as a rational stomach, and at the same time provide what is needed to keep the physical and spiritual man alive and in good condition. But I have said nothing as yet of desserts, and although in my opinion fruit is the best dessert at all times, to which ices and cream may be added on special occasions, you do wish to know of, at least, a restricted number of light desserts.

Some of them are quite wholesome.   They also are the means of adding agreeably to the necessary variety in our daily food, and as such, as well as in an economical view, are even to be recommended.   For to-day, however, I will not keep your attention any longer, but close this already too amplified epistle.

LETTER XXI

Lo, as at English feasts, so I regreet
The daintiest last, to make the end most sweet.
—SHAKESPEARE.

IF I am opposed to pies and heavy puddings, it is principally for hygienic reasons. But, aside from this, I deem them wasteful, inasmuch as the outlay for their production far exceeds the nourishment derived from them for the human system. To make good pies and all the old-fashioned English puddings, we need much butter, suet, raisins, almonds, and similar fruit, all of which is high-priced, and sure to tax one's digestive powers. And you know that only such food nourishes as is properly digested. It is different, however, with the lighter kinds of farinaceous food, and all the delightful trifles I comprise under the head of light desserts. To prepare them we use milk, eggs, cereals, and fresh fruit, — all of them nourishing, pleasant to the palate, and easily digested. If any fat is needed for their production, it is butter, and not much of it. You will remember that in indicating to you the daily rations for adults, I mentioned Professor C. Voit's *dictum*, that the required 6.9 ounces of pure muscle (meat) can be replaced by dairy produce and eggs. I would advise that, especially in hot summer weather, a more frequent use should be made of this sort of diet. To give you a comparative idea of the food-values you would thus deal with, I note down the following schedule : —

Valuation of food-matters for light desserts.

	ALBUM.	CARBOH.	FATS.	WATER.	MIN. MATTERS.	CELLULOSE.
Eggs	12.5	0.0	12.0	74.5	1.0	0.0
Milk (new)	3.4	4.8	3.6	87.5	0.7	0.0
" (skimmed)	3.1	4.8	0.7	90.7	0.7	0.0
Butter.........	0.6	0.6	83.3	14.5	1.0	0.0

173

	ALBUM.	CARBOH.	FATS.	WATER.	MIN. MATTERS.	CELLULOSE.
Wheat flour....	10.5	72.5	1.5	14.5	1.0	0.5
" bread ..	7.0	55.2	0.5	36.0	1.0	0.3
Cornstarch	1.0	83.6		15.0	0.4	
Farina	11.0	71.5	1.5	15.0	0.5	0.5
Rice	8.0	76.5	1.0	13.0	1.0	0.5
Sugar		99.0			1.0	
Fruit (fresh) ...	0.5	10.0		85.0	0.5	4.0
" (dried)...	2.5	55.0	1.0	30.0	1.5	10.0

You will find some repetitions in the above, while other substances are added to aid you in gaining a clearer valuation of the foods employed in the following recipes. I begin with the simplest and at the same time the most economical of all desserts — with a German recipe for *Arme Ritter*, poor knights, dating from the middle ages, when it sometimes was also called " Beggar-man." Let us suppose that since then it has gained by transformation; but, at any rate, I never saw it go begging when placed on the family table. I make it when slices of stale bread have accumulated in the bread-box. I shape them as evenly as possible, and not larger than the palm of my hand. Then I place them side by side on some large platters, and pour over them a thin batter consisting of milk, one egg, a pinch of salt, and a little flour, — about a scant tablespoonful for a pint of milk, but no more than the bread will take up. This batter I beat with an egg-beater, and take one-half of it in which to soak the slices of bread for about half an hour; then I turn the slices with the cake-lifter, and pour the rest of the batter over them. After another half-hour's soaking they are ready to be browned in a large frying-pan by means of a little butter over a brisk fire. The pan and butter must be hot before putting in the bread. Put in as many at a time as the pan will hold; turn them as soon as they are of a golden brown underneath, and brown them on the other side as well, adding a little more butter. When done, heap them on a hot dish, dust some sugar over them, and serve with a fruit sauce or some stewed fruit.

The most economical dessert.

Another simple dessert is pancakes. I have already given you a recipe for them in my last, when speaking about eggs.[1] They may be served with powdered sugar and lemons quartered, the juice to be eaten squeezed Pancakes; how to serve them. on the sugared pancakes; or with stewed fruit, as well as a fruit sauce; or you may spread some fruit jelly or jam on each cake separately, and roll it up by means of a silver fork. You then serve them lying side by side.

Some of the most delicate of desserts are made and served in cups. There are cups on purpose for them, but small coffee-cups will do instead. For a custard take as many Desserts served in cups. cupfuls of milk as you have cups to fill. Place the milk over a moderate fire, and when it begins to boil add for each cup a scanty tablespoonful of sugar and a few drops of almond essence. Take also one egg for each cup, beat light, and stir into the milk. Now fill your cups and place them into a *bain-marie*, *i.e.* in a shallow pan, which you fill with boiling water from the tea-kettle, up to three-quarters the height of the cups. Cover the pan with a second one, and leave it standing where the water keeps boiling moderately. When the surface of the mixture begins to thicken, which will be in about ten minutes, you quickly remove the pan from the fire and take the cups out of the water; for, if the water is allowed to boil too rapidly or too long, the custards will be spoiled. Serve cold.

For coffee *crème* in cups take three-quarters of a pint of milk, let it come to a boil, then pour into it two ounces of ground mocha. Cover up and put in a warm place, where it will draw — not boil. Leave it there for about ten minutes, then strain, and add the yolks of five eggs beaten light beforehand, and two ounces of sugar. Beat the whole vigorously, fill into cups, and finish in the *bain-marie*. For chocolate *crème* take two and a half ounces of chocolate, one pint of milk, four eggs, and two and a half ounces of sugar. Let the chocolate dissolve in the hot milk, and proceed as before.

[1] See p. 168.

When you happen to have saved the whites of three eggs, try this dessert, which I will call Mount Blanc: Take one pint

Recipe for Mount Blanc.

of milk and put it on to boil. Meanwhile beat your three whites to a stiff snow — stiff enough for a spoon to stand in it upright.[1] When the milk boils, add one ounce of sugar, some vanilla essence, and one and a half ounces of cornstarch dissolved in a little milk. Stir over the fire until large bubbles make their appearance. Remove from the fire, and mix into it the snow of the whites, not by stirring, which would undo it, but by mixing it from side to side. Fill into a mould previously dipped into cold water, and set away to get cold. Turn it out on a dish, and serve with either a fruit or a wine sauce.

Here is a snow *crème*, quickly made: Take one pint of cream, the whites of two eggs, two tablespoonfuls of sweet

Snow *crème*.

white wine (or one of arrack), sugar to taste, a pinch of grated lemon or orange peel, and beat the whole until stiff. Fill into glass cups or stem glasses.

Another delicacy which you serve in glasses, is raspberry

Raspberry foam.

foam. Take three tablespoonfuls of raspberry syrup or jelly, the whites of six eggs, and three tablespoonfuls of sugar. Beat with the egg-beater until quite stiff. Then fill into glasses and serve. This is sufficient for ten persons.

In berry time you will find the following a very acceptable recipe: Take one pint of juice squeezed either from raspber-

Recipe for a very delicate dessert.

ries or red currants; add four ounces of sugar, and water sufficient to make altogether one quart of liquid. Let it come to a boil, then stir into it one cupful of fine farina, soaked previously in cold water, the superfluous water being poured off. Stir well, to avoid lumps, and keep stirring until the farina is done (about five to ten minutes). Fill into a mould dipped in cold water, and when cool set on ice. Serve with cream. If wanted particularly nice, fill into a ring mould, and when turned out heap some

[1] See p. 183.

whipped cream up in the centre. This recipe hails from Denmark, where it is called *Rodgrod*, — red groats.

Some of the finest dessert dishes are made with the addition of whipped cream. In the cities it can be bought at the confectioners, but the best is always made at home. You need for it fresh cream, not over a day old. Put *Whipped cream,* it in a large bowl or tureen, and set it on the ice *and how to make* *it.* for at least one hour. Then beat with an egg-whip, and as the foam forms remove it with a skimmer into a colander which has been placed over another bowl. Return the liquid cream which drops into the latter to the cream you whip, and continue in this way until all your cream has turned to foam. If the cream should not get as stiff as desirable, add to it a pinch of pulverized gum tragacanth bought at a reliable druggist's. It eases the whipping considerably, and does not detract from the taste of the cream. If you wish, you may now sweeten your whipped cream and flavor it. To do the latter there is vanilla, grated chocolate, fruit marmalade or jelly, fresh raspberries or strawberries, etc., which *A dish of* you mix with your cream by stirring gently. *whipped cream* *and fruit.* Such flavored cream is a nice dessert in itself, when heaped up pyramid-like on a dish and served with fruit or cake. One pint of cream will make whips enough for six persons. A very pretty dish is obtained, for instance, in this way: Heap berries up in a crystal bowl, dust sugar over them freely, and then cover them up with sweetened whipped cream (take five ounces of sugar for one pint of cream). Put on the ice for one or two hours, and before serving garnish with a rim of extra large berries.

To make a Russian *crème* you also need whipped cream. Take three tablespoonfuls of powdered sugar and two eggs. Put in a large bowl and stir for half an hour, *Recipe for* when it will be quite thick. Add one tablespoon- *Russian crème.* ful of best brandy (or arrack), and one pint of whipped cream. Mix gently, and serve at once. This is enough for five or six persons.

For a chocolate *bavaroise* (or *crème*) take one pint of milk,

boil with half a pound of chocolate and a quarter of a pound of sugar. Flavor with vanilla. When cold add one ounce of
Chocolate bavaroise. gelatine, which previously has been dissolved in water. Whip until the mixture begins to stiffen, then add a pint or a little more of whipped cream, which stir into it lightly. Put on ice.

As to gelatine, it is a pretty safe rule to take one cupful to one and a half of cold water for every ounce of gelatine.
Proportions for the use of gelatine. Mix the two, and put in a warm place. Stir from time to time until the gelatine is quite dissolved. For stiffening a pint of liquid you generally need a scant ounce of gelatine in summer, while during the cold season a little over half an ounce is sufficient. This rule applies especially to jellies. For a *crème* less will do.

To vary, I will now give you a recipe for Russian rice. Take a quarter of a pound of rice. You will remember how to
Russian rice. boil it, with all the seeds left whole, and yet tender.[1] When you have thus cooked it in water (no salt), put it on a sieve to get dry and cold. Then transfer it to a crystal dish. Take a quarter of a pound of sugar, moisten it with a gill of water, and boil it until a thickish sirup is obtained (about fifteen to twenty minutes). When somewhat cool add to it a wineglassful of Jamaica rum, or arrack, and pour over the rice in the glass dish. Garnish with preserved or canned fruit, — peaches, apricots or cherries, — or with different kinds of fruit.

A very pretty dessert dish is a *macédoine* of fruit. You will very likely make it only when you expect invited guests.
Several ways in which to make a macédoine of fruit. It will be then worth the trouble. You can do it in different ways. Take either fresh, or canned, or preserved fruit; and you may make it with a jelly or without. Anyway, take the prettiest fruit at your command, and of different colors. Stone the cherries, leave the berries whole, but cut the larger fruit into nice pieces, — either in halves, quarters, or halved quarters. Put all your

[1] See p. 85.

fruit into a deep dish, pour over it a bottle of a light white wine, and set aside. Now take half a pound of sugar, and cook with one glassful of water until it makes a thick sirup. If your fruit is fresh, drop it little by little into the boiling sirup, and let it simmer for a little while; if canned or preserved, drop it in after the sirup has been removed from the fire, and merely let it steep for a while. Then take out the fruit with a skimmer, put into a large bowl, pour over it the wine in which previously it has soaked, and finally add the sirup. Let stand for four hours, when put in a vessel filled with ice, to chill thoroughly, and when served add small pieces of ice to the *macédoine*. This is Mademoiselle Françoise's recipe.

I will give you another one made with jelly. Take three-quarters of a pound of sugar, and cook it with half a pint of water for fifteen minutes. Add the grated peel of three lemons, and their juice; a pint and a half of California Marsala, and two ounces of gelatine. Put through a flannel bag until clear. Have a mould ready packed in ice, pour in some of the jelly; when stiff, add a layer of fruit; pour in some more jelly; let it get stiff; add more fruit, and so on until all is used up. Finish with jelly, and turn out when ready to be served. If you take fresh fruit for this dish, do not cook it; if canned or preserved fruit, see that it is well drained of its juice. Save the latter, and use it, when you have occasion, for fruit sauces, jellies, etc.

If made with preserved fruit, you might put as a first layer (after the jelly) some macaroons, as a second some candied orange peel arranged in a star-like pattern, and as a third layer slices of quince or any other dark red fruit.

It will take some time before you have tried all these recipes. If you are successful, you will be able hereafter to avail yourself of any other recipe which may strike your fancy. A little practice is all you need. I will add now merely a few more recipes for baked puddings of a light kind.

This apple pudding is exceedingly delicate: Peel, core, and quarter some tart apples. Boil them with a little water until soft.   Mash them with a spoon, and take as much of them as will make a quarter of a pound.   Add the same weight of butter and sugar while still hot.   Then, after it gets cool, mix with it three eggs beaten to a foam, and the grated peel of one lemon.   Butter a pudding-form, dust it over with powdered sugar, and fill into it your mixture.   The form must be high enough to allow the rising of the pudding.   Bake in a quick oven for about half an hour. Try by inserting a straw (or a wooden toothpick) into the centre.   If nothing attaches to it when pulled out, the baking is done.   Remember this for other occasions.   Serve at once.

A light apple pudding.

For a white of egg pudding take four whites and beat them to a stiff snow.   Now mix two tablespoonfuls of apricot (or some other) marmalade with an ounce and a half of sugar, and add it carefully to the snow.   Fill the whole into a buttered china dish, and bake in a slow oven for about half an hour.   Serve immediately in the dish baked in.

White of egg pudding.

For a simple custard pudding take one pint of milk, stir into it gradually one tablespoonful of flour, the yolks of six eggs beaten light, sugar to taste, a flavoring of vanilla or lemon, and a teaspoonful of brandy. Finally mix with it a teaspoonful of melted butter (which may be warm, but must not be hot), and pour into a buttered dish. Bake in a moderately hot oven.

Custard pudding.

A lemon pudding also is a simple affair.   Take for it a quarter of a pound of sugar, and mix with the yolks of five eggs, stirring   continually.   When   quite   foamy   add quickly the juice of one lemon, and then the whites of the eggs, beaten to a stiff snow.   Put into a buttered form, which it must not fill any more than three-quarters, since the mixture will rise considerably.   Bake about fifteen to twenty minutes, and serve at once.

Lemon pudding.

Finally, I give you this recipe for a rice pudding: Take a quarter of a pound of rice, and boil it in a pint of milk until thick.   Meanwhile beat half a pound of butter to a cream,[1]

---

[1] See p. 183.

add one by one the yolks of eight eggs, a quarter of a pound of sugar, the grated peel of half a lemon, and last of all the rice, which must be cold. When thoroughly mixed, Rice pudding. add the whites of the eggs beaten to a snow. Bake in a buttered form, and turn out on a cake-plate. Serve warm with a fruit sauce. This is a very nice pudding. It may also be made of farina instead of rice.

I must not close this letter before giving you a few recipes for the sauces mentioned. For a wine sauce, take one whole egg and the yolks of two, a heaped teaspoonful A wine sauce. of flour, two ounces of sugar, and half a pint of white wine. Beat with an egg-whip over the fire until just before the point of boiling. Serve hot or cold, as you please.

A very simple sauce is made by first sweetening some cream, then adding the juice of a lemon, which will thicken the cream.

For fruit sauces, the easiest way is to take home-made fruit sirup, and thin it with cold water. Or, if the sauce is to be hot, thin the sirup first with water, and when it Fruit sauces. comes to a boil add a teaspoonful of cornstarch dissolved in water. Stir while boiling until the cornstarch is done, which will be in two or three minutes.

This last recipe for a claret sauce is excellent: Take one tablespoonful of powdered sugar, as much of Claret sauce. raspberry or currant jelly, and one glassful of claret. Stir until it slightly thickens. But do not put it on the fire.

From the almost endless number of nice recipes for light desserts, I have chosen for you what I consider easy for a beginner, and withal good and wholesome. May it give you as much pleasure to carry out these recipes as it gave me pleasure to write them down.

LETTER XXII

Wouldst thou both eat thy cake and have it?
—SHAKESPEARE.

ONE thing brings forth another. Therefore, when I made up my mind to teach you some simple desserts, I as much as bound myself to add a lesson about cakes, since some of the former do seem to call for some kind of cake to complete the course. It is also, in fact, a great convenience for a hospitably inclined housewife to have cake ready at all hours. If put in a porcelain crock well covered, or in a tin box, cake of all sorts will keep for days and weeks, and is always at hand to be offered to unexpected guests, or ready for any other emergency. To produce good cake is, however, an art by itself, and not so easy as people generally suppose. But if you set about to do it methodically, and are observant of certain strict rules, there is no reason why you should not in time excel in it as well as in the other culinary branches. Only do not devote to the baking of cakes any more time than is necessary to keep yourself reasonably well supplied. For cake, as your judgment will tell you after all my teachings, is not actual food; it is merely one of those pleasant auxiliaries by which we bring variety into the routine of our indispensable fare.

As to the rules, the flour to be used must be the finest and best. See that it is dry, and yet not so dry as to make it **Rules for baking cake.** seem like dust when taken up in your hand and allowed to sift through your fingers. Flour, if kept in a damp place, or a warm one, will spoil easily, and thus be unfit to use. Get the other ingredients also of the purest and best. Your sugar likewise has to be dry and well powdered; your butter must be the freshest, and if too much

182

salted will have to be worked over in cold water, in order to sweeten it. Break each egg separately into a cup before using it, so as to test its freshness. Be careful in breaking eggs and separating the yolks and whites, for any particle of the former mixed with the latter will prevent these from getting stiff when whipped. To whip the whites to a snow, put them into a deep bowl or, better still, into an open-mouthed pitcher. By then using an egg-beater and plying it without stopping, a stiff snow will readily form. Test its stiffness by introducing a table-spoon: if it will stand up by itself, your snow is just right. Do not touch it again until mixed into the cake batter. It is better to have one person stir the batter, and another whip the whites, and have the snow done the minute it is wanted. But if this is impracticable, whip your snow before you stir your batter, and set it in a basin of cold water to keep. When a recipe tells you to beat butter to a cream, do as follows: Weigh your butter first, then put it in the dish in which your cake is to be stirred. Place it near the stove for about an hour beforehand to get soft, but do not let it melt. Use a flat wooden spoon with a long handle for stirring, and do it vigor-ously in one and the same direction, until the butter is white and foamy. When adding eggs, let them have about the same temperature as the butter, or the latter might curdle. To fur-ther avoid this, add one egg at a time, alternating with a spoon-ful of sugar, and mix thoroughly before adding the next. Beat all cake batter in one direction, and with uniform alacrity. Your success depends a good deal on this. The snow of the whites is not added until the last moment. Do not stir it in, but mix from the sides of the vessel toward the middle by gen-tle strokes. The batter when finished must be baked at once. Another important factor in baking is the fire. It ought to be looked after at least an hour beforehand, and be in such a condition as to need no handling during the time of baking. Most cakes need a moderately hot oven, and some even a cool one. A good old test is, to put a piece of thick paper into the oven, to shut the door, and open it again after five minutes. If the paper is light brown, the oven is moderately hot; and if yellow, the oven is cool. Now, as to forms for baking, it is advisable to have one or, better, two sheet-iron pans with low rims, just fitting into your oven, for small cakes either to be put directly upon them or for holding a number of small cake moulds; besides, to have a round tin form with a straight rim an inch to an inch and a half high, and another one with a rim as high as your forefinger. Lastly, have one of copper (or tin) fluted and turban-shaped. Your forms must be kept immaculately clean, perfectly dry, and, to receive the cake batter, must be well buttered inside and dusted over either with cracker-dust or powdered sugar, except when directed otherwise. For buttering the form, I first melt a little butter, then I use a soft painter's brush (kept for this sole purpose) to give the form a coating of the butter. Get ready your form (or forms) before beginning with the cake, so as to have no delay when the latter is to be baked. After the baking is done, do not turn out your cake until it has stood a while to cool off, or it might not come out unharmed. Even when turned out, do not let it get cold all at once, for fear it might settle down. Keep all these rules in your mind, for I shall not reiterate them.

The recipes I have selected for your benefit are mostly old and tried ones, handed down in the family for generations. They are the most wholesome, too, as far as cake goes. The first, a very simple one, is associated with mother's and grandmother's cake-box, readily opened to the *sesame* of bright eyes begging and little chubby hands outstretched. I will call the recipe German drop cakes. Take half a pound of sugar, half a pound of flour, two eggs, and the yolks of another two. Beat sugar and eggs together for half an hour, then add the flour, and stir until thoroughly mixed. Instead of all wheat flour, you may take half and half wheat flour and cornstarch, which will make the cakes somewhat more delicate. Have ready a sheet-iron pan, give it a very thin coating of butter, and from a teaspoon drop upon it little heaps of batter. Have sufficient space between them, for they will run and get, at least, double the original size. Bake in a slow oven in about half an hour. They must not get brown, but look a pale yellow. Loosen them with the blade of a knife after they have somewhat cooled off, and let them get quite cold on a platter before removing them to the cake-box. They will keep for a month.

Another cake which may be kept for a long time is Israel cake. Take for it half a pound of butter, half a pound of sugar, half an ounce of cornstarch, three-quarters   Israel cake. of a pound of wheat flour (both good weight), and three eggs. Beat the butter to a cream, add eggs and sugar, and the flour at the very last. Stir for half an hour. The batter ought to be rather stiff. Butter a shallow pan ; fill into it the batter, which smooth evenly with the blade of a knife, then dust over it some sugar, and, if you wish it, some almonds cut into fine shreds. Bake in a slow oven for about half an hour. The cake must be of a light yellow. Cut it into squares, or strips an inch and a half by three inches, while warm.

A plain cake made very quickly is called Jenny Lind cake. The reason why it was called after the great singer is not evident to me. That it should have been because   Jenny Lind cake. she was plain of features, I am not willing to believe ; let us rather suppose that her sweet and simple nature suggested it. Take for this cake, two cups of flour, one and a half of sugar, a half a cup of butter, one of cream, two eggs, one teaspoonful of baking powder. Mix the latter with the flour. Beat the butter to a cream, and add the rest in quick succession. Stir until light, and bake in a deep form, and in a hot oven for about half an hour.

This latter cake would be much more deserving the name of the following, called Lightning cake. Take a quarter of a pound of butter ; beat to a cream ; add one   Lightning cake. after the other a quarter-pound of sugar, the yolks of three eggs, a quarter-pound of flour, a flavoring of lemon peel, and the stiff snow of the whites of three eggs. Put into a round form and bake a quarter of an hour. When cold, powder sugar over the cake, and ornament it with preserved fruit. Or cover it with icing, of which later. You also may bake two such cakes, place one on top of the other, and spread jelly or marmalade between. A little later I will give you the recipe of another layer cake; but first I wish to make you acquainted with a most excellent sponge cake and a sand cake, so called from its fine crumbly texture.

For Sponge cake take half a pound of sugar, the yolks of ten eggs, and stir for half an hour. Add the grated peel of half a lemon (or any other flavoring), and a quarter of a pound of cornstarch, and lastly the stiff snow of five eggs. Bake in a high form in a moderately hot oven, for from half to three-quarters of an hour. The top must feel firm and dry to the touch.

Sponge cake.

For Sand cake, which will keep in good condition for many days, take half a pound of butter; beat to a cream, when add the yolks of five eggs and half a pound of sugar. Stir for half an hour, and then add gradually half a pound of cornstarch, one sherry-glassful of Jamaica rum, the grated peel of half a lemon, and lastly the stiff snow of three eggs. Bake like the sponge cake. It is best made a couple of days before cutting it.

Sand cake.

This Chocolate cake also is very good: Take a quarter of a pound of butter, beat to a cream, add the yolks of six eggs, a half a pound of sugar, and stir for half an hour. Then add a quarter of a pound of grated chocolate, two tablespoonfuls of cocoa powder, some vanilla flavoring, four scant ounces of cornstarch, and at last the stiff snow of the six whites of egg. Bake in a form like the preceding cakes, but have the oven hot. It will take about three-quarters of an hour before it is done.

Chocolate cake.

Now for the layer cake, which I deem an extra good one. Its name is Vienna cake. Take for it one pound of butter, beaten to a cream, the yolks of seven eggs, and seven whole eggs. Add one yolk and one whole egg at a time, and after all are mixed in, add gradually one pound of sugar. Stir for half an hour, then add one pound of the finest possible wheat flour, and the grated peel of one lemon. This cake requires a hot oven. Baked in a large,

Vienna cake.

round, and shallow form, it will make four to five layers, each baked separately until of a light brown. You might, however, divide the above amount of batter into six or eight smaller layers (for which of course smaller forms are required — two being put in the oven at one time), and thus make two layer cakes with different filling and icing for each. After the layers are cold, trim them so as to fit nicely one on top of the other, and if too much browned in places, shave off what is objectionable. Now spread a thin layer of fruit jelly or marmalade (raspberry is the nicest), or some other kind of filling, between each layer of cake, and finish the top with icing. Spread it evenly over the entire outside of the cake, except, of course, its bottom. You are now no longer bound by strict rules, weights, and measures. Your fancy comes into play to select, decorate, and even invent. You may make a cake filling of any of the whipped creams I have indicated to you in my last letter. Or you may use for it the *crèmes* I gave you the recipes for, adding, perhaps, a little gelatine to prevent their running. But, mind you, the creams will not keep any longer than a day or two. After that they will get sour. You might also take some of the icing you mean to use and fill your cake with it. I will speak about icings presently, but wish to give you first the recipes for two particularly nice fillings.

The first is a Nut filling: Take two ounces of sugar, and make a boiled sirup of it with three tablespoonfuls of water, to which add three ounces of walnuts (or hazel- Two nice cake nuts), peeled and pounded fine in a mortar, with fillings. the addition of a tablespoonful of cream. Add half a teaspoonful of vanilla essence, and one ounce of candied orange peel minced. Stir until thick.

The second is an Orange filling, for which take the peel of one orange, cut off very thin and soak it in the juice squeezed from the orange for fifteen minutes. Remove the peel, and add the juice to two ounces of sugar; add the yolks of two eggs, beaten to a foam. Add also one teaspoonful of flour, and one gill of white wine. Stir the whole over the fire until it thickens. Then let get somewhat cool, and mix with it the stiff snow of one white of egg.

A simple icing is made by taking two ounces of powdered sugar and one white of egg, stirring both together for fifteen minutes. Add either lemon, orange, or any other kind of fruit juice, according to your fancy. When done, spread it over your cake in a thin sheet, and put in a place where it will dry. A Chocolate icing is easiest made thus : Take a quarter of a pound of chocolate, break up, and soften in a warm place ; mix with two ounces of sugar and, stirring well, gradually add the whites of two eggs.

Cake icings and ornamenting.

To ornament your cakes after they are iced, you take one or more kinds of preserved or candied fruit, arrange them in patterns, with leaves cut out of candied citron or orange rind. Add, if you will go to that extent, some beading and arabesquing of icing (of a different color if you prefer) by putting a teaspoonful at a time into a funnel-shaped paper bag, with an opening about as large as a pinhead.

To make the most of my remaining space, I now give you in quick succession a number of recipes of small cakes and tidbits, which you may ornament likewise as your fancy leads you. First of all I will mention that you may use the recipes for sponge and sand cakes to make pretty little tarts, baked in small tin or copper moulds, which come with raised patterns. The only difference I would counsel is, to take all the whites for the snow, instead of part of them. It will make the tarts lighter. For that reason you must be particular not to fill the moulds more than three-quarters full. After turning out the tarts, ice them, and dust over them, before the icing hardens, some chopped pistachio-nuts (or almonds). This is merely in the way of a suggestion.

Small cakes or tarts.

For Chocolate tarts take a quarter of a pound of sugar, an ounce and a half of grated chocolate, and the yolks of six eggs. Stir for a quarter of an hour; add three ounces of cornstarch and the whites beaten to a snow.

Portuguese Drop Cake. — Take butter, eggs, sugar, and flour, of equal weight. Beat the butter to a cream, add the eggs, sugar, and flour. Stir for half an hour, and drop in little heaps size of a walnut on a sheet-iron pan, which previously you slightly dust over with flour. Then take a preserved cherry for each drop cake, place it in the centre, and press down far enough to fix it in its place. Bake in a moderately hot oven.

Sugar Wafers. — Take sugar the weight of two eggs, and flour the weight of one egg. Stir the sugar with the addition of three eggs for a quarter of an hour, then add the flour and half a teaspoonful of minced orange peel, or candied orange flowers. Put in little heaps on a very thinly buttered sheet-iron pan, three inches apart. Dust them over with granulated sugar, and bake in a moderately hot oven. Remove them from the pan while hot, and bend them over a rounded stick in the shape of a scroll. Or shape them like a cornucopia and fill with whipped cream just before serving.

To make Macaroons take half a pound of blanched and skinned almonds, of which five or six may be bitter. Pound them to a paste in a mortar with the addition of the whites of three eggs. Add to this paste   Macaroons. ten ounces of sugar, and stir for a quarter of an hour. Put in little round or oblong heaps on a sheet of white paper dusted over with flour. Dust granulated sugar over them, and bake in a slow oven.

Filets de Vent. — Take six ounces of sugar, the white of one egg, the grated peel of half a lemon (or some vanilla flavoring), and stir until like a thick icing. Bake in little heaps on paper, and in a slow oven.

Kisses. — Take one tablespoonful of sugar to every white of one egg; flavor with cinnamon, vanilla, lemon, or whatever you choose. Beat with a spoon until quite light. Drop in tiny heaps on a sheet of white paper, and bake in a very cool oven. They must not brown, but get hard on top.

Meringues. — Proceed in the same way, with this difference : beat the whites to a stiff snow first, then add the sugar little by little. Put oval heaps the size of half an egg on paper. Have a board underneath the paper, and place both board and paper into a very slow oven to bake the meringues. After they get glazed on top, which will be in about twenty-five to thirty minutes, remove them from the paper, and if not hollow inside, take out from below what is soft with a teaspoon. Fill the space left with fruit jelly, or whipped cream flavored. Put two and two together, and serve.

Little bits of cake or confectionery are called *bouchées* (mouthfuls). They make a nice show and are not difficult to get up.

Bouchées. Especially, if you should happen to have some remnants of sand cake, or any other kind of a rather solid texture. Cut them into slices three-quarters of an inch thick, spread with marmalade or some other filling, place two and two together, cut into pieces about an inch and a half square, or into lozenges, and cover over with icing. Dust minced pistachio-nuts, almonds, or candied orange peel on top, or garnish in some other way.

For *bouchées* of another kind take the yolks of three eggs, add seven teaspoonfuls of sugar, and three heaped tablespoonfuls of flour. Stir until foamy, then add the snow of the three whites. Rub flour over a baking-board and roll out to a thin sheet. Rub flour also over the rolling-pin you use. Then take a sherry glass, dip it into flour, and cut out round pieces, which you bake on buttered paper. Place two and two upon each other, with a filling between, and cover with a thick chocolate icing. Or fill with raspberry jelly, and cover with icing made with raspberry sirup thickened by mixing with sugar sirup. Dip the *bouchées* into it, and put in the oven for about two minutes to dry.

I would count candied fruit also as *bouchées*. It is easily made, and, both by itself as well as for ornamenting, is a great delicacy

How to candy fruit. for those who like sweets. But you understand that all this is a luxury, in which to indulge only occasionally. Take any kind of fresh fruit, divide those which are too large into halves, and boil in water until tender. Drain, and make a sirup — a pint of water to a pound of sugar — which boil until by dipping a wooden skewer into cold water, then into the boiling sirup and back again into the cold water, you can whirl the sirup sticking to the skewer into a globule, which will crack in breaking off.   In this sirup you drop your fruit, allowing it to boil up a few times.   Then remove from the fire, and let the fruit remain in the sirup for twenty-four hours, when place the fruit side by side on a wide colander by means of a skimmer.   Dust powdered sugar over it, and set the colander in a lukewarm oven over night.   When dry, the fruit is done.   For nuts, oranges, and chestnuts, you do somewhat differently.   The oranges you divide into sections, the walnuts you cut into halves, the chestnuts you boil and peel; and one like the other you merely immerse into the sirup described, then take them out again, and put aside for the sugar to dry.

To candy orange peel, take the whole thickness.   Cut into even sections before peeling; boil in water until tender, then put into cold water, and let it remain in it for two or   Candied orange peel. three hours.   Drain, and for each half a pound of peel take ten ounces of sugar.   Add water to the latter, and boil for about five minutes, then pour over the peel, and let stand over night.   On the following day boil peel and sirup until the former gets transparent, and the latter thick.   Remove the peel on to some paper, and let it get dry.   You may also put it into glass jars, pour the sirup over it, and keep it tied up. In any case, save the sirup ; it will do you good service for one thing or another.

Will this do for you?   There are hundreds more of nice recipes for cakes and sweetmeats, but too much of a good thing is merely embarrassing.   Therefore I close this subject.

LETTER XXIII

O, 'tis most sweet.
—SHAKESPEARE.

IN the last two letters I made mention more than once of
preserves, — especially jellies, marmalades, and sirup, necessary for carrying out certain recipes for cake and light desserts.
I deem it good policy to have a store laid in of those preserves, each kind in its season, and home-made. It is done
with comparatively little expense, and, moreover, they are far
better than those bought at the dealers'. I will give you here
a restricted number of recipes for putting up fruit; as many
as I think you will need for the present. They are recipes
well-tried many a time over. First of all, however, I have to
enjoin on you the following precepts : For putting
Rules for putting up stores of preserves. up any kind of stores, be sure that the strictest
cleanliness prevails in regard to the food you
use, as well as to everything coming in contact with it. The
more rigidly this rule is carried out, the more certain you
will be to exclude all germs disastrous to your complete success. See that your preserving-kettle be porcelain-lined, and
never used for any other purpose. Your skimmer also ought
to be of porcelain, and the spoon you use of shining silver.
Whatever it is you put up must be of the freshest and best.
Cleanse it carefully, and drain it well after washing in cold
water. The sugar also must be the best and purest, and if
vinegar is used, buy only prime cider vinegar which is neither
too mild nor too strong. If a recipe calls for sirup in which
to cook the fruit, you prepare it by putting a pint of water to
every pound of sugar into your preserving-kettle. Put it on
the fire and, stirring from time to time, let it come to a boil.
Take off the scum that rises, and continue to do so until your
sugar is clear, when it will be ready for further use.

Have your glassware for receiving your preserves ready at hand when they are done. It also will have to be scrupulously clean, and dry at the same time. I put my glass jars or jelly-glasses in a place where they will get thoroughly hot, and fit to receive the boiling fruit, when intended to be put up air-tight. You must make sure, however, that no draft of cool air strikes the glass, or it will crack in spite of former care. Wipe the edges of it clean with a towel dipped into hot water ; then secure the lids to keep out the air, and after the glass gets cool tighten the screws once more.

The first of all fresh fruit are strawberries, but they are diffi-cult to preserve on account of their volatile aroma, which makes them so delicious when eaten fresh from the vines. They are not the fruit for you to waste time and money on. When cherries come, however, get some of the Sour cherries put dark, sour kind, and put them up air-tight. They up air-tight. are delicious as a *compote* in winter, and far more whole-some than fruit put up in the over-sweet, old-fashioned way. Stone your fruit, then weigh it, and for every pound of it take half a pound of sugar. Put both together into your kettle, and place over a moderate fire. Let boil for about twenty minutes, stirring from time to time, and taking off the scum which rises. If you have more juice than needed for filling your jars with fruit, add to every pint of juice which is left half a pound more of sugar; boil it for a minute or two longer, and fill into bottles, which seal up. It makes an excel-lent pudding sauce, and will do for some desserts, when fruit sirup is mentioned.

To put up blackhearts I can recommend the following : Take them whole, merely removing the stems, and for every three pounds of cherries take one pound of sugar Blackhearts put and one cupful of vinegar. When boiling, watch. up air-tight. the cherries, and just as soon as they get tender, which will be in about ten or fifteen minutes, take them off the fire, skim, and fill them hot into air-tight jars. They ought to look plump and natural. They are delicious for use in winter. You can put up plums the same way, if they are fully ripe. If you wish them perfect, you peel them before cooking. By pouring boiling water over the plums, and letting them remain in it until you can bear your hand in the water, the skins will peel off without much trouble.

After cherry time we have raspberries, blackberries, and currants to gather in for future use. The following recipe is Raspberry and equally good for raspberry and for blackberry blackberry jam. jam: Take three-quarters of a pound of sugar for every pound of berries. Put over a slow fire, and allow to boil for twenty minutes from the time boiling commences. Fill hot into air-tight jars. The raspberry jam is improved by taking part currants, one-third of the latter and two-thirds of raspberries.

To make raspberry sirup squeeze the berries through a napkin until all the juice is extracted. Boil the latter for fifteen How to make minutes, skimming continually, and then add one raspberry sirup. pound of sugar for every pint of juice. Let boil up once with the sugar, and take off the fire. Fill into bottles, cork up, and seal. This sirup retains all the flavor of the berries, and is delicious as a beverage, mixed with water, and for cooking purposes. For jelly you proceed in the Jellies of rasp- same way, except that you allow the juice to boil berries, black- berries, and for fully two minutes longer after the sugar has been currants. added. Fill in jelly-glasses; cover them loosely with sheets of white paper, and let the jelly get firm. Then cut round pieces of white paper to fit into the apertures of the glasses. Moisten these pieces with brandy, and place directly over the jelly. Finally, paste white paper over the tops of the glasses, and your jelly is ready to store away. Blackberry jelly, which is very good and wholesome, is made in the same way. For currant jelly I can recommend this recipe : Squeeze all the juice out of some red currants, and for every pint of it take one pound of sugar. Choose the best granulated, and pound it in a mortar to a powder. Pass it through the finest sieve you can procure, so as to be quite sure that no coarse particles remain. Then put the sugar in a deep porcelain bowl, and into a heated oven to get dry and hot, but not so hot as to melt. When quite hot, take it out and, while stirring the sugar incessantly, pour your juice into it by degrees, a small quantity at a time. As soon as the juice is all absorbed and the sugar entirely dissolved, the jelly will be ready to fill into glasses, and to be put away. If done carefully this jelly surpasses every other kind in color and flavor. It will keep as long as three years. I will mention here that it is a good plan to mark all your preserves with your name, what kind it is, and the date, especially the latter.

When peaches make their appearance in plenty, I counsel you to buy several basketfuls at a time, and select the most perfect ones for putting up "fresh," while of the specky or inferior ones you make a thin marmalade, or rather a *compote*, for which I have my own recipe. Free the peaches of their skins and stones. The perfect ones you cut into halves, and make a sirup for them. To every pound of fruit you take one-quarter of a pound of sugar, and to every pound of the latter a very scanty pint of water. After the sirup is clear, drop into the boiling liquid your halves of peaches, and allow them to boil up just once. Then remove the kettle from the fire, and as quickly as possible drop your fruit, piece by piece, into your hot jars, fill them up with the sirup, and screw the lids down on them. Peaches done in this way will have almost the full aroma of the fresh fruit, when opened in winter. The same is the case with finely flavored pears, which I peel, cut into halves, take out the cores, but let the stems remain on the corresponding halves. Then I proceed in the same manner as stated in regard to peaches. I have done even cantelope in this way with success.

For the peach marmalade you proceed thus: After your fruit is peeled and stoned you cut it into small pieces, which may be as irregular as you please. Then weigh it, and for every pound of it take one-quarter of a pound of sugar, provided the peaches are fully ripe. If not, take two ounces more of sugar for each pound of fruit. Put the latter into a tureen and mix it with your sugar. Put in a cool place until the next day. Open four peach stones out of every dozen stones you have taken from your fruit, and take out the kernels. Free them of their brown skins, which you can do easily after having scalded them with boiling water. Keep the kernels until you put your sugared peaches over the fire next morning. Then add them to the peaches, which will have plenty of juice of their own by this time. Boil them over a moderate fire for twenty minutes, stirring and skimming frequently. Fill into air-tight jars. This mild preserve has never failed to find favor when placed on my table.

I add a first-rate recipe for brandy peaches, of which you might do well to put up a half-gallon jarful. Accompanied A recipe for by ice-cream they furnish you with a choice desbrandy peaches. sert course for a little dinner party. Take fruit which is fully ripe, and yet firm and speckless. Pour boiling water over it, and leave it covered over for a few minutes. Then take out one peach after another, and with a clean crash towel rub as much of the skin off as you can without seriously breaking it. Have ready some large, open-mouthed glass jars, fill them with your peaches, sprinkling granulated sugar over them sufficient to cover them slightly. Put a thick sprinkling of sugar on top, and then fill the jars up with the best white California brandy. Screw up air-tight, and set away.

Tedious as it is to put up quinces, I consider them fully worth the trouble they cause, and would advise you to try the following way of making a fine preserve of sliced quinces, a jelly, and a stiff marmalade, all out of the same fruit at the same How to preserve time. Peel your quinces, quarter and core them, quinces. being careful to save the seeds. Take all the perfect parts and divide in even slices. Make a sirup, taking equal parts of sugar and fruit, and when ready drop into the boiling liquid the sliced quinces. Cook slowly, and skim well. When the quinces turn red and look clear, they are done. Remove them with a skimmer, and put into jars. Boil the sirup until thick, and almost like a jelly, when pour over the fruit, and screw up the jars. Some add a lemon sliced thin, and freed from all seeds, to the quinces as soon as they begin to turn red. This is a matter of taste. While the slices are cooking, take a second kettle or pan, put into it the parings, cores, and seeds, add water sufficient to cover them. When perfectly soft strain through a clean napkin. Meanwhile cut up all remaining imperfect parts of your quinces into small pieces, and when your kettle is empty put them in, add the liquor drained from cores and parings, and cook until quite soft. Drain again, mash the quince through a sieve, weigh it, and put once more into your kettle. Add sugar, three-quarters of a pound to a pound of the quince, and a cupful of the drained liquor for every pound of fruit. Boil until thick, stirring pretty much all the time to prevent scorching. Fill into cups and glasses. It will turn out firm, and, eaten with cream, is delicious. Now have your kettle cleaned, in order to make your jelly. Take the remaining liquor from parings, etc., and for every pint of it add one pound of sugar. Boil, skimming frequently, until it jellies. Test it by letting a drop from your spoon fall on a cold plate. If it turns into jelly remove your kettle from the fire at once. Quinces jelly easily; be careful, therefore, to watch the right moment, lest your jelly should turn to sirup.

I believe this is all you will need of sweet preserves, without running the risk of being extravagant. There are but a few recipes for pickles which I would like you to know. The material for them is cheap, and you will not find the like of these pickles in any market. Aside from being refreshing when eaten with meat, they will serve you for making and trimming salads and various dishes. They are of the wholesome kind, too, — not overcharged with hot spice. The recipe for pickled beets I gave you before, when speaking about salads.[1] I now have for you

The Sea-captain's Pickled Cucumbers. — You will find them the best you ever ate. For fifty cucumbers take half a pint of salt. Put into a vessel large enough to hold them; add the salt, and pour boiling water over them sufficient to cover them up. Let stand over night, then wipe them dry,

[1] See p. 154.

and arrange in large stone jars or crocks. Boil vinegar sufficient to cover your cucumbers. Just before it comes to a boil throw in your spice, viz. for every two quarts of vinegar half an ounce of mace, one ounce of black pepper seeds, one ounce of mustard seeds, and a quarter of a horseradish root cut into slices. Pour vinegar and spices over your cucumbers boiling hot, and when cold tie up and keep in a cool place. The following is a recipe for

Tarragon Gherkins. — Take cucumbers not larger than your little finger, wash them, and rub them all over with a fine brush, then put them in brine strong enough to bear an egg, for twenty-four hours, when drain, and dry them with a clean towel. Arrange them in either glass or small stone jars layerwise, and put between each layer about half a dozen black pepper seeds and a sprig of tarragon. You may also add a bit of summer savory, and some shallots, or tiny onions whole, but this is not necessary. Now boil vinegar and pour it over the cucumbers boiling hot. Lay a few shavings of horseradish on top of each jar; it will help to keep the pickles. Tie paper over them when cold, and in a week try a pickle. If lacking in salt, add some to the vinegar. They will keep all winter if kept in a cool place.

A good old-fashioned relish, which looks appetizing in a glass dish, and will also serve as part of a mixed winter salad, is

Pickled Cabbage. — Take a firm head of cabbage. Cut it into the thinnest shreds, as for salad; then chop fine. Put into a large bowl, and mix a heaped tablespoonful of salt with it. Let stand over night; and next morning drain well. Mince one small onion; chop two red bull-nose peppers (of which first remove the seeds); add one tablespoonful of white and one of black mustard seed, a sprinkle of celery seed, a few whole cloves, and a dozen or more black pepper seeds. Mix all this with the chopped cabbage; pack into a stone jar; cover the whole with a cabbage leaf, and fill up with boiling hot vinegar.

I add the recipe for a very nice sweet pickle, to eat with cooked ham or any other kind of salt or cured meat.

Spiced Pumpkin. — Peel the pumpkin, remove the seeds, and cut the marrow into pieces about half an inch wide, two inches long, and as thick as wide. Cover with vinegar in a porcelain vessel. Let stand over night in a cool place. The following day drain off the vinegar, and throw it away. Then take half a pound of sugar and four tablespoonfuls of vinegar for every pound of pumpkin, and place on the stove to boil until the latter begins to look clear and glassy. Add the following spice before it is quite done : three cloves, a small stick of cinnamon, and the peel of half a lemon for every pound of pumpkin. Put into glass jars, and if the sirup is not thick enough when the pumpkin is done, cook it a while longer, before pouring it over the latter. The rinds of watermelon may be done in the same way, after peeling off the hard green outside.

Of the various catsups which can be made at home, I counsel you to make but the following, since it is easiest, and better than any you buy.

Tomato Catsup. — After washing ripe tomatoes, scald and peel them ; then measure, and for half a peck of them take one scant cupful of salt, two roots of horseradish grated, one ounce each of black and white mustard seed ; four red peppers, three onions, one ounce of nasturtiums, all chopped fine ; half an ounce of celery seed, one teaspoonful each of ground black pepper and cloves ; and one tablespoonful of ground cinnamon. Press off the juice of the tomatoes, and add to the latter all the other ingredients. After mixing thoroughly, pour over the whole one quart of vinegar ; fill into bottles, and cork and seal well. You will notice that no cooking is needed to make this catsup. You may leave out the nasturtiums, if more convenient, and also the celery seed, since some people object to the latter.

There is one more item you might add to your stores, and that is tarragon vinegar, since you can make it with little trouble so much cheaper than you buy it.

Tarragon Vinegar. — Take a quart bottle, fill it with the best cider vinegar, and add about five ounces of tarragon leaves, after having stripped them off their stems, and dried in a warm but shady spot. If you choose, you may also add a teaspoon-ful of salt, a few shallots, and a little pimpernel. In France they add instead, some lemon peel and a few cloves. But this as good as neutralizes the flavor of tarragon. Your vinegar once prepared, you cork your bottle, and put it for a fortnight in a place where it will be exposed to the sun. After that time filter your vinegar through a clean piece of flannel or linen, and put it away, tightly corked, for use.

It seems to me that now I might safely leave you to your-self. You have succeeded already, with the help I lent you in these letters, in giving a dinner party, which has delighted every one permitted to be your guest ; your husband, I am told, looks well and cheerful, thanks to his wife's art, and his purse, as you write to me, is not the loser for the good fare on your table. Well, my friend, is there anything still to add to my teachings ? I will await your answer.

LETTER XXIV

Unsightly dishes always spoil
The most delicious morsel,
Serve it, though modestly, with grace:
Your guests will sup with pleasure.

YOUR wish is granted: I will give you all the assistance I can, to get up an evening entertainment which does not overstep your means, and yet will please the most fastidious of your friends. I will suggest to you various dishes and relishes the cost of which is moderate, while it remains for you to act on these suggestions, and with your taste and skill to make the most of them, not forgetting to serve your menu in the most tempting manner possible. No pains must be spared, of course, but head and hands be devoted to the task.

I have always found that pickled oysters were welcome at evening parties. Panned or scalloped oysters also are very nice; but, they require the presence of a good cook in the kitchen, while pickled oysters can be Pickled oysters. made a day or so before the entertainment. I have here for you a very good recipe: To pickle a hundred oysters, drain off the liquor; put it on the fire to boil; remove the scum rising, and when clear add the necessary salt (which you must prove by tasting), a teacupful of vinegar, a tablespoonful of black pepper seeds, and two or three blades of mace. Let boil up, then add the oysters after having picked them over carefully to remove fragments of shell. Let simmer for five minutes, and put either in glass jars or a large tureen covered up. Serve in a large glass bowl.

I merely need to remind you here of the mixed salads — chicken, Italian, lobster, etc. — which you have learned to make by this time. The *chef-d'œuvre* which, I am sure, you will produce, is a fit centre-piece for your table, and will serve you better than an expensive mass of flowers. Now you have oysters and a salad; and, to set off these two chief dishes, I counsel to have several plates with sandwiches of different kinds, both inviting to the eye and appetizing to the palate. It is about as much of an art to make the sandwiches I mean as it is to *compose* a salad. But, after once mastering the art, you will never be at a loss to give your supper or lunch table an enticing aspect.

To prepare yourself for these sandwiches you have to go to work in several ways. First of all you have the choice of several kinds of mixed butter for spreading them, which can be made days beforehand, since that sort of preparation will keep. Here are three recipes.

Sandwiches, and how to make them.

Mustard Butter. — Take two tablespoonfuls of mustard (I would choose the French) for every piece of butter the size of an egg. See that the butter is soft — not hard — and work the two ingredients together, by means of a stone mortar and pestle, until perfectly blended. The two following you work in the same way.

Anchovy Butter. — Take one teaspoonful of anchovy paste to butter the size of an egg. If you should find that the anchovy flavor were not predominant enough, add a little more paste.

Sardine and Herb Butter combined is the best looking, as well as the best flavored of the three. The ingredients are salted sardines three ounces, butter a quarter of a pound, minced parsley a scant tablespoonful, and minced tarragon a teaspoonful. Wash the sardines well, but do not soak them; split them and remove the bones; then cut them into fine strips, and finally chop them as fine as possible. Mix and rub together all the ingredients until thoroughly blended.

The two latter kinds of butter, when spread on bread, are palatable enough without anything else. But, used as a foundation or envelope for meat, fish, salad, etc., all three kinds will lend a delightfully *piquant* flavor to either substance.

Next, order your bread the day before you need it, lest it
will be too spongy to slice down nicely. Order some long,
round loaves of French bread, and some square and oblong
loaves of home-made (or Vienna) bread. The former, when
sliced, will furnish you with small, disk-like pieces, surrounded
by a crisp brown crust, which many persons like. For those
who do not, you will have the other kind of bread, of which
you may trim off the crust, after slicing it. All slices must, of
course, be as thin as possible. I would, however, take part
of the trimmed slices, and toast them slightly on the under side.
I will tell you later for what purpose. The slices from the
home-made bread are too large to use whole. Therefore, cut
them either crosswise, so as to form two triangular pieces,
or lengthwise, which will give you two oblong ones. Now
butter some with butter pure and simple, and some with one
or another kind of mixed butter; and then set about to finish
them in different ways, — something for the individual taste of
each guest. Have ready boiled tongue, ham, veal, etc., all
chopped up fine, and each by itself. Make use of boiled or
roasted meat you may have on hand. In the large cities you
can buy any quantity of cooked ham, tongue, etc., which saves
work. Or buy the potted meats, of which some, however,
are very highly spiced. With them you can do nothing more
than spread over buttered bread. But the chopped meat
you may heap up on the latter; and you may mix it with a
mayonnaise, or a *sauce ravigote*,[1] thickened by a little gelatine.
Then, provide some capers, pickled cucumbers, both chopped
fine, some olives (of the small kind), some hard-boiled eggs,
grated cheese, and, if you will take the additional trouble,
some amber-colored *aspic*, either chopped or cut into dice,
and use for garnishing. Cut the eggs into slices; keep the
rings of whites thus obtained intact, excepting the end pieces,
which you mince; and rub the yellow into fine crumbs. All
this — and more which I have not mentioned — is your material
with which to do what you please, provided you produce the

[1] See p. 74.

most enticing and satisfactory *bouchées* your guests have ever tasted. I will suggest a way of doing it. Have two large round plates and two smaller ones; have each covered with a fringed napkin or doily. Put in the centre of the large plates (or dishes), respectively, a little pyramid of olives and pink radishes. Surround them with disk-like pieces of buttered bread. Put in the centre of each of these pieces a ring of white of egg (hard-boiled), and in the centre of it some minced tongue, while on the outside you rim the white of egg with the crumbled yolk, with a caper set on top of it in short intervals, like so many beads. Put, also, a caper in the very centre, on top of the minced tongue. These sandwiches you surround by others of triangular shape. It takes two rows of them to form a ribbon-like rim: the first row you place point outward; the second row point inward (toward the centre of the plate). Have the first row of triangles toasted on the under side; spread caviare on the upper side, and place upon it one-half of a thin slice of lemon. For the second row of triangles, I advise ham and white of egg, both minced and kept separate, so as to form two smaller triangles on each of the larger triangles of bread. (Do not forget that each piece of bread must first of all be buttered.) Around this double row I would place a band of oblong pieces of bread, toasted on the under side, spread with fresh butter on top, and the latter covered with grated cheese of two kinds; for instance, Gruyère on one slice and Chester on the next. Take a knife, and with it smooth over and press down all minced and chopped ingredients, so as to make them cling to the buttered bread. Finally, garnish with a few sprigs of tarragon, little bunches of watercress, or a wreath of smilax and some stray flowers of mignonette, and your sandwiches will look tempting enough even for a person who has dined. The two smaller plates I would fill with doubled sandwiches, *i.e.* two and two put together, the inside of each piece of bread being spread with mixed butter of one kind or the other. Between these two covers I would put some chopped meat, either by itself, or mixed with a mayonnaise, or with the simple addition of some chopped pickles. Arrange these sandwiches symmetrically, one above the other, either forming a high square, or an octagon, or pyramid. Garnish with greens, and a flower here and there.

If you think your guests would like to treat themselves to an indigestion by following the fashion and munching some salted almonds, which certainly are very palatable, Recipe for I will be your accomplice, and give you here the salted almonds. recipe: Take the best and largest almonds in market. Scald them with boiling water; let stand until cool, when the brown skins will pull off readily. Wash them in cold water, put on a clean towel, and rub them dry. For a pint of them, take two teaspoonfuls of olive oil (or of melted butter); mix and put them on a shallow sheet-iron pan; distribute evenly, and dust them over with a tablespoonful of salt. Place them in a slow oven; and, after about five to ten minutes, stir them up, add another tablespoonful of salt, and put back in the oven until they have turned slightly brown. Stir again, and remove on a sheet of paper, to get cool.

You now will have to deliberate whether it might be best for you to order ice-cream for the *finale* of your entertainment, or to get up yourself a sweet and yet cooling dish. If not in a position to get a really good ice-cream, I would rather do the latter. For this purpose I recommend to you a *macédoine* of fruit, for which I gave you more than one recipe.[1] To accompany it, have some nice cake, or *bouchées* of cake, and be sure to choose some in which you have succeeded before. Or have simply some sweet wafers, which you buy in small tin boxes. Now, if you add to all this a cooling beverage, you may consider your menu complete for the evening. I know of several rather inexpensive beverages, the recipes of which might be of use to you now and on future occasions. They are the following: —

Tea Punch. — Take five heaped teaspoonfuls of black tea. Have your teapot hot before you put it in. Pour over it

[1] See p. 178.

enough boiling water to cover. Allow to draw for three minutes, then fill up with boiling water. Let draw for two minutes, and pour through a tea sieve into a pitcher which will
hold two quarts. Fill the teapot up with *boiling* water again
and again, allowing it each time to draw for two or three minutes, until your pitcher is full. Meanwhile, heat a bottle of
California table claret (which need not cost any more than
twenty cents a bottle), until just before boiling; put half a
pound of sugar into the punch-bowl, add the peel and juice
of one lemon, and pour over it the hot claret and the tea.
Finally, add half a pint of arrack. This economical punch is
equally good cold or hot. If you wish it cold, set it in ice for
several hours before serving.

Cardinal Punch. — Take three bottles of light Rhine or
Moselle wine, and pour it over a small soup-plateful of fresh
fruit which has been sugared for about an hour beforehand.
The best fruit to take is either oranges, peaches, pineapple, or
strawberries — the three former to be divided into even slices.
Add sugar to taste. Do not sweeten too much — about one
pound of sugar altogether. Let stand, covered up, for two
hours, then add half a bottle of cheap claret. Put in ice to
chill thoroughly, and when being served add — the recipe says
a bottle of champagne, which I convert into — a bottle of
Apollinaris kept on ice. The latter has the same sparkling
effect, and the punch does not lose by it in quality.

Snow Punch. — Take two pounds of sugar, and boil with
one quart of water for twenty minutes; then pour over the
peels of three oranges shaved off very thin; cover up, and
let stand for one hour. Add the juice of four lemons, and
pour through a hair sieve. Put into a covered vessel and pack
in ice and salt for several hours. Before serving, add the
whites of six eggs, and whip until quite foamy, when finally
add, still whipping, six tiny glassfuls of Jamaica rum or mara-
schino cordial. Serve from a bowl, or in glasses filled in the
pantry.

Ambrosia. — Take one quart of milk, add vanilla extract sufficient to give it a pleasant flavor, half a wineglassful of cherry

brandy (Kirsch), half a small pineapple cut into very small pieces, and sugar to taste. Let stand covered up and on ice for three hours. This drink is served in small glasses at court parties in Berlin.

A very refreshing drink also, when kept on ice, is Almond Milk. To make it, take one pound of sweet and one dozen bitter almonds. Scald, skin, and drop them into Almond milk. cold water. Drain, and pound them, with the addition of some water, in a mortar until in very small fragments. Put them into a bowl and mix with cold water to the consistency of thin mush. Let stand for about fifteen minutes, then squeeze the liquid through a very clean napkin (there must be no starch or indigo in it). Put more water on the almonds; let stand, and squeeze again. Add the liquid you obtain to the former. The almonds are now of no further use. Sweeten the almond milk to taste, and flavor with orange-flower essence, rose water, or vanilla. By adding a little fresh milk, the color is improved.

But if you will not go to the extent of all this trouble and expense, a beverage made simply of raspberry juice or sirup mixed with water, and chilled on ice, is also an agreeable and refreshing drink.

Now, before ending my advisory correspondence on the art of cooking, — which has taken a larger scope than I at first intended, — I will note down, for your guidance, a few menus for small lunch and dinner parties, keeping in view the limited means you have to deal with, in league with your art.

MENUS FOR LUNCHEONS

No. 1

Amber-colored broth, in cups, with cheese crusts.
Lobster cutlets.
Salpicon royal, on shells.
Chicken croquettes, with celery salad, mayonnaise dressing.
Coffee *crème*, in cups, with small cakes.

No. 2

Velvety soup, in cups.
Minced veal kidneys on *sauté*ed bread.
Risotto.
Backhaendl (fried chicken), with fried parsley.
Salad of lettuce, string-beans, and beets,
French dressing.
Snow *crème*, with *bouchées* of cake.

No. 3

Raw-meat soup, in cups.
Oyster patties.
Sweetbreads stewed in sauce allemande.
Chicken in jelly, with green salad, French dressing.
Raspberry water ice, with sweet wafers.

No. 4

Chicken *purée* soup, in cups.
Eggs on shells.
Beefsteak with mushrooms in brown sauce.
Meringues filled with whipped cream.

MENUS FOR DINNERS

No. 1

Flour soup No. 1., with asparagus tips.
Boiled salmon, with sauce *génoise*, small potatoes,
pickled gherkins (or cucumber salad).
Ragoût of sweetbreads in a ring of *croûtons*.
Cauliflower surrounded by green peas, boiled rice,
and broiled lamb chops.
Roast chickens stuffed with oysters, lettuce salad,
French dressing.
Russian *crème*, with macaroons.
Neufchâtel cheese, crackers.
Fruit.
Coffee.

No. 2

Green pea soup, with dice of custard.
Ringed pike, small potatoes with melted butter and parsley,
mustard sauce.
Macaroni *à la Milanaise*.
Roast beef, small roasted potatoes,
purée of spinach.
Game birds, with green salad, French dressing.
Raspberry foam, with sugar wafers.
Edam cheese, crackers.
Fruit.
Coffee.

No. 3

Julienne soup, with marrow balls.
Panned oysters on shells.
Chicken fricassee.
Saddle of mutton, mashed potatoes with green herbs,
chestnut *purée*, currant jelly.
Cauliflower with boiled lobster, sauce *ravigote*.
Salad of lettuce and water-cress,
French dressing.
Macédoine of fruit, with small sponge cakes.
Fromage de Brie, crackers.
Fruit.
Coffee.

No. 4

Soup with moulded rice.
Striped bass, stuffed and baked, potatoes,
sauce *hollandaise*.
Mixed *ragoût* in pastry shell.
Filet of beef *à la jardinière*.
Scalloped oysters, green salad, French dressing.
Ice-cream, *bouchées*.
Gorconzola, crackers.
Fruit.
Coffee.

I leave it to your judgment to change or modify these menus in relation to the guests you are going to entertain. You will not have less than three and no more than nine at table — a number between that of the Graces and the Muses (according to the old saying), and they will be either intimate friends, or friends farther removed whom you wish to compliment. Your bill of fare will have to be regulated to suit these different circumstances.

And now I have, indeed, come to the end.

For my farewell I present you with a motto full of wisdom to put over your kitchen mantel : —

> " Es kommt alles auf die Bereitung an,
> Sagte Hans, und spickte eine Kroete."

> (It all depends on how it's done,
> Quoth Jack, a-larding of a toad.)

INDEX

A

Acid dissolves gelatine, 79.
Albuminoids, in general, 9; — in daily rations, 9; — in Rumford Soup, 21; — in various soups, 22; — in various meats, 43; — in rice, 84; — in vegetables, 106; — in different fish, 128; — in eggs, 164; — in cheese, 170; — in light desserts, 174.
Almonds, salted, 205; — milk, 207.
Ambrosia, 207.
Anorganic substances, 9.
Arme Ritter, 174.
Asparagus, soup, 31; — shavings, dried, 34; how to cook —, 113; difference in —, 113; — *en petits pois*, 113; — combines well with, 113.
Aspic, uses of, 79; recipe for —, 79; — in a *plat de goût*, 79.

B

Backhaendl. See Chicken.
Baked rice, 87; — potatoes, 100; — lobster, 145.
Baking. See Cake.
Balls, bread, 27; sponge —, 28; marrow —, 28; forcemeat —, 28; codfish —, 140; fish — for lobster fricassee, 145.
Barley, nutritive value, 11; — soup No. 1, 24; — soup No. 2, 25.
Baronius, Cardinal, 2.
Batter for frying, 78.
Bavarian recipe for ham dumplings, 28; — — for potato noodles, 102; — — for potato balloons, 103.
Bavaroise. See *Crème.*

Beans, dried, nutritive value, 11; string —, nutritive value, 11; black or Mexican — soup, 33; dried — soup, 34; to cook string —, 109; to cook Lima —, 109.
Béchamel, 72.
Beef, roast, 44; — braised, 46; value of different cuts of —, 47; filet of — à *la jardinière*, 47; how to use remnants of —, 48; — *en matelote*, 48; loss in weight, 49; *stufato à l'italienne*, with macaroni, 92.
Beefsteak, how to broil, 44; to use remnants of —, 48.
Beef-tea, nutritive value, 11.
Beets, as a vegetable, 121; how to pickle —, 154.
Beverages, fermented, nutritive value, 11.
Blackberry jam, 194; — jelly, 194.
Bloaters. See Herring.
Bluefish *en matelote*, 137.
Boil, how to, meat, 14; — mutton, 56; — ham, 62; — tongue, 63; — rice, 85; — macaroni, 89; — cauliflower, 112; — fish, 130; — lobster, 143; loss of weight in boiling, 49.
Bombe à la Sardanapale, 116.
Bones, left over, 7; — waste material, 49.
Bouchées, 190.
Bouille-abaisse, 136.
Braise, how to, meat, 45; — beef, 46.
Bread-box, the, 7; stale — added to soups, 19; — as accessories to soups, 27; — balls, for soup, 27; wheat —, nutritive value, 11; 174; — for sandwiches, 203.
Breast of mutton. See Mutton.

Typography by J. S. Cushing & Co., Boston, U.S.A.

Presswork by Berwick & Smith, Boston, U.S.A.

ST. DUNSTAN'S HOUSE, FETTER LANE,
LONDON, E.C. 1892.

Select List of Books in all Departments of Literature

PUBLISHED BY

Sampson Low, Marston & Company, Ld.

ABBEY and PARSONS, *Quiet Life*, from drawings; motive by Austin Dobson, 31s. 6d.

ABBOTT, CHARLES C., *Waste Land Wanderings*, 10s. 6d.

ABERDEEN, EARL OF. See Prime Ministers.

ABNEY, CAPT., *Thebes and its Greater Temples*, 40 photos. 63s.

—— and CUNNINGHAM, *Pioneers of the Alps*, new ed. 21s.

About in the World. See Gentle Life Series.

—— *Some Fellows*, from my note-book, by "an Eton boy," 2s. 6d.; new edit. 1s.

ADAMS, CHARLES K., *Historical Literature*, 12s. 6d.

ADDISON, *Sir Roger de Coverley*, from the "Spectator," 6s.

AGASSIZ, ALEX., *Three Cruises of the "Blake,"* illust. 2 vols. 42s.

ALBERT, PRINCE. See Bayard Series.

ALCOTT, L. M. *Jo's Boys*, a sequel to "Little Men," 5s.

—— *Life, Letters and Journals*, by Ednah D. Cheney, 6s.

—— *Lulu's Library*, a story for girls, 3s. 6d.

—— *Old-fashioned Thanksgiving Day*, 3s. 6d.

—— *Proverb Stories*, 3s. 6d.

ALCOTT, L. M., *Recollections of my Childhood's Days*, 3s. 6d.

—— *Silver Pitchers*, 3s. 6d.

—— *Spinning-wheel Stories*, 5s.

—— See also Low's Standard Series and Rose Library.

ALDAM, W. H., *Flies and Fly-making*, with actual specimens on cardboard, 63s.

ALDEN, W. L. See Low's Standard Series.

ALFORD, LADY MARIAN, *Needlework as Art*, 21s.; l. p. 84s.

ALGER, J. G., *Englishmen in the French Revolution*, 7s. 6d.

Amateur Angler in Dove Dale, a three weeks' holiday, by E. M. 1s. 6d., 1s. and 5s.

ANDERSEN, H. C., *Fairy Tales*, illust. in colour by E. V. B. 25s., new edit. 5s.

—— *Fairy Tales*, illust. by Scandinavian artists, 6s.

ANDERSON, W., *Pictorial Arts of Japan*, 4 parts, 168s.; artist's proofs, 252s.

ANDRES, *Varnishes, Lacquers, Siccatives, & Sealing-wax*, 12s. 6d.

Angler's strange Experiences, by Cotswold Isys, new edit., 3s. 6d.

ANNESLEY, C., *Standard Opera Glass*, the plots of eighty operas, 3rd edit., 2s. 6d.

Annual American Catalogue of Books,.1886-89, each 10s. 6d., half morocco, 14s.

—— 1890, cloth, 15s., half morocco, oloth sides, 18s.

Antipodean Notes; a nine months' tour, by Wanderer, 7s. 6d.

APPLETON, *European Guide,* new edit., 2 parts, 10s. each.

ARCHER, W., *English Dramatists of To-day,* 8s. 6d.

ARLOT'S *Coach Painting,* from the French by A. A. Fesquet, 6s.

ARMYTAGE, HON. MRS., *Wars of Queen Victoria's Reign,* 5s.

ARNOLD, E., *Birthday Book;* by Kath. L. and Constance Arnold, 4s. 6d.

—— E. L. L., *Summer Holiday in Scandinavia,* 10s. 6d.

—— *On the Indian Hills,* Coffee Planting, &c., 2 vols. 24s.

—— R., *Ammonia and Ammonium Compounds,* illust. 5s.

Artistic Japan, text, woodcuts, and coloured plates, vols. I.-VI., 15s. each.

ASBJÖRNSEN, P. C., *Round the Yule Log,* 7s. 6d.; new edit. 5s.

ASHE, R. P., *Two Kings of Uganda;* six years in Eastern Equatorial Africa, 6s.; new edit. 3s. 6d.

—— *Uganda, England's latest Charge,* stiff cover, 1s.

ASHTON, F. T., *Designing fancy Cotton and Woollen Cloths,* illust. 50s.

ATCHISON, C. C., *Winter Cruise in Summer Seas;* "how I found " health, 16s.

ATKINSON, J. B. *Overbeck.* See Great Artists.

ATTWELL, *Italian Masters,* especially in the National Gallery, 3s. 6d.

AUDSLEY, G. A., *Chromolithography,* 44 coloured plates and text, 63s.

—— *Ornamental Arts of Japan,* 2 vols. morocco, 23l. 2s.; four parts, 15l. 15s.

—— W. and G. A., *Ornament in all Styles,* 31s. 6d.

AUERBACH, B., *Brigitta* (B. Tauchnitz), 2s.; sewed, 1s. 6d.

—— *On the Height* (B. Tauchnitz), 3 vols. 6s.; sewed, 4s. 6d.

—— *Spinoza* (B. Tauchnitz), 2 vols. 4s.

AUSTRALIA. See F. Countries.

AUSTRIA. See F. Countries.

Autumn Cruise in the Ægean, by one of the party. See " Fitzpatrick."

BACH. See Great Musicians.

BACON. See English Philosophers.

—— DELIA, *Biography,* 10s. 6d.

BADDELEY, W. ST. CLAIR, *Love's Vintage;* sonnets and lyrics, 5s.

—— *Tchay and Chianti,* a short visit to Russia and Finland, 5s.

—— *Travel-tide,* 7s. 6d.

BAKER, JAMES, *John Westacott,* new edit. 6s. and 3s. 6d.

BALDWIN, J., *Story of Siegfried,* illust. 6s.

—— *Story of Roland,* illust. 6s.

—— *Story of the Golden Age,* illust. 6s.

—— J. D., *Ancient America,* illust. 10s. 6d.

Ballad Stories. See Bayard Series.

Ballads of the Cid, edited by Rev. Gerrard Lewis, 3s. 6d.

BALLANTYNE, T., *Essays.* See Bayard Series.

BALLIN, ADA S., *Science of Dress*, illust. 6s.

BAMFORD, A. J., *Turbans and Tails*, 7s. 6d.

BANCROFT, G., *History of America*, new edit. 6 vols. 73s. 6d.

Barbizon Painters, by J. W. Mollett—I. Millet, T. Rousseau, and Diaz, 3s. 6d. II. Corot, Daubigny and Dupré, 3s. 6d.; the two in one vol. 7s. 6d.

BARING-GOULD. See Foreign Countries.

BARLOW, A., *Weaving*, new edit. 25s.

—— P. W., *Kaipara, New Z.*, 6s.

—— W., *Matter and Force*, 12s.

BARRETT. See Gr. Musicians.

BARROW, J., *Mountain Ascents*, new edit. 5s.

BASSETT, *Legends of the Sea*, 7s. 6d.

BATHGATE, A., *Waitaruna, New Zealand*, 5s.

Bayard Series, edited by the late J. Hain Friswell; flexible cloth extra, 2s. 6d. each.
Chevalier Bayard, by Berville.
De Joinville, St. Louis.
Essays of Cowley.
Abdallah, by Laboullaye.
Table-Talk of Napoleon.
Vathek, by Beckford.
Cavalier and Puritan Songs.
Words of Wellington.
Johnson's Rasselas.
Hazlitt's Round Table.
Browne's Religio Medici.
Ballad Stories of the Affections, by Robert Buchanan.
Coleridge's Christabel, &c.
Chesterfield's Letters.
Essays in Mosaic, by T. Ballantyne.
My Uncle Toby.
Rochefoucauld, Reflections.
Socrates, Memoirs from Xenophon.
Prince Albert's Precepts.

BEACONSFIELD, *Public Life*, 3s. 6d.

—— See also Prime Ministers.

BEAUGRAND, *Young Naturalists*, new edit. 5s.

BECKER, A.L., *First German Book*, 1s.; *Exercises*, 1s.; *Key to both*, 2s. 6d.; *German Idioms*, 1s. 6d.

BECKFORD. See Bayard Series.

BEECHER, H. W., *Biography*, new edit. 10s. 6d.

BEETHOVEN. See Great Musicians.

BEHNKE, E., *Child's Voice*, 3s. 6d.

BELL, *Obeah, Witchcraft in the West Indies*, 2s. 6d.

BELLENGER & WITCOMB'S *French and English Conversations*, new edit. Paris, bds. 2s.

BENJAMIN, *Atlantic Islands as health, &c., resorts*. 16s.

BERLIOZ. See Gr. Musicians.

BERVILLE. See Bayard Series.

BIART, *Young Naturalist*, new edit. 7s. 6d.

—— *Involuntary Voyage*, 7s. 6d. and 5s.

—— *Two Friends*, translated by Mary de Hauteville, 7s. 6d.
See also Low's Standard Books.

BICKERSTETH, ASHLEY, B.A., *Outlines of Roman History*, 2s. 6d.

—— E. H., Exon., *Clergyman in his Home*, 1s.

—— *From Year to Year*, original poetical pieces, morocco or calf, 10s. 6d.; padded roan, 6s.; roan, 5s.; cloth, 3s. 6d.

—— *Hymnal Companion*, full lists post free.

—— *Master's Home Call*, new edit. 1s.

—— *Octave of Hymns*, sewn, 3d., with music, 1s.

BICKERSTETH, E. H., Exon., *Reef, Parables,* &c., illust. 7s. 6d. and 2s. 6d.

—— *Shadowed Home,* n. ed. 5s.

BIGELOW, John, *France and the Confederate Navy,* an international episode, 7s. 6d.

BILBROUGH, *'Twixt France and Spain,* 7s. 6d.

BILLROTH, *Care of the Sick,* 6s.

BIRD, F. J., *Dyer's Companion,* 42s.

—— F. S., *Land of Dykes and Windmills,* 12s. 6d.

—— H. E., *Chess Practice,* 2s. 6d.

BISHOP. See Nursing Record Series.

BLACK, Robert, *Horse Racing in France,* 14s.

—— W., *Donald Ross of Heimra,* 3 vols. 31s. 6d.

—— Novels, new and uniform edition in monthly vols. 2s. 6d. ea.

—— See Low's Standard Novels.

BLACKBURN, C. F., *Catalogue Titles, Index Entries,* &c. 14s.

—— H., *Art in the Mountains,* new edit. 5s.

—— *Artists and Arabs,* 7s. 6d.

—— *Breton Folk,* new issue, 10s. 6d.

—— *Harz Mountains,* 12s.

—— *Normandy Picturesque,* 16s.

—— *Pyrenees,* illust. by Gustave Doré, new edit. 7s. 6d.

BLACKMORE, R. D., *Georgics,* 4s. 6d.; cheap edit. 1s.

—— *Lorna Doone, édit. de luxe,* 35s., 31s. 6d. & 21s.

—— *Lorna Doone,* illust. by W. Small, 7s. 6d.

—— *Springhaven,* illust. 12s.; new edit. 7s. 6d. & 6s.

—— See also Low's Standard Novels.

BLAIKIE, *How to get Strong,* new edit. 5s.

—— *Sound Bodies for our Boys and Girls,* 2s. 6d.

BLOOMFIELD. See Choice Editions.

Bobby, a Story, by Vesper, 1s.

BOCK, *Head Hunters of Borneo,* 36s.

—— *Temples & Elephants,* 21s.

BONAPARTE, Mad. Patterson, *Life,* 10s. 6d.

BONWICK, James, *Colonial Days,* 2s. 6d.

—— *Colonies,* 1s. ea.; 1 vol. 5s.

—— *Daily Life of the Tasmanians,* 12s. 6d.

—— *First Twenty Years of Australia,* 5s.

—— *Last of the Tasmanians,* 16s.

—— *Port Philip,* 21s.

—— *Lost Tasmanian Race,* 4s.

BOSANQUET, C., *Blossoms from the King's Garden,* 6s.

—— *Jehoshaphat,* 1s.

—— *Lenten Meditations,* I. 1s. 6d.; II. 2s.

—— *Tender Grass for Lambs,* 2s. 6d.

BOULTON, N. W. *Rebellions,* Canadian life, 9s.

BOURKE, *On the Border with Crook,* illust., roy. 8vo, 21s.

—— *Snake Dance of Arizona,* 21s.

BOUSSENARD. See Low's Standard Books.

BOWEN, F., *Modern Philosophy,* new ed. 16s.

BOWER. See English Philosophers.

—— *Law of Electric Lighting,* 12s. 6d.

BOYESEN, H. H., *Against Heavy Odds,* 5s.

—— *History of Norway,* 7s. 6d.

BOYESEN, *Modern Vikings*, 6s.
Boy's Froissart, King Arthur, Mabinogian, Percy, see "Lanier."

BRADSHAW, *New Zealand as it is*, 12s. 6d.

—— *New Zealand of To-day*, 14s.

BRANNT, *Fats and Oils*, 35s.

—— *Soap and Candles*, 35s.

—— *Vinegar, Acetates*, 25s.

—— *Distillation of Alcohol*, 12s. 6d.

—— *Metal Worker's Receipts*, 12s. 6d.

—— *Metallic Alloys*, 12s. 6d.

—— and WAHL, *Techno-Chemical Receipt Book*, 10s. 6d.

BRASSEY, LADY, *Tahiti*, 21s.

BRÉMONT. See Low's Standard Novels.

BRETON, JULES, *Life of an Artist*, an autobiography, 7s. 6d.

BRISSE, *Menus and Recipes*, new edit. 5s.

Britons in Brittany, by G. H. F. 2s. 6d.

BROCK-ARNOLD. See Great Artists.

BROOKS, NOAH, *Boy Settlers*, 6s.

BROWN, A. J., *Rejected of Men*, 3s. 6d.

—— A. S. *Madeira and Canary Islands for Invalids*, 2s. 6d.

—— *Northern Atlantic*, for travellers, 4s. 6d.

—— ROBERT. See Low's Standard Novels.

BROWNE, LENNOX, and BEHNKE, *Voice, Song, & Speech*, 15s. ; new edit. 5s.

—— *Voice Use*, 3s. 6d.

—— SIR T. See Bayard Series.

BRYCE, G., *Manitoba*, 7s. 6d.

—— *Short History of the Canadian People*, 7s. 6d.

BUCHANAN, R. See Bayard Series.

BULKELEY, OWEN T., *Lesser Antilles*, 2s. 6d.

BUNYAN. See Low's Standard Series.

BURDETT-COUTTS, *Brookfield Stud*, 5s.

BURGOYNE, *Operations in Egypt*, 5s.

BURNABY, F. See Low's Standard Library.

—— MRS., *High Alps in Winter*, 14s.

BURNLEY, JAMES, *History of Wool*, 21s.

BUTLER, COL. SIR W. F., *Campaign of the Cataracts*, 18s.

—— *Red Cloud*, 7s. 6d. & 5s.

—— See also Low's Standard Books.

BUXTON, ETHEL M. WILMOT, *Wee Folk*, 5s.

—— See also Illust. Text Books.

BYNNER. See Low's Standard Novels.

CABLE, G. W., *Bonaventure*, 5s.

CADOGAN, LADY A., *Drawing-room Comedies*, illust. 10s. 6d., acting edit. 6d.

—— *Illustrated Games of Patience*, col. diagrams, 12s. 6d.

—— *New Games of Patience*, with coloured diagrams, 12s. 6d.

CAHUN. See Low's Standard Books.

CALDECOTT, RANDOLPH, *Memoir*, by H. Blackburn, new edit. 7s. 6d. and 5s.

—— *Sketches*, pict. bds. 2s. 6d.

CALL, ANNIE PAYSON, *Power through Repose*, 3s. 6d.

CALLAN, H., M.A., *Wanderings on Wheel and Foot through Europe*, 1s. 6d.

Cambridge Trifles, 2s. 6d.

Cambridge Staircase, 2s. 6d.

CAMPBELL, LADY COLIN, *Book of the Running Brook*, 5s.

—— T. See Choice Editions.

CANTERBURY, ARCHBISHOP. See Preachers.

CARLETON, WILL, *City Ballads*, illust. 12s. 6d.

—— *City Legends*, ill. 12s. 6d.

—— *Farm Festivals*, ill. 12s. 6d.

—— See also Rose Library.

CARLYLE, *Irish Journey in 1849*, 7s. 6d.

CARNEGIE, ANDREW, *American Four-in-hand in Britain*, 10s. 6d.; also 1s.

—— *Round the World*, 10s. 6d.

—— *Triumphant Democracy*, 6s.; new edit. 1s. 6d.; paper, 1s.

CAROVÉ, *Story without an End*, illust. by E. V. B., 7s. 6d.

Celebrated Racehorses, 4 vols. 126s.

CÉLIÈRE. See Low's Standard Books.

Changed Cross,&c., poems, 2s.6d.

Chant-book Companion to the Common Prayer, 2s.; organ ed. 4s.

CHAPIN, *Mountaineering in Colorado*, 10s. 6d.

CHAPLIN, J. G., *Bookkeeping*, 2s. 6d.

CHATTOCK, *Notes on Etching* new edit. 10s. 6d.

CHERUBINI. See Great Musicians.

CHESTERFIELD. See Bayard Series.

Choice Editions of choice books, illustrated by C. W. Cope, R.A., T. Creswick, R.A., E. Duncan, Birket Foster, J. C. Horsley, A.R.A., G. Hicks, R. Redgrave, R.A., O. Stonehouse, F. Tayler, G. Thomas, H. G. Townsend,

Choice Editions—continued.

E. H. Wehnert, Harrison Weir, &c., cloth extra gilt, gilt edges, 2s. 6d. each; re-issue, 1s. each.

Bloomfield's Farmer's Boy.

Campbell's Pleasures of Hope.

Coleridge's Ancient Mariner.

Goldsmith's Deserted Village.

Goldsmith's Vicar of Wakefield.

Gray's Elegy in a Churchyard.

Keats' Eve of St. Agnes.

Milton's Allegro.

Poetry of Nature, by H. Weir.

Rogers' Pleasures of Memory.

Shakespeare's Songs and Sonnets.

Elizabethan Songs and Sonnets.

Tennyson's May Queen.

Wordsworth's Pastoral Poems.

CHREIMAN, *Physical Culture of Women*, 1s.

CLARK, A., *A Dark Place of the Earth*, 6s.

—— Mrs. K. M., *Southern Cross Fairy Tale*, 5s.

CLARKE, C. C., *Writers, and Letters*, 10s. 6d.

—— PERCY, *Three Diggers*, 6s.

—— *Valley Council;* from T. Bateman's Journal, 6s.

Classified Catalogue of English-printed Educational Works, 3rd edit. 6s.

Claude le Lorrain. See Great Artists.

CLOUGH, A. H., *Plutarch's Lives*, one vol. 18s.

COLERIDGE, C. R., *English Squire*, 6s.

—— S. T. See Choice Editions and Bayard Series.

COLLINGWOOD, H. See Low's Standard Books.

COLLINSON, Adm. SIR R., *H.M.S. Enterprise in Search of Franklin*, 14s.

CONDER, J., *Flowers of Japan; Decoration*, coloured Japanese Plates, 42s. nett.

CORREGGIO. See Great Artists.

COWLEY. See Bayard Series.

COX, DAVID. See Great Artists.

COZZENS, F., *American Yachts*, pfs. 21*l.*; art. pfs. 31*l.* 10*s.*

—— See also Low's Standard Books.

CRADDOCK. See Low's Standard Novels.

CREW, B. J., *Petroleum*, 21*s.*

CRISTIANI, R. S., *Soap and Candles*, 42*s.*

—— *Perfumery*, 25*s.*

CROKER, MRS. B. M. See Low's Standard Novels.

CROUCH, A. P., *Glimpses of Feverland* (West Africa), 6*s.*

—— *On a Surf-bound Coast*, 7*s.* 6*d.*; new edit. 5*s.*

CRUIKSHANK, G. See Great Artists.

CUDWORTH, W., *Abraham Sharp*, 26*s.*

CUMBERLAND, STUART, *Thought-reader's Thoughts*, 10*s.* 6*d.*

—— See also Low's Standard Novels.

CUNDALL, F. See Great Artists.

—— J., *Shakespeare*, 3*s.* 6*d.*, 5*s.* and 2*s.*

CURTIN, J., *Myths of the Russians*, 10*s.* 6*d.*

CURTIS, C. B., *Velazquez and Murillo*, with etchings, 31*s.* 6*d.* and 63*s.*

CUSHING, W., *Anonyms*, 2 vols. 52*s.* 6*d.*

—— *Initials and Pseudonyms*, 25*s.*; ser. II., 21*s.*

CUTCLIFFE, H. C., *Trout Fishing*, new edit. 3*s.* 6*d.*

DALY, MRS. D., *Digging, Squatting, &c., in N. S. Australia*, 12*s.*

D'ANVERS, N., *Architecture and Sculpture*, new edit. 5*s.*

—— *Elementary Art, Architecture, Sculpture, Painting*, new edit. 10*s.* 6*d.*

—— *Elementary History of Music*, 2*s.* 6*d.*

—— *Painting*, by F. Cundall, 6*s.*

DAUDET, A., *My Brother Jack*, 7*s.* 6*d.*; also 5*s.*

—— *Port Tarascon*, by H. James, 7*s.* 6*d.*; new edit. 5*s.*

DAVIES, C., *Modern Whist*, 4*s.*

DAVIS, C. T., *Bricks, Tiles, &c.*, new edit. 25*s.*

—— *Manufacture of Leather*, 52*s.* 6*d.*

—— *Manufacture of Paper*, 28*s.*

—— *Steam Boiler Incrustation*, 8*s.* 6*d.*

—— G. B., *International Law*, 10*s.* 6*d.*

DAWIDOWSKY, *Glue, Gelatine, &c.*, 12*s.* 6*d.*

Day of my Life, by an Eton boy, new edit. 2*s.* 6*d.*; also 1*s.*

DE JOINVILLE. See Bayard Series.

DE LEON, EDWIN, *Under the Stars and Under the Crescent*, 2 vols. 12*s.*; new edit. 6*s.*

DELLA ROBBIA. See Great Artists.

Denmark and Iceland. See Foreign Countries.

DENNETT, R. E., *Seven Years among the Fjort*, 7*s.* 6*d.*

DERRY (Bishop of). See Preachers.

DE WINT. See Great Artists.

DIGGLE, J. W., *Bishop Fraser's Lancashire Life*, new edit. 12*s.* 6*d.*; popular ed. 3*s.* 6*d.*

—— *Sermons for Daily Life*, 5*s*

DOBSON, Austin, *Hogarth*, with a bibliography, &c., of prints, illust. 24s.; l. paper 52s. 6d.
—— See also Great Artists.

DODGE, Mrs., *Hans Brinker, the Silver Skates*, new edit. 5s., 3s. 6d.. 2s. 6d. ; text only, 1s.

DONKIN, J. G., *Trooper and Redskin; N. W. mounted police*, Canada, 8s. 6d.

DONNELLY, Ignatius, *Atlantis, the Antediluvian World*, new edit. 12s. 6d.
—— *Cæsar's Column*, authorized edition, 3s. 6d.
—— *Doctor Huguet*, 3s. 6d.
—— *Great Cryptogram*, Bacon's Cipher in Shakespeare, 2 vols. 30s.
—— *Ragnarok : the Age of Fire and Gravel*, 12s. 6d.

DORÉ, Gustave, *Life and Reminiscences*, by Blanche Roosevelt, fully illust. 24s.

DOS PASSOS, J. R., *Law of Stockbrokers and Stock Exchanges*, 35s.

DOUDNEY, Sarah, *Godiva Durleigh*, 3 vols. 31s. 6d.

DOUGALL, J. D., *Shooting Appliances, Practice, &c.*, 10s. 6d.; new edit. 7s. 6d.

DOUGHTY, H. M., *Friesland Meres and the Netherlands*, new edit. illust. 10s. 6d.

DOVETON, F. B., *Poems and Snatches of Songs*, 5s. ; new edit. 3s. 6d.

DU CHAILLU, Paul. See Low's Standard Books.

DUNCKLEY ("Verax.") See Prime Ministers.

DUNDERDALE, George, *Prairie and Bush*, 6s.

Dürer. See Great Artists.

DYKES, J. Oswald. See Preachers.

Echoes from the Heart, 3s. 6d.

EDEN, C. H. See Foreign Countries.

EDMONDS, C., *Poetry of the Anti-Jacobin*, new edit. 7s. 6d. and 21s.

Educational Catalogue. See Classified Catalogue.

EDWARDS, *American Steam Engineer*, 12s. 6d.
—— *Modern Locomotive Engines*, 12s. 6d.
—— *Steam Engineer's Guide*, 12s. 6d.
—— H. Sutherland. See Great Musicians.
—— M. B., *Dream of Millions, &c.*, 1s.
—— See Low's Standard Novels.

EGGLESTON, G. Cary, *Juggernaut*, 6s.

Egypt. See Foreign Countries.

Elizabethan Songs. See Choice Editions.

EMERSON, Dr. P. H., *East Coast Yarns*, 1s.
—— *English Idylls*, new ed. 2s.
—— *Naturalistic Photography*, new edit. 5s.
—— *Pictures of East Anglian Life*; plates and vignettes, 105s. and 147s.
—— and GOODALL, *Life on the Norfolk Broads*, plates, 126s. and 210s.
—— *Wild Life on a Tidal Water*, copper plates, ord. edit. 25s. ; édit. de luxe, 63s.
—— R. W., by G. W. COOKE, 8s. 6d.
—— *Birthday Book*, 3s. 6d.
—— *In Concord*, a memoir, 7s. 6d.

English Catalogue, 1863-71, 42s.; 1872-80, 42s. ; 1881-9, 52s. 6d.; 5s. yearly.

English Catalogue, Index vol.
1837-56, 26s.; 1856-76, 42s.;
1874-80, 18s.

―――― *Etchings,* vol. v. 45s. ; vi.,
25s.; vii., 25s.; viii., 42s.

English Philosophers, edited by
E. B. Ivan Müller, M.A., 3s. 6d.
each.

Bacon, by Fowler.

Hamilton, by Monck.

Hartley and James Mill, by Bower.

Shaftesbury & Hutcheson; Fowler.

Adam Smith, by J. A. Farrer.

ERCKMANN-CHATRIAN.
See Low's Standard Books.

ERICHSON, *Life,* by W. C.
Church, 2 vols. 24s.

ESMARCH, F., *Handbook of
Surgery,* 24s.

Essays on English Writers.
See Gentle Life Series.

EVANS, G. E., *Repentance of
Magdalene Despar, &c.,* poems,
5s.

―――― S. & F., *Upper Ten, a
story,* 1s.

―――― W. E., *Songs of the Birds,*
n. ed. 6s.

EVELYN, J., *An Inca Queen,*
5s.

―――― JOHN, *Life of Mrs. Godol-
phin,* 7s. 6d.

EVES, C. W., *West Indies,*
n. ed. 7s. 6d.

FAIRBAIRN, A. M. See
Preachers.

Familiar Words. See Gentle
Life Series.

FARINI, G. A., *Kalahari
Desert,* 21s.

FARRAR, C. S., *History of
Sculpture, &c.,* 6s.

―――― MAURICE, *Minnesota,* 6s.

FAURIEL, *Last Days of the
Consulate,* 10s. 6d.

FAY, T., *Three Germanys,* 2
vols. 35s.

FEILDEN, H. ST. J., *Some
Public Schools,* 2s. 6d.

―――― Mrs., *My African Home,*
7s. 6d.

FENN, G. MANVILLE. See
Low's Standard Books.

FENNELL, J. G., *Book of the
Roach,* n. ed. 2s.

FFORDE, B., *Subaltern, Police-
man, and the Little Girl.* 1s.

―――― *Trotter, a Poona Mystery,*
1s.

FIELD, MAUNSELL B., *Memo-
ries,* 10s. 6d.

FIELDS, JAMES T., *Memoirs,*
12s. 6d.

―――― *Yesterdays with Authors,*
16s.; also 10s. 6d.

Figure Painters of Holland.
See Great Artists.

FINCK, HENRY T., *Pacific
Coast Scenic Tour,* 10s. 6d.

FITCH, LUCY. See Nursing
Record Series, 1s.

FITZGERALD. See Foreign
Countries.

―――― PERCY, *Book Fancier,* 5s.
and 12s. 6d.

FITZPATRICK, T., *Autumn
Cruise in the Ægean,* 10s. 6d

―――― *Transatlantic Holiday,*
10s. 6d.

FLEMING, S., *England and
Canada,* 6s.

*Foreign Countries and British
Colonies,* descriptive handbooks
edited by F. S. Pulling, M.A.
Each volume is the work of a
writer who has special acquaint-
ance with the subject, 3s. 6d.

Australia, by Fitzgerald.

Austria-Hungary, by Kay.

Denmark and Iceland, by E. C. Otté.

Egypt, by S. L. Poole.

France, by Miss Roberts.

Germany, by L. Sergeant.

Greece, by S. Baring Gould.

Foreign Countries, &c.—cont.
Japan, by Mossman.
Peru, by R. Markham.
Russia, by Morfill.
Spain, by Webster.
Sweden and Norway, by Woods.
West Indies, by C. H. Eden.

FOREMAN, J., *Philippine Islands*, 21s.

FOTHERINGHAM, L. M., *Nyassaland*, 7s. 6d.

FOWLER, *Japan, China, and India*, 10s. 6d.

FRA ANGELICO. See Great Artists.

FRA BARTOLOMMEO, AL-BERTINELLI, and ANDREA DEL SARTO. See Great Artists.

FRANC, MAUD JEANNE, *Beatrice Melton*, 4s.
—— *Emily's Choice*, n. ed. 5s.
—— *Golden Gifts*, 4s.
—— *Hall's Vineyard*, 4s.
—— *Into the Light*, 4s.
—— *John's Wife*, 4s.
—— *Little Mercy; for better, for worse*, 4s.
—— *Marian, a Tale*, n. ed. 5s.
—— *Master of Ralston*, 4s.
—— *Minnie's Mission, a Temperance Tale*, 4s.
—— *No longer a Child*, 4s.
—— *Silken Cords and Iron Fetters, a Tale*, 4s.
—— *Two Sides to Every Question*, 4s.
—— *Vermont Vale*, 5s.
A plainer edition is published at 2s. 6d.

France. See Foreign Countries.

FRANCIS, F., *War, Waves, and Wanderings*, 2 vols. 24s.
—— See also Low's Standard Series.

Frank's Ranche ; or, My Holiday in the Rockies, n. ed. 5s.

FRANKEL, JULIUS, *Starch Glucose, &c.*, 18s.

FRASER, BISHOP, *Lancashire Life*, n. ed. 12s. 6d.; popular ed. 3s. 6d.

FREEMAN, J., *Melbourne Life, lights and shadows*, 6s.

FRENCH, F., *Home Fairies and Heart Flowers*, illust. 24s.

French and English Birthday Book, by Kate D. Clark, 7s. 6d.

French Revolution, Letters from Paris, translated, 10s. 6d.

Fresh Woods and Pastures New, by the Author of "An Angler's Days," 5s., 1s. 6d., 1s.

FRIEZE, *Duprè, Florentine Sculptor*, 7s. 6d.

FRISWELL, J. H. See Gentle Life Series.

Froissart for Boys, by Lanier, new ed. 7s. 6d.

FROUDE, J. A. See Prime Ministers.

Gainsborough and Constable. See Great Artists.

GASPARIN, *Sunny Fields and Shady Woods*, 6s.

GEFFCKEN, *British Empire*, 7s. 6d.

Generation of Judges, n. e. 7s. 6d.

Gentle Life Series, edited by J. Hain Friswell, sm. 8vo. 6s. per vol.; calf extra, 10s. 6d. ea.; 16mo, 2s. 6d., except when price is given.
Gentle Life.
About in the World.
Like unto Christ.
Familiar Words, 6s.; also 3s. 6d.
Montaigne's Essays.
Sidney's Arcadia, 6s.
Gentle Life, second series.
Varia; readings, 10s. 6d.
Silent hour; essays.
Half-length Portraits.
Essays on English Writers.
Other People's Windows, 6s. & 2s. 6d.
A Man's Thoughts.

George Eliot, by G. W. Cooke, 10s. 6d.

Germany. See Foreign Countries.

GESSI, ROMOLO PASHA, *Seven Years in the Soudan,* 18s.

GHIBERTI & DONATELLO. See Great Artists.

GILES, E., *Australia Twice Traversed,* 1872-76, 2 vols. 30s.

GILL, J. See Low's Readers.

GILLESPIE, W. M., *Surveying,* n. ed. 21s.

Giotto, by Harry Quilter, illust. 15s.

—— See also Great Artists.

GIRDLESTONE, C., *Private Devotions,* 2s.

GLADSTONE. See Prime Ministers.

GLENELG, P., *Devil and the Doctor,* 1s.

GLOVER, R., *Light of the World,* n. ed., 2s. 6d.

GLÜCK. See Great Musicians.

Goethe's Faustus, in orig. rhyme, by Huth, 5s.

—— *Prosa,* by C. A. Buchheim (Low's German Series), 3s. 6d.

GOLDSMITH, O., *She Stoops to Conquer,* by Austin Dobson, illust. by E. A. Abbey, 84s.

—— See also Choice Editions.

GOOCH, FANNY C., *Mexicans,* 16s.

GOODALL, *Life and Landscape on the Norfolk Broads,* 126s. and 210s.

—— &EMERSON, *Pictures of East Anglian Life,* £5 5s. and £7 7s.

GOODMAN, E. J., *The Best Tour in Norway,* 6s.

—— N. & A., *Fen Skating,* 5s.

GOODYEAR, W. H., *Grammar of the Lotus, Ornament and Sun Worship,* 63s. nett.

GORDON, J. E. H., *Physical Treatise on Electricity and Magnetism.* 3rd ed. 2 vols. 42s.

—— *Electric Lighting,* 18s.

—— *School Electricity,* 5s.

—— Mrs. J. E. H., *Decorative Electricity,* illust. 12s.

GOWER, LORD RONALD, *Handbook to the Art Galleries of Belgium and Holland,* 5s.

—— *Northbrook Gallery,* 63s. and 105s.

—— *Portraits at Castle Howard.* 2 vols. 126s.

—— See also Great Artists.

GRAESSI, *Italian Dictionary,* 3s. 6d.; roan, 5s.

GRAY, T. See Choice Eds.

Great Artists, Biographies, illustrated, emblematical binding, 3s. 6d. per vol. except where the price is given.

Barbizon School, 2 vols.

Claude le Lorrain.

Correggio, 2s. 6d.

Cox and De Wint.

George Cruikshank.

Della Robbia and Cellini, 2s. 6d.

Albrecht Dürer.

Figure Paintings of Holland.

Fra Angelico, Masaccio, &c.

Fra Bartolommeo, &c.

Gainsborough and Constable.

Ghiberti and Donatello, 2s. 6d.

Giotto, by H. Quilter, 15s.

Hogarth, by A. Dobson.

Hans Holbein.

Landscape Painters of Holland.

Landseer.

Leonardo da Vinci.

Little Masters of Germany, by Scott; éd. de luxe, 10s. 6d.

Mantegna and Francia.

Meissonier, 2s. 6d.

Michelangelo.

Mulready.

Murillo, by Minor, 2s. 6d.

Overbeck.

Raphael.

Great Artists—continued.
Rembrandt.
Reynolds.
Romney and Lawrence, 2s. 6d.
Rubens, by Kett.
Tintoretto, by Osler.
Titian, by Heath.
Turner, by Monkhouse.
Vandyck and Hals.
Velasquez.
Vernet & Delaroche.
Watteau, by Mollett, 2s. 6d.
Wilkie, by Mollett.

Great Musicians, edited by F. Hueffer. A series of biographies, 3s. each:—
Bach, by Poole.
Beethoven.
*Berlioz.
Cherubini.
English Church Composers.
*Glück.
Handel.
Haydn.
*Marcello.
Mendelssohn.
Mozart.
*Palestrina and the Roman School.
Purcell.
Rossini and Modern Italian School.
Schubert.
Schumann.
Richard Wagner.
Weber.

Are not yet published.

Greece. See Foreign Countries.

GRIEB, *German Dictionary*, n. ed. 2 vols. 21s.

GRIMM, H., *Literature*, 8s. 6d.

GROHMANN, *Camps in the Rockies*, 12s. 6d.

GROVES, J. Percy. See Low's Standard Books.

GUIZOT, *History of England*, illust. 3 vols. re-issue at 10s. 6d. per vol.

—— *History of France*, illust. re-issue, 8 vols. 10s. 6d. each.

—— Abridged by G. Masson, 5s.

GUYON, Madame, *Life*, 6s.

HADLEY, J., *Roman Law*, 7s. 6d.

Half-length Portraits. See Gentle Life Series.

HALFORD, F. M., *Dry Fly-fishing*, n. ed. 25s.

—— *Floating Flies*, 15s. & 30s.

HALL, *How to Live Long*, 2s.

HALSEY, F. A., *Slide Valve Gears*, 8s. 6d.

HAMILTON. See English Philosophers.

—— E. *Fly-fishing*, 6s. and 10s. 6d.

—— *Riverside Naturalist*, 14s.

HAMILTON'S *Mexican Handbook*, 8s. 6d.

HANDEL. See Great Musicians.

HANDS, T., *Numerical Exercises in Chemistry*, 2s. 6d.; without ans. 2s.; ans. sep. 6d.

Handy Guide to Dry-fly Fishing, by Cotswold Isys, 1s.

Handy Guide Book to Japanese Islands, 6s. 6d.

HARDY, A. S., *Passe-rose*, 6s.

—— Thos. See Low's Standard Novels.

HARKUT, F., *Conspirator*, 6s.

HARLAND, Marion, *Home Kitchen*, 5s.

Harper's Young People, vols. I.–VII. 7s. 6d. each; gilt 8s.

HARRIES, A. See Nursing Record Series.

HARRIS, W. B., *Land of the African Sultan*, 10s. 6d.; l. p. 31s. 6d.

HARRISON, Mary, *Modern Cookery*, 6s.

—— *Skilful Cook*, n. ed. 5s.

—— Mrs. B. *Old-fashioned Fairy Book*, 6s.

—— W., *London Houses*, Illust. n. edit. 1s. 6d., 6s. net; & 2s. 6d.

HARTLEY and MILL. See English Philosophers.

HATTON, JOSEPH, *Journalistic London*, 12s. 6d.

—— See also Low's Standard Novels.

HAWEIS, H.R., *Broad Church*, 6s.

—— *Poets in the Pulpit*, 10s. 6d. new edit. 6s.; also 3s. 6d.

—— Mrs., *Housekeeping*, 2s. 6d.

—— *Beautiful Houses*, 4s., new edit. 1s.

HAYDN. See Great Musicians.

HAZLITT, W., *Round Table*, 2s 6d.

HEAD, PERCY R. See Illus. Text Books and Great Artists.

HEARD, A.F., *Russian Church*, 16s.

HEARN, L., *Youma*, 5s.

HEATH, F. G., *Fern World*, 12s. 6d., new edit. 6s.

—— GERTRUDE, *Tell us Why*, 2s. 6d.

HELDMANN, B., *Mutiny of the "Leander,"* 7s. 6d. and 5s.

—— See also Low's Standard Books for Boys.

HENTY, G. A., *Hidden Foe*, 2 vols. 21s.

—— See also Low's Standard Books for Boys.

—— RICHMOND, *Australiana*, 5s.

HERBERT, T., *Salads and Sandwiches*, 6d.

HICKS, C. S., *Our Boys, and what to do with Them; Merchant Service*, 5s.

—— *Yachts, Boats, and Canoes*, 10s. 6d.

HIGGINSON, T. W., *Atlantic Essays*, 6s.

—— *History of the U.S.*, illust. 14s.

HILL, A. STAVELEY, *From Home to Home in N.-W. Canada*, 21s., new edit. 7s. 6d.

—— G. B., *Footsteps of Johnson*, 63s,; *édition de luxe*, 147s.

HINMAN, R., *Eclectic Physical Geography*, 5s.

Hints on proving Wills without Professional Assistance, n. ed. 1s.

HOEY, Mrs. CASHEL. See Low's Standard Novels.

HOFFER, *Caoutchouc & Gutta Percha*, 12s. 6d.

HOGARTH. See Gr. Artists.

HOLBEIN. See Great Artists.

HOLDER, CHARLES F., *Ivory King*, 8s. 6d.

—— *Living Lights*, 8s. 6d.

—— *Marvels of Animal Life*, 8s. 6d.

HOLM, SAXE, *Draxy Miller*, 2s. 6d. and 2s.

HOLMES, O. WENDELL, *Before the Curfew*, 5s.

—— *Over the Tea Cups*, 6s.

—— *Iron Gate, &c., Poems*, 6s.

—— *Last Leaf*, 42s.

—— *Mechanism in Thought and Morals*, 1s. 6d.

—— *Mortal Antipathy*, 8s. 6d., 2s. and 1s.

—— *Our Hundred Days in Europe*, new edit. 6s.; l. paper 15s.

—— *Poetical Works*, new edit., 2 vols. 10s. 6d.

—— *Works*, prose, 10 vols.; poetry, 4 vols.; 14 vols. 84s. Limited large paper edit., 14 vols. 294s. nett.

—— See also Low's Standard Novels and Rose Library.

HOLUB, E., *South Africa*, 2 vols. 42s.

HOPKINS, MANLEY, *Treatise on the Cardinal Numbers*, 2s. 6d.

Horace in Latin, with Smart's literal translation, 2s. 6d. ; translation only, 1s. 6d.

HORETZKY, C., *Canada on the Pacific*, 5s.

How and where to Fish in Ireland, by H. Regan, 3s. 6d.

HOWARD, BLANCHE W., *Tony the Maid*, 3s. 6d.

—— See also Low's Standard Novels.

HOWELLS, W. D., *Suburban Sketches*, 7s. 6d.

—— *Undiscovered Country*, 3s. 6d. and 1s.

HOWORTH, H. H., *Glacial Nightmare*, 18s.

—— *Mammoth and the Flood*, 18s.

HUDSON, N. H., *Purple Land that England Lost;* Banda Oriental 2 vols. 21s. : 1 vol. 6s.

HUEFFER. E. See Great Musicians.

HUGHES, HUGH PRICE. See Preachers.

HUME, F., *Creature of the Night*, 1s.

Humorous Art at the Naval Exhibition, 1s.

HUMPHREYS, JENNET, *Some Little Britons in Brittany*, 2s. 6d.

Hundred Greatest Men, new edit. one vol. 21s.

HUNTINGDON, *The Squire's Nieces*, 2s. 6d. (Playtime Library.)

HYDE, *Hundred Years by Post*, 1s.

Hymnal Companion to the Book of Common Prayer, separate lists gratis.

Iceland. See Foreign Countries.

Illustrated Text-Books of Art-Education, edit. by E. J. Poynter, R.A., illust. 5s. each.

Architecture, Classic and Early Christian.

Illust. Text-Books—continued.

Architecture, Gothic and Renaissance.

German, Flemish, and Dutch Painting.

Painting, Classic and Italian.

Painting, English and American.

Sculpture, modern.

Sculpture, by G. Redford.

Spanish and French artists.

INDERWICK, F. A., *Interregnum*, 10s. 6d.

—— *Sidelights on the Stuarts*, new edit. 7s. 6d.

INGELOW, JEAN. See Low's Standard Novels.

INGLIS, *Our New Zealand Cousins*, 6s.

—— *Sport and Work on the Nepaul Frontier*, 21s.

—— *Tent Life in Tiger Land*, 18s.

IRVING, W., *Little Britain*, 10s. 6d. and 6s.

—— *Works*, "Geoffrey Crayon" edit. 27 vols. 16l. 16s.

JACKSON, J., *Handwriting in Relation to Hygiene*, 3d.

—— *New Style Vertical Writing Copy-Books*, Series I. 1—8, 2d. and 1d. each.

—— *New Code Copy-Books*, 22 Nos. 2d. each.

—— *Shorthand of Arithmetic*, Companion to all Arithmetics, 1s. 6d.

—— L., *Ten Centuries of European Progress*, with maps, 12s. 6d.

JAMES, CROAKE, *Law and Lawyers*, new edit. 7s. 6d.

—— HENRY. See Daudet, A.

JAMES and MOLE'S *French Dictionary*, 3s. 6d. cloth ; roan, 5s.

JAMES, *German Dictionary*, 3s. 6d. cloth ; roan 5s.

JANVIER, *Aztec Treasure House*, 7s. 6d. ; new edit. 5s.

Japan. See Foreign Countries.

JEFFERIES, RICHARD, *Amaryllis at the Fair*, 7s. 6d.

—— *Bevis*, new edit. 5s.

JEPHSON, A. J. M., *Emin Pasha* relief expedition, 21s.

JERDON. See Low's Standard Series.

JOHNSTON, H.H., *The Congo*, 21s.

JOHNSTON-LAVIS, H. J., *South Italian Volcanoes*, 15s.

JOHNSTONE, D. L., *Land of the Mountain Kingdom*, new edit. 3s. 6d. and 2s. 6d.

JONES, MRS. HERBERT, *Sandringham, Past and Present*, illust., new edit. 8s. 6d.

JULIEN, F., *Conversational French Reader*, 2s. 6d.

—— *English Student's French Examiner*, 2s.

—— *First Lessons in Conversational French Grammar*, n. ed. 1s.

—— *French at Home and at School*, Book I. accidence, 2s.; key, 3s.

—— *Petites Leçons de Conversation et de Grammaire*, n. ed. 3s.

—— *Petites Leçons*, with phrases, 3s. 6d.

—— *Phrases of Daily Use*, separately, 6d.

KARR, H. W. SETON, *Shores and Alps of Alaska*, 16s.

KARSLAND, VEVA, *Women and their Work*, 1s.

KAY. See Foreign Countries.

KENNEDY, E. B., *Blacks and Bushrangers*, new edit. 5s., 3s. 6d. and 2s. 6d.

KERR, W. M., *Far Interior, the Cape, Zambesi, &c.*, 2 vols. 32s.

KERSHAW, S. W., *Protestants from France in their English Home*, 6s.

KETT, C. W., *Rubens*, 3s. 6d.

Khedives and Pashas, 7s. 6d.

KILNER, E. A., *Four Welsh Counties*, 5s.

King and Commons. See Cavalier in Bayard Series.

KINGSLEY, R. G., *Children of Westminster Abbey*, 5s.

KINGSTON. See Low's Standard Books.

KIPLING, RUDYARD, *Soldiers Three, &c.*, stories, 1s.

—— *Story of the Gadsbys*, new edit. 1s.

—— *In Black and White, &c.*, stories, 1s.

—— *Wee Willie Winkie, &c.*, stories, 1s.

—— *Under the Deodars, &c.*, stories, 1s.

—— *Phantom Rickshaw, &c.*, stories, 1s.

⁎⁎* The six collections of stories may also be had in 2 vols. 3s. 6d. each.

—— *Stories*, Library Edition, 2 vols. 6s. each.

KIRKALDY, W. G., *David Kirkaldy's Mechanical Testing*, 84s.

KNIGHT, A. L., *In the Web of Destiny*, 7s. 6d.

—— E. F., *Cruise of the Falcon*, new edit. 3s. 6d.

—— E. J., *Albania and Montenegro*, 12s. 6d.

—— V. C., *Church Unity*, 5s.

KNOX, T. W., *Boy Travellers*, new edit. 5s.

KNOX-LITTLE, W. J., *Sermons*, 3s. 6d.

KUNHARDT, C. P., *Small Yachts*, new edit. 50s.

—— *Steam Yachts*, 16s.

KWONG, *English Phrases*, 21s.

LABOULLAYE, E., *Abdallah*, 2s. 6d.

LALANNE, *Etching*, 12s. 6d.

LAMB, CHAS., *Essays of Elia*, with designs by C. O. Murray, 6s.

LAMBERT, *Angling Literature*, 3s. 6d.

Landscape Painters of Holland. See Great Artists.

LANDSEER. See Great Artists.

LANGLEY, S. P., *New Astronomy*, 10s. 6d.

LANIER, S., *Boy's Froissart*, 7s. 6d.; *King Arthur*, 7s. 6d.; *Mabinogion*, 7s. 6d.; *Percy*, 7s. 6d.

LANSDELL, HENRY, *Through Siberia*, 1 v. 15s. and 10s. 6d.

—— *Russia in Central Asia*, 2 vols. 42s.

—— *Through Central Asia*, 12s.

LARDEN, W., *School Course on Heat*, n. ed. 5s.

LAURIE, A., *Secret of the Magian, the Mystery of Ecbatana*, illus. 6s. See also Low's Standard Books.

LAWRENCE, SERGEANT, *Autobiography*, 6s.

—— and ROMNEY. See Great Artists.

LAYARD, MRS., *West Indies*, 2s. 6d.

LEA, H. C., *Inquisition*, 3 vols. 42s.

LEARED, A., *Marocco*, n. ed. 16s.

LEAVITT, *New World Tragedies*, 7s. 6d.

LEFFINGWELL, W. B., *Shooting*, 18s.

—— *Wild Fowl Shooting*, 10s. 6d.

LEFROY, W., DEAN. See Preachers.

LELAND, C. G., *Algonquin Legends*, 8s.

LEMON, M., *Small House over the Water*, 6s.

Leo XIII. Life, 18s.

Leonardo da Vinci. See Great Artists.

—— *Literary Works*, by J. P. Richter, 2 vols. 252s.

LIEBER, *Telegraphic Cipher*, 42s. nett.

Like unto Christ. See Gentle Life Series.

LITTLE, ARCH. J., *Yang-tse Gorges*, n. ed., 10s. 6d.

Little Masters of Germany. See Great Artists.

LONGFELLOW, *Miles Standish*, illus. 21s.

—— *Maidenhood*, with col. pl. 2s. 6d.; gilt edges, 3s. 6d.

—— *Nuremberg*, photogr. illu. 31s. 6d.

—— *Song of Hiawatha*, illust. 21s.

LOOMIS, E., *Astronomy*, n. ed. 8s. 6d.

LORNE, MARQUIS OF, *Canada and Scotland*, 7s. 6d.

—— *Palmerston.* See Prime Ministers.

Louis, St. See Bayard Series.

Low's French Readers, edit. by C. F. Clifton, I. 3d., II. 3d., III. 6d.

—— *German Series.* See Goethe, Meissner, Sandars, and Schiller.

—— *London Charities*, annually, 1s. 6d.; sewed, 1s.

—— *Illustrated Germ. Primer*, 1s.

—— *Infant Primers*, I. illus. 3d.; II. illus. 6d. and 7d.

—— *Pocket Encyclopædia*, with plates, 3s. 6d.; roan, 4s. 6d.

—— *Readers*, I., 9d.; II., 10d.; III., 1s.; IV., 1s. 3d.; V., 1s. 4d.; VI., 1s. 6d.

Low's Select Parchment Series.

Aldrich (T. B.) Friar Jerome's Beautiful Book, 3s. 6d.

Lewis (Rev. Gerrard), Ballads of the Cid, 2s. 6d.

Whittier (J. G.) The King's Missive. 3s. 6d.

Low's Stand. Library of Travel (except where price is stated), per volume, 7s. 6d.

1. Butler, Great Lone Land; also 3s. 6d.
2. —— Wild North Land.
3. Stanley (H. M.) Coomassie, 3s. 6d.
4. —— How I Found Livingstone; also 3s. 6d.
5. —— Through the Dark Continent, 1 vol. illust., 12s. 6d.; also 3s. 6d.
8. MacGahan (J. A.) Oxus.
9. Spry, voyage, *Challenger.*
10. Burnaby's Asia Minor, 10s. 6d.
11. Schweinfurth's Heart of Africa, 2 vols. 15s.; also 3s. 6d. each.
12. Marshall (W.) Through America.
13. Lansdell (H). Through Siberia, 10s. 6d.
14. Coote, South by East, 10s. 6d.
15. Knight, Cruise of the *Falcon,* also 3s. 6d.
16. Thomson (Joseph) Through Masai Land.
19. Ashe (R. P.) Two Kings of Uganda, 3s. 6d.

Low's Standard Novels (except where price is stated), 6s.

Baker, John Westacott.

Black (W.) Craig Royston.
—— Daughter of Heth.
—— House Boat.
—— In Far Lochaber.
—— In Silk Attire.
—— Kilmeny.
—— Lady Siverdale's Sweetheart.
—— New Prince Fortunatus.
—— Penance of John Logan.
—— Stand Fast, Craig Royston!
—— Sunrise.
—— Three Feathers.

Low's Stand. Novels—continued

Blackmore (R. D.) Alice Lorraine.
—— Christowell.
—— Clara Vaughan.
—— Cradock Nowell.
—— Cripps the Carrier.
—— Ereme, or My Father's Sins.
—— Kit and Kitty.
—— Lorna Doone.
—— Mary Anerley.
—— Sir Thomas Upmore.
—— Springhaven.

Brémont, Gentleman Digger.

Brown (Robert) Jack Abbott's Log.

Bynner, Agnes Surriage.
—— Begum's Daughter.

Cable (G. W.) Bonaventure, 5s.

Coleridge (C. R.) English Squire.

Craddock, Despot of Broomsedge.

Croker (Mrs. B. M.) Some One Else.

Cumberland (Stuart) Vasty Deep.

De Leon, Under the Stars and Crescent.

Edwards (Miss Betham) Half-way.

Eggleston, Juggernaut.

French Heiress in her own Chateau.

Gilliat (E.) Story of the Dragonnades.

Hardy (A. S.) Passe-rose.
—— (Thos.) Far from the Madding.
—— Hand of Ethelberta.
—— Laodicean.
—— Mayor of Casterbridge.
—— Pair of Blue Eyes.
—— Return of the Native.
—— Trumpet-Major.
—— Two on a Tower.

Harkut, Conspirator.

Hatton (J.) Old House at Sandwich.
—— Three Recruits.

Hoey (Mrs. Cashel) Golden Sorrow.
—— Out of Court.
—— Stern Chase.

Howard (Blanche W.) Open Door.

Ingelow (Jean) Don John.
—— John Jerome, 5s.
—— Sarah de Berenger.

Lathrop, Newport, 5s.

Mac Donald (Geo.) Adela Cathcart.
—— Guild Court.

Low's Stand. Novels—continued.
Mac Donald (Geo.) Mary Marston.
—— Orts.
—— Stephen Archer, &c.
—— The Vicar's Daughter.
—— Weighed and Wanting.
Macmaster, Our Pleasant Vices.
Macquoid (Mrs.) Diane.
Musgrave (Mrs.) Miriam.
Osborn, Spell of Ashtaroth, 5s.
Prince Maskiloff.
Riddell (Mrs.) Alaric Spenceley.
—— Daisies and Buttercups.
—— Senior Partner.
—— Struggle for Fame.
Russell (W. Clark) Betwixt the
　Forelands.
—— Frozen Pirate.
—— Jack's Courtship.
—— John Holdsworth.
—— Little Loo.
—— My Watch Below.
—— Ocean Free Lance.
—— Sailor's Sweetheart.
—— Sea Queen.
—— Strange Voyage.
—— The Lady Maud.
—— Wreck of the *Grosvenor.*
Steuart, Kilgroom.
Stockton (F. R.) Ardis Claverden.
—— Bee-man of Orn, 5s.
—— Hundredth Man.
—— The late Mrs. Null.
Stoker, Snake's Pass.
Stowe (Mrs.) Old Town Folk.
—— Poganuc People.
Thomas, House on the Scar.
Thomson, Ulu, an African Ro-
　mance.
Tourgee, Murvale Eastman.
Tytler (S.) Duchess Frances.
Vane, From the Dead.
Wallace (Lew.) Ben Hur.
Warner, Little Journey in the
　World.
Woolson (Constance Fenimore)
　Anne.
—— East Angles.
—— For the Major, 5s.
—— Jupiter Lights.

　　See also Sea Stories.

Low's Stand. Novels, new issue
　at short intervals, 2s. 6d. and 2s.
Blackmore, Alice Lorraine.
—— Christowell.
—— Clara Vaughan.
—— Cripps the Carrier.
—— Kit and Kitty.
—— Lorna Doone.
—— Mary Anerley.
—— Tommy Upmore.
Cable, Bonaventure.
Croker, Some One Else.
Cumberland, Vasty Deep.
Do Leon, Under the Stars.
Edwards, Half-way.
Hardy, Laodicean.
—— Madding Crowd.
—— Mayor of Casterbridge.
—— Trumpet-Major,
—— Two on a Tower.
Hatton, Old House at Sandwich.
—— Three Recruits.
Hoey, Golden Sorrow.
—— Out of Court.
—— Stern Chase.
Holmes, Guardian Angel.
Ingelow, John Jerome.
—— Sarah de Berenger.
Mac Donald, Adela Cathcart.
—— Guild Court.
—— Stephen Archer.
—— Vicar's Daughter.
Oliphant, Innocent.
Riddell, Daisies and Buttercups.
—— Senior Partner.
Stockton, Bee-man of Orn, 5s.
—— Dusantes.
—— Mrs. Lecks and Mrs. Aleshine.
Stowe, Dred.
—— Old Town Folk.
—— Poganuc People.'
Thomson, Ulu.
Walford, Her Great Idea, &c.,
　Stories.
Low's German Series, a gradu-
　ated course. See " German."
Low's Readers. See English
　Reader and French Reader.
Low's Standard Books for Boys,
　with numerous illustrations,
　2s. 6d. each; gilt edges, 3s. 6d.

Low's Stand. Books for Boys—continued.

Adventures in New Guinea: the Narrative of Louis Tregance.

Biart (Lucien) Adventures of a Young Naturalist.

—— My Rambles in the New World.

Boussenard, Crusoes of Guiana.

—— Gold Seekers, a sequel to the above.

Butler (Col. Sir Wm., K.C.B.) Red Cloud, the Solitary Sioux: a Tale of the Great Prairie.

Cahun (Leon) Adventures of Captain Mago.

—— Blue Banner.

Célière, Startling Exploits of the Doctor.

Chaillu (Paul du) Wild Life under the Equator.

Collingwood (Harry) Under the Meteor Flag.

—— Voyage of the *Aurora*.

Cozzens (S.W.) Marvellous Country.

Dodge (Mrs.) Hans Brinker; or, The Silver Skates.

Du Chaillu (Paul) Stories of the Gorilla Country.

Erckmann - Chatrian, Brothers Rantzau.

Fenn (G. Manville) Off to the Wilds.

—— Silver Cañon.

Groves (Percy) Charmouth Grange; a Tale of the 17th Century.

Heldmann (B.) Mutiny on Board the Ship *Leander*.

Henty (G. A.) Cornet of Horse: a Tale of Marlborough's Wars.

—— Jack Archer; a Tale of the Crimea.

—— Winning his Spurs: a Tale of the Crusades.

Johnstone (D. Lawson) Mountain Kingdom.

Kennedy (E. B.) Blacks and Bushrangers in Queensland.

Kingston (W. H. G.) Ben Burton; or, Born and Bred at Sea.

—— Captain Magford; or, Our Salt and Fresh Water Tutors.

—— Dick Cheveley.

—— Heir of Kilfinnan.

Low's Stand. Books for Boys—continued.

Kingston (W. H. G.) Snowshoes and Canoes.

—— Two Supercargoes.

—— With Axe and Rifle on the Western Prairies.

Laurie (A.) Conquest of the Moon.

—— New York to Brest in Seven Hours.

MacGregor (John) A Thousand Miles in the *Rob Roy* Canoe on Rivers and Lakes of Europe.

Maclean (H. E.) Maid of the Ship *Golden Age.*

Meunier, Great Hunting Grounds of the World.

Muller, Noble Words and Deeds.

Perelaer, The Three Deserters; or, Ran Away from the Dutch.

Reed (Talbot Baines) Sir Ludar: a Tale of the Days of the Good Queen Bess.

Rousselet (Louis) Drummer-boy: a Story of the Time of Washington.

—— King of the Tigers.

—— Serpent Charmer.

—— Son of the Constable of France.

Russell (W. Clark) Frozen Pirates.

Stanley, My Kalulu—Prince, King and Slave.

Winder (F. H.) Lost in Africa.

Low's Standard Series of Books by popular writers, cloth gilt, 2s.; gilt edges, 2s. 6d. each.

Alcott (L. M.) A Rose in Bloom.

—— An Old-Fashioned Girl.

—— Aunt Jo's Scrap Bag.

—— Eight Cousins, illust.

—— Jack and Jill.

—— Jimmy's Cruise.

—— Little Men.

—— Little Women and Little Women Wedded.

—— Lulu's Library, illust.

—— Shawl Straps.

—— Silver Pitchers.

—— Spinning-Wheel Stories.

—— Under the Lilacs, illust.

—— Work and Beginning Again, ill.

Low's Stand. Series—continued.
Alden (W. L.) Jimmy Brown, illust.
—— Trying to Find Europe.
Bunyan (John) Pilgrim's Progress, (extra volume), gilt, 2s.
De Witt (Madame) An Only Sister.
Francis (Francis) Eric and Ethel, illust.
Holm (Saxe) Draxy Miller's Dowry.
Jerdon (Gert.) Keyhole Country, illust.
Robinson (Phil) In My Indian Garden.
—— Under the Punkah.
Roe (E. P.) Nature's Serial Story.
Saintine, Picciola.
Samuels, Forecastle to Cabin, illust.
Sandeau (Jules) Seagull Rock.
Stowe (Mrs.) Dred.
—— Ghost in the Mill, &c.
—— My Wife and I.
—— We and our Neighbours.
See also Low's Standard Series.
Tooley (Mrs.) Life of Harriet Beecher Stowe.
Warner (C. Dudley) In the Wilderness.
—— My Summer in a Garden.
Whitney (Mrs.) A Summer in Leslie Goldthwaite's Life.
—— Faith Gartney's Girlhood.
—— Hitherto.
—— Real Folks.
—— The Gayworthys.
—— We Girls.
—— The Other Girls : a Sequel.
** A new illustrated list of books for boys and girls, with portraits of celebrated authors, sent post free on application.
LOWELL, J. R., *Among my Books*, Series I. and II., 7s. 6d. each.
—— *My Study Windows*, n. ed. 1s.
—— *Vision of Sir Launfal*, illus. 63s.
MACDONALD, A., *Our Sceptred Isle*, 3s. 6d.
—— D., *Oceania*, 6s.

MACDONALD, Geo., *Castle Warlock, a Homely Romance*, 3 vols. 31s. 6d.
—— See also Low's Standard Novels.
—— Sir John A., *Life*.
MACDOWALL, Alex. B., *Curve Pictures of London*, 1s.
MACGAHAN, J. A., *Oxus*, 7s. 6d.
MACGOUN, *Commercial Correspondence*, 5s.
MACGREGOR, J., *Rob Roy in the Baltic*, n. ed. 3s. 6d. and 2s. 6d.
—— *Rob Roy Canoe*, new edit., 3s. 6d. and 2s. 6d.
—— *Yawl Rob Roy*, new edit., 3s. 6d. and 2s. 6d.
MACKENNA, *Brave Men in Action*, 10s. 6d.
MACKENZIE, Sir Morell, *Fatal Illness of Frederick the Noble*, 2s. 6d.
MACKINNON and SHAD-BOLT, *South African Campaign*, 50s.
MACLAREN,A. See Preachers.
MACLEAN, H. E. See Low's Standard Books.
MACMASTER. See Low's Standard Novels.
MACMURDO, E., *History of Portugal*, 21s.; II. 21s.; III. 21s.
MAHAN, A. T., *Influence of Sea Power on History*, 18s.
Maid of Florence, 10s. 6d.
MAIN, Mrs.,*High Life*, 10s. 6d.
—— See also Burnaby, Mrs.
MALAN, A. N., *Cobbler of Cornikeranium*, 5s.
—— C. F. de M., *Eric and Connie's Cruise*, 5s.
Man's Thoughts. See Gentle Life Series.
MANLEY, J. J., *Fish and Fishing*, 6s.

MANTEGNA and FRANCIA. See Great Artists.

MARCH, F. A., *Comparative Anglo-Saxon Grammar,* 12s.

—— *Anglo-Saxon Reader,* 7s. 6d.

MARKHAM, ADM., *Naval Career,* 14s.

—— *Whaling Cruise,* new edit. 7s. 6d.

—— C. R., *Peru.* See Foreign Countries.

—— *Fighting Veres,* 18s.

—— *War Between Peru and Chili,* 10s. 6d.

MARSH, G. P., *Lectures on the English Language,* 18s.

—— *Origin and History of the English Language,* 18s.

MARSHALL, W. G., *Through America,* new edit. 7s. 6d.

MARSTON, E., *How Stanley wrote " In Darkest Africa,"* 1s.

—— See also Amateur Angler, Frank's Ranche, and Fresh Woods.

—— W., *Eminent Actors,* n. ed. 6s.

MARTIN, J. W., *Float Fishing and Spinning,* new edit. 2s.

Massage. See Nursing Record Series.

MATTHEWS, J. W., *Incwadi Yami,* 14s.

MAURY, M. F., *Life,* 12s. 6d.

—— *Physical Geography and Meteorology of the Sea,* new ed. 6s.

MEISSNER, A. L., *Children's Own German Book* (Low's Series), 1s. 6d.

—— *First German Reader* (Low's Series), 1s. 6d.

—— *Second German Reader* (Low's Series), 1s. 6d.

MEISSONIER. See Great Artists.

MELBOURNE, LORD. See Prime Ministers.

MELIO, G. L., *Swedish Drill,* 1s. 6d.

MENDELSSOHN *Family,* 1729-1847, Letters and Journals, 2 vols. 30s.; new edit. 30s.

—— See also Great Musicians.

MERRIFIELD, J., *Nautical Astronomy,* 7s. 6d.

MERRYLEES, J., *Carlsbad,* 7s. 6d. and 9s.

MESNEY,W., *Tungking,*3s. 6d.

Metal Workers' Recipes and Processes, by W. T. Brannt,12s.6d.

MEUNIER, V. See Low's Standard Books.

Michelangelo. See Great Artists.

MILFORD, P. *Ned Stafford's Experiences,* 5s.

MILL, JAMES. See English Philosophers.

MILLS, J., *Alternative Elementary Chemistry,* 1s. 6d.

—— *Chemistry Based on the Science and Art Syllabus,* 2s. 6d.

—— *Elementary Chemistry,* answers, 2 vols. 1s. each.

MILTON'S *Allegro.* See Choice Editions.

MITCHELL, D.G.(Ik. Marvel) *English Lands, Letters and Kings,* 2 vols. 6s. each.

—— *Writings,* new edit. per vol. 5s.

MITFORD, J., *Letters,* 3s. 6d.

—— MISS, *Our Village,* illust. 5s.

Modern Etchings, 63s. & 31s.6d.

MOLLETT, J. W., *Dictionary of Words in Art and Archæology,* illust. 15s.

—— *Etched Examples,* 31s. 6d. and 63s.

—— See also Great Artists.

MONCK. See English Philosophers.

MONEY, E., *The Truth About America*, 5s. ; new edit. 2s. 6d.

MONKHOUSE. See G. Artists.

Montaigne's Essays, revised by J. Hain Friswell, 2s. 6d.

—— See Gentle Life Series.

MOORE, J. M., *New Zealand for Emigrant, Invalid, and Tourist*, 5s.

MORFILL, W. R., *Russia*, 3s. 6d.

MORLEY, HENRY, *English Literature in the Reign of Victoria*, 2s. 6d.

—— *Five Centuries of English Literature*, 2s.

MORSE, E. S., *Japanese Homes*, new edit. 10s. 6d.

MORTEN, *Hospital Life*, 1s.

MORTIMER, J., *Chess Player's Pocket-Book*, new edit. 1s.

MORWOOD, V.S., *Our Gipsies*, 18s.

MOSS, F. J., *Great South Sea*, 8s. 6d.

MOSSMAN, S., *Japan*, 3s. 6d.

MOTTI, PIETRO, *Elementary Russian Grammar*, 2s. 6d.

—— *Russian Conversation Grammar*, 5s. ; Key, 2s.

MOULE, H. C. G., *Sermons*, 3s. 6d.

MOXLEY, *West India Sanatorium, and Barbados*, 3s. 6d.

MOXON, W., *Pilocereus Senilis*, 3s. 6d.

MOZART, 3s. Gr. Musicians.

MÜLLER, E. See Low's Standard Books.

MULLIN, J.P., *Moulding and Pattern Making*, 12s. 6d.

MULREADY, 3s. 6d. Great Artists.

MURILLO. See Great Artists.

MUSGRAVE, MRS. See Low's Standard Novels.

—— *Savage London*, n. e. 3s. 6d.

My Comforter, &c., Religious Poems, 2s. 6d.

Napoleon I. See Bayard Series.

Napoleon I. and Marie Louise, 7s. 6d.

NELSON, WOLFRED, *Panama*, 6s.

Nelson's Words and Deeds, 3s. 6d.

NETHERCOTE, *Pytchley Hunt*, 8s. 6d.

New Democracy, 1s.

New Zealand, chromos, by Barraud, 168s.

NICHOLSON, *British Association Work and Workers*, 1s.

Nineteenth Century, a Monthly Review, 2s. 6d. per No.

NISBET, HUME, *Life and Nature Studies*, 6s.

NIXON, *Story of the Transvaal*, 12s. 6d.

Nordenskiöld's Voyage, trans. 21s.

NORDHOFF, C., *California*, new edit. 12s. 6d.

NORRIS, RACHEL, *Nursing Notes*, 2s.

NORTH, W., *Roman Fever*, 25s.

Northern Fairy Tales, 5s.

NORTON, C. L., *Florida*, 5s.

NORWAY, G., *How Martin Drake Found his Father* illus. 5s.

NUGENT'S *French Dictionary*, new edit. 3s.

Nuggets of the Gough, 3s.

Nursing Record Series, text books and manuals. Edited by Charles F. Rideal.

1. Lectures to Nurses on Antiseptics in Surgery. By E. Stanmore Bishop. With coloured plates, 2s.

Nursing Record Series—contin.
2. Nursing Notes. Medical and Surgical information. For Hospital Nurses, &c. With illustrations and a glossary of terms. By Rachel Norris (*née* Williams), late Acting Superintendent of Royal Victoria Military Hospital at Suez, 2s.
3. Practical Electro-Therapeutics. By Arthur Harries, M.D., and H. Newman Lawrence. With photographs and diagrams, 1s. 6d.
4. Massage for Beginners. Simple and easy directions for learning and remembering the different movements. By Lucy Fitch, 1s.

O'BRIEN, *Fifty Years of Concession to Ireland*, vol. i. 16s.; vol. ii. 16s.

—— *Irish Land Question*, 2s.

OGDEN, James, *Fly-tying*, 2s. 6d.

O'GRADY, *Bardic Literature of Ireland*, 1s.

—— *History of Ireland*, vol. i. 7s. 6d.; ii. 7s. 6d.

Old Masters in Photo. 73s. 6d.

Orient Line Guide, new edit. 2s. 6d.

ORLEBAR, *Sancta Christina*, 5s.

Other People's Windows. See Gentle Life Series.

OTTÉ, *Denmark and Iceland*, 3s. 6d. Foreign Countries.

Our Little Ones in Heaven, 5s.

Out of School at Eton, 2s. 6d.

OVERBECK. See Great Artists.

OWEN, Douglas, *Marine Insurance*, 15s.

Oxford Days, by a M.A., 2s. 6d.

PALGRAVE, *Chairman's Handbook*, new edit. 2s.

—— *Oliver Cromwell*, 10s. 6d.

PALLISER, *China Collector's Companion*, 5s.

—— *History of Lace*, n. ed. 21s.

PANTON, *Homes of Taste*, 2s. 6d.

PARKE, *Emin Pasha Relief Expedition*, 21s.

PARKER, E. H., *Chinese Account of the Opium War*, 1s. 6d.

PARSONS, J., *Principles of Partnership*, 31s. 6d.

—— T. P., *Marine Insurance*, 2 vols. 63s.

PEACH, *Annals of Swainswick*, 10s. 6d.

Peel. See Prime Ministers.

PELLESCHI, G., *Gran Chaco*, 8s. 6d.

PENNELL, H. C., *Fishing Tackle*, 2s.

—— *Sporting Fish*, 15s. & 30s.

Penny Postage Jubilee, 1s.

PERRY, Nora, *Another Flock of Girls*, illus. by Birch & Copeland, 7s. 6d.

Peru, 3s. 6d. Foreign Countries.

PHELPS, E. S., *Struggle for Immortality*, 5s.

—— Samuel, *Life*, by W. M. Phelps and Forbes-Robertson, 12s.

PHILLIMORE, C. M., *Italian Literature*, new. edit. 3s. 6d.

PHILLIPPS, W. M., *English Elegies*, 5s.

PHILLIPS, L. P., *Dictionary of Biographical Reference*, new. edit. 25s.

—— W., *Law of Insurance*, 2 vols. 73s. 6d.

PHILPOT, H. J., *Diabetes Mellitus*, 5s.

—— *Diet Tables*, 1s. each.

Picture Gallery of British Art. I. to VI. 18s. each.

—— *Modern Art*, 3 vols. 31s. 6d. each.

PINTO, *How I Crossed Africa,* 2 vols. 42s.

Playtime Library. See Humphrey and Huntingdon.

Pleasant History of Reynard the Fox, trans. by T. Roscoe, illus. 7s. 6d.

POCOCK, R., *Gravesend Historian,* 5s.

POE, by E. C. Stedman, 3s. 6d.

—— *Raven,* ill. by G. Doré, 63s.

Poems of the Inner Life, 5s.

Poetry of Nature. See Choice Editions.

Poetry of the Anti-Jacobin, 7s. 6d. and 21s.

POOLE, *Somerset Customs and Legends,* 5s.

—— S. LANE, *Egypt,* 3s. 6d. Foreign Countries.

POPE, *Select Poetical Works,* (Bernhard Tauchnitz Collection), 2s.

PORCHER, A., *Juvenile French Plays,* 1s.

Portraits of Racehorses, 4 vols. 126s.

POSSELT, *Structure of Fibres,* 63s.

—— *Textile Design,* illust. 28s.

POYNTER. See Illustrated Text Books.

Preachers of the Age, 3s. 6d. ea.

Living Theology, by His Grace the Archbishop of Canterbury.

The Conquering Christ, by Rev. A. Maclaren.

Verbum Crucis, by the Bishop of Derry.

Ethical Christianity, by H. P. Hughes.

Sermons, by Canon W. J. Knox-Little.

Light and Peace, by H. R. Reynolds. Faith and Duty, by A. M. Fairbairn. Plain Words on Great Themes, by J. O. Dykes.

Sermons, by the Bishop of Ripon.

Preachers of the Age—continued.

Sermons, by Rev. C. H. Spurgeon.

Agoniæ Christi, by Dean Lefroy, of Norwich.

Sermons, by H. C. G. Moule, M.A. *Volumes will follow in quick succession by other well-known men.*

Prime Ministers, a series of political biographies, edited by Stuart J. Reid, 3s. 6d. each.

1. Earl of Beaconsfield, by J. Anthony Froude.
2. Viscount Melbourne, by Henry Dunckley ("*Verax*").
3. Sir Robert Peel, by Justin McCarthy.
4. Viscount Palmerston, by the Marquis of Lorne.
5. Earl Russell, by Stuart J. Reid.
6. Right Hon. W. E. Gladstone, by G. W. E. Russell.
7. Earl of Aberdeen, by Sir Arthur Gordon.
8. Marquis of Salisbury, by H. D. Traill.
9. Earl of Derby, by George Saintsbury.

** An edition, limited to 250 copies, is issued on hand-made paper, medium 8vo, bound in half vellum, cloth sides, gilt top. Price for the 9 vols. 4l. 4s. nett.

Prince Maskiloff. See Low's Standard Novels.

Prince of Nursery Playmates, new edit. 2s. 6d.

PRITT, T. N., *Country Trout Flies,* 10s. 6d.

Reynolds. See Great Artists.

Purcell. See Great Musicians.

QUILTER, H., *Giotto, Life, &c.* 15s.

RAMBAUD, *History of Russia,* new edit., 3 vols. 21s.

RAPHAEL. See Great Artists.

REDFORD, *Sculpture.* See Illustrated Text-books.

REDGRAVE, *Engl. Painters,* 10s. 6d. and 12s.

REED, Sir E. J., *Modern Ships of War*, 10s. 6d.

—— T. B., *Roger Ingleton, Minor*, 5s.

—— *Sir Ludar.* See Low's Standard Books.

REID, Mayne, Capt., *Stories of Strange Adventures*, illust. 5s.

—— Stuart J. See Prime Ministers.

—— T. Wemyss, *Land of the Bey*, 10s. 6d.

Remarkable Bindings in British Museum, 168s.; 94s. 6d.; 73s. 6d. and 63s.

REMBRANDT. See Great Artists.

Reminiscences of a Boyhood, 6s.

REMUSAT, *Memoirs*, Vols. I. and II. new ed. 16s. each.

—— *Select Letters*, 16s.

REYNOLDS. See Gr. Artists.

—— Henry R., *Light & Peace, &c. Sermons*, 3s. 6d.

RICHARDS, J. W., *Aluminium*, new edit. 21s.

RICHARDSON, *Choice of Books*, 3s. 6d.

RICHTER, J. P., *Italian Art*, 42s.

—— See also Great Artists.

RIDDELL. See Low's Standard Novels.

RIDEAL, *Women of the Time*, 14s.

RIFFAULT, *Colours for Painting*, 31s. 6d.

RIIS, *How the Other Half Lives*, 10s. 6d.

RIPON, Bp. of. See Preachers.

ROBERTS, Miss, *France*. See Foreign Countries.

—— W., *English Bookselling*, earlier history, 7s. 6d.

ROBIDA, A., *Toilette*, coloured, 7s. 6d.

ROBINSON, "*Romeo*" *Coates*, 7s. 6d.

—— *Noah's Ark*, n. ed. 3s. 6d.

—— *Sinners & Saints*, 10s. 6d.

—— See also Low's Standard Series.

—— *Wealth and its Sources*, 5s.

—— W. C., *Law of Patents*, 3 vols. 105s.

ROCHEFOUCAULD. See Bayard Series.

ROCKSTRO, *History of Music*, new ed. 14s.

RODRIGUES, *Panama Canal*, 5s.

ROE, E. P. See Low's Standard Series.

ROGERS, S. See Choice Editions.

ROLFE, *Pompeii*, 7s. 6d.

Romantic Stories of the Legal Profession, 7s. 6d.

ROMNEY. See Great Artists.

ROOSEVELT, Blanche R. *Home Life of Longfellow*, 7s. 6d.

ROSE, J., *Mechanical Drawing*, 16s.

—— *Practical Machinist*, new ed. 12s. 6d.

—— *Key to Engines*, 8s. 6d.

—— *Modern Steam Engines*, 31s. 6d.

—— *Steam Boilers*, 12s. 6d.

Rose Library. Popular Literature of all countries, per vol. 1s., unless the price is given.

Alcott (L. M.) Eight Cousins, 2s.; cloth, 3s. 6d.

—— Jack and Jill, 2s.; cloth, 5s.

—— Jimmy's cruise in the Pinafore, 2s.; cloth, 3s. 6d.

—— Little Women.

—— Little Women Wedded; Nos. 4 and 5 in 1 vol. cloth, 3s. 6d.

—— Little Men, 2s.; cloth gilt, 3s. 6d.

Rose Library—continued.

Alcott (L. M.) Old-fashioned Girls, 2s.; cloth, 3s. 6d.
—— Rose in Bloom, 2s. ; cl. 3s. 6d.
—— Silver Pitchers.
—— Under the Lilacs, 2s. ; cloth, 3s. 6d.
—— Work, A Story of Experience, 2 vols. in 1, cloth, 3s. 6d.
Stowe (Mrs.) Pearl of Orr's Island.
—— Minister's Wooing.
—— We and Our Neighbours, 2s.
—— My Wife and I, 2s.
Dodge (Mrs.) Hans Brinker, or, The Silver Skates, 1s. ; cloth, 5s. ; 3s. 6d. ; 2s. 6d.
Lowell (J. R.) My Study Windows.
Holmes (Oliver Wendell) Guardian Angel, cloth, 2s.
Warner (C. D.) My Summer in a Garden, cloth, 2s.
Stowe (Mrs.) Dred, 2s. ; cloth gilt, 3s. 6d.
Carleton (W.) City Ballads, 2 vols. in 1, cloth gilt, 2s. 6d.
—— Legends, 2 vols. in 1, cloth gilt, 2s. 6d.
—— Farm Ballads, 6d. and 9d. ; 3 vols. in 1, cloth gilt, 3s. 6d.
—— Farm Festivals, 3 vols. in 1, cloth gilt, 3s. 6d.
—— Farm Legends, 3 vols. in 1, cloth gilt, 3s. 6d.
Clients of Dr. Bernagius, 2 vols.
Howells (W. D.) Undiscovered Country.
Clay (C. M.) Baby Rue.
—— Story of Helen Troy.
Whitney (Mrs.) Hitherto, 2 vols. cloth, 3s. 6d.
Fawcett (E.) Gentleman of Leisure.
Butler, Nothing to Wear.
ROSS, MARS, *Cantabria*, 21s.
ROSSINI, &c., See Great Musicians.
Rothschilds, by J. Reeves, 7s. 6d.
Roughing it after Gold, by Rux, new edit. 1s.
ROUSSELET. See Low's Standard Books.

ROWBOTHAM, F. J., *Prairie Land*, 5s.
Royal Naval Exhibition, a souvenir, illus. 1s.
RUBENS. See Great Artists.
RUGGLES, H. J., *Shakespeare's Method*, 7s. 6d.
RUSSELL, G.W. E., *Gladstone*. See Prime Ministers.
—— W. CLARK, Mrs. *Dines' Jewels*, 2s. 6d.
—— *Nelson's Words and Deeds*, 3s. 6d.
—— *Sailor's Language*, illus. 3s. 6d.
—— See also Low's Standard Novels and Sea Stories.
—— W. HOWARD, *Prince of Wales' Tour*, illust. 52s. 6d. and 84s.
Russia. See Foreign Countries.
Saints and their Symbols, 3s. 6d.
SAINTSBURY, G., *Earl of Derby.* See Prime Ministers.
SAINTINE, *Picciola*, 2s. 6d. and 2s. See Low's Standard Series.
SALISBURY, LORD. See Prime Ministers.
SAMUELS. See Low's Standard Series.
SANDARS, *German Primer*, 1s.
SANDEAU, *Seagull Rock*, 2s. and 2s. 6d. Low's Standard Series.
SANDLANDS, *How to Develop Vocal Power*, 1s.
SAUER, *European Commerce*, 5s.
—— *Italian Grammar* (Key, 2s.), 5s.
—— *Spanish Dialogues*, 2s. 6d.
—— *Spanish Grammar* (Key, 2s.), 5s.
—— *Spanish Reader*, new edit. 3s. 6d.
SAUNDERS, J., *Jaspar Deane*, 10s. 6d.

SCHAACK, M. J., *Anarchy*, 16s.

SCHAUERMANN, -*Ornament* for technical schools, 10s. 6d.

SCHERER, *Essays in English Literature*, by G. Saintsbury, 6s.

SCHERR, *English Literature*, history, 8s. 6d.

SCHILLER'S *Prosa*, selections by Buchheim. Low's Series 2s. 6d.

SCHUBERT. See Great Musicians.

SCHUMANN. See Great Musicians.

SCHWEINFURTH. See Low's Standard Library.

Scientific Education of Dogs, 6s.

SCOTT, LEADER, *Renaissance of Art in Italy*, 31s. 6d.

—— See also Illust. Text-books.

—— SIR GILBERT, *Autobiography*, 18s.

—— W. B. See Great Artists.

SELMA, ROBERT, *Poems*, 5s.

SERGEANT, L. See Foreign Countries.

Shadow of the Rock, 2s. 6d.

SHAFTESBURY. See English Philosophers.

SHAKESPEARE, ed. by R. G. White, 3 vols. 36s.; *édit. de luxe*, 63s.

—— *Annals; Life & Work*, 2s.

—— *Hamlet*, 1603, also 1604, 7s. 6d.

—— *Hamlet*, by Karl Elze, 12s. 6d.

—— *Heroines*, by living painters, 105s.; artists' proofs, 630s.

—— *Macbeth*, with etchings, 105s. and 52s. 6d.

—— *Songs and Sonnets*. See Choice Editions.

—— *Taming of the Shrew*, adapted for drawing-room, paper wrapper, 1s.

SHEPHERD, *British School of Painting*, 2nd edit. 5s.; 3rd edit. sewed, 1s.

SHERIDAN, *Rivals*, col. plates, 52s. 6d. nett; art. pr. 105s. nett.

SHIELDS, G. O., *Big Game of North America*, 21s.

—— *Cruisings in the Cascades*, 10s. 6d.

SHOCK, W. H., *Steam Boilers*, 73s. 6d.

SIDNEY. See Gentle Life Series.

Silent Hour. See Gentle Life Series.

SIMKIN, *Our Armies*, plates in imitation of water-colour (5 parts at 1s.), 6s.

SIMSON, *Ecuador and the Putumayor*, 8s. 6d.

SKOTTOWE, *Hanoverian Kings*, new edit. 3s. 6d.

SLOANE, T. O., *Home Experiments*, 6s.

SMITH, HAMILTON, and LEGROS' *French Dictionary*, 2 vols. 16s., 21s., and 22s.

SMITH, EDWARD, *Cobbett*, 2 vols. 24s.

—— G., *Assyria*, 18s.

—— *Chaldean Account of Genesis*, new edit. by Sayce, 18s.

—— GERARD. See Illustrated Text Books.

—— T. ROGER. See Illustrated Text Books.

Socrates. See Bayard Series.

SOMERSET, *Our Village Life*, 5s.

Spain. See Foreign Countries.

SPAYTH, *Draught Player*, new edit. 12s. 6d.

SPIERS, *French Dictionary*, 2 vols. 18s., half bound, 2 vols. 21s.

SPRY. See Low's Stand. Library.

SPURGEON, C. H. See Preachers.

STANLEY, H. M., *Congo*, 2 vols. 42s. and 21s.

—— *In Darkest Africa*, 2 vols., 42s.

—— *Emin's Rescue*, 1s.

—— See also Low's Standard Library and Low's Standard Books.

START, *Exercises in Mensuration*, 8d.

STEPHENS, F. G., *Celebrated Flemish and French Pictures*, with notes, 28s.

—— See also Great Artists.

STERNE. See Bayard Series.

STERRY, J. Ashby, *Cucumber Chronicles*, 5s.

STEUART, J. A., *Letters to Living Authors*, new edit. 2s. 6d.; édit. de luxe, 10s. 6d.

—— See also Low's Standard Novels.

STEVENS, J. W., *Practical Workings of the Leather Manufacture*, illust. 18s.

—— T., *Around the World on a Bicycle*, over 100 illust. 16s.; part II. 16s.

STEWART, Dugald, *Outlines of Moral Philosophy*, 3s. 6d.

STOCKTON, F. R., *Casting Away of Mrs. Lecks*, 1s.

—— *The Dusantes*, a sequel, 1s.

—— *Merry Chanter*, 2s. 6d.

—— *Personally Conducted*, illust. by Joseph Pennell, 7s. 6d.

—— *Rudder Grangers Abroad*, 2s. 6d.

—— *Squirrel Inn*, illust. 6s.

—— *Story of Viteau*, illust. 5s. new edit. 3s. 6d.

—— *Three Burglars*, 1s. & 2s.

—— See also Low's Standard Novels.

STORER, F. H., *Agriculture*, 2 vols., 25s.

STOWE, Edwin. See Great Artists.

—— Mrs., *Flowers and Fruit from Her Writings*, 3s. 6d.

—— *Life . . . her own Words . . . Letters and Original Composition*, 15s.

—— *Life*, told for boys and girls, by S. A. Tooley, 5s., new edit. 2s. 6d. and 2s.

—— *Little Foxes*, cheap edit. 1s.; 4s. 6d.

—— *Minister's Wooing*, 1s.

—— *Pearl of Orr's Island*, 3s. 6d. and 1s.

—— *Uncle Tom's Cabin*, with 126 new illust. 2 vols. 18s.

—— See also Low's Standard Novels and Low's Standard Series.

STRACHAN, J., *New Guinea*, 12s.

STRANAHAN, *French Painting*, 21s.

STRICKLAND, F., *Engadine*, new edit. 5s.

STUTFIELD, *El Maghreb*, ride through Morocco, 8s. 6d.

SUMNER, C., *Memoir*, new edit. 2 vols. 36s.

Sweden and Norway. See Foreign Countries.

Sylvanus Redivivus, 10s. 6d.

SZCZEPANSKI, *Technical Literature*, a directory, 2s

TAINE, H. A., *Origines*, I. Ancient Régime, French Revolution, 3 vols.; Modern Régime, vol. I. 16s.

TAYLOR, H., *English Constitution*, 18s.

—— R. L., *Analysis Tables*, 1s.

—— *Chemistry*, 1s. 6d.

Techno-Chemical Receipt Book, 10s. 6d.

TENNYSON. See Choice Editions.

Ten Years of a Sailor's Life, 7*s.* 6*d.*

THAUSING, *Malt and Beer,* 45*s.*

THEAKSTON, *British Angling Flies,* 5*s.*

Thomas à Kempis Birthday-Book, 3*s.* 6*d.*

—— *Daily Text-Book,* 2*s.* 6*d.*

—— See also Gentle Life Series.

THOMAS, BERTHA, *House on the Scar, Tale of South Devon,* 6*s.*

THOMSON, JOSEPH. See Low's Standard Library and Low's Standard Novels.

—— W., *Algebra,* 5*s.* ; without Answers, 4*s.* 6*d.* ; Key, 1*s.* 6*d.*

THORNTON, W. PUGIN, *Heads, and what they tell us,* 1*s.*

THORODSEN, J. P., *Lad and Lass,* 6*s.*

TICKNOR, G., *Memoir,* new edit. 2 vols. 21*s.*

TILESTON, MARY W., *Daily Strength,* 4*s.* 6*l.*

TINTORETTO. See Great Artists.

TITIAN. See Great Artists.

TODD, *Life,* by J. E. Todd, 12*s.*

TOURGEE. See Low's Standard Novels.

TOY, C. H., *Judaism,* 14*s.*

Tracks in Norway, 2*s.*, n. ed. 1*s.*

TRAILL. See Prime Ministers.

Transactions of the Hong Kong Medical Society, vol. I. 12*s.* 6*d.*

TROMHOLT, *Aurora Borealis,* 2 vols., 30*s.*

TUCKER, *Eastern Europe,* 15*s.*

TUCKERMAN, B., *English Fiction,* 8*s.* 6*d.*

—— *Lafayette,* 2 vols. 12*s.*

TURNER, J. M. W. See Gr. Artists.

TYSON, *Arctic Adventures,* 25*s.*

TYTLER, SARAH. See Low's Standard Novels.

—— M. C., *American Literature,* vols. I. and II. 24*s.*

UPTON, II., *Dairy Farming,* 2*s.*

Valley Council, by P. Clarke, 6*s.*

VANDYCK and HALS. See Great Artists.

VANE, DENZIL, *Lynn's Court Mystery,* 1*s.*

—— See also Low's Standard Novels.

Vane, Young Sir Harry, 18*s.*

VELAZQUEZ. See Gr. Artists.

—— and MURILLO, by C. B. Curtis, with etchings, 31*s.* 6*d.* and 63*s.*

VERE, SIR F., *Fighting Veres,* 18*s.*

VERNE, J., *Works by.* See page 31.

Vernet and Delaroche. See Great Artists.

VERSCHUUR, G., *At the Antipodes,* 7*s.* 6*d.*

VIGNY, *Cinq Mars,* with etchings, 2 vols. 30*s.*

VINCENT, F., *Through and through the Tropics,* 10*s.* 6*d.*

—— MRS. H., 40,000 *Miles over Land and Water,* 2 vols. 21*s.*; also 3*s.* 6*d.*

VIOLLET-LE-DUC, *Architecture,* 2 vols. 31*s.* 6*d.* each.

WAGNER. See Gr. Musicians.

WALERY, *Our Celebrities,* vol. II. part i., 30*s.*

WALFORD, MRS. L. B. See Low's Standard Novels.

WALL, *Tombs of the Kings of England,* 21*s.*

WALLACE, L., *Ben Hur,* 2*s.* 6*d.*

—— *Boyhood of Christ,* 15*s.*

—— See also Low's Stand. Novs.

WALLACE, R., *Rural Economy of Australia and New Zealand*, illust. 21s. nett.

WALLER, C. H., *Names on the Gates of Pearl*, 3s. 6d.

—— *Silver Sockets*, 6s.

WALTON, *Angler*, Lea and Dove edit. by R. B. Marston, with photos., 210s. and 105s.

—— *Wallet-book*, 21s. & 42s.

—— T. H., *Coal-mining*, 25s.

WARNER, C. D., *Their Pilgrimage*, illust. by C. S. Reinhard, 7s. 6d.

—— See also Low's Standard Novels and Low's Standard Series.

WARREN, W. F., *Paradise Found, Cradle of the Human Race*, illust. 12s. 6d.

WASHBURNE, *Recollections (Siege of Paris, &c.)*, 2 vols. 36s.

WATTEAU. See Great Artists.

WEBER. See Great Musicians.

WEBSTER, *Spain*. See Foreign Countries and British Colonies.

WELLINGTON. See Bayard Series.

WELLS, H. P., *Salmon Fisherman*, 6s.

—— *Fly-rods and Tackle*, 10s. 6d.

—— J. W., *Brazil*, 2 vols. 32s.

WENZEL, *Chemical Products of the German Empire*, 25s.

West Indies. See Foreign Countries.

WESTGARTH, *Australasian Progress*, 12s.

WESTOBY, *Postage Stamps; a descriptive Catalogue*, 6s.

WHITE, RHODA E., *From Infancy to Womanhood*, 10s. 6d.

—— R. GRANT, *England without and within*, new ed. 10s. 6d.

—— *Every-day English*, 10s. 6d.

WHITE, R. GRANT, *Studies in Shakespeare*, 10s. 6d.

—— *Words and their Uses*, new edit. 5s.

—— W., *Our English Homer, Shakespeare and his Plays*, 6s.

WHITNEY, MRS. See Low's Standard Series.

WHITTIER, *St. Gregory's Guest*, 5s.

—— *Text and Verse for Every Day in the Year*, selections, 1s. 6d.

WHYTE, *Asia to Europe*, 12s.

WIKOFF, *Four Civilizations*, 6s.

WILKES, G., *Shakespeare*, 16s.

WILKIE. See Great Artists.

WILLS, *Persia as it is*, 8s. 6d.

WILSON, *Health for the People*, 7s. 6d.

WINDER, *Lost in Africa.* See Low's Standard Books.

WINSOR, J., *Columbus*, 21s.

—— *History of America*, 8 vols. per vol. 30s. and 63s.

WITTHAUS, *Chemistry*, 16s.

WOOD, *Sweden and Norway.* See Foreign Countries.

WOLLYS, *Vegetable Kingdom*, 5s.

WOOLSEY, *Communism and Socialism*, 7s. 6d.

—— *International Law*, 6th ed. 18s.

—— *Political Science*, 2 vols. 30s.

WOOLSON, C. FENIMORE. See Low's Standard Novels.

WORDSWORTH. See Choice Editions.

Wreck of the " Grosvenor," 6d.

WRIGHT, H., *Friendship of God*, 6s.

—— T., *Town of Cowper*, 6s.

WRIGLEY, *Algiers Illust.* 45s

Written to Order, 6s.

BOOKS BY JULES VERNE.

LARGE CROWN 8vo. WORKS.	Containing 350 to 600 pp. and from 50 to 100 full-page illustrations.		Containing the whole of the text with some illustrations.	
	Handsome cloth binding, gilt edges.	Plainer binding, plain edges.	Cloth binding, gilt edges, smaller type.	Limp cloth.
	s. d.	s. d.	s. d.	s. d.
20,000 Leagues under the Sea. Parts I. and II.	10 6	5 0	3 6	2 0
Hector Servadac	10 6	5 0	3 6	2 0
The Fur Country	10 6	5 0	3 6	2 0
The Earth to the Moon and a Trip round it	10 6	5 0	2 vols., 2s. ea.	2 vols., 1s. ea.
Michael Strogoff	10 6	5 0	3 6	2 0
Dick Sands, the Boy Captain	10 6	5 0	3 6	2 0
Five Weeks in a Balloon	7 6	3 6	2 0	1 0
Adventures of Three Englishmen and Three Russians	7 6	3 6	2 0	1 0
Round the World in Eighty Days	7 6	3 6	2 0	1 0
A Floating City	7 6	3 6	2 0	1 0
The Blockade Runners			2 0	1 0
Dr. Ox's Experiment	—	—	2 0	1 0
A Winter amid the Ice	—	—	2 0	1 0
Survivors of the "Chancellor".	7 6	3 6	3 6	2 0
Martin Paz			2 0	1 0
The Mysterious Island, 3 vols.:—	22 6	10 6	6 0	3 0
I. Dropped from the Clouds	7 6	3 6	2 0	1 0
II. Abandoned	7 6	3 6	2 0	1 0
III. Secret of the Island	7 6	3 6	2 0	1 0
The Child of the Cavern	7 6	3 6	2 0	1 0
The Begum's Fortune	7 6	3 6	2 0	1 0
The Tribulations of a Chinaman	7 6	3 6	2 0	1 0
The Steam House, 2 vols.:—				
I. Demon of Cawnpore	7 6	3 6	2 0	1 0
II. Tigers and Traitors	7 6	3 6	2 0	1 0
The Giant Raft, 2 vols.:—				
I. 800 Leagues on the Amazon	7 6	3 6	2 0	1 0
II. The Cryptogram	7 6	3 6	2 0	1 0
The Green Ray	5 0	3 6	2 0	1 0
Godfrey Morgan	7 6	3 6	2 0	1 0
Kéraban the Inflexible:—				
I. Captain of the "Guidara"	7 6	3 6	2 0	1 0
II. Scarpante the Spy	7 6	3 6	2 0	1 0
The Archipelago on Fire	7 6	3 6	2 0	1 0
The Vanished Diamond	7 6	3 6	2 0	1 0
Mathias Sandorf	10 6	5 0	3 6	2 vols 1 0 each
Lottery Ticket	7 6	3 6	2 0	1 0
The Clipper of the Clouds	7 6	3 6	2 0	1 0
North against South	7 6	3 6		
Adrift in the Pacific	6 0	3 6		
The Flight to France	7 6	3 6		
The Purchase of the North Pole	6 0			
A Family without a Name	6 0			
César Cascabel	6 0			

CELEBRATED TRAVELS AND TRAVELLERS. 3 vols. 8vo, 600 pp., 100 full-page illustrations, 7s. 6d., gilt edges, 9s. each:—(1) THE EXPLORATION OF THE WORLD. (2) THE GREAT NAVIGATORS OF THE EIGHTEENTH CENTURY. (3) THE GREAT EXPLORERS OF THE NINETEENTH CENTURY.